HEAD OF THE DRAGON

Book Three in the GAILSONE Series

***

A novel by Casey Glanders

Ordering Information:

Quantity sales. Special discounts are available on quantity purchases by corporations, associations, and others. For details, contact the publisher at the address above or visit gailsone.com.

Orders by U.S. trade bookstores and wholesalers. Please contact Casey Glanders at cjglanders@gmail.com or visit www.gailsone.com.

This is a work of fiction. Any resemblance to any persons, living or dead, is purely coincidental.

No superheroes were harmed in the writing of this publication.

Printed in the United States of America

Also by this author:

Big In Japan

Blood & Rust

A Night at the Opera

Date Night

Blackbird's Song

The Impossible Door

Black Days

Hit

Red Rook

Old Ghosts

Ifrit

Paint the Town Red

No Man's Land

The Impossible Door

Rare Gems

Turnabout

For my Family

Chapters

"Oh. Yes, well. I just don't see this one that often. The Reflection is a sign of many things, but this early in the reading, it's hard to say. It feels like you'll meet someone who reflects parts of you that you wish were not there. It could also mean a glimpse into your darker half, or maybe that you'll meet your evil twin? Rather hard to say."

- Kappa-san

Big In Japan

Prologue:

The Grey

The evening air outside was cold, and the rain had only just stopped falling on the dark Manhattan streets. Inside a quiet, one-bedroom apartment the heater rattled as it valiantly fought against the outside chill. Jesse Darling, aka Darkane, Master of Mysticism, lit a clove cigarette and glanced at the nude woman sleeping at his side. Her form was half covered in a sea of blankets, and the yellow light pouring through the blinds curved over her body as she softly snored. He moved some of her chestnut hair out of her face and tried to adjust the flat pillow under his neck without waking her. Her name was Candice, a bartender at a local pub he liked to frequent. They had been dating off and on for about six months, and currently they were very on. He counted the tattoos along her arm, and idly traced one of a rose that went to her shoulder blade. He took a long drag, making sure to flick the gold ash into a cheap, green ashtray on the cluttered nightstand.

Jesse had wanted to get some sleep, but found it impossible. There were too many voices on the wind, and they all had grave things to say. Some were hushed, muted whispers, but some were loud, blaring warnings about the future. Many were chants or songs, which always annoyed Jesse. He hated dealing with the chanting spirits; they always demanded songs in exchange for their knowledge, and Jesse detested singing.

It was hard to make sense of all the messages he was receiving, but he knew enough. He had asked about Superior Force, his super-powered teammate in the Collective Good. Jesse's involvement in the Collective Good was something that nowadays he viewed as a necessary evil. Initially, he had joined for the women and prestige, but eventually the responsibility of keeping the world safe outweighed even the allure of sex and stardom, and one morning Jessie discovered, much to his horror, that he was fully committed to the organization he had once referred to as, "a bunch of fucking wankers." Still, membership had its perks. With the money he earned as a full-time member on the roster, he was easily able to acquire the materials he needed for his spell work.

Superior Force had gone missing after desperately trying to defuse what the press was calling "the Catastrophe", when dozens of bombings had rocked the world, all designed to entrap the most powerful being on the planet. Whatever they had done, it had worked. No one had seen or heard from Superior Force in weeks, and whenever Jesse asked the wind, all he received were songs of ice, darkness, and the sound of soft crying. It unsettled him, and that was saying something for a man who would take tea with demons.

He took another drag from his cigarette, and tried to focus. The smoke that slowly poured from his chapped lips twirled into a circle, and within it Jesse saw the air flicker and glow. An image appeared, fleeting and disjointed, of a young girl with glowing, white eyes. He thought she looked familiar, but he couldn't quite place her. Her lips were moving. He tried to focus, and the wind whispered, *"For all of them!"* Then there was silence as the smoke circle broke apart.

More and more, his visions had been like this. It unsettled him. As a magic user he was used to vague symbolism, but these felt more like clear pieces of broken glass that were reflecting an image in a mirror. He had shards, but not enough to really know what was happening. When he had brought this to the attention of the local Spiritual Magistrate, she had laughed hysterically in his face, offered him an orange soda, and then kicked him out the door. Sadly, this was about par for the course when dealing with Nana Schulz, but still, Jesse had hoped for *something* of value.

Candice rolled over and nuzzled him as she sighed in her sleep. She smelled like cheap beer, coconut oil, and cigarette smoke. Even after showering, it was hard to get the smell of the bar out of her hair and skin, but Jesse didn't mind. He thought that added to her allure, and as he lay there thinking about it, he traced her side and seriously debated waking her up. They had recently grown more serious, and he found he didn't mind it. She was hard-working, and trying to get an online degree in event management. They'd had a rough patch a while back, but she had gotten cleaned up (mostly), and things were good. It was a new feeling for Jesse, and he was secretly waiting for the rug to be pulled out from under him.

As he lay there, he felt something shift. Something was off, and the voices that whispered in the night changed their song. This only happened when a choice was coming that could alter Jesse's fate, and typically it was a bad one. He glanced again at Candice, and then scooted himself out of the bed to find his pants. If trouble was going to find him, he preferred it not be at his flat, and not while he was sober.

Jesse stepped onto the slick concrete sidewalk in front of his apartment building, and pulled up the collar on his coat. He wanted some regular cigarettes, some beer, and potentially a burrito. There was nothing decent to eat at his place, and he figured he could bring something back for Candice when she woke up. Pulling his coat closed, Jesse did his best to pretend the cold wasn't bothering him as he made his way to the corner Duane Reade pharmacy.

The store was warm, and the blue fluorescents gave everything a dull, faded look. There was a mom holding a newborn in what passed for the grocery isle, looking desperately for some generic formula while her infant screamed in her arms. There was a wino cruising the beer stand, and a man buying some smokes at the counter. Aside from that, it wasn't that crowded.

Jesse grabbed a warm six-pack, a bag of ice, three microwave burritos, and waited patiently behind the man buying cigarettes as the young girl working the counter tried to understand the man through a thick accent. Jesse was letting his mind wander when he heard the all-too-familiar sound of a shotgun being pumped behind him, and then the obligatory screaming that followed.

"On the ground! On the fucking ground now!" It was the wino. Jesse turned to see him pointing the shotgun right at his face. The wino was shaking, and had some drool on the side of his mouth and chin. His eyes were wide and bloodshot, and looked vacant. Jesse nodded and smiled.

"Hey man, it's cool. We're all cool here."

The wino turned his shotgun towards the young mother. She was clinging to her newborn who was still shrieking in her arms. The mother was on her knees and sobbing as the wino snapped, "Shut that kid up! Shut him up now! Do it!"

"Please don't hurt us, please..." the mother choked out. Jesse cleared his throat to get the wino's attention. The wino swung back around to see Jesse with his hands up and a smile on his face.

"Hey man, it's cool. You smoke?" Jesse glanced to his right hand, which was holding a pack of cloves. The wino didn't even register that the crinkled pack hadn't been there a moment ago. "You want one? You mind if I have one?"

"Just keep your hands up!" The wino screamed. "You, empty the register! Now!" He pointed his gun at the girl working the register. The man buying cigarettes was already on the ground, his hands covering his head.

"Don't bother with that," Jesse said. He calmly put his hands down and fished in his pocket for his lighter. "And would you please put your gun down? You're scaring folks."

The wino put the barrel of the shotgun so close to Jesse's face that the mage could smell the gunpowder residue left over from a previous outing. Jesse took a drag off his clove and nodded to the wino. "You can pull that trigger all you like. While you were fucking around, I turned the shells into copper lumps. Go on, try it."

The wino pulled the trigger, but nothing happened. He tried several more times while Jesse blew a long strand of purple smoke from his lips. The smoke trailed around the confused wino, and then materialized into a coiled mass of snakes. The wino let out a gargled scream as the snakes slithered around his flailing limbs and into his coat. He crashed into a display of energy drinks as he scrambled out the door. Jesse watched as the man dove onto the sidewalk, rolling and screaming, before scrambling to his feet and taking off into the night.

Satisfied, Jesse approached the young lady behind the counter and then pointed behind her. "Pack of Luckys?"

The young woman blinked, not quite registering what was going on.

***

The street was eerily deserted as a lone cab splashed through potholes and rounded a corner, leaving Jesse alone with his thoughts. The whispers had said something would happen tonight, that there was a splitting of paths. Jesse wondered if they had meant the wino. The man did have a gun, after all. If the young mother hadn't distracted him, Jesse wouldn't have had time to quickly cast the alchemical spell that transmuted his rounds. Could that have been what they were on about? Jesse shivered and frowned. It seemed too trivial, and not at all like something that warranted this level of caution. He clutched his plastic bag of food and booze, and trudged back towards his apartment.

As he slouched down the empty sidewalk, he noticed the sound of his uncomfortable metal-clasped boots as they clanged on the wet pavement beneath him. His torn leather pants and ratty shirt offered little protection from the harsh evening chill, and his thin black trench coat didn't add much, either. He had debated changing his look, but he found that showmanship was just as much a part of the job as actual crime fighting, and he had an established image with the masses. Plus, Candice thought it was hot, so why mess with a good thing?

All of this ran through Jesse's head as he tried to block out the constant whooshing sound of cars flying by at high speeds. It was getting to the point that he was considering casting a red-light spell, just to mess with the evening drivers. He glanced up at a nearby traffic signal, wet his lips, and slid his hands out of his pockets. As he pulled back his collar to get a better view, he finally looked around, and then froze.

The street was completely empty. Slowly, his mind began to register that for a Friday night in New York, this was unheard of. Also, he realized it had been empty since he left the convenience store. In fact, he couldn't recall seeing any vehicles, save for a solitary cab that had flashed by him before he entered the store, but the sound continued.

"What the hell is this?" Darkane mumbled in a voice made rough by too many cigarettes. The puddles around him were still sloshing with ripples, showing a recent disturbance. Aside from that, the whooshing sound had suddenly stopped. He was enveloped in silence. Even the wind had hushed, and for a man who was connected to Shamanistic magic, that always boded ill.

As a cold chill trickled down his spine, he turned around to see a figure in a dark trench coat and fedora calmly standing a good 10 meters behind him. The figure's hands were resting in his pockets, and nothing about this man stood out as particularly dangerous, aside from the fact that he was obviously there for the young mage, and that he also seemed unfazed by the lack of people and traffic. While the man didn't look all that threatening, Darkane tensed as he got a look at the man's face. There were no features visible- it was nothing more than a blank surface.

"Hey," Jesse said in as calm of a voice as he could muster. "Sweet getup. I dig the face."

The figure said nothing. He just continued to stare at Jesse. At least, Jesse guessed he was staring; it's hard to tell when a person doesn't have any eyes. Jesse tried to play it off and grinned at the figure. "S'cool man. I get it. You're not a talker. You smoke?"

Jesse reached into a side pocket to pull out a special crumpled pack of cloves. The cigarettes were actually filled with a powerful mixture of ground gemstones, cursed bones, and several ingredients from a lower plane that very few had access to. Jesse had learned long ago to hide his weapons in plain sight, and for some reason, people were usually stupid enough to let him have at least one smoke. He went to fish one out from its crinkled wrapping and reached for his lighter. The mixture would be enough to give him a boost in magical abilities, and with it, he would be able to get off one or two powerful spells. If nothing else, he could use it to create an emergency portal.

Jesse smiled, and then went white as a sheet as the cigarette disappeared from his mouth. "Wha? What the fu..?" He looked at the man in gray. His coat was only slightly rumpled, but there he stood, still ten meters away, now calmly holding up the cigarette in his hand. He crumpled it, and a purple cloud of screaming smoke momentarily erupted from the tobacco before vanishing on the wind.

"Okay, cool. Not much for smoking. I dig." Jesse was beginning to get nervous. He reached into his coat for another talisman, a homemade version of an Infinity knife. He had crafted it from a werewolf's bones back when he was still heavy into nature-based magic. He felt around his hidden weapon's pocket, but his hands grasped empty air. He looked again to the figure, who was now holding the knife up by the blade. The man calmly twirled it in his hand and continued to otherwise stand perfectly still, waiting for Jesse to make another move.

"Okay, asshole. You wanna play with the Master of Mystics? Fine. Le...le..." Jesse tried to speak, but his words came in a gurgle. He coughed up some blood, and when he reached for his throat, he found his hand covered in red. Horrified, he glanced towards the man in grey. The knife in the man's hand was now dripping with blood from the slice across Jesse's throat.

Jesse panicked. Most of his spells required a verbal component, but he had some he could still try. He reached for his dream bag, a container of extra dimensional dust, but it was gone. The pouches and containers he had hidden throughout his boots, belt, and coat were all missing. He glanced back to the man and saw all of his trinkets, necklaces, vials, and every other magical knick-knack he possessed piled at the man's feet. Somehow, the man had managed to take every single weapon Jesse had on his person without him realizing it. Even Jesse's shopping bag lay there in the pile of dangerous archaic magical weaponry.

Jesse felt the world slipping away and his vision going black. He tried to hold his throat closed with one hand while he dropped to his knees and began to quickly trace a circle around him with his own blood. It was risky and usually involved some form of infernal pact, but he was desperate. Jesse started to sob as he nearly finished the circle, only to suddenly feel a sharp, tight pressure in his chest. He looked down to see the hilt of the knife sticking out of the front of his shirt. The blade had pierced him through the heart and had protruded out the other side, staining his coat. He suddenly thought of Candice, sleeping soundly in his apartment. He could see her face clearly, and try as he might, that was the only thing his mind seemed to want to focus on. He wondered, as he felt himself slipping away and into the blackness, why such a mundane, ordinary thing would suddenly be all he could see. In his ears, the voices of the night were whispering again. They were singing again, but this time the song was clear. It was his requiem. It was laced with the warnings they had uttered before, when he was safe and warm in his bed, and hadn't paid attention.

Jesse fell backwards and crumpled to the ground. The figure in grey stood there for a moment, as if to make sure the legendary Darkane was truly dead. Then, he calmly slipped a smart phone out of his pocket. He took a snap shot of the dead mage, sent it via a text, and then gently tucked the cell phone away.

In the blink of an eye, he was gone. Seconds later, traffic resumed travelling down the now-busy New York street.

Chapter One

"I'm in charge."

Then

***

'So, this is how I'm going to die.'

The thought danced through Alice's mind as she struggled against the leather restraints binding her to the cold, metal table. Despite her panic, the thought was eerily calm, as though she were an observer — and not likely to be sliced and diced at any moment. Unfortunately, Alice recognized her surroundings. She was in a Purge O/E room. The Operations and Experimentation wing was one she had been familiar with since Prometheus had first brought her on board a few months ago, but she had actively worked to avoid it. Now the frightened teenager found herself trapped there, stripped down to a white tank top and her underwear, and terrified for what was going to happen next.

"I'm sorry!" Alice screamed as the masked Purge soldiers that had carted her in once again checked her restraints. Above her, a large, white disc hummed in the ceiling. Every time Alice tried to turn on her entropy powers and rot through her restraints, the disc above her hummed louder. Alice tried pulling away, but the bonds were tight, and she was powerless to fight back. She had not eaten or drunk for over 24 hours. Still, she managed to pour every ounce of energy she had into straining against her unyielding bonds.

As she vainly fought, the soldiers carefully attached sensors to her bare skin. The wires from the sensor pads fed into a massive computer terminal on wheels that was running on the far side of the room. As soon as Alice was connected, the machine began to display a haphazard readout of energy signatures. Beside the terminals stood a series of vats, tubes, and boiling, green chemicals in a large, oval-shaped pool with walls three feet high. The fumes from the chemicals was acrid and nauseating, burning Alice's nose and mouth with each gasp she took.

"I'm sorry," Alice cried out again. "I didn't mean to! It was an accident! Please!" The soldiers, satisfied that Alice wasn't going anywhere, signaled towards a wall-length mirror that the room was secure. A moment, later a door slid open, and Prometheus slowly entered the room. He was using a cane and looked physically drained, but focused. His gray uniform drooped on his gaunt frame, and his blond hair looked slightly mussed, but, aside from that, he maintained an almost regal air about him as he moved. Behind him came a stout, bald man in thick, Coke-bottle glasses, dressed in a white surgeon's coat and green latex gloves.

"Prometheus!" Alice cried out. "Alexi! Please! Please let me out. I swear, I didn't mean to do it. It was a mistake! I swear! It was just a mistake!"

Prometheus walked to Alice and caressed the side of her face as she whimpered. "I'm sorry, my dear, but I'm afraid I can't do that. You've become too dangerous to let you roam free."

"I've got it under control," Alice said, hyperventilating. "Seriously. It was a one-time mistake. I've got it under control. Please believe me."

"I want to, I really do. However," Prometheus stepped back and put his weight on his cane. "It was most definitely not a 'one-time mistake.' You've had too many accidents, too many flare ups, and this latest one was the last straw."

"It was just a..."

"You rotted a man's arm off," Prometheus sighed. "He was trying to help you out of the landing craft, and the second you touched him, he started to disintegrate. That was the fifth Purge soldier you've maimed since I brought you on. The fifth. Three of them have already died from their injuries. I won't have my army crippled because you cannot control yourself."

"Please," Alice sobbed. "I can do this. Please. I don't want to die."

"Oh, Alice," Prometheus said in a soft voice. "I promise, I won't let you die. I'm just going to have Dr. Tolarius fix you, my dear. Once he's done, you'll finally have the control you always wanted over your gift."

Behind Prometheus, Dr. Tolarius was busy looking over the readouts that he was receiving from his sensor array. "Sir," the small, round doctor said in a quiet voice, "a word."

"We'll be right back, Alice. Please don't worry." Prometheus patted Alice on the head, and then followed Tolarius back into the darkened viewing room on the other side of the mirror. "Yes, Doctor?"

"You should know that in truth, there is a very low probability that she will live," Tolarius bluntly stated. "This procedure is, to put it mildly, experimental. I have never encountered a life form like her before. Her powers are incredible, and *extremely* dangerous. The inhibitor is taxed to the breaking point from trying to keep her subdued." Tolarius gestured to the large disc above them, which was whining and vibrating.

"Be that as it may," Prometheus said as he watched Alice through the glass. "I will not let her go. Doctor, I've hunted for someone like her for years. She is, without a doubt, the most perfect magical specimen the Purge has ever seen. There has *never* been another magic user like her, and I refuse to see her gift wasted."

"That is the only reason I'm letting you push me on this," Tolarius grumbled. "Project Grail wasn't anywhere close to being ready. You're lucky I've already made the progress I have."

"I think you're underselling yourself, Doctor," Prometheus said.

Tolarius sighed and rubbed his eyes under his glasses. "To even make the *possibility* of this work, I had to destroy every Phoenix on Earth. Even with that, and let me reemphasize this point, I cannot guarantee this will be successful. You understand that, correct? That if this doesn't work, we have essentially thrown away any chance we had of keeping you stable?"

Prometheus shrugged. "If this works, then we can move on to tending my situation." He glanced down at his cane. "If not, then I suppose I won't have to worry much longer."

Tolarius turned and observed Alice as she began to scream for Prometheus. "This will destroy her, you know. Completely and totally. She'll be a useless husk after this."

"No, she won't," Prometheus said. He gestured to the far side of the room where an old woman in a floral hat watched the proceedings with mild interest. "I've called in a favor with the Spiritual Magistrate. She will personally oversee the spiritual side of the operation. You do your job, and she'll do hers. I will have the General I've always dreamed of."

Tolarius glanced at Prometheus. "I did not think you enjoyed using magic."

"I don't," Prometheus grumbled. "But, I enjoy losing even less. Your science is amazing, Herr Doctor. Still, for what we are attempting, we will need some mystical help." Prometheus looked to Alice, who was glancing around in a panic. "This woman, once under control, will be the greatest weapon the Purge has ever seen."

"Agreed," Tolarius said. "Provided this works."

"Provided this works," Prometheus said with a nod.

They both watched Alice for a moment, each mulling over their own hopes for the operation. Finally, Prometheus sighed, tapped his cane against the floor, and said, "Let's not waste any more time. Thank you for sharing your concerns with me."

"Oh, one more thing. May I record this for posterity?" Tolarius asked. "If this works, it will make for a marvelous reference."

"Be my guest," Prometheus said. "It's not like she'll remember."

"You there," Tolarius called to a soldier standing near the door. "Bring in my media crew. I want this all documented. Record all of it. Every detail."

"Sir," the soldier said with a brisk salute.

Meanwhile, on the freezing metal slab of the operating table, Alice had broken out into a cold sweat. She was breathing fast and shallow, and watching, wide-eyed, as Tolarius reentered the room, walking past several, wall-mounted cameras that stayed focused on Alice. Their lights were blinding, and Alice did her best to turn her head away. She looked to the old woman standing off to the side, but the Spiritual Magistrate completely ignored Alice's pleas for help, and instead turned her attention to Dr. Tolarius.

"If this works," Nana Schulz, the Magistrate for North America, aid to Tolarius. "I'll provide you with the necessary tools to do this yourself in the future."

"Oh?" Tolarius asked, slightly intrigued. "You don't plan on helping in the future? If it's a matter of price..."

Nana Schulz shook her head. "No, it's not that. This is leaving me with a bad taste in my mouth, that's all. I'd prefer not to come back here again. Still," she glanced down at the helpless Alice as her voice became quiet. "A deal's a deal."

Tolarius nodded in agreement as he stood over Alice. "Now, my dear," Tolarius said to the panicked teenager as he reached for a scalpel. "I apologize, but my sample material must be kept as clean as possible. Unfortunately, that means no anesthetic can be in your system. I'm sure you understand."

Alice looked at the black lenses of the cameras that were only a few feet away, and started to cry. Over and over, she whispered to herself as Tolarius started with a long incision on Alice's side "Feel free to comment on how this feels," Tolarius said to her. "For science, of course."

"I can do this," she said, both to Tolarius and to herself. "Please, I can control it. Please," she whispered, tears streaming down her face as the procedure began. "It's true. I'm in control."

"I'm in charge."

Chapter Two

Terror is Profit

Now

***

In Tucson, Arizona, a green and white, ranch-style home with a row of stone-rimmed shrubs sat in an unassuming suburban cul-de-sac. The garage was open. Inside, Dr. Edward Tolarius sat at a dimly-lit work bench, fiddling with his latest invention. Small, stout and bald, he appeared to be in his late 60's. He had looked like this for years, and, as a result, people who knew him were typically wrong about his age. Despite this, his health had deteriorated from his years of working in damp environments, submarines and underwater bases, which led to a wet cough that occasionally contained flecks of blood.

His health had been in decline for some time, but it wasn't until the collapse of the Purge that he decided to peacefully retire and move to Arizona, where the dry, hot climate could work its magic. His neighbors were friendly enough, and he carried enough legitimate patents to keep himself financially comfortable. Also, he still had roughly five million in US currency tucked away in multiple airport security lockers, but that was being saved for a rainy day.

Edward twisted his tiny Phillips screwdriver a quarter-turn, sealed a battery compartment, and smiled. In front of him was a small, egg-shaped device with several LED lights and a set of tiny buttons. It looked simplistic (and almost crude, considering its creator), but the Doctor smiled all the same. This was his hobby now, building little things, tiny things he could sell, or use around the house, or in the community. No more tidal cannons or liquid metal submersibles. He was retired, but that didn't mean he couldn't tinker.

A small LCD screen beside his workbench chimed with a proximity alert. Dr. Tolarius glanced at it, and touched the small, glowing screen. He saw the bio-ID listing and punched in the 'Stand Down' code for his home defense system. A few minutes later, he noticed a shadow fall across his workbench, and smiled to himself.

"I have to say, when I set out to locate the great and powerful Dr. Tolarius, this is not what I was expecting to find. What's that little thing do?" The voice was female, bold, and eerily familiar to Tolarius. He smiled and nodded as he cupped his latest invention in his hands.

"It's a microwave disruptor, but a very low-frequency one. It only knocks out cellular devices. I get so tired of going to the movies and having my time interrupted. This one, in particular, is a special request."

"It's hard to think of you going to the movies."

Tolarius chuckled. "Like you, I'm retired, my dear. Besides, I can't imagine what you would expect to find. After all, I'm old, out of shape and...Alice?" Tolarius turned and blinked in surprise at the site of the young blonde woman in the white and pink jumpsuit standing in the entrance to his garage. She stood with her arms crossed in front of her chest, and the look of someone only pretending to be calm on her face.

"Don't feel bad, I get that a lot." Anna said with a smirk and a shrug. She calmly strolled into the open garage and looked around at the walls. Interspersed with the weed whacker, lawnmower and other gardening tools, she noticed a plasma rifle, several Infinity knives, and what looked like a leaf blower with a thorium reactor attached to its side. "I see you've kept busy."

Dr. Tolarius stood and took a hesitant step towards Anna as he adjusted his glasses. "You're not, you're…"

"By the way, congratulations on your son's election. You must be very proud. So, I'm looking for something," Anna said, ignoring the doctor as he stuttered in wide-eyed shock. "An old invention of yours. I'm hoping you still have it. If not, I'll happily pay a commission to have you rebuild it. The Purge is nothing if not upfront with its business. Terror is Profit, yada-yada."

"What do you want?"

Anna came to a stop and glanced around the garage. "I was looking for a controller unit, preferably the neuro-adaptive model? Bluetooth? I know it was officially destroyed by Superior Force back in the day, but I also know that it was an invention you were proud of, so chances are you took the time to rebuild it, and possibly perfect it. I am looking to purchase it, and maybe some other tech."

Edward glanced around his garage. "Most of my inventions are around you. You'll notice that there is a lack of neuro-controllers."

Anna shrugged and smiled. "Whatever. I call bullshit. If anything, you probably rebuilt it into a more compact form. I read your research, and from what I could gather, you and Prometheus were looking at ways to miniaturize a version of the controller tech before your lab was destroyed."

"Prometheus asked, I did the looking, and yes, I *did* manage to make it smaller. The problem is the delivery system. I managed to get it to the size of a quarter, but in order to properly work, you need a nanite infusion for the radio control to be fluid."

"And it worked?" Anna asked.

Tolarius nodded. "Oh, it worked. The problem was it tended to fry the wearer. It was 100% lethal. Still is, though I've managed to increase the effectiveness a bit. Should last for several days, maybe a week if you're lucky. In the end though, your test subject better not be important to you."

"Is the device for sale?"

Tolarius eyed the woman for a moment. He calmly set his screwdriver on his workbench, wiped his hands on his shirt, and adjusted his thick bifocals. He then stood, the hand with the egg-shaped device sliding into his pocket. "I have made it a point to avoid doing business with the Purge, or any other organization for that matter, since the death of Prometheus. At my age, I have found it is best not to stir the pot."

Anna considered the doctor's words. "That's technically not a no. I can understand your hesitation. We are, after all, talking about tech that only you could perfect. I can see how you wouldn't want trouble knocking on your door."

The doctor nodded and wiped some sweat from his face. "I'm doing my best to live a quiet life, and I would prefer to avoid getting back into old habits."

"What if I told you what it was for? Would that sweeten the deal?" Anna asked. She put her hand on her hip, and flashed a smug smile.

Edward shrugged. "You could. I can't guarantee that it will."

Anna's grin turned predatory "What if I were to use it to destroy the Collective Good?"

Dr. Tolarius, once the scourge of the West Coast and most feared of the world's mad scientists, took off his glasses and stared at Anna. "Are you insane?"

"This is the big push, Doctor. The Purge is hedging its bets. We've already done the impossible; Superior Force has been defeated. The Red Guard was defeated, and with a few more well-timed tweaks, we can... well, that would be telling. We're on the verge of the greatest victory in the history of mankind, but we need a push, a little distraction before our final act. That's where your controller comes in."

Tolarius nodded. "I've been following your exploits. Only a fool wouldn't be able to see this for what it is. Still, from what I've gathered, the Purge has got to be exhausted, both in finances and in resources. How are you planning to accomplish your victory? My weaponry is impressive, but I'm a realist, my dear. It's simply not enough. Besides, from what I saw, you've already destroyed my energy collector."

"Oh, I know. This toy may get trashed too. Like I said, it's all a distraction. The real threat will come from the north."

Tolarius stared at Anna for a solid ten seconds before he said in a quiet voice, "My God, you are completely insane. You can't. You absolutely *cannot do* what you are suggesting. You have no idea, not the faintest, of what your actions will result in."

"My actions," Anna said while puffing up her chest with pride, "will result in the Purge securing its stranglehold over North America. From there, the Black Cloak, the Dead Talon, and all others will follow suit. We will carve a new empire, one that Prometheus, for all his posturing, was never able to achieve."

Tolarius shook his head. "No. What you will do is completely destroy this planet. You go through with your plan, and the Earth will be reduced to a charred ball floating dead in space. There's a reason the *Metatron* was never used, you stupid little girl. There's a *reason* Prometheus left it under the ice and walked away. You activate her, and the world will die. You will die. Everything," Tolarius gestured around his garage, "will simply die, and that will be your new empire, you foolish, insane child."

Anna's expression darkened. "So, does that mean you're refusing to help me?"

Tolarius shrugged. "On the contrary, you can have your toy. For a modest fee, of course."

Anna nodded. "Of course. Pray tell, why the capriciousness?"

Tolarius walked to a red Stanley toolbox beside a pegboard that held a rake, some clippers, and a hoe. He slid out the large, bottom drawer and took out a small, black box. After carefully checking its contents, he shut the lid, seemingly satisfied.

"This is the Purge nanite controller I was asked to create. I haven't officially tested it, but I can assure you my technology works. It's extremely Plug-and-Play; there's even a flash drive. You can use it in conjunction with most major operating systems. There is a help file that opens with the first activation, depending on what you're connecting to. I would suggest reading it."

Tolarius held the box out to Anna, along with what looked like a small credit swiper. Anna grumbled as she took a small card out of her belt and quickly slid it in the reader. After a tiny light on the side turned green, Tolarius smiled and nodded. "Thank you for your patronage."

Anna looked at the small box with a frown. "Seriously? That's it?"

"That's it. Don't be so put out. Most of my clientele weren't able to handle anything beyond what you have there. I designed for the most simple-minded of idiots to be able to take advantage of my work. It's why I was the best."

Anna shrugged. "Okay, I'll buy that. Still, you haven't answered my question."

Dr. Tolarius smiled as he headed back to his workbench. "First, there's no long-term benefit to using that technology. Even if you found someone that you could make the most of that with, your window of effectiveness will be extremely limited, and it's only good for one use. Secondly, there is no earthly way you can power the *Metatron*. The only substance on the planet that could get her to fly would be Thorium-27. Considering that it's not native to our dimension and that *Alice Gailsone,*" Tolarius emphasized the name and smiled, which made Anna bristle. "Has destroyed the Impossible Door, I fail to see how you intend to get your hands on anything that could provide enough power to do what you need. You're setting yourself up for failure, but I suppose that's to be expected, considering who you are. Pity."

Anna was shaking slightly, but kept her voice steady. "Big talk from an old man futzing around in his garage. You have no idea who I am, or what I'm capable of."

Tolarius let out a loud laugh. "I have no idea? My dear, who do you think made you the way you are? Who do you think designed your cryogenic prison? I know *exactly* who you are. You are a discarded waste product from what was easily the greatest biological achievement of my career. You're the proverbial leftover meatloaf in Prometheus's fridge. There's nothing left in you but some unearned recognition, and a veritable dictionary of mental disorders. Go have fun with your little toy, dear. Have fun when the Collective Good rips your spine out, and shows it to you before they finish what Prometheus never got around to doing. Although, in his defense, he did tend to forget about things after each...vacation."

Tolarius turned his attention back to his workbench, reaching for an old set of switches that he had laying off to the side. He picked up his screwdriver, and set to work disassembling them. "Run along, little leftover. Run along and kill yourself gloriously. I will be watching it on television."

Anna was shaking with rage, but still managed to keep herself from lashing out. She fought the urge to take her Infinity blade and slit the bloated, mad scientist from his genitals to his jaw, and instead closed her eyes, counted to ten, and tucked the controller into a pouch on her belt. In a calm, almost friendly voice, she said, "You really should learn to be more polite to a lady, Dr. Tolarius. Sometimes, we have friends."

Tolarius caught some movement out of the corner of his eye. He turned his head and saw Totallus; large, shiny and in a skin-tight black and purple bodysuit with a V slit exposing his chest, standing in the garage doorway.

"My, my. You *do* like to play with dangerous toys. There's a reason the Purge kept the Mark IV program limited to just a few models, and it wasn't budget. I suppose you've read that, as well?"

"I see you recognize my good friend, Totallus." Anna gestured to the silent, motionless android. "He is going to remove your body parts with his shiny, metallic fingers - one by one - unless you refund the purchase of the controller, and apologize for your harsh words."

Tolarius chuckled again, and reached into his pocket. He held up his tiny egg for Anna to see. "You know, this really is some of my better work. Simplistic, but good, nonetheless. See these three buttons here? The first one knocks out cell phones."

"The money, old man. Now." Anna was gritting her teeth as Tolarius continued in a tone that said he 100% did not care.

"The second button can knock out a wide array of electrical devices. Perfect for when too much is going on, like at a town hall meeting, or when people won't stop speeding in the cul-de-sac."

"I will fucking kill you if I have to! I will do it with my bare hands!" Anna was shaking with rage, but still, Tolarius didn't seem to notice.

Finally, Tolarius looked Anna in the eye and nodded. "I was right to have you put in that tube. My mistake was recommending to Prometheus that he keep you in case we needed to do what we did again, but I don't make mistakes like he did. I got it right the first time, where his pride wouldn't let him admit he was a colossal fuckup at genetic manipulation. You were stripped bare, sweetie, right down to your bones. Down to your very soul. Anything we left in you was by accident. In fact, I'm surprised your brain wasn't reduced to pudding when we were finished. There's nothing special about you, and that won't change, even if you use a hundred amplifiers."

Dr. Tolarius held up his egg and pressed the third button.

The light in the garage went out. Totallus suddenly staggered and collapsed to the floor, a gargled, digital cry emanating from his mouth as he fell. Anna glanced over in horror at her metallic protector as he lay motionless on the concrete floor. Around her, she could hear the absence of electrical activity. In her shock at losing her bodyguard, she started to back away from the mad doctor.

"What did you do?" She asked in a half-hysterical yell.

"The third button is a high-level EMP. I may be retired, but I'm not stupid. Sorry about your credit cards, by the way. That's why I know my controller will work, but that it, like your plan, is ultimately going to fail."

Anna glared at Tolarius with large, hot tears running down her face. "You just fried this?! Why? Just to be an asshole?"

Tolarius reached in his pocket and took out his car keys. He held them up and flashed a smirk. "Oh, don't worry. I shield my work, and that includes the case for your new toy." He pressed a button on his key fob, and immediately, the garage door light turned blood red. Anna whirled around as the walls of the garage slid, moved, or spun around to reveal row after row of menacing cannons, all humming with power, and all pointed in her direction.

Anna froze. "You don't mock me. *No one* mocks me. I'm going to kill you, old man."

"No, you won't." Tolarius said in an angry voice. "You will pick up that billion-dollar piece of garbage on my floor, take your worthless toy, and go back to your insane, delusional fantasies. That, or I will do what Prometheus should have done years ago."

Anna glared, her entire body shaking with rage. She marched over to where she had set the Collector and picked it up. Then, she slowly backed out of the garage. Instantly, four heavily-armed Purge shock troops moved in to collect the downed Totallus. The troops kept a leery eye on the scowling old man, and the dozens of massive guns that were positioned in the walls around him, now pointed squarely at their heads.

There was a growing roar of wind, and Tolarius shielded his eyes as a small hovercraft descended in his driveway, next to his maroon Cadillac. The shock troops loaded the prone android on board, and Anna followed, her new toys clutched close to her chest.

"She's going to kill you, you know," Tolarius called out to the young blonde as she boarded the vessel. Anna didn't turn around, but she did clutch the devices tighter as she entered the craft, and took her seat. The back hatch closed with a hydraulic whirr, and, a moment later, the hovercraft lifted off and sped north over the neighborhood with a high-pitched whine.

As she sat in her jump seat, her prized still clutched to her person, Anna felt her tears flow freely at Tolarius's words. "Get me to Manhattan, now!" she snapped at the pilot. "It's time to get things rolling. Any word from Kogoura?"

"He radioed while you were out. The *Metatron* has begun its initial power up, Ma'am," the pilot replied.

"Good. Get me to New York ASAP. I have business there before things get started," Anna said. She gripped the equipment in her hands so tightly that blood was starting to run down her palms. In a quiet voice, she whispered her mantra over and over, "I'm better than her. I'm better than her. I know it. I'm better than *her*..."

Tolarius watched the hovercraft roar out of his drive, and fly off into the hazy, blue sky of the morning. A neighbor that he vaguely knew named Joana was standing with her pug by his mailbox, watching the large ship as it swiftly disappeared on the horizon. Her dog barked wildly at the floating menace, and then peed in victory on Joana's wooden mailbox post.

Tolarius sighed and turned his attention back to his workbench. He picked up the set of switches from his table, poked at them, poked again, and then tossed them to the side. With a grunt, he reached for the dark green wall phone that hung near a pegboard in his garage. He then dug a small, creased address book out of his back pocket, and flipped through the worn pages until he found what he was after. He dialed carefully (Tolarius *hated* redialing. It was a pet peeve) and then waited.

"Hello," he said when the line picked up. "Yes, hello. It has been a while, hasn't it? I'm sorry to bother you, but do you have a moment? There's something I think you should know..."

***

Two days later, the office of the newly appointed Senator George Harding Carter was dark, save for the lights of the city that poured in through the penthouse office windows. Carter hadn't liked Stengles much, but he had to admire the man's sense of style when it came to flaunting power. The office had a commanding view of the Manhattan skyline, and the young senator had to admit that he felt a rush of power each time he looked out on the city at night. With a smug grin, he chuckled to himself and sipped from a tumbler of scotch.

"Enjoying the view?" From the shadows behind the senator, a blonde woman with her hair cut in a familiar-looking bob emerged. She was in a white body suit with pink highlights running down the sides, and the grin on her face, illuminated by the lights of the city, was Cheshire-like in appearance.

Carter felt his smile vanish, but didn't turn to face his guest. "And hello to you, too. I don't suppose they've covered knocking at the new Purge, have they? How did you get in here, anyway?"

General Anna May drifted to Carter's side and stopped to admire the view with the young, platinum-haired man. Carter noticed that she smelled of jasmine, and that her suit was partially unzipped in the front. With some degree of effort, he avoided looking at her, and tried to focus on the city. Anna noticed this, and laughed to herself. "I have a teleporter. She's in the lobby on her smart phone."

"What do you want? I'm busy tonight."

Anna let out a chuckle and glanced at the senator. "Busy? Doing what? Drinking the taxpayers' money away?"

Carter gave a mock toast with his glass. Some of the scotch sloshed out, running down his fingers. "I'm in charge of a superhuman shit storm of a state. Fuck NOT drinking at work. Besides, if you must know," George said, as he took a sip of his drink, "I'm waiting on a call. Something of mutual interest."

"Really?" Anna said with a raised eyebrow. "Could that have anything to do with the favor you owe us for bankrolling your election, Mr. Carter?" Anna reached over and gently took the glass of scotch from George's hand, took a sip, and let out a little gasp. "Oh, very smooth. Nice. Did we pay for this, too?"

"As a matter of fact," George said as his pocket buzzed. He took out his smart phone, checked it, nodded and then tucked it away. "Yes. I've taken measures to clean things up once and for all with the Collective Good."

"Your predecessor claimed he could do that, too." Anna pointed out as she downed the rest of the scotch. "And then he was taken out by a broken data geek and a 12-year-old girl. Honestly, it hasn't done a lot to restore my faith in New York senators. Tell me, what wonderful new plan am I paying for?"

"Stengles was a joke," Carter said with a snort. "He couldn't tell his asshole from his elbow. When I do something, I get the job done the first time."

Anna nodded. "Just like your father. By the way, how is Dr. Tolarius?"

George stiffened at the name of his estranged father. "I wouldn't know. We don't talk."

"Well," Anna said with a grin. "It just so happens that *I* do. And he told me something very interesting the other day. It seems, and stop me if you already know this, but it seems that a Totallus went missing from a warehouse in New Jersey this week. Can you believe that?"

George glanced at Anna and shrugged. "So what?"

"Well," Anna said as she carefully placed the empty tumbler on the mahogany desk behind them and turned to lean against the window, facing George. "It just so happens that they can only be activated by a very short list of people. People that are genetically coded to interface with them. People like you, Mr. Carter."

"Again, so what?" George asked flippantly. "Even if I did 'borrow' a Totallus, which I'm not saying I did, what would it matter? Are you here to bitch at me about how your little terrorist organization is running out of money?"

"Not at all," Anna said with a sly smile. "I just wanted to point out that we're on a time-table. You see, I'm not like my predecessor, either. I like to get things done, and done quickly. In just a couple of days, the skies of this city will rain red with blood. My grand plan is almost upon us, and when I'm finished, you, my brave Mr. Carter, will come swooping in to save the day. You will rebuild this shattered city, and help its citizens to stand united. Of course, they'll rally behind the man who saved them, who lifted them up. That's you, by the way. Just so we're clear."

"I gathered," George said, dryly. "Look, I've taken steps to move the Collective Good off the table. It's cost me a lot of money and favors, but I've brought in a friend to get the job done right. Just remember that I want something special in return."

Anna grinned and put her hands behind her as she leaned back on the glass. "Anything in particular you desire, Mr. Carter?"

George stepped back and reached for a folder on his desk. "As a matter of fact, there is. Here."

He handed the folder to Anna, who took it, opened it, and frowned. Inside was a picture of a 12-year-old girl with shoulder-length brown hair and light brown freckles on her cheeks. "You want a child?"

"Her name is Holly Bedford," George said as his smile vanished. "I want you to find her, and I want you to bring her home."

Chapter Three

Just one little shot?

As wisps of moonlight danced along the shores of the Hudson, four women (well, three women and one android, technically) were quickly and quietly moving into position for their first official Collective Good team assignment. It was early evening, and the construction crews at the Jacob K. Javits Convention Center had packed up several hours ago. The facility had been partially closed following some recent superhuman activity in the area, and many of the glass panels that lined its expansive lobby area were in the process of being replaced. As the evening boat traffic started making its way down the river, the lights from the passing ships reflected off the beautiful, clear walls of the facility, casting crimson and yellow patterns across the walls and floors.

The city lights were briefly joined by a soft purple glow from somewhere above the massive glass ceiling. Quietly, a small pile of sand started to form in the middle of the lobby. It was gently raining down from the center of the purple glow overhead, and formed a neat pile on the floor below. A moment later, two shapes made a swift and silent descent into the darkened convention center. Both were women, clad in black stealth suits. The first had a pale face, obscured by a black and white domino mask, and bobbed purple hair. The second, an Asian woman with sheathed blades crisscrossed along her back, landed with the grace and silence of a cat beside the former.

Alice Gailsone, former second-in-command of the Purge and one-time supervillain, gave three gentle taps to a button on her wrist. The former terrorist extraordinaire turned to her companion, the deadly assassin Aika Fukijima, also known as The Lotus. Aika was Alice's personal assistant, which meant that (sometimes) she was involved with the tedium of day-to-day business life, as Alice was currently the owner of *Rare Gems*, a gem procurement facility in Brooklyn. While working with Alice at Rare Gems was admittedly boring, the purple-haired woman made up for it by inviting Aika along on some of her side missions for the Collective Good. Personally, Aika didn't care why or for how long Alice intended on working for the world's premiere superhero organization, as long as she was able to get out and put her skills to good use.

They nodded to each other before darting across the floor of the lobby, mindful of the security cameras and their slow, arcing patterns. Within moments, they were in a side hall, standing in front of a janitor's closet. Alice touched the door's lock with a finger that glowed purple. Instantly, the metal lock rotted away into flecks of dust from Alice's entropy magic. Alice gave the now-unlocked door a light nudge. Beside her, Aika drew her katana and held it at the ready.

Their efforts were rewarded with a long stairway, followed by a dark passageway that led several stories below the massive complex. Alice and Aika moved as quietly as they could, making sure to take their time as they descended into the inky blackness of the stairwell. Alice led the way, using the night-vision lenses on her domino mask to see where she was going.

The night-vision painted the stairwell in brilliant shades of green for Alice, and she was grateful for the assist. Ever since signing on with the Collective Good, she had been quietly impressed with the level of technology and quality they had put into her equipment. Her goggles, for instance, could cycle through night-vision, thermal, infrared, and six other settings Alice hadn't even bothered with yet. Aside from a few hiccups when she started, she was now thoroughly happy with her new outfit. It was a visual copy of her old one; a black body suit with a purple gemstone on the chest, a utility belt for her equipment, and some rather comfy footwear. The fabric was an experimental breathable Kevlar weave, built to absorb impact, and slick enough to help deflect a blade attack. It had been modified heavily by R&D to withstand numerous forms of assault, and, so far, Alice was pleased. Her hands were left uncovered, as any gloves she wore would rot off as soon as she used her powers. Her face was left mostly uncovered, save for a domino mask. This left most of her face plainly visible, but honestly, Alice didn't mind this. In fact, she considered it something of a trademark for her former badass villainess persona as Dyspell, the Most Dangerous Woman in the World.

Alice nearly jumped when she felt Aika's hand on her shoulder. Slightly flustered, Alice turned and saw the grim-faced assassin holding the wall with her other hand. Silently, Aika squeezed Alice's shoulder again, and then pointed towards their feet. Alice glanced towards the floor, and after a couple of seconds, noticed a thin strand of piano wire about two more steps down. She looked back at Aika, who must have felt her move. Aika just pointed down again and frowned, not wanting to speak.

Carefully, Alice stepped over the wire, checked to see where it was attached, and then gently touched the sensor it with her finger. A small flash of purple light momentarily glimmered in the darkness, and the sensor rotted away. Alice motioned Aika to let her know it was safe, and they continued on until they reached the bottom level.

Alice paused at the last step and reached out to stop Aika. The floor looked slightly askew, and Alice searched the walls until she found a small switch behind a false wall tile. She flipped it, and they both heard a small clank come from beneath the floor.

Satisfied that things were safe, they continued on until they reached a thick, metal door. Alice put her finger to the lock and focused. She carefully rotted through the metal, and as quietly as they could the two ladies opened the door to reveal a wider, well-lit passageway that spilled out into a massive oval chamber.

The room looked more like an amphitheater than the storage room their schematics had hinted at, complete with fancy, red velvet stadium seating. The well-lit chamber had a concrete floor and was separated into an inner and outer area by a curved wall of what looked like Plexiglas. On the outside, following the rows of seats, was a beautiful oak bar, some empty wine glasses, and various bits of waterlogged, colored paper that were scattered across the floor. Within the Plexiglas section, Alice and Aika could see the concrete flooring was stained dark red in random, asymmetrical blobs.

"The room is clear," Aika said in a low voice. "Whoever was behind this is gone."

Alice notably relaxed and touched the side of her mask to deactivate her night vision. "Or at the very least, they're done for the night. Blackbird, we're in."

Alice put her finger to her ear as she heard a garbled "copy that" come through her receiver. Alice frowned. Their tech was stellar, but the walls were so thick that the signal on her earpiece was only barely coming through.

"Why did you rot the sensor?" Aika asked as they looked around.

Alice shrugged. "I didn't feel like forgetting about it on the way out. Also, it was really cool."

Aika grumbled, "'Cool spy things' cannot be the answer for every reckless decision you make."

"Sure it can," Alice said with a smirk.

"Dyspell," Aika called, mindful of using her code name in the field, "Over here."

Alice headed over to Aika, who had found an entrance to the inner chamber, and was kneeling by one of the dried splatters. "This happened recently. Two hours old, at the most."

"You can tell that by looking?"

Aika glanced at Alice. "I am not unfamiliar with blood," she calmly stated. "This happened tonight. Careful, the floor is slippery."

Alice touched the floor, feeling the red, sticky residue. "Agreed. I'm surprised they pulled up stakes so quickly."

"They did not," Aika said as she looked around. "They were merely done for the night. They would not have left so much evidence behind, otherwise. The main crew is gone for the evening. Anyone we find will be from the graveyard shift, which I imagine will be here shortly."

Alice nodded and relaxed a bit. "Or the cleanup crew, which one would think would have been here by now. Well, that means all that awesome stealth was for nothing. By the way, how'd you know about the wire on the stairs?"

Aika glanced at Alice. "There was an indent in the wall. I took it to be a signal."

Alice grinned and turned her attention back to the room. She slipped out her PhoneBuddy and started to record. "Cool. Just let me get this for Blackbird. You seeing this, BB?"

Over their earpieces, a crackly voice answered, "Feed is coming through. Is this through your goggle feed?"

Alice shook her head for a second before sighing. "Nope. PhoneBuddy. Better resolution."

"...You couldn't figure out the GUI, could you?"

Alice growled under her breath as Victoria changed the subject. "Looks like our tip-off was on the money."

"Sure does," Alice murmured. "No sign of anyone yet. Looks like they vacated. Lotus, grab a blood sample?"

Aika was already scraping some of the blood on the floor into a vial, and then carefully tucking it into her utility belt. "Done."

Blackbird's voice chimed in again. "You can see better than me. What's your opinion? Is this a one-off?"

Alice shook her head, and then remembered that Victoria Green, aka Blackbird, couldn't see her. "Not likely. The main passage was rigged, and the walls, the seating, and especially the lighting all suggest careful planning. That might mean there's an alternate way in for the staff."

"Anything else?" Victoria asked.

Alice continued. "Someone put up some serious money for this. The combat ring looks to be Plexiglas, but I'd bet money it's actually some form of clear alloy to prevent anyone from escaping."

Aika took a closer look and ran her hand along the surface. "This is not glass. It feels like Aluminum oxynitride."

Alice raised an eyebrow. "Transparent aluminum? That's a bit extreme."

"Can you pan the inner chamber?" Victoria asked.

Alice turned her PhoneBuddy towards the chamber. "Yeah, everything here looks perfect. There's an open ceiling with a massive lighting rig. Anything that happened in this arena was clearly visible, no matter where you were standing. Also," Alice panned over to a far wall, where a high-end video camera was stationed on a stand. "Their video setup is still here, and it looks like it was set for a live feed."

Alice yelped as a shuriken flew by her head, shattering the camera's lens. She turned to see Aika standing calmly behind her. "I didn't say it was on! There's no blinky light!"

Aika gave her a look that said she 100% did not care. "And now, we are sure."

Alice and Aika could both hear Blackbird sighing through their commlinks. "A live feed means something was posted to the web. I'll have my people do a search."

Alice shook her head, despite the fact that Victoria couldn't see her. "Let me save you some time. Eedee?"

Over the comm came a chipper voice. "Already on it, mom! I'm checking the Purge FTP sites we used to frequent. I'm also checking for any video uploads, recent feeds, and activity on any Bitcoin accounts we used to use."

"Thanks, and don't call me Mom." Alice smiled, and tucked her PhoneBuddy into her pocket. "If anything is posted, Eedee should be able to find it."

"Provided this was the Purge," Victoria noted. "And provided they're still using the same accounts. Also, you can track Bitcoins?"

"*You* can't?" Alice asked with a small, sly grin.

Eedee chimed in. "Sorry. I looked, but aside from some chatter, I don't see any video uploads. Most of the FTP sites are down, too. Probably from blowing up so many Purge bases."

"Eedee," Victoria cut in. "Can you get me that chatter? Every little bit helps."

"Roger dodger!" Eedee happily replied.

Alice shrugged. "Well, I'm not surprised. This new Purge does seem a little more haphazard than mine was. If I had to guess, they're running low on resources at this point, especially after wasting so many of their bases during that whole mess with Superior Force. If it is them, I'm betting they haven't considered anything so trivial as setting up new FTP servers, or they don't care."

"Or they were not the ones to host it," Aika said. She was looking around the arena. "This area does not provide a lot of room for maneuverability. Also, the blood splatters indicate that a good portion of the victim's blood ended up on their assailant. This is not an ideal gladiatorial pit."

Alice nodded as she walked up beside Aika. She had noticed the small enclosure as well. "I agree. It's an execution chamber. I'm just glad we got here after everyone left. I...huh."

Alice bent down, and picked something small and white off the floor. After rubbing it between her fingers, she popped the flecks of crystal in her mouth.

"Did you just eat something off the floor of an execution chamber?" Aika asked in a voice that said she wasn't all that surprised.

"Shut up," Alice said. "Huh. Epsom salt. Why the hell would Epsom salt be on a kill floor?"

"We have been here long enough," Aika pointed out. "As I have said, if this is a regular event, then someone should be along to clean the room."

As if on cue, they were interrupted by the sound of a door opening on the far side of the room. They both looked up in time to see a janitor, who stood frozen in his tracks. They stared at one another in dumbstruck silence for several moments before Alice smiled and waved.

"Hi," she said in her friendliest tone.

The janitor dropped his mop and ran back out the door, screaming for help.

"That could have gone better," Alice mumbled, as she and Aika took off after him. He had a good lead on them, but they were closing the gap pretty quickly. Aika slipped a shuriken out from her belt and, as they sprinted down the hall, she flung it at the screaming janitor. The man let out a gargled cry as he stumbled forward and collapsed, the throwing star lodged firmly in the back of his head.

Alice glared at Aika. "Dude! He was a janitor! You don't have to kill the janitors!"

"Who killed what now?" Victoria's voice chimed in over their commlink.

"No one!" Alice quickly chirped. "No one's killing anyone! We're all alive. Over. Yes. Good." She then glared at Aika, who shrugged.

"We needed to stop him, so I stopped him," Aika said in a bored tone. Strolling down the hallway, she stopped to lean down and pluck her weapon out of the back of the man's skull. Alice, still frustrated, grumbled to herself as she followed along.

"We could have asked him who he works for. This should not be a conversation. We're good...we're less-bad guys now. We don't need to kill cleaning crews!"

"You are a 'less-bad guy'," Aika pointed out. "I just happen to be in your service. I...did you hear that?"

They both looked down the hallway. Just beyond a bend, they could hear sounds, voices, and movement.

Both women now moved with a sense of urgency. They knew that if the janitor had been shouting for someone, then there must have been someone to hear him.

'That, or he panicked,' Alice thought to herself.

As they rounded a corner, the hallway opened up into a larger staging area lined with tables, gurneys, blood-soaked bandages and cabinets stocked with a helter-skelter array of medical supplies. There were several mutilated bodies on some of the tables, but what caught both ladies' attention was the small group of medical examiners gathered around a far table.

One of the doctors, a woman with curly brown hair poking out from under a net, let out a surprised cry. "Shit! There *is* someone here. Security!"

All three doctors stopped what they were doing, and, despite looking alarmed, Alice and Aika both noticed that they weren't running. One kept glancing at the wall, screaming, "This isn't right! This isn't what..!" She was cut off when a second later, a panel to a side room chimed, and a woman stepped out. She looked to be Latina, roughly mid-20s, and was wearing a short blue dress with matching tights. A silver sash hung on her hip, and in her right hand was a katana.

Alice tensed as she recognized the woman's outfit, but Aika put her hand out to stop her. The Latina woman glanced at Alice, but then locked her glare on Aika, who returned the favor. They studied each other for a moment before the newcomer said, "You're the Lotus, aren't you?"

Aika nodded. "And you are one of the Sisters of Avalon. Malice, correct?"

The woman, Malice, nodded. "Our reputation precedes us. This is honestly unexpected. I was told that... you know what? It doesn't matter. I've been longing for a chance to face you. Hell, everyone in the Sisterhood has heard stories about you. This is a dream come true."

Aika brought her sword up in a ready stance. "No," she said in a low voice. "It is not."

In a blur, the two women were on each other, swords flashing in a shower of sparks. Alice was almost entranced by the action, until she noticed that one of the doctors had grabbed a flash drive out of a laptop that was on their operating table, and were using this as an opportunity to escape. Wasting no time, Alice took off after them with a shout. "Hey! Get back here! Guys!" Alice said over her comm. "I have doctors on the run!"

"That's cool," came a calm reply over the comms. "When they're topside, we'll take 'em."

Aika paid her employer little notice as she continued to lock blades with the smiling warrior. They fought with a vicious caution, each diving at the other, striking and slashing, blocking and parrying, and then retreating for several moments. Then they would begin again, as if in some timed, insane dance.

Malice grinned, and nodded towards Aika's arm. "So, the legendary Lotus can be cut. Working for that traitor has made you soft."

Aika didn't have to glance at her arm to know that Malice had managed to get in a quick slice. "Maybe," Aika said in a casual tone.

They leapt at each other again, blades clanging and sliding across each other in a silver blur. Malice went for what looked like an obvious opening in Aika's defenses, then blinked as a flash of silver momentarily flickered in front of her. She blinked again, and Lotus was standing a good three meters away.

Malice opened her mouth to comment, but found it was filled with blood. She gagged and dropped her sword. She brought her trembling hands to her neck, which had been neatly sliced open in a neat, red line.

"Or maybe I wanted to make you feel confident," Aika said as she shook the thin strand of crimson from her sword. Malice fell to the ground, gasping and choking to death at Aika's feet. Aika, her face a picture of calm, let out a small sigh.

"You were very skilled," she said in a quiet voice. "Thank you for the honor of fighting you."

"Oh, she was just okay," a voice called out. Aika glanced up to see two other women standing in the passageway. One, a blonde, was holding a naginata. The other, a tall woman with skin the color of midnight and long, shiny brown hair, was twirling two sais in her hands as she smirked. "We sent her out first to see how you'd fare. Now, it's our turn."

Aika sighed as she reminded herself that the Black Cloak, the top European-based terrorist agency, always made a point to recruit *three* female assassins to serve as the Sisters of Avalon.

With a nod, Aika tightened her grip on her blade. "Very well, let us begin."

***

Alice was panting from exhaustion as she chased the three doctors down the hall. Two of them were young, a man and a woman, while the third was older, pudgy, and, in Alice's opinion, exhibiting far too much energy for someone his age. Alice was starting to suspect there was something more to the older doctor when he suddenly stopped and turned to face her. Alice slowed up and grumbled as she watched the two younger doctors make a break for a hatchway.

"Go," the older doctor called over his shoulder. "I've got this."

Alice slipped into a fighting stance. "Two bogeys are slipping though."

"Calling some friends?" The older doctor smiled at Alice and stretched. "You know, when we were told we were getting protection from the Black Cloak, I thought it was a bit ridiculous. Unnecessary, really. We have our own means of keeping ourselves safe."

Alice, having had more than her share of experience with psychotic doctors, stayed frosty. Every muscle in her body was coiled as she waited for the older man to make his move. She felt a cold feeling of anticipated dread wash over her. "You're not going to quietly surrender, are you?"

The doctor smiled and shrugged. "Not really. By the way, you may want to run away now."

Alice smiled and inched her hand towards her side, where a Glock was patiently waiting in its holster. The doctor saw this and flicked his wrist. Alice stared as the doctor was now holding a small, glowing green vial of liquid.

"Not bad, eh? I used to moonlight as a stage magician in college. Nothing fancy, just sleight of hand."

Alice's eyes widened as she recognized the contents of the vial. "Don't," she said. "Look, I know this seems like a good idea to you right now, but trust me, you don't want to do this. The change is permanent."

The doctor laughed, popping the cork on the vial. "Maybe in your day, but we've done our homework, little lady." Alice sighed and felt her stomach drop into her shoes as the doctor chugged the glowing liquid.

Alice whispered in a slightly shaking voice, "I need Eedee. Right now, please."

"I'm kind of busy at the moment, Mom!" Eedee's voice was broken by static and the sound of high winds.

Alice swallowed and mumbled, "Don't call me Mom."

In front of her, the doctor had grown to a hulking brute nearly three times his original size. His skin was an oozing mass of wires, metal, and green sludge. His head had warped into what looked to be a gigantic dog only with a mouth that was lined with a seemingly impossible number of sharp, metallic teeth. The slimy, humongous beast slammed its clawed hands into the tiled floor, cracking it as it did so.

Alice had some prior experience with techno-shifters. The Thorium-based nanite solution had been developed as a super serum by the Purge to be sold on the black market, and then further weaponized by a local crime lord who called himself Obsidian. The results, no matter how the drug was synthesized, were always the same. A massive, homicidal were-beast covered in wires, metal, and slime, and powered almost completely by mindless rage. The creatures were so dangerous and unpredictable that Alice and Prometheus had pulled the plug on the project years ago.

Alice had squared off against techno-weres in the past, but this one was larger, and sported considerably more spikes along its limbs and back than even Alice was used to. Also, Alice noted that his drool was melting through the floor. The techno beast snarled at Alice, and for a moment, the pale woman thought that his curling black lips almost looked like a smile.

Alice cracked her knuckles and focused her powers. Her hands started to glow purple as she clenched her fists and assumed a ready stance. "I'm sorry," Alice said as the beast coiled. "If you can understand me right now, I'm so sorry."

A heartbeat later, the monster pounced.

***

Outside, there was the sound of a clank from the concrete walkway along the calm, black waters of the river. A sewer grate that was near the walkway's ledge opened outward, and the two younger doctors, a young man with short hair and a Pakistani woman, both climbed out.

"We got away," the man said to himself. He was shaking, and had to hold himself as his partner sealed the manhole hatch behind them.

"No, we got out. We're getting away, so let's not blow it. Come on!" She grabbed him by the arm, and the two of them made their way to a small nearby pier. There was a speedboat tied to the docks, quietly floating as the river's water lapped against its side. She climbed in while he started to untie the craft.

"Would you hurry it up?" the woman hissed. She searched a compartment for the boat's keys, and quickly started it up as the man was on his last rope.

"Calm down," he said. "We got away. Dr. Pierce said he would hold her off, so I don't see why you're..."

He was cut off by the sound of a loud crack, followed by the woman screaming and clutching her shoulder. He saw a large, red stain grow across her white coat. A second later, there was a second crack, followed by the windshield of the boat shattering. Without wasting any time, the woman threw the boat into full reverse and cranked the wheel. She pulled out and shifted the boat into full speed, just as a third loud crack was heard. This time, the speedometer exploded into a hundred pieces of shattered plastic.

Behind her, the female doctor could hear her partner yelling for her. "Cindy! There's a flying woman behind us!"

Cindy glanced back and cursed. Hovering close behind them was what appeared to be a curvy blonde in a skintight blue suit. She was calling out to them, but it was hard to hear over the roar of the boat's engine.

"She's telling us to stop," the man called out.

"Derrick, the plasma cannon under the seat! Use it!" Cindy snapped back. She was heading downriver and trying to make it out into the harbor, but they still had a ways to go, and the flying woman was easily keeping up.

Derrick lifted the back row of seats to reveal a small compartment, and inside, a large, silver, shoulder-mounted cannon. He quickly turned it on, waited for the small green activation light on its side to start glowing, and then hoisted the cannon onto his shoulder. He let the auto sights line the woman up through the bright red digital scope on the cannon's side. As soon as the cannon in his hands chimed, he pulled the trigger.

***

Eedee had been watching with Allison from across the river when she suddenly perked up. "Hey! Look over there! There are two people coming out of the ground!"

Allison, who had been scanning the rooftop of the convention center through her sniper scope, tilted her gun downward and grinned. She had been on the lookout since she had gotten Alice's signal that they had made it inside safely. "Why, there sure are. Good job, Eedee. Hey, Blackbird?" Allison asked "I've got two bogeys. Authorization to terminate?"

"Negative," Victoria's voice chimed in her ear. "Bogeys needed for questioning. Detain only."

Alison watched as they headed for a nearby speedboat. "What about just shooting one of them? Can I shoot one of them?"

"Negative. Detain only."

Allison lined up the man's head between her crosshairs. "The why in God's name am I here? I'm a sharpshooter. It's what I do. Come on. Just one little shot? I can wound. You know I can wound."

"Allison..." Victoria grumbled. Allison had been offered no less than three different code names, only to turn them all down. The only one she was hot on was the Mistress of Death, which Victoria flat-out refused to use.

"Something small, like a shoulder? Please?"

"No. You might kill one of them on accident, and tonight is already a cluster fuck. Just send Eedee."

"Spoilsport."

"…You just want to shoot something, don't you?"

"…Maybe."

There was the unmistakable sound of a defeated sigh. "Just fucking send Eedee."

Beside Allison, Eeedee asked, "How would shooting them help, exactly?"

Allison shrugged. "They will be so scared that they will surrender."

Eedee watched as the woman climbed into the boat. "I really don't see how that works. I'd think they'd just run for it."

Allison shrugged. "If they do, I'll just keep shooting the boat until one of them gets in the way. Problem solved."

"You want me to just go get them for you? Miss Blackbird said to go get them. Can I go now?" Eedee asked. The bubbly android was already floating a good two feet off the rooftop.

"…Yeah, you probably should. I'm making a bad choice. Go get in position. I miiiight just give 'em a warning shot. See if they're smart, or if they run." Allison tweaked her scope and adjusted for wind. Beside her, she heard a whoosh, and knew that Eedee was already on her way.

The auburn-haired woman adjusted her cap, took a sip from her juice box, and tried to keep the adrenaline surging through her from making her bounce in place. She hadn't been given a lot of excuses to break out the sniper rifle lately, short of scoping out coffee houses for potential dates with her new boyfriend. Brandon Vitags (also known as the Red Guard) had readily offered to help with the mission. Allison, while touched at his eagerness, politely declined. Even though he was superhuman, she found that she was always distracted when he was along. It was silly, but she was always convinced that she needed to keep an eye on him and make sure he was safe. Never mind that he was nearly indestructible and a cosmic warrior. He was hers, and she tended to worry.

Allison adjusted her red-rimmed glasses and started humming the theme to *Green Acres*. The classic comedy jingle always put her in a good mood, and she liked associating that good mood with shooting things. She waited until the two doctors were ready to take off, and, despite Victoria's insistence, was about to squeeze off a round when she heard the crack of a gunshot. Allison's eyes widened to the size of dinner plate as she watched the woman in the boat reel back, her arm now red with blood.

"What the fuck?" Allison mumbled. She felt a cold chill pass over her body as a second shot hit the boat. A moment later, the two scientists were unmoored, and Eedee was giving pursuit down the Hudson.

"What's going on?" Victoria asked.

"It wasn't me."

"Allison?"

"IT WASN'T ME, OKAY?"

Eedee's voice crackled over the comms. "Hey, I thought you said you weren't going to shoot them!"

"ALLISON!" Victoria's voice was so loud there was reverb in Allison's earpiece.

"One sec," She mumbled as she swung her rifle up and around. There were a lot of vantage points nearby, and the shot could have come from several different angles. Still, Allison was counting on the shooter not being as careful as her. Allison switched the night vision on her scope on and hurriedly scanned the area across from the convention center. Sure enough, she saw what looked like a man standing on top of a nearby office complex, rifle in hand.

Allison drew a bead on the other shooter. She hadn't adjusted for the shot, and Victoria wouldn't stop yelling in her ear. Allison did a quick assessment for wind, aimed at the man's torso, and pulled the trigger. With no small level of satisfaction, Allison grinned as she saw the man fly backwards, his gun dropping to the ground. Her grin turned to a frown when a second later, the man got up and started running for the rooftop access door.

"Huh. That wasn't what I was going for," Allison mumbled. A small voice in the back of her head that suspiciously sounded like Eedee pointed out that she was lucky she had only grazed the man, and that he would be worth more to them alive. Allison then reminded the small voice that this was a rare opportunity to legally shoot someone, and to shut the fuck up.

"Did you just shoot someone again? Allison?" Victoria asked in a warning tone.

"'Again' implies I shot someone already. Yeah, I shot a sniper on a roof catty corner to here. Checking targets." Grumbling, Allison ignored the voice in her ear, and quickly adjusted her angle to follow the boat. Wind was down, but visibility was an issue, and her scope could only offer so much under these conditions. Sighing, she lowered the scope and then looked back to the office building adjacent to her vantage point. "They're out of range. All yours, Eedee."

"Roger dodger!" Eedee said back. Allison grinned, and turned her attention back to the convention center. She was miffed at missing, but only to a point. The shot was a difficult one to pull off on the fly, and Allison had at least (kind of) hit him. She was also pissed about the boat, but if the Mark IV Totallus was on the case, then Allison had little to worry about.

"Should have just shot 'em both when they popped up," Allison grumbled. "Victoria, Eedee's apprehending the bogeys. I'm going after the..." Allison was making her way to the access door for her own roof when a bright blue flash from the boat caught her attention. "Holy shit! They've got a plasma cannon!"

***

Eedee was trying to call out to the people in the boat, but wasn't sure if they could hear her or not. They seemed pretty panicked, and the boat's engine was awfully loud. She pulled in a little closer and called out, "Excuse me? Please stop your boat. My friend will happily stop shooting at you if you would be kind enough to surrender. Please? Hello?"

Eedee watched as the man moved to the back of the boat and pulled something large and shiny out of the back row storage bin. "Huh," she said as she auto-zoomed on the weapon. "A 141-TA Plasma Cannon, military graAAAACCK!" Eedee screamed as she quickly dodged a bright blue beam of energy. A moment later, she dodged again, spinning in the air as the man with the cannon let off a rapid succession of blasts.

Eedee was moving as fast as she could while trying to keep up a random dodging pattern. She knew that the 141-TA's locking system was pattern-based, and that she could avoid being shot if she managed to add enough random variables to stay ahead of the locking system by .05 seconds. It wasn't a commonly known flaw, but Eedee was grateful for the timing variance. It was enough that she could keep out of range, but all it would take is one lucky shot and she'd end up with a hole through her torso.

Over the comm, Eedee heard the panicked voice of Alice say, "I need Eedee. Right now, please."

"I'm kind of busy at the moment, Mom!" Eedee's shouted as she dodged a blast. The plasma bolt meant for the flying android instead slammed into the side of a restaurant, which exploded a moment later.

"Please stop shooting at me!" she desperately called out. Beneath her, the speedboat was going at top speed, cutting through the wake of a larger shipping vessel and bouncing wildly. The shooter was having trouble keeping his balance, but he wasn't letting that stop him from trying to shoot her down. He kept on rattling off shots, and Eedee was growing more and more alarmed.

"Blackbird?" She asked as she did a fast barrel roll to avoid a shot.

"...Go ahead, Eedee," Blackbird replied.

Eedee dove, but she could feel the heat from the plasma burst that went through the space where her head had just been. "How badly do we need these people alive?"

"Pretty bad. The facility was deserted. These three were working overtime, so they're our best leads. We need them for questioning, and we need their data. Why?"

Eedee dove low, skimming the water behind the boat. She strayed left to avoid a shot, and then cringed as she felt the heat from an explosion behind her. The plasma blast had slammed into the side of a tanker that was shipping something flammable, and the entire Hudson was now awash with uneven orange light as the ship went up in a colossal fireball.

"What was that?" Blackbird asked, alarmed. "I could hear that loud and clear through your comms. Eedee, what did you do?"

"Nothing! I swear! That was them! That was all them!"

"Look, just shut them down," Blackbird's patience was beginning to sound strained on the comm. "Just try not to kill them, and not like Allison tries."

"I heard that," Allison chimed in.

"I know you did. We're having a talk when you get back."

Eedee winced at the string of cursing coming from Allison's comm. "Um, Blackbird? You should know that the 141-TA has a common production flaw related to overheating from continued use, and they are continually using it."

"How long until the flaw kicks in?"

Eedee shrugged as she flew and quickly climbed to avoid another shot. "Assuming they keep this level of intensity up, about 20 seconds, give or take."

"Take them down hard, Eedee. We need them."

Eedee nodded. "Roger dodger!" And with that, she did a high-speed nosedive into the black waters below.

***

Alice was holding her side to cover the large scratch along her abdomen. The hallway was wide enough to move, but not wide enough for a proper fight. The techno-were had been quicker than any she had faced before, and it wasn't staying still long enough for her to get in a good grip. She had already unloaded her sidearm into it, but that just seemed to make it mad. All she needed was one touch, and the beast would be done for. The problem was that it seemed to know that on some level, and had done its best to keep out of reach.

Alice slashed with her hands at the monster, but was unable to get near enough. In response, several cables shot out of the beast's back and started whipping through the air at Alice, slicing into her outfit. Alice let out a short cry as she managed to get a hold of one of the cables, which instantly rotted to dust in her grip.

"Come on, just get a little closer. Nice, tasty girl over here," Alice taunted. For emphasis, she gestured to herself and grinned. The techno-were continued to growl and slowly advance, sprouting more cables as it did so.

Alice considered her options. The creature wasn't getting close enough for a touch-based attack, so short of doing something ridiculous, she would have to go with her ranged options. She slid her PhoneBuddy out of her pocket, eyed the creature, and smiled.

"PhoneBuddy, fire!" she yelled as the tiny cell phone erupted with electrical energy. The blast hit the creature in the face, who immediately shook it off.

"Well, shit."

Alice slumped as the monster advanced again. She tucked and rolled out of the way as one of the metal cables lashed out at her, and instead left a wide gash in the hallway wall. Alice wasted no time as she slid one of her newer additions, a pack of detonation tape, out of her belt. It was meant for opening doorways (or walls, for that matter), but Alice had discovered in practicing with it that the roll could be used all at once, if necessary. She slammed the roll against the ground as hard as she could, which activated the pressure countdown on the small, black dots that lined the tape roll. She then threw it at the monster and sprinted the opposite direction.

The explosion threw Alice forward several feet, and she gasped as the hallway filled with fire and smoke. She slammed rather unceremoniously into the floor, and did a poorly-executed roll before coming up coughing. Behind her, she could hear something that sounded like static and screaming combined into one horrible wail. She looked back, and through the smoke she could see the techno-were, burning and charging through the hallway towards where she was standing. One of its eyes was gone, and its left side looked stripped. Through the missing swath of flesh, Alice could see a mess of wires and muscle that was hemorrhaging blood, oil, and a thick, green sludge.

Before Alice could react, the monster was on top of her. Alice tried to focus, but the beast was insanely fast. She barely had time to shift her weight, and put her shoulder into its mouth as opposed to her neck, before the techno-were knocked her onto her back, slamming her to the floor. Alice screamed, and then drove her hand up and into its neck. Her skin was glowing bright purple, and her hand moved through the beast like its skin was made from soft butter. The beast howled, and in a desperate attempt to stop her, clamped down even harder.

Alice gritted her teeth, and forced herself not to pass out from pain. The hallway was thick with black smoke, and the only light was coming from the quickly spreading fire, as it lapped at the cheap plaster walls and ceiling tiles. Alice could barely breathe, but she kept focused on the task at hand. She ripped her hand through the side of the monster's neck, pulled her hand back into a fist, and slammed it through the monster's skull.

"Fucking DIE!" Alice screamed as the techno-were started to convulse. Its eyes rolled up in its head as its jaw loosened on her shoulder, and she focused her powers through her shoulder to quickly loosen the creature's metallic teeth from her skin. Coughing, dizzy and feeling a bit disoriented, Alice crawled out from under the dead monster, and tried to get to her feet. She was about to fall forward, but was unexpectedly caught.

Alice glanced up to see Aika, completely covered in blood, and sporting a gash along her cheek. Her outfit was nearly shredded from tiny cuts and slices, and her hair was so matted with blood that it looked like one solid, black blob attached to her head. Behind Aika, Alice noted there was a trail of red that had dribbled off her clothing as she walked.

"Hey," Alice said in a hoarse voice. "So, how's your evening going?"

"We should leave," Aika said in a steady voice. She moved to Alice's good side, and looped the pale woman's arm over her own shoulder. "Come. This way."

Aika led Alice back the way they had come. Alice was a bit out of it, but instantly snapped to it when she saw the medical lab. It was a complete disaster. The tables had been knocked over, there were large swaths of blood covering the walls, and off to the side, what looked like a sai buried in a computer screen. There was a woman who looked like she was impaled on a naginata, and across the room, following a haphazard smear trail of blood, was a woman slumped against the wall with a sai firmly in her skull.

"You've been busy," Alice whistled. "Are these the Sisters of Avalon?"

"They *were*," Aika said in a calm tone.

Alice glanced at her, clearly impressed. "You took down all three of them?"

Aika made her way back to the main arena chamber. Already, the medical room was filling with smoke from the hallway behind them. "Yes," was Aika's only reply.

"Aika, that OWOWOWHOLYSHITSHIFTYOURWEIGHT!" Alice cried out, as Aika quickly adjusted herself.

"Is that better?" Aika asked. Alice, who was covered in a sheen of cold sweat, nodded.

"Yeah, yeah. I don't think that fucker broke my collarbone, but it still stings. Oh, and I'm dealing with a touch of rust poison, so if I barf on you, I apologize in advance."

"Can't you break it down?"

They started up the stairway as the lights behind them started to flicker.

"Yeah, but it's still gonna take a while. Rust is a bitch to get rid of. Mostly, it just breaks down into more rust. Give me five minutes, and I'll be gold."

Aika glanced over. "You defeated a techno-were."

Alice smiled and nodded. "Hell yes, I did. I'm still the most dangerous wohUUURAARRFFF!"

Aika quickly braced Alice against the wall as the former villain made good on her earlier threat. After a good thirty seconds of purging, a shaking and coughing Alice gave Aika a thumbs-up, and they continued their cautious ascent of the stairs.

***

Cindy glanced back at Derrick, who was looking around wildly. "Well? Did you get her?"

Derrick shook his head, and headed to the front of the boat. He stood beside Cindy, using her seat to brace himself as they made their way down the river. Several fire patrol boats sped past them as they went.

"I think so, but I'm not sure! One second she was there, and the next, she disappeared!"

Cindy nodded. "Good work. Let's dock and ditch this thing. We've got to get back to..."

Cindy's words ended in screaming as their boat suddenly lifted out of the water. Underneath, soaking wet and frowning, was Eedee, who was now hovering a good 20 feet above the Hudson with the speedboat firmly held above her.

"Sorry about this, but you're both under arrest!" Eedee called out. She quickly scanned the shoreline for a place big enough to drop a speedboat, and spotted a parking lot. "Just hold on, I'm going to put you down, and then you can go to jail. One sec."

In the boat, Derrick was hyperventilating as he dropped the plasma cannon. "We're dead!" He kept repeating to himself. "We're fucking dead! They'll find out, and then there'll be no place for us to go. Cindy, what should we..?"

Derrick's eyes widened in horror as he saw Cindy pick up the plasma cannon and point it at their feet. "Cindy, don't!"

"Derrick, we can swim to shore. Just hold on!"

Cindy flipped the side switch to reactivate the cannon, which now had a flashing red light where the green one had been before. Derrick reached out to stop her, practically screaming, "No, the gun's too hot! It'll..."

That was as much as Derrick got out before Cindy pulled the trigger. Instead of a plasma blast, the gun sparked, sputtered, and then emitted a high-pitched whine. Cindy's eyes widened as the cabin of the boat was awash in a blue light before the cannon exploded, taking the boat with it.

As Allison was charging across the dark lawn that separated her from the other sniper, she let out a long string of expletives as she watched the boat explode. "Eedee, come in," Allison said over the comm channel. "Eedee? Eedee, do you copy?"

"What's happening?" Victoria asked in a concerned voice. "Allison? Report!"

Allison looked at the long line of burning buildings along the Hudson, the blazing tanker inferno, and then over to the convention center. The massive glass enclosure was awash with flickering orange light as she saw Alice and Aika stumble out the front.

Allison was about to respond when she looked up to see Eedee, whose entire top half was black, frizzy, and smoking, while her bottom half was covered in a thick, slimy mix of river water and mud.

"Allison, do you copy?"

"...Yeah. Um, I think we're done for tonight."

"Say again? Allison? Hello?"

Allison took her earpiece out and watched as Eedee landed next to her. She fished a towel out of her pack and handed it to Eedee, who tried to wipe some of the soot from her face. She glanced to the other building, and then shook her head. The other sniper had too much of a lead, and the forensic team could find what they needed when they followed up. With a feeling of defeat, the team stood and watched as the shoreline of the Hudson burned. Eedee was the first to break the silence.

"We're going to get fired for this, aren't we?"

Allison shrugged and took a sip from her juice box. She glanced at the building where the other sniper had been, and sighed. He was probably long gone by now, anyway. "Yeah, probably."

Chapter Four

"It wasn't me!"

***

Victoria Green, vice president of Tanner Industries, believed in maintaining a professional appearance at all times. It was something her grandmother had taught her; if you look the part, you tend to act the part. That was why even though it was going on 2:00am, she was the very picture of professionalism in her trademark green suit. Her black hair was freshly combed, and her tea had just been served by the tireless graveyard staff of Tanner Tower. Despite all of this, she was about three seconds from completely losing her shit.

As calmly as she could, Victoria leaned back in her chair and examined each of the women before her. She tapped her fingers together as her eyes drifted from Alice, who was bandaged up and favoring her left shoulder, to Aika, who looked like something out of a horror movie, to Eedee, who smelled like burned plastic and fuel, to Allison, who looked like she wanted to be anywhere else but there. After glancing at each of the women in front of her, she carefully picked up a steaming cup of tea that was perched on the edge of her desk, took a long, loud sip, and then set it down.

"So," Victoria began. She reached out and gently opened a folder on her desk. Inside were photos of the devastation along the Hudson. "First off, I would like to thank you for immediately reporting in. I appreciate promptness, and I know that all of our time is valuable. Plus, it's very late, to the point that it is very early, and I think we'd all like to get some sleep." Victoria set the pictures down and picked up a television remote from her desk. She pointed towards a large monitor on her far wall, and turned it on to show a live report of the fires along the river. "Who would like to go first?"

"The tip was a good one," Alice started off in her most professional tone. "All we had was that it was some kind of death-fueled underground sporting event. The actual setup was something worse. It was," Alice paused for a moment. "It looked a lot like one of my old Purge plans. We took some video and grabbed some samples for the lab."

At this, Aika fished the vial of blood she had collected out of her utility belt and set it on Victoria's desk.

"Thank you," Victoria said with a nod. "Please, continue."

Alice swallowed. She had used that tone often enough when she had been the one in the chair. "Well, we found some workers that were staying late, and they proceeded to run. Aika was held up by the goddamn Sisters of Avalon, who had been hired to provide security."

Victoria gave an impressed whistle, and glanced at Aika, who nodded. "Their presence alone confirms the tip was genuine. I don't suppose any of them were left alive for questioning?"

Aika looked at Victoria. The Asian assassin was covered head to toe in dried – and drying – blood. Without blinking, she said "No."

Victoria nodded with a sigh, and looked over some notes she had scribbled down. "Back to the doctors. You stumbled on three that were working late. Is this correct?"

Alice nodded. "Yeah. I gave chase until the oldest in the group turned into a damn techno-were. Hence the shoulder." Alice pointed to her wounds. Victoria eyed Alice's arm, and nodded.

"Yes, you poor dear," Victoria said in the most detached voice she could manage. "That looks horrible. We'll be sure to get that treated in a sec, but first, how did this lead to the convention center, and all the evidence of what was going on, burning to the ground?"

Alice scratched the back of her head and coughed. "During the fight, I used my exploding door tape to try to slow the thing down."

Victoria pointed to the monitors. "Tape did that?"

"It's, um, it's very powerful tape."

The rest of the women nodded in agreement.

Victoria sighed and rubbed her forehead. "This was against a nanite-infused techno monster, correct?"

Alice nodded. "Yes."

"So, why didn't you just use your belt's EMP?"

Alice closed her eyes. Victoria made a 'tsk' sound through her teeth as she stared at the former terrorist.

"You forgot about the EMP, didn't you?"

"Now, hold on a minute," Alice blurted out. "Let's say you're me, and you've got a choice between some boring old EMP and some awesome exploding tape. Which would..?"

Victoria put her hand to her head, and rubbed her temple. "The EMP."

"Well, then, you're a very boring person, and I pity your life."

"Alice!" Victoria barked, and then stopped herself. "Please. Look, I get it. Heat of the moment. Monster coming at you. I get it."

"Besides," Alice said with a shrug, immediately followed by a wince. "I tried my PhoneBuddy on it, and it did nothing. The nanite membrane was electrostatic resistant. The EMP would have put me in the dark with that thing, and in that scenario, I probably would have died. That left my filament, which was useless in close quarters, my Glock which was fuck-all useless, and my taser net, which would have done jack. I couldn't get near him because he had a ranged attack in a confined space, so this seemed like the best possible option."

Alice smirked, and then noticed the others looking at her. "What? Yes, I actually *did* remember the fucking thing this time, I just made a split-second field decision. Geez, I'm impulsive, not stupid."

Victoria held up a hand. "That's enough. Honestly, as upset as I am, that logic sort of makes sense. I know what it's like to be stuck against something that seems impossible to kill. Moving on." Victoria turned her glare on Allison.

"I gave you one command. One. Do you remember what it was?"

Allison frowned. "It wasn't me."

Victoria ignored her as she continued. "And what did you do?"

"It wasn't me!"

Victoria rubbed her face. "I was on the comm. I heard everything. A warning shot? Look, the next time you disobey like that, at least take out a damn kneecap or something and make it so they can't get away."

Allison perked up, but Victoria immediately cut her off. "No, that does not mean you have carte blanche to shoot people in the knees."

Allison crossed her arms and pouted. "Killjoy."

"Allison, we needed them alive. We really, *really* needed them alive. They were our best lead."

Allison frowned and snapped back, "I told you, it. Wasn't. Me. There was a second shooter. I pegged him, but he got away."

Victoria raised an eyebrow at that. "You're telling me you missed?"

"Hell no, I didn't miss!" Allison nearly yelled. "I nailed him with less than five seconds to adjust for distance, wind, and bearings. I got him in the upper left torso. Find me six people on this continent that can do that, I fucking dare you! I..." Allison took a breath, calmed herself, and continued. "Bastard was wearing body armor, otherwise he'd be a stain. You can send a team up there to check and back my story."

"Okay, fine," Victoria said. "I just figured that..."

"Look," Allison said through her teeth. "I know my rep, but you should know that above all else, I follow orders and do my job. I know how to play the good soldier, and I do it very, very well. Besides," Allison said as she crossed her arms and gave Eedee a smirk. "I wasn't the one who blew up the boat."

"Oh no," Eedee said, slightly angry. "Don't even suggest that was my fault. I was repeatedly asking them to stop, and they tried to kill me with a 141-TA. *That's* what killed them; the gun overheated and blew. I had them contained, and they exploded." To emphasize the point, Eedee made a "pschew" noise and made a jazz hands gesture.

Victoria leaned back in her seat and pondered this. "Eedee, I know you were trying to avoid their shots, but don't you have any ranged attacks?"

Eedee shook her head. "Not really. I mean, I did, but after your techs helped to rebuild me, they went offline. They said I was too much of a threat to keep my pew-pews."

"Your...ah. Lasers. Got it." Victoria sighed and nodded. "Okay. Head on down to tech after this and I'll see about getting you something. Sorry, I forgot that we took those out. Remind me, what are you fitted for? Eye lasers? Repulsor blasts?"

At this, Alice shook her head. "We determined after the Mark III that eye beams were an awful idea. They overheat too easily and are a bitch to keep charged. The excessive heat was overloading the neuro circuits and causing them to go haywire. Plus, in practical combat scenarios we noticed they tended to lead to other...structural weaknesses. Now a Totallus's hands are another story. Eedee's wiring can easily support an ionic attack, and she was wired for an energy transfer cannon via her palms, but that's about it."

"Okay, good to know. Eedee," Victora asked, "How many shots did they get off, including the one that blew up the boat?"

Eedee blinked. "They got off 11."

Victoria closed her eyes, lost in thought. "Aren't the 141's Purge tech?"

"Yeah," Alice nodded, thinking. "We copied a NATO patent and modified it. They had a tendency to explode in the field if overused."

"So, what constituted overuse?"

"About 30 shots. They needed a cool-down period after 20 or so."

"So, why did it only take 11 shots for a 141-TA to overheat to the point of detonation?"

All five women fell silent as they processed that.

"It was a setup," Aika said.

Alice nodded. "Why in God's name would they have firepower like that in the back of their boat? It's bulky, takes time to charge, it's conspicuous as Hell, and it's known to have problems when wet."

Allison joined in. "But if you were panicked, you wouldn't think about that, would you?"

Victoria continued. "And if you wanted to distract any law enforcement, or Collective Good members for that matter, a plasma cannon would cause so much damage that you probably wouldn't even notice that it had detonated after only a few shots. Eedee," Victoria asked, "What is the probability of escape on the Hudson when being pursued?"

"Gosh, that's taking a lot of variables into account. The sheer number of different scenarios..."

"Short version. What was the probability they would escape *you*?"

Eedee smiled. ".04%, boss."

"The gun was insurance. It was never meant to stop you. It was meant to destroy any leftovers that were stupid enough to get caught."

Alice thought about this. "Tonight was a setup for us?"

Victoria shook her head. "More like whoever is running this wanted to make sure that their tracks were covered. First off, Alice, most of the infrastructure for that convention center was glass, steel, and concrete. The section you were in was built from highly flammable materials, and it was also the only place in the entire building without any fire extinguishers. Didn't you find it odd that the building went up so quickly?"

Alice nodded as Victoria turned her attention to Aika. "And you. If I were to hire you, would it be for evening security?"

Aika made a sound that almost sounded like a snort. Victoria smiled and said, "Okay, noted. So, why were all three of the Sisters of Avalon there? Aren't they the European version of you?"

Aika bristled. "They are hardly 'me'."

Victoria sighed. "I meant they belonged to the European equivalent of your assassin's guild."

Aika nodded in agreement. "They were not security. They were there to clean up."

Victoria again glanced at the television. "No other workers. None. Just those three, and they seemed pretty panicked when they saw you. And one of them had a techno serum. Okay." Victoria stood and turned to stare out her window at the shimmering lights of Manhattan. "So, if someone was planning on wiping everyone out, then why were we there? I think it's safe to say that tip was fed to us, but why?"

Alice glanced at the television. "It was a setup. We were setup to look incompetent."

Victoria nodded. "That's a good theory. I'll..."

"No, look at the TV. We were fucking set up."

At this, all of them turned to see Eedee holding a speedboat in midair, followed by a blinding explosion. Victoria turned up the volume in time to hear, "...confirmed that this was the work of a Purge weapon of mass destruction, known as a Totallus. Sources claim that this was in fact an act sponsored by the Collective Good, and that they have been secretly funding the continued operation of a Purge terror cell right here in New York. More on this as it develops. To recap, dozens perished tonight in a blatant act of terror as..."

Victoria shut the television off. Eedee hugged herself and glanced at the fuming businesswoman. "I'm sorry," she said in a meek voice.

Victoria looked to Eedee, and shook her head. "Not your fault. We were played. I thought the tip was too good to be true, but I ignored my gut. That footage was dead-on, Eedee. The camera work was too clear for it to be anything but planned. This whole thing was just... dammit."

Victoria closed her eyes and leaned onto her desk. "We're making some changes. First off, Allison, you're off the active roster, and will report to my office tomorrow for reassignment."

"Ex-fucking-*scuse* me?" Allison blurted. She was quickly cut off by an extremely loud, and pissed, Victoria.

"THAT IS ENOUGH," the raven-haired superhero growled. "You will report to my office tomorrow morning for reassignment, and this is not open for discussion! Do I make myself clear?"

Allison stiffened, and then nodded. Victoria waited for the younger woman to say something, but Allison remained surprisingly silent. The others were looking at Allison with worried expressions. They all knew that out of all of them, Allison was the most likely to revel in the chance to use her skill sets.

"Now," Victoria said in a calm voice, "I realize tonight was a botch, but looking at the situation objectively, I don't think it was your fault. Allison, Aika, Eedee, you're excused. And Aika? Eedee? For God's sake, use the spa to shower off. You both look like Hell."

Aika nodded her thanks, and the bubbly android gave a cheerful salute. They followed the dejected Allison out of the office, leaving Alice alone with Victoria. Alice watched them leave, and then turned to face Victoria. "That was kind of harsh, wasn't it?"

"I need Allison for a side project. Besides," Victoria said as she slumped in her chair, "I'm losing Collective Good members faster than I can blink. Right now, I need Allison the genius, not Allison the assassin."

Alice sighed. "I can see that. Just let me have her tomorrow morning for our training session?"

"Alice..." Victoria said in a warning tone.

Alice put up her hands. "I need her for an object lesson, and then she's yours. Promise."

Victoria was about to argue, but then she threw her hands up. "Fine, but I *need* her. I'm short-handed on good agents, so I'm stealing your best."

Alice nodded, and then shuffled her feet. "So, why am I still here, and not with a healer?"

"I already called for a healer. Nick is on night duty. He should be here shortly."

Alice nodded. "Didn't he heal me before?"

"Couple of times, probably. Nick is one of our top healers, so yeah. I'm surprised the Kevlar didn't hold up. Tea?" Victoria gestured to the silver tea service on her desk.

Alice tried to shrug, but the pain in her collarbone stopped her. Instead she nodded as she accepted the cup Victoria was pouring for her. "Pretty sure it did, actually. Kevlar doesn't do a whole helluva lot of good when something is trying to crush you. Still, it helped. Techno-weres tend to drool a compound acid, so I think that Kevlar weave is the only reason I still have an arm."

Victoria studied the fabric for a moment, and then turned her attention back to Alice. "Look, Alice." Victoria said. "I think you should know something. The reason I jumped the gun tonight with your team."

"You told us," Alice said. "You thought there was a potential hostage situation, and this seemed like a strong lead."

Victoria closed the file on her desk, and then handed it to Alice. "It's not just that. I...look. Over the last week, several Collective Good agents have gone missing. A week ago, Yeager went off the grid while working a lead with a rumored death cult on the East Side. Shortly after that, Aquatica vanished tailing a cargo ship about 30 nautical miles off the coast, and on top of *that*, tonight Darkane didn't report in. I sent Brandon and Suzie to check on Yeager, and look at what they found."

Alice looked over the photos in the folder. They showed a destroyed apartment, with several stains marked off, complete with exhibit tags. "You sent your two strongest players to investigate a disappearance?"

"I sent the Red Guard and Miss Major because, honestly, short of Poseidon, I am out of heroes. Alice, over half of my entire team is gone, and I have no idea who is doing this."

Alice set the folder down, and thought about it. "Makes sense. You want to do it easy, you take out the small fry. It would make sense to remove Yeager, and even Darkane, provided that he's actually missing and not being an ass. Now, Aquatica? That's a bit left-field. Was she even supposed to be working?"

Victoria shook her head. "It was supposed to be Poseidon, but he was called away. Chris only works for us part-time, and he has his own company to run."

"So, Aquatica was taken instead. Okay. Next, Brandon would make sense. Dangerous to keep on the board, but easy to take out if you know what you're doing. That leaves Blackthorne, you, and Suzie. Blackthorne, I notice, isn't here."

Alan Tanner, aka Blackthorne, had been conspicuously absent from the meetings Alice had been involved with lately. She wasn't sure if she had done something to offend him, or if there was more going on, but honestly, she found that she didn't really mind. She could tell that there was some friction between the illustrious industrialist-superhero and Victoria, and Alice hated being in the middle of things. She glanced at Victoria's abdomen, which was slightly larger than it had been several weeks ago.

"No, he's not, is he?" Victoria said. She noticed the glance, and casually placed her file over her stomach, blocking Alice's stare. "That was my doing. I've asked him to lay off things for a while. I... need some space for the time being."

"How are you holding up?"

Victoria glanced at Alice, and then dropped the file on her desk. "12 weeks in."

"Morning sickness?"

Victoria rubbed her temples. "Not as much, now. The only reason I didn't completely lose my temper tonight is because I perpetually feel like I'm going to barf." She smacked the side of a clear, crystal dish filled with brown, wrapped hard candies. "I keep eating these stupid ginger candies, and they do nothing. NOTHING! I want a pizza, and some pickles, and a beer and some more beer, some fucking strawberry ice cream, or just some beans and cheese."

"Hey," Alice said, leaning against the giant, oak desk. "It's cool. You wanna go down to the gym and throw a few punches? Might cheer you up? Hell, I won't even dodge, if it'll make you feel better."

Victoria frowned and pointed. "You're way too fucked up for sparring."

"Dude, that's what makes it work for you!" Allison said. She held out her wounded arm and let it hang limp. "Look, I'm prone. Prooone." For emphasis, she let her arm swing back and forth.

Victoria bit her lip, but then shook her head. "Thanks, but no. I just want to vomit, and get some rest. Look, back to the matter at hand. The Collective Good is, for the most part, destroyed. The public doesn't know it yet, but, aside from Brandon and Suzie, you and your family are the premier heroes left in New York City. Alan is... he has been so flighty lately that I don't feel responsible including him as an active member."

"You think they're dead?"

Victoria nodded. "I have to assume so. Someone is trying very hard to ruin us. If you were me, and you didn't have access to your family, who would you have sent in tonight?"

Alice tapped her chin, and thought about it. Meanwhile, there was a light knock on the door. A young Asian man popped his head in and waved. "Hey. Heard someone got messed up again."

Alice and Victoria waved to Nick, who smiled and gestured for Alice to have a seat in one of the chairs facing Victoria's desk.

"Hey, stranger," Nick said to Alice. Alice smiled back.

"Hey, yourself. You taking any classes this semester?"

"Full load. Bio-chem, some anatomy. Here, have a seat." She plopped down, and braced herself. Nick put his hands on Alice's wounded shoulder and focused. A white light emanated from his hands, and Alice bit back a scream. Victoria watched as Alice's eyes teared up from the pain, and then slammed shut as Nick finished up.

"There you go. That will be $5,000."

"Such a smooth talker," Alice said through her teeth. "No wonder I can barely keep myself contained."

Victoria pointed to the door. "Submit a work order. You know the drill."

"Yes, ma'am," Nick said with a mock salute. He patted Alice on the shoulder, which caused her to wince. "Take it easy. You had a severed tendon, and those get a little stiff if you keep sewing them up. I recommend a trip to the spa, and some sessions with a physical therapist."

Alice nodded, and gave the healer a strained smile. "Thanks for patching me up, Nick."

Nick shrugged. "Lady, thank *you*. Your fuckups are paying my way through college."

Alice frowned slightly as Nick made his way out the door. Victoria looked at Alice's freshly-healed shoulder. There was a slight discoloration in the pale flesh where jagged teeth had punctured the skin, but, aside from that, she looked fine. "Nick's gotten pretty good at fixing you up."

Alice leaned back and laughed. "Shit, that kid has spent so much time repairing my skin and fixing my wounds that I've become desensitized to him. After the cruise, he had to work on me so much that when he accidentally walked in on me at the hospital after a shower, I didn't even bother with a towel. He's seen everything so much he didn't even care, either. Just kept munching on a burrito, gestured to the bed, and said, 'thanks for stripping ahead of time.' I tell ya, nothing else makes a girl feel attractive.

"And in answer to your question from before; I would have been scared about thinning the herd, and would have sent Brandon. Honestly, between the techno-were and the Sisters of Avalon, I don't know that he would have made it out of there."

"Neither do I. By sending in your team, we messed things up for them tonight."

Alice gestured behind her. "So, how long before it's public that my family is your only viable source for superheroes?"

Victoria looked at the liquor cabinet in the corner of the office, and silently wished she could raid it. "Not long. This would have been more than enough to take Brandon down. Everything about this was designed to help smear the Collective Good. While they might not have bargained on all of you, the end result is the same. We're being taken apart in every way." She noticed Alice yawning, and yawned in sympathy. "Hey, why don't you get some rest? Isn't tomorrow a big day at your place?"

Alice grinned and nodded. "Holly's first day at public school. Little shit is so excited that she's ready to pop. Allison has been going nuts, too. She's in full-on mom mode."

Alice expected some kind of positive response from Victoria, or at least a nod of acknowledgement, but Victoria just sat there and stared at Alice. Alice fidgeted for a bit and said, "What? Is there something on my face?"

Victoria tapped her fingers together for a bit as she thought about the best way to say what she wanted to. "Alice, what I'm about to say stays between us, understand? You don't tell Aika, and you definitely do not tell Allison. Understood?"

Alice stopped smiling and nodded. "Hey, you got it, boss. What's up?"

Victoria glanced to the side as if nervous about how to continue, took a breath, and said, "So, as you know, for the last few months, we've been working pretty heavily with Holly here at Tanner Tower."

Alice nodded. "She's made remarkable progress for someone her age."

"Her progress is amazing for anyone, age notwithstanding," Victoria said. "Allison brought her in stating she was a mid-level telepath, but she's not. She's off the damn charts. It's not just telepathy, either. In observation, we've seen projection, mental manipulation, memory alteration, even signs of telekinesis."

Victoria fished a file out of her side drawer and tossed it to Alice, who flipped through and did a quick scan.

"Damn," Alice said in an impressed tone. "Girl has got it going on. Where was all of this when we needed her? Why didn't she use more of this when the Tower was taken over last month?"

"She did," Victoria said as she took the file back from Alice. "Remember? You asked her for help with that half-vampire."

"Well, yeah," Alice said with a shrug. "But she didn't, I mean...she..."

Alice blinked as if clearing away some cobwebs. As she started to think back, Victoria continued, "She created a complete imaginary scenario where your jewelry shop was destroyed. She projected the force of the explosion, the smell, the heat, everything. It was so real that the vampire was genuinely stunned when you revealed yourself. Alice," Victoria leaned in. "No one on file can do that. No one can get close to implanting a complete false memory like that, and this 12-year-old girl did it with ease."

Alice shook her head. "But we were training her, so it makes sense that she'd be able to pull something like that off."

"It's not the only time," Victoria said. She flipped to several photos in the file in front of her. "We haven't noticed. No one has, but the camera doesn't lie. Half the time when we were training her, she wasn't even there."

Victoria showed Alice several pictures of various Collective Good members, and one of herself, standing in an empty room and addressing someone who wasn't there. Alice studied the pictures for several seconds before setting them down, and letting out a long sigh. "She's playing us," Alice growled.

Victoria shook her head. "Not the way you're thinking. To me, this feels like psychic hooky. I would have killed for that power in school." Alice snorted, while Victoria smiled. "I truly believe she's a good kid, but she's damaged goods, Alice. She was subjected to God only knows what level of physical and psychological torture for years, and who can say how much she manipulated her environment to help her cope?" Victoria tossed the picture of herself across the desk.

"Noted," Alice said. "Still, this raises the question, how much of what we've dealt with concerning her is real?"

Victoria shrugged. "I honestly don't know at this point, but I do know that Allison loves her dearly, and that she would shut down if I showed this to her. I think," Victoria bit her lip as she searched for the right words. "I think that Holly is *trying* to be a good kid, but I think that the temptation of her powers is eventually going to be too much. I think she's already showing cracks here and there by making us see and believe what we're comfortable with, and by making us flat-out forget what she doesn't want us to remember."

"Okay, you've sold me," Alice said. "What's your plan?"

Victoria took a small, wooden box out of her desk and opened it. Inside was a small, steel syringe and next to it, several clear bottles. Each was marked with a plain white sticker and a serial number.

"This is something we've been working on for a while," Victoria said. "What do you do when you've got a metahuman so powerful that you can't rely on external Inhibitors to do the job? You put the Inhibitors inside of them. This is a nanite compound stored in a saline solution that will permanently inhibit anyone that is injected with it. There is no known reversal process."

Alice stared at the vials on Victoria's desk, and felt a shudder go down her spine. "How long have you had these?" She asked.

"We finalized the first batch two days before we asked you to start," Victoria said. "It was originally intended for you."

The silence in the room grew so thick that it was almost tangible. The ticking from the scuffed, worn wristwatch Victoria's grandmother had given her could be heard as both women debated what to say next. Finally, Alice broke the silence.

"Give her a chance," Alice said quietly. "She's a young girl with a lot of bad in her past, and her power is so incredible that she may not fully realize what she's doing. Instead of stripping her of it, you should help her."

"We've been helping her," Victoria said. "If I hadn't seen her progressing positively, I would have injected her myself months ago."

Alice clenched her fists, and, for a moment, Victoria expected the purple-haired woman to explode. Instead, Alice reached over and gently closed the lid of the box. "Who else knows about this?"

"You, me, and Alan." Victoria said as she put the box back in her desk. "I've had to work to keep this blocked from Holly. Alan was the one who came up with the compound."

Alice turned to leave. As she reached the door, she looked over her shoulder. "I don't blame you for making that, by the way," she said in a quiet voice. "I would have too, if I were you. Thank you for not using it on us."

"I'll give her one more chance," Victoria said, "but if she goes over the edge, or if I deem her to be too great a threat, then I'm using the nanites."

"No, you won't." Alice said. "I don't... we don't hurt kids, Vic. It's my one rule. You know that."

"This won't kill her," Victoria said. "Hell, it probably won't even hurt. It just stops your powers for working."

"Permanently," Alice added.

Victoria nodded. "Permanently."

Alice stared at the injection kit for several seconds before responding a defeated voice, "If things get that bad, I'll do it myself." Victoria was about to protest, but Alice cut her off. "Allison really likes you. She looks up to you. Hell, she's even gone on patrol as you to help cover. You do this to her girl, and she will never forgive you. In fact, she'll most likely kill you, but me?" Alice shrugged. "She's used to hating me. If things get bad, I'll do it."

Victoria was about to say more, but Alice suddenly let out a huge yawn and stretched. It was as if a spell had been broken, and instantly, both women were back to their normal selves.

Victoria pointed to the door. "Get out of here, would you? Get some rest, and I'll see you in the morning."

Alice nodded. "If you need anything at all, give me a call, okay? Don't hesitate."

"Thanks, but I think I've got things covered." Victoria said with a strained smile. "Now, shoo."

Alice didn't argue. As soon as the door closed, Victoria slumped back into her chair, wiping her face with her hands. Not wanting to give into sleep, exhaustion, or the emotions that had been threatening to overtake her lately, she resumed poring over her work. She continued to flip through the folders that were stacked in piles across her desk. There was one for each member of the Collective Good that had gone missing. Aquatica, Yeager, and, underneath those, one marked Blackthorne.

Chapter Five

Trucker Speed

Allison fidgeted and checked her watch for the seventh time as she waited for the bus to arrive. According to said watch, her PhoneBuddy, and the clock on the wall in the store, bus 223 would be along in exactly 5 minutes to take Holly to Margaret Mead Middle School. Allison had already researched the teachers, the staff, looked up criminal histories and scouted out six different escape routes from the school. She had identified what hallways Holly should avoid in the event of a situation, and had spent a minimum of three hours detailing out maps showing what areas of the school to head to for shelter in the event of different emergencies, which she then reviewed with Holly via PowerPoint. This didn't even account for the extensive criminal background checks on each member of the teaching staff. Now, as she stood outside with Holly and Eedee, she started frantically going over her preparations yet again.

Holly, meanwhile, had prepared for school by going shopping with Alice and Allison to pick out a backpack, school supplies and a new wardrobe. At least, she tried to, but after the two older women got into a heated debate in the middle of the department store about the practicality of Kevlar weave in an undershirt, Holly had slipped away and dialed Victoria Green, who took her shopping that afternoon. After multiple talks with Allison about safety, boys, paying attention in class, knife fighting techniques, hand-to-hand, boys again, the importance of technology in the classroom and finally respecting your teachers, Allison had to admit that she couldn't think of anything more to do to prepare Holly for the public school system.

Holly was in a white, long-sleeved blouse with a plaid skirt and black tights. She wore red suspenders (as a fashion statement), and her shoulder-length brown hair was in a loose ponytail that bobbed as she looked at Allison.

"Are you gonna be okay?" Holly asked as she gave Allison's hand a squeeze.

Allison looked to Holly and smiled. "Sure, squirt. I'm just...I haven't been to school in a long time, and my memories are a bit fuzzy. I remember that it could be fun, that teachers could be indifferent to what goes on around them, that...**boys**. Have we talked about boys?"

Holly took a breath, and counted internally to three. Aunt Alice had taught her that it helped when dealing with Allison. "*Yes*, and I'm not a stranger to all that. Do you *remember* my last job? I had to sit in a smelly hotel room, and psychically tune in while politicians had sex with planted hookers next door. Then those same hookers would treat me to ice cream before our boss would shake them down and make me tell him everything I had learned. I have been mentally connected to so much old-person stuff that I couldn't go near a boy right now if I wanted to, so...*yes*, we have talked about boys and *yes*, I think I know what I need to know."

Allison stood next to Holly and stared straight ahead with a tense look on her face for a moment. Then, she relaxed completely. "Thank *God*," she said.

Holly glanced at her. "I just summed up the Hell that was my life before I met you and you say, 'thank God'?"

Allison nodded. "Yep. I can sleep easy knowing I don't have to worry about you with a boy."

Holly thought on this. Without looking at her guardian, she said, "You are a terrible person, Miss Gailsone."

Allison nodded. "Terrible stock, Miss Gailsone."

The two continued to stand in somewhat-awkward silence. Eedee, who had mostly been observing, turned to Holly and said, "I wanna go to school, too."

Holly smiled at the bubbly killer android. Truth be known, she was still a little unsettled by Eedee. When Holly looked at people, she didn't just see them, she saw their thoughts and feelings as well. It painted people in layers that had depth and color to them that Holly had difficulty putting into words.

Eedee, on the other hand, was an artificial life form. Her brain wasn't exactly organic, and try as she might, Holly couldn't get anything off of her. When she spoke to Eedee, all she saw was what her eyes told her. Even though she knew the android was capable of emotions, and even though they were now (kind of) friends, it still unsettled Holly that she couldn't read Eedee. She was a flat, gray island in a sea of glowing, flowing colors and song.

Suddenly, Allison tensed up as she saw the bus round the corner. "Okay, you're good? You need anything? You have my credit card? Don't use my credit card. You have your books? The gun I gave you? Everything?"

Eedee blanched. "Allison! What the heck?!"

Holly hugged her and said, "Pretty sure I can't bring a gun to school. They'd expel me and arrest you. I'll be fine, okay? I'll be fine."

"Allison!" Eedee snapped. "She can't bring a freaking gun to school!"

"She'll be fine," a voice said from behind Allison. All three women turned to see Alice Gailsone standing behind them. She held out a bag with a Hello Kitty sticker on the side and directed a large grin towards Holly. Under her other arm was a large box. "You'll be fine, hon. I promise. Here, it's full of oatmeal pies. Eat them all, or buy some friends. Your call."

Holly looked from Alice to Allison for approval. Allison nodded and, after an awkward pause, gave Holly a quick kiss on the forehead. "Be good. Kick ass. Come home safe."

Holly blushed a little, smiled and nodded as she took the bag from Alice, who then ruffled the young girl's hair. Before getting on the bus, Holly stared at Allison for a moment. Allison suddenly smiled warmly, and nodded back. Alice, more intrigued than confused, watched the exchange, and wondered if they were simply using nonverbals, or if Holly was talking to Allison via telepathy. The two women and one killer android then watched as Holly boarded the giant, yellow bus and made her way to a seat near the front. Allison waved to Holly, who smiled and waved back as the bus gave a hydraulic hiss, and rolled down the road to its next stop.

Allison stood and watched until the bus rounded a corner. She stood for several moments more, just watching where the bus had turned out of sight. It was still very early in the morning, and the sun had not fully peeked over the skyline. The sleepy Brooklyn street was still painted in shades of half-lit gray, and the air was cool, waiting for the warmth of the sun to flow over the rooftops and paint the block with vibrancy.

Allison was nervous, scared and a little bit annoyed that her charge, who she had promised she would be there for (and who she had actually *died* at one point to protect) was going to be out of her sight for the next seven hours.

Allison glanced at the gigantic stone golem that stood outside the gem store. Looking around to make sure no one was really paying attention, she stepped over to the ten-foot tall Japanese statue and whispered, "Fudo, go and watch Holly's school. Anything bad happens, you bring her home. Anyone gets in your way, fucking murder them."

Allison stepped back and stared at Fudo, who did not move an inch. As Allison sighed in frustration, Eedee tapped her on the shoulder. Allison glanced at her as Eedee mouthed the word, "please".

"Ah," Allison said. She leaned in again. "Please go and watch Holly's school. Please bring her home if bad things happen. Please murder anyone who gets in your way."

Fudo continued to stand perfectly still.

Allison gave a long sigh. "Could you please go and keep an eye on her from a safe distance, and do nothing that would cause a random passerby harm unless you had no choice?"

She looked up as the golem nodded its head. Allison smirked as Fudo freed himself from his favorite spot in front of the store, and slowly lumbered down the New York sidewalk

Allison watched Fudo leave, and fidgeted. While the golem would protect Holly, Allison still wanted to do more, and not actually being there that morning was eating her up inside. At that moment, she didn't care that she had things to do. It agitated her to the point that she was considering setting up a sniper's nest across from the school when Alice once again cut in.

"She'll be fine. It's the other kids I'd worry about." Allison turned again towards Alice, who stood with her arms crossed, and a small smile on her face. She was dressed in a blood red business suit with a low-cut cream blouse and a gold band necklace, complete with a sparkling diamond resting just above her very pale cleavage. Her red pencil skirt was offset by black pantyhose and bright red pumps. On top of that, Allison noted that Alice's cheeks were flushed, her lips were a rich shade of red and her eyes were brighter than usual. Allison stared at her boss for a good ten seconds.

"I still worry. That's normal, I think. Yeah," Allison said in a distracted voice. "Is your shoulder okay? What time did you make it in last night and - are you wearing makeup?"

Alice nodded and grinned. "Yep. Gotta be professional today. Um... did you just send Fudo across Brooklyn? In broad daylight? I... you know what? Why not? Here, hold this," Alice shoved a giant box of doughnuts into Allison's arms. Alice opened the front door to *Rare Gems*, the small, yellow-brick gem exchange store that Allison and Holly lived above with Aika and Eedee. It was the family business, in that Alice and Allison both ran the shop. Also in the sense that they owned it, and that Alice oftentimes slept upstairs in lieu of going back to her one-bedroom flat.

"You look good, mom!" Eedee said is a chipper voice. Alice nearly tripped at the comment.

"Don't call me Mom. Now, get in the store, Eedee."

"Yes, momm-ma'am. Yes, ma'am!" Eedee said, as she skipped in behind the two women.

Alice sighed and turned on the orange-and-blue neon OPEN sign in the window. Allison followed her in, still curious as to why her boss was so dressed up. Behind the counter, Aika was already brewing coffee. Allison almost let out a snicker at seeing the deadly and feared Lotus changing a coffee filter, but then thought better of it. After all, the woman tended to wear loose-fitting clothing, and Allison counted no less than a dozen places where a decent-sized blade could be tucked on the petite Japanese woman's frame.

Alice unlocked the jewelry case covers, and prepped the main lobby for a day of business while Eedee immediately descended on the customer waiting area. Allison carefully set the box of doughnuts down and continued to watch her boss energetically hop from case to case. "Are you okay? Because you're not usually here this early. Or even awake this early, for that matter. And you never wear red. Purple, black, white, cream, but never, ever red. And last night! What gives?"

Aika quietly eyed both her housemate and her employer as she poured out three cups of coffee. Allison was right, this *was* a bit early for Alice, and she wasn't quite acting or dressing like herself. Plus, as tired as Allison was, she knew that Alice had to be even moreso. After Alice finished with her morning rounds, she looked around and then made eye contact with Aika.

"Ohayou, Aika-san!" Alice said in a chipper voice. Aika gritted her teeth slightly at her boss's attempt at being cultural and nodded a 'good morning' back. Alice, either not noticing or not caring, smiled and then headed to the counter where Allison was busy digging out a bear claw from the doughnut box.

"So," Alice said, "I have been up since five this morning. Did you know that there even *is* a five in the morning? It shocked the hell out of me, too."

"We didn't get out of the tower until after two. What's up? Also, how are you even conscious?" Allison asked, mildly concerned. Alice was not accustomed to getting up early if work didn't call for it, let alone after a botched mission.

"Trucker speed," Alice cheerfully replied. "Lots and lots of trucker speed. Anyway, we need to talk. All four of us." Allison paused in mid-bite while Aika calmly sipped her coffee. Eedee, thrilled at being included, bounced over to join the conversation.

"What about?" Allison mumbled through her food. Immediately, she scrambled to catch the falling piece of doughnut from her mouth. Aika, without missing a beat, passed her a napkin as Allison flailed.

"About the store. There may need to be some changes with *Rare Gems* that require your attention." Allison swallowed, and focused on Alice. Already, she had a feeling where this was going. Alice reached into the breast pocket of her suit and pulled out her PhoneBuddy. After a few swipes, she brought up a packed calendar, and turned it to show the others.

"I met with Victoria last night after you all left, and as a result, my duties have marginally increased. Here is my current calendar of appointments for *Rare Gems* for the next month, and here," she swiped to another calendar screen, also packed with appointments, "is what Victoria has laid out for me concerning the Collective Good. You'll notice that both schedules are impossible to accomplish at the same time."

Allison glanced at the Victoria schedule, and snorted. "Fuck it," she said as she carefully took another bite. "You owe them nothing. They made one promise, and managed to fuck it up in record time. Money aside, we're fine, boss. Just let them hang."

Aika nodded in agreement. "There is nothing binding you to them at this point. Allison is correct; you should cut ties. We can find another way to save your mother."

Alice sighed, and put her PhoneBuddy away. "You're just pissed you got transferred. And this is Victoria we're talking about. I thought you were all friends."

"Work-friends," Allison mumbled through her doughnut.

"I respect her, and I like flying her plane," Aika said in agreement.

Alice rolled her eyes. "Anyway, I would love to up and quit, but there are a couple of facts you're not taking into consideration. First, I've already researched every possible avenue on the planet, and short of shifting reality as we know it, there is no other way to cure my mother. The cancer has spread, and at her age, chemo would deteriorate her too rapidly." Alice glared at Allison. "We are *not* shifting reality. Do I make myself clear, young lady?"

Allison stuck out her tongue at Alice. "Could happen," she said with a grumble.

"Second," Alice continued, "There's the matter of the Open Hand Act. As long as we're registered, we have to be careful about how we behave, otherwise its three hots and a cot in the moon gulag."

"There's a moon gulag?" Allison asked.

"Cool!" Eedee chirped.

Alice nodded. "I know, right? Can't cure cancer, but we can build a freaking lunar prison. Brave new world."

"Did Victoria threaten to put me in the moon gulag?" Allison asked.

"Maybe. Quit shooting random assholes. Anyway, problem three, we're..."

"I didn't fucking shoot that lady!"

"...We're also all technically members of the Collective Good. That means if we want to be able to use our abilities and/or shoot someone in the face legally, we need to do what we can to keep that status."

Allison nodded, "I *do* enjoy shooting people..."

"Yes, I know. Please stop for now. Fourth, someone tried to jack us last night. I don't know what's going on, or who is behind this, but they're getting bolder. If it's the same crew that murdered Phil's friends, they're acting in my name. I want to meet this mystery person and shake her hand before I rot her fucking face off. Her and her fucking tin-can murderbot."

"He killed Laura," Eedee said in a lower voice. All three women turned their attention to the young-looking blonde. She was staring out the window at the traffic going by. "The Totallus. He killed my friend. She was my best friend in the whole world. She gave me my name."

Eedee turned her attention towards Alice. "When the time comes, he's mine. You can have the girl, but my brother is *mine*."

Eedee started to flex the arm that the tech crew at Tanner Tower had redone, but Allison put out a hand and gently took her shoulder. "Hey, don't go off in here, okay? Time and place. This isn't it, alright?"

Eedee looked at Allison and relaxed. She smiled and said, "Thanks, sis. I appreciate it."

Allison looked at Eedee with eyes the size of dinner plates. "WOAH. Woah. We need to define some verbiage here. I like you, and you may be a good house mate, but I am *not* your sister."

Eedee glanced from Allison to Alice, and then back to Allison with a confused look on her face. "But, she's your mom too, right? I thought you were her daughter."

"Niece," Allison corrected.

Eedee scrunched her face. "But when I accessed the sealed adoption records, I could have sworn I saw…"

"**Niece**," Both women said.

Eedee shrugged. "Okay. Whatever, cousin!"

"Christ," Alice muttered under her breath. She could already feel a stress headache coming on, and her day had yet to officially start. "So, back to our previous conversation…"

Aika calmly nodded. "Agreed. While I do not like the thought, based on what happened last night, you are correct. It may not be wise to break ties with the Collective Good at this time."

Alice nodded. "Great! That means we either need to train the two of you," she pointed at Allison and Aika, "on the finer points of dealing full-time with my distributors, or we need to hire a network of reps."

"Reps," Allison said instantly.

"Reps," Aika parroted.

"I can work the counter!" Eedee cheered.

Alice blinked.

"Come on guys, it's not that bad! You get to travel, *hell* no, Eedee, there's good money involved, *usually* no one tries to kill you…"

Allison shook her head. "No can do, boss. I'll mind the store, but I hate travel, and you know damn good and well it would be a matter of time before I got all stabby."

Alice shrugged. "To be honest, you get us business when you're stabby. When you don't follow through with it, you make a helluva saleswoman."

Allison smoothed out her white, button-up blouse and adjusted her red-rimmed glasses. "Tell you what; I'll act as your manager until this whole mess is done with, but then I'm out, and Cindy gets promoted. I work as-needed. Deal?"

"But, I'm good with people, and I waited tables! How much harder could this possibly be?" Eedee said with a pout.

Alice shook her head no. "Not good enough. You're too nice. I need girls who are ruthless."

Eedee opened her mouth, but Alice stopped her. "Ruthless doesn't mean using lasers on clients. See, this is what I'm talking about. Allison already knows that."

Allison smirked, "Do I?"

Alice cleared her throat. "Next, I may need your help, all of you." Alice pointed at Allison and Aika. "To add to our woes, there's one more problem on the table. Fifth, the issue of new recruits."

Aika nodded. "The gentleman in the red coat?"

Alice nodded back. "Yep. Phil and his new bunch are being hunted by this new psycho-bitch player and as creepy as he is, I count Phil as one of my friends. I owe him, and I respect the fact that he's usually able to handle his business, so if he's coming to me all but begging for help, help he will get."

"Plus, you did murder his kid."

Everyone glanced at Allison, who looked around and shrugged. "I'm just sayin.' What? Are we just going to pretend that entire thing didn't freaking happen?"

Alice cleared her throat, and grabbed a doughnut. "Kinda trying to. Yeah."

"So, what? We're helping another Gellery? Why? Is this just because you're feeling guilty, or because you were banging his son?"

Aika let out a whistle. "While I admit I am not entirely versed on American culture, even I know you should not have said that."

Alice closed her eyes and mentally counted to ten. "Allison, my past with his family aside, Phil is my friend. I can't just leave him hanging."

Allison slammed her fist on the counter, causing both Aika and Alice to jump. "The hell you can't! You *always* do this! You go on and on about keeping a low profile, about not sticking our necks out and staying safe. Then you turn right around, and put us all at massive personal risk! This is becoming habit for you, and it's pissing me off! Dammit, we're supposed to be *done*! I work to distance myself from killing people, and then you're all, 'hey, let's go fuck something up over here!' and I do it, and then you get mad because I keep doing it! And then you tell me to back off! I have had to go through therapy, group counseling, medications, treatments, *organized FUCKING retreats* to deal with the mountain of shit I had to cope with when we quit and you...you...YOU CAN'T KEEP FUCKING DOING THIS TO ME!"

Allison slammed her fist into the glass case beside her so hard that it shattered. She was hyperventilating, and both Alice and Aika watched as she closed her eyes and focused, her hand still frozen in place.

"I'm bleeding, aren't I?"

Alice nodded. "Yep."

Allison looked at the slick, red ball of flesh that was her right hand. There were several glass shards sticking out of it at random angles.

"Well. That...I could have managed my aggressions better, couldn't I? I think I need to go to the back. I think I need to get into the first aid kit, and then call Victoria for a healer."

Allison closed her eyes, and took a deep breath before continuing in a level voice. "My charge is starting her first day of school. This is a very emotional day for me. I think I need to excuse myself for a moment. Yes. Please, excuse me."

Alice moved aside as Allison quickly walked to the back. A thin trail of blood followed her as she went. Eedee, worried about Allison, floated after her.

"Her therapy sessions have done wonders," Alice commented. Aika glanced to Alice and raised an eyebrow. "Seriously!" Alice countered, "A couple of years ago, we would have wound up in a Mexican standoff. Now, she just breaks things."

"She is very wound up about this," Aika noted. Alice nodded.

"I don't blame her. This is her second chance at the whole 'mommy' thing."

Aika shot Alice a surprised look. Alice nodded, and kept her eyes on the door. "It was back in the Purge. She got pregnant. The dad was nice enough. Respectful, smart, polite. I liked him. I thought he was good for her. They would have fucked it up, no doubt, but still. I was happy that she was happy. And then I kind-of, sort-of, accidentally ruined it for her. It isn't something she willingly talks about."

"Then why are you telling me?" Aika asked.

"Because," Alice said with a glance, "we're family, and you should know why she's so moody about all this. Here she is, new kid, new guy in her life, the whole package. This is her second chance at a life she honestly never thought she deserved. She's terrified she'll lose it."

"Should not she be the one to tell me this?"

Alice shrugged. "Eh, probably. I'm not good with boundaries."

Aika nodded in agreement. They stood in silence for a moment before something clicked with Aika.

"I am family?" Aika asked with a raised eyebrow.

Alice coughed, and turned her attention back to her calendar. "If you haven't figured that out yet, then we need to have a little heart-to-heart, hon."

A moment later, Allison emerged from the back with a thick bandage around her hand. She glanced at the display case and mumbled, "Sorry about that." Eedee immediately floated to the side to get a vacuum.

Alice shrugged and gestured to the broom in the corner. "Then clean it up. Eedee, quit floating. You need to pass for human here. Allison? If nothing else comes up after your chore list is done, why don't you go text Brandon and decompress for two minutes. Only two minutes."

"...Why?"

"We've got a busy day."

Allison shook her head. "No, why are you being this nice?"

Alice looked from Allison to the bandaged hand. "Oh, no reason. I was just concerned a bit, is all."

"That would imply that you had empathy. Or a soul."

Alice shrugged, and got out her PhoneBuddy. "Think what you like. By the way, while we're on this little side-note, here are said chore lists for the day."

A few swipes on her screen, and she was done. Allison and Aika both reached for their chirping phones, and both frowned when they saw their screens. Allison promptly shook her head and said, "Sorry, but I'm already booked to be with Brandon this morning. Like, for actual work that I am quite possibly late to."

"You want me to secure convention bookings?" Aika said in a tone that screamed she couldn't care less. "Need I remind you that I am not technically an employee here?"

Alice nodded. "Oh, just suck it up and help out. You live here, too. Go do normal people stuff. It'll be good for you. Promise. Now get. I need you finished and present at your last listed activities by 11. Allison, Victoria filled me in. I just need you at 11. Beyond that, go play cops and robbers."

Aika raised an eyebrow. "Get what?"

Alice made a shooing gesture. "Get! As in, get out and do things. It's slang."

Allison put her PhoneBuddy away. "Ignore her backward hick-speak. She spent her childhood in Bumfuck, Nebraska."

"It was Kansas," Alice said with a frown. "And I am not a hick. My lineage just so happens to be that of farmers, travelling magicians, overly-religious zealots, you know. Usual background for a Midwest girl. Now...please get on with your days."

Grumbling, both former assassins accepted the assigned tasks on their PhoneBuddies and headed out. Eeedee looked from the two disgruntled women to Alice. "What about me?" Eedee asked in a chipper tone. Alice considered the killer android. She was about to tell her to go self-occupy for the morning, but then thought better of it. After all, it had been a long time since she had command of a Totallus, and Alice had forgotten how convenient they could be to have around.

"Eedee, remind me. How many computations can you do per second?"

Eedee flashed a wide grin. "How many do you need? 'Cause I betcha I can top it!"

Alice allowed herself a small smile. "I bet you can. Do you know the tax laws for New York?"

Eedee paused and cocked her head. A few seconds later, she looked at Alice and nodded. "Now I do. Just downloaded it."

"Perfect. Clear your calendar until 11, hon. You're my new accountant."

Eedee clapped her hands excitedly. Alice shot her a curious glance. "You're excited about balancing my books?"

"Well, no," Eedee said with a huge grin, "but you included me in something, and that makes me feel special. And you called me 'hon,' which I've noticed you only do with people that you care about."

Alice thought about it and then shrugged it off. "Whatever. Now, I...Eedee, quit floating!"

Eedee stopped and gently lowered herself to the ground. "So," Eedee asked. "Were you planning on telling them what was on your calendar for 11:00?"

Alice shot her a glare. "Are you snooping in my files?"

Eedee shook her head, and grabbed a pen and notepad off of Alice's desk. "No, but I am synced to your PhoneBuddies. In fact, I run a nightly backup of your data."

Alice blinked. "I thought I did that on my laptop."

"Nah. Victoria had me install an app that could manage it. She figured I was safer than a regular computer."

Alice nodded thoughtfully. "Well, she's not wrong. And to answer your questions, I was going to tell them until Allison got her hand slapped. Now, I'm saving it for a surprise. Trust me," Alice said as she opened a laptop, and fired up her accounting software. "This will totally brighten her day."

Chapter Six

Soaking Wet and Covered in Blood

Dr. Susan Gordon stood in the lobby of Aegaeon Holdings, LLC and checked her Phonebuddy for what felt like the hundredth time. She had called off work for this meeting, and when you're the senior neurosurgeon for a children's hospital, people tended to notice when you were gone. Add to that her frequent quick 'breaks' when she would disappear to handle something as Miss Major, and her employment was something she saw as put at risk.

Of course, it helped that Alan Tanner sat on the hospital's board of directors. It also helped that she was fairly well-known in the field of neurosurgery as one of the leading pioneers in non-invasive techniques, and her work in genetic research at Morgan Stanley's Children's Hospital was regarded by many in the field of medicine as something akin to wizardry. Still, Susan tended to worry. She valued her private life and her career, and she took an immense personal satisfaction in being able to do what she did.

As Miss Major, the tiny female powerhouse of the Collective Good, she was second only to Superior Force in terms of strength. Her blue and white costume had become a familiar sight above the New York skyline. Still, she had never seen that as something special. She had been born with her superhuman abilities, and while she was proud of the fact that she was one of the few African American heroes, let alone a woman, she didn't see either of those things as what really defined her.

Her skill as a surgeon, and her work as a genetic researcher, was something she had earned through endless hours of hard work, and her superpowers (while admittedly *very* impressive) had nothing to do with those accomplishments. Because of this, anything that directly interfered with her career, short of a life-threatening situation that demanded Miss Major's presence, was something she regularly didn't have time for.

Susan adjusted her fake glasses, and took a deep breath. While considered short by most standards, Dr. Gordon still cut an imposing figure in her navy business suit. The fact that she was agitated by being made to wait was only adding to her persona. She glanced again at the secretary and asked, "Look, is there any way you could try buzzing him again? This meeting was his idea, and I've got a lot of work to do."

"I'm sorry, ma'am. Mr. Ellswood is particular about people barging in on him. I'll try him again." The secretary once again pressed a green button on her desk, and both ladies were rewarded with silence.

"If you wouldn't mind waiting just a few more minutes, I'm sure he's just finishing up with his meeting…"

"Please," Susan snorted. "I've worked with Chris long enough to know 'meeting' is code word for mid-morning screw. Look, if he needs me to leave work, and then just leaves me hanging, then he can go fu…"

Susan was interrupted by a chime from the secretary's phone. "Oh," the relieved assistant said. "Delayed text. It's this building, ma'am. My apologies. It looks like he just finished up about ten minutes ago. Mr. Ellswood will see you now."

"About fucking time," Susan muttered as she stepped into the private elevator that led to Chris's office. As CEO and Founder of Aegaeon Holdings, Chris had the entire top floor of the 22-story skyscraper devoted to his private offices, and he preferred that any visitors enter via the express elevator in his assistant's lobby. Susan had heard him mention in a Collective Good meeting that it was for intimidating potential business rivals. Susan figured it was because he was an asshole.

The elevator chimed, and an irate Dr. Gordon stormed off the elevator ready to verbally tear the aquatic super hero down. "Look, the next time you decide to bang one of your interns, don't do it when…I…"

Susan froze. The gigantic office was completely destroyed. A far window was shattered, letting in a strong, cold breeze. The blinds were bent and rattled with every gust, and there were random papers fluttering around the massive office space. Chris's desk was overturned and shoved to one side, and there were small fires burning in the dark green carpet. Still, this wasn't what stopped Susan cold.

Standing in the middle of the ruined office was a Totallus. Susan recognized it immediately as an older model, but still dangerous. The gigantic, silver-skinned man was in a bright, skin-tight purple suit with a gigantic T on the front. Chris was covered in blood and bruises, and was lying motionless at the android's feet.

In a heartbeat, Susan was airborne and bracing herself as the Totallus charged, slamming into her head-on. Susan grunted and did her best to hold her ground, but the robot was extremely strong. It grabbed her and forced her down, causing Susan to slam into the ground. She nimbly dodged a punch that went through the floor, shattering the concrete where her head had been only moments before. She shifted her weight, and shoved the robot up and off her, and then rolled away.

The Totallus instantly scrambled to its feet and made to grab Susan, but, instead of running, she rushed the robot and punched it square in the jaw. The Totallus went reeling back, and was sent flying across the office. It crashed into a support pillar, which buckled, but didn't give way. The Totallus braced itself against it, and righted itself in time to see Susan streak towards it, her fists in front of her like a battering ram. She slammed into the robot's chest and kept going, letting their momentum carry them. They shattered a window on the south side of the office as they went tumbling into the open air.

Susan winced as the Totallus brought its fists down on her back, like a hammer. She kept her grip on the android, and flew as fast as she could towards the open ocean. The Totallus, realizing what she was trying to do, attempted to grab her face and pull her head back. Susan gritted her teeth and flew faster. A few seconds later, they found themselves over the waters of the Upper Bay. Without wasting a second, she forced the two of them down into the water as fast as she could fly.

They crashed into the choppy surface with the force of a small explosion. Susan held her breath as they dove into the salty, black waters of the Atlantic, and forced them to move even faster. The Totallus was scrambling now, trying desperately to stop Susan, but she had it in an iron grip. No matter how hard it hit her, she wasn't letting go. They slammed into the ocean floor with such force that their impact created a momentary air bubble. As the water rushed to fill the void, Susan pummeled the android with a series of lightning fast punches that were focused on its head. The android tried to fight back, but Susan was a hurricane. She only stopped when there was a bright flash, and a flurry of bubbles from the Totallus's face. It opened its mouth as if to scream, and a black film of oily bubbles emerged as small flashes of light flickered behind its eyes.

Susan hovered for a moment underwater to make sure the robot was done before grabbing its head and ripping it off its body. She took the two pieces of Totallus in hand and flew upwards, breaking the surface like a missile. She flew back to Chris's office in seconds, tossing the broken android off to the side as she landed.

"Chris!" she cried as she landed beside him. She tried to check his vitals, which, due to his physiology, was nearly impossible. The older man was swollen from being pummeled by the Totallus. His face was barely recognizable, and he was bleeding from his eyes, nose, ears, and mouth.

Susan suspected that there was some internal bleeding, and, from the sound of his breathing he had punctured a lung. He had so many obvious breaks that Susan was terrified to pick him up. She looked around and saw the remains of Chris's gigantic desk. She darted over. and proceeded to rip the top of it off. She then brought it back to Chris, and did her best to slide it under him.

Chris made a noise, but Susan couldn't tell if he was conscious. She glanced around for something to secure him with, but was coming up empty. Then, she looked back at the Totallus. She grabbed the body of the android and, in one swift motion, ripped it in two with her bare hands. She then grabbed some arterial cables and used them to quickly tie Chris to the wooden plank.

"Alright, you dirty old man. Let's try to not die, okay?" Susan said in a strained voice. She honestly wasn't sure if Chris would survive, but she knew that with the severity of his condition there was no way he would make it if she waited for the ambulance. Tanner Tower had decent medical facilities, but it was across town, and for injuries this severe, she needed specialists. Bellevue was the closest option, and they had a good trauma ward that she had worked with in the past. She considered using Tanner Tower anyway, but at that moment, she heard Chris gag, and then noticed that he had stopped breathing. (Side note: add something here.) Without a second thought, she lifted Chris on his makeshift stretcher and took off into the mid-morning sky.

In less than two minutes, they landed on the helipad for Bellevue hospital. Susan kept Chris level and screamed at the dumbfounded attendant, "Get me a stretcher, now!" The EMT's were already on hand, having been waiting for the medical copter to arrive from a wreck on the west end. Susan helped them slide Chris onto a gurney, and rushed them inside. Around her were the terrifying and familiar words she remembered from working trauma in her youth.

"He's not breathing!"

"No pulse. Prepping for shock. Get me 150mg of Amiodarone ready to go."

"Ready with the adrenaline."

"Clear!"

Susan flinched at the sight of her colleague's body jumping in place from the pulse of electricity. A second later, needles were in his arm and fingers were to his neck. Susan checked, and felt a rush of hope as she detected a faint pulse. "Slight pulse. More Amiodarone. Another 150mg."

One of the EMT's looked up, alarmed. "He's had the maximum. He can't..."

"He's a superhuman," Susan snapped. "He's not super-strong, but his metabolism is enhanced. We need to get him into surgery, and we need to get him wet."

"Ma'am?"

Susan nearly bent the handle on the gurney. "He's Poseidon! Water helps him! Get a wet blanket and put it over him, now!"

"Ma'am!" the frightened EMT nodded and ran for the bathroom. Susan followed them to the doors of the trauma ward, where two men in green surgical scrubs were waiting.

Susan felt a hand on her shoulder, and turned to see Dr. Kendal, one of her old advisers, standing there. He had a thinning mess of white hair, and was a little more wrinkled than she remembered, but aside from that, she instantly felt relief at having him there.

"Susan," the older doctor warned. "You can't go in there. It's not your ward."

Susan deflated a bit. "I know. This was the closest option, and he was dying. I didn't know where else to take him in time."

"You did good, Susie," Dr. Kendal said with a soft pat on her shoulder. Susan smiled, and then looked around. Several nurses were looking at her, and she realized to her horror that she wasn't dressed as Miss Major. Instead, she was standing there soaking wet and covered in blood. She had landed on the helipad not as Miss Major, but as Susan Gordon. Her secret was out.

Susan looked around as her stomach tightened. "They all saw me," she said to herself in a small voice. "Oh, my God. They saw me. They saw..."

"They saw a committed doctor arrive with a patient," Dr. Kendal said in a voice slightly louder than it needed to be. "And what's so odd about that? Now, why don't you get back to your own ward? I still have your contact info at Morgan Stanley. I'll let you know how he turns out."

Susan shook his head. "I brought him in, I should be here. I should..."

Dr. Kendal took her by the hand and patted it. "Susan, I will see to his care myself. Now, you should probably leave before someone who doesn't work here and knows you makes a connection, don't you agree?"

Susan looked at her old mentor, and then gave him a quick kiss on the cheek. "How long have you known?"

He laughed and squeezed her hand. "You really think those glasses are fooling anyone? Now, get out of here before someone makes a fuss."

Susan nodded and smiled, relief washing over her. "Thank you, Geoff."

"Go on, Suzie. I'll tend your friend." Susan nodded, wiped a tear from her eye as she laughed in relief, and took off back the way she had come. Dr. Kendal watched her go, and then headed into prep for surgery.

Chapter Seven

"I thought I saw a rat."

Holly Gailsone checked her class listings, and did her best to navigate the crowded halls of Margaret Mead Middle School. Having grown up in New York, she was used to being around lots of people, but it still made her a little edgy. As a telepath, she had to work to keep other people's thoughts out of her head. Holly likened it to building a sandcastle, and digging a moat as the tide came in. The tide wasn't going to stop, and the water made the work maddening, but if you took a break, your castle would crumble. That was how Holly felt as she did her best to look normal and squeeze through the noisy, vibrant hallway before her.

She located her locker and read the combination off a crumpled Post-it. Beside her was a girl roughly her size dressed *completely* in black. Black combat boots, black leggings, a black skirt, and a black leather jacket over what Holly noted was a Black Flag tee-shirt. The girl's pale wrists were covered in metal bracelets, and her oval face was hidden behind a thick layer of pale makeup. Her hair was dyed completely black to match everything else, and was done up in two tight balls on top of her head. Holly tried to ignore the thoughts that were rolling off the girl like cold waves.

Holly added some vanity items to her locker's interior that Victoria had helped her pick out (a mirror, a plastic door-shelf, and a tiny erase board). She then casually stepped back just before the girl in black 'accidently' swung her bag around, missing Holly by inches. The bag swished by Holly and crashed into the locker instead, knocking down the items Holly had just hung up.

"Oops," the girl said in a sarcastic voice. "Sorry, Princess. Didn't mean to fuck up your stuff."

Holly looked at her for a moment. The other girl met her stare and tensed, her eyes wide and her nose flaring. Holly was looking at her thoughts, which were a jumbled, frenzied mess. She wanted to be mad, but that was the problem with being a telepath; when you constantly knew *why* people were the way they were, it became difficult to hold a grudge.

"It's cool," Holly said with a smile. She extended her hand. "I'm Holly, and no, I'm not a cheerleader."

The goth girl blinked. Holly could see her teetering on how to respond. She looked a little deeper, and saw a slick, pale coat of fear and insecurity behind her angry, swirling thoughts. Holly bit her lip and said, "Let me try again. I am very new here and..." Holly probed a bit deeper, and picked up on some colorful phrases floating around in the girl's mind. She sounded like Aunt Allison after a bad practice session. Holly adjusted her speech pattern to make the girl feel more comfortable. "...And I have no idea where the fuck anything is. At all. I might be screwed. Um, do you know where room 104 is?"

In point of fact, Holly knew exactly where it was because the goth girl knew where it was, and Holly could see it plain as day in her mind. The goth paused, and then slowly extended her hand to shake Holly's. "Yeah, I'm actually heading there. Name's Jean."

Holly smiled, relieved that Jean had decided to be nice. "Pleased to meet you, Jean."

Jean glanced at Holly, and then at the locker she had just slammed into. "Sorry about that. I, um, I guess I wasn't looking."

Holly shrugged. "Hey, it's my first day here. I figure it goes with the territory. So, is it always this crowded?"

Holly carefully bent to get her belongings off the ground. She could hear six different guys behind her, all checking her out. Holly was starting to regret the skirt, knee-length though it may have been. Jean bent down to help as well. Together, they cleaned what little Holly had and put it back in the locker.

"Yeah, pretty much. I mean, it's a school. That's what they do here. Where'd you transfer from?"

Again, Holly sensed a spike in anger and curiosity from Jean. She did a quick read, and decided on the best course of action for dealing with this new, potential friend; brutal honesty.

"I was a ward of the state after my mom was killed. I did a lot of not-school and had some, um, foster parents that weren't around a lot. This is my first real school experience in years."

Jean softened instantly, and Holly felt the sympathy roll of the girl in soft, blue waves. "Oh, sorry. That, um, that sucks, I guess."

Holly shrugged. "It's cool, now. I have a new, um, I got adopted recently, and so, it's cool."

Jean nodded, and Holly closed her locker.

"Well, don't think that because you've got a sob story that I'm gonna give a shit. Come on, your class is this way, Princess." Jean waved her on, but Holly could feel a small, flicker of liking in the angry girl, so she smiled and followed.

A few moments later, Holly noticed a locker that looked like someone had taken a hammer to it. There was spray paint over it, and the kids in the hallway were doing their best not to stare. Holly took one look at the destroyed door and felt the blood drain out of her face. Across the locker in ugly, red letters was the word FREAK.

"What happened?" Holly asked. She noticed Jean bristle at the question.

"It wasn't his fault. Roger wasn't dangerous, just different. They knew it, too. If he had been dangerous, they would have stayed away. You know what he could do? He made plants grow. That was it. He called it being herbakinetic." Jean took a breath and did her best to keep from shaking with rage. "They cornered him two days ago, and beat him so bad that they put him in the hospital. The principal blamed him for it, and now he's expelled. All because some assholes destroyed a bunch of stuff a couple weeks ago."

Holly swallowed, and kept her comments to herself. She had seen on the news that the night Superior Force vanished had been catastrophic for a lot of major cities. Politicians and talk show hosts were blaming not only him, but the entire Collective Good for the deaths. The media claimed that the event was avoidable, and that the heroes should have stepped up to do more. Public opinion agreed, and Holly had noticed that she and Allison no longer went to Tanner Tower, unless there was an emergency. Instead, Victoria would come to them. She also noticed that Brandon, the Red Guard, had been assigned to their shop as an almost permanent fixture. Holly knew this was because of other, Allison-related reasons, but again, kept her mouth shut. After all, if her aunt wanted to have some fun, then who was she to judge?

'I just wish she would keep it down,' Holly mentally grumbled to herself.

The voices around her were chaotic, scattered, and annoyingly shallow. By the time Holly made it to Physics 100, she had witnessed five infidelities, twelve blackmail-worthy secrets, heard over thirty Twitter posts. Holly maintained her composure. She made a mental note to stay the hell away from a boy she identified as Peter, and to *maybe* drop a pencil by a boy named Travis (she may have exaggerated her disdain for boys to her aunt, just a little). Hearing people's thoughts was nothing new for her, but the idea of being around people that thought like this all day, *every day*, was a bit much.

Holly sat in the seat beside Jean, and did her best to pretend to pay attention to the teacher. She looked around and smiled to herself. *'It's boring, but thank God. Thank God for a boring life. I can do this. I can so handle this.'*

After a few moments, she cleared her mind and concentrated. She could 'see' the class around her, a swirling mess of thoughts, fantasies and emotions. She wasn't a pro at using her powers (that was changing, courtesy of Ms. Green's funded tutoring sessions), but she knew how to block out a bit, and she could get a general feel for who was thinking what. She was interrupted when a note hit her in the side of the head. She was so focused on listening to people that she jumped in surprise, which caused the teacher to stop in his lecture and stare at her.

"Sorry," she said in a small voice. "I, um, thought I saw a rat."

The teacher, a balding man in a brown jacket, adjusted his thick spectacles, and glared at Holly. Holly slunk in her seat as best she could, already wishing she had invisibility powers instead of psychic ones. Once the teacher went back to the board, she reached down and felt around on the ugly, cream-colored tile floor until she found the wadded-up piece of paper. Slowly, she slid back up and unfolded it.

Pay attention!

Holly looked bedside her at Jean, who was glancing at her and at the teacher. Holly was confused, but then focused. She saw a series of images, all of her teacher berating and verbally abusing the students in his class. She realized that she had been tuning him out, and that Jean had caught it before he could notice. Holly kept one eye on the teacher, and scribbled a quick note back. She let it roll off her desk, and watched as Jean leaned over to get something out of her bag, and came up with a pencil and note.

Lunch? I have oatmeal pies.

Jean looked at the note, and then at Holly. After a second, she smiled and nodded.

"Thanks, Aunt Alice," Holly mumbled to herself with a small smile. Beside her, Jean was busy taking notes.

***

At lunch, Holly grabbed a seat at the table furthest from the lunch line. Being the new girl, it was fairly easy for her to get privacy. She had been distracted throughout the morning, and as a result, she hadn't done a whole lot to reach out to her classmates. She was busy picking at the faux potatoes on her green tray when someone dropped a tray across from her. Holly looked up, and saw Jean standing and staring expectantly. Holly took the bag of oatmeal pies out of her backpack and tossed one to Jean, who sat down with a nod.

"So, is it always this boring?" Holly asked. Jean nodded.

"Yeah, pretty much. Nice job on almost getting busted five minutes into class, by the way."

Holly blushed. "Sorry about that."

Jean shrugged, and took a bite of her pie. "Hey, s'cool. I did the same."

They sat in silence, both focusing on their lunches. Holly knew Jean meant she zoned out, but it still felt nice to pretend that maybe she meant she was busy using some fantastic set of powers, too.

"So," Holly finally asked. "How long have you been a foster kid?"

Jean shot Holly a look that spoke volumes. Holly, realizing that she had slipped up, quickly covered. "I mean, you lightened up a lot when I mentioned the foster thing. I just figured, you know, that you were, um, sorry?"

Jean stared at Holly for a second, and then relaxed. "Four years in the system. On my fifth set of parents. They're okay, I guess. Not gonna adopt me anytime soon, though. Guess that's just for you spoiled little rich kids."

Holly sighed. She knew this game. "My last, um, foster mom was a hooker. So I get it, you know."

Jean whistled. "Damn, okay. That wins."

Holly looked at her tray of food. "I don't think it's a contest."

There was an awkward silence. It was broken when a deep, male voice asked, "Hey Jean! Who's your friend?"

Holly saw Jean visibly stiffen, and felt nervousness start to roll off of her. A tall, muscular jock appeared at the side of their table, complete with short, neatly trimmed hair and a NY Knicks jersey. "Hey, Brent," Jean said in a stilted voice. "Um, this is Holly. She's, um, she's new here and stuff."

Brent smiled at Holly. "Sup? I'm Brent." He offered his hand, which Holly shook. She looked from Brent to Jean, and then back again.

"So Jeany," Brent said, "we still on for this weekend? My mom's out of town, and Matt and Tyler said they can score us some beer. You still wanna come?"

Jean reddened, and kept her eyes focused on her tray. "Um, yeah! Yeah, that would be great. I'd like that. Sure."

Brent grinned, and then glanced at Holly. "Sorry, wasn't tryin' to be rude. So, um, it's a date?"

"Sure," Jean said, her voice cracking slightly. "A date."

"Alright! Okay, so I'll, um, I'll see you then!"

Holly watched as Brent wandered across the lunchroom to a table with several other large, grinning jocks. They patted each other and nodded, and Holly was tempted to try to 'listen in' a little more, but her attention was back on Jean, who was grinning and beet red.

"Is that your boyfriend?" Holly asked. She already knew the answer, but had to ask. Jean dug into her casserole and scooped out a chunk of something that resembled food. "Are we old enough to even have boyfriends?"

"Jesus, have you been in a bubble?" Jean said. She was doing her best to not smile, which made her smile even more obvious to Holly.

"Have you, um, you know…" Holly was trying to find the right way to ask her new friend what she wanted to. Jean glanced at Holly.

"We haven't gone out or anything. I just, um, he just…"

Holly raised an eyebrow. "Now who sounds like they live in a bubble? Seriously? I meant have you gone out in the past? Is he even nice?"

"No, but he's hot. That counts for a lot. Come on," Jean said with a frown. "Not all guys are, you know, *bad*."

Holly put her face in her hands. "Oh my God. Don't be that girl."

Jean glanced over at the boys and blushed. "Besides," she continued, "he's into me. I don't know why, but he's into me. I'm not gonna spoil that. You don't know what's up here. What's your problem, anyway? Jealous?""

Holly frowned and glanced back at the group of boys. "When you're raised by women who get raped on a regular basis, you learn to be a little distrustful."

Jean instantly backed off. "Look, I like you, Princess. You come off as a good person to me, and you brought pies, which makes you awesome in my book, but don't spoil this for me, okay? He's perfect, and I've been wanting a date with him for months. Ever since I saw him at Tyler's pool party and he… why am I saying all this out loud?"

Holly blushed. "I, um, I think I unconsciously do that to people. Personality and stuff. I'm sorry."

Jean considered Holly. "Gimmie another pie, and we'll call it even."

"Just like that?" Holly tossed her another pie.

"I don't have a lot of friends," Jean said quietly. "And you seem nice. And you talk to me. And hey, like I said, you brought me pies."

Holly smiled. "Hey, you wanna hang out after class? My aunt wants me home immediately, but maybe we can hang out afterwards?"

Jean smiled back. "Yeah, I think I'd like that. We can hit Toby's for some coffee. I can swing by later, if that's cool. Where do you live?"

Holly nodded. "Yeah, that's cool. I live above a jewelry shop."

Jean shook her head in mock disgust. "Fucking princess. I knew it."

Holly sensed the humor, and did her best to sound cocky. "Yep. Tower room and everything. Now quit bitching, and give me your number."

Holly ignored the insults running through Jean's head, and took out her PhoneBuddy. She looked calm, but inside, she was ecstatic. For the first time in a long time, she was making a friend her age, and it felt wonderful. Still, she couldn't shake the feeling that something about all of this was wrong. When Brent had come over to their table and started flirting, Holly had tried to focus on him, but there was a lot of other noise and it made it hard to pick anything out, so she kept at it. The more she looked, the more she felt uneasy. She hadn't been able to pin anything down off of Brent, because there had been waves of lust, liking, insecurity, fear, joy, and about every other emotion one could think of rolling off of Jean.

Holly glanced back at Brent, who throughout their entire conversation had not given off one thought, one emotion, or even one inkling that he liked Jean in any way. She shuddered, and then resumed focusing on her pies.

***

Meanwhile, Brent was busy texting on his own phone. Sneaking a few close-up pics of the new girl had been easy. Jean had provided enough of a distraction that Holly hadn't noticed the phone in his hand. Smiling to himself, Brent sent the image along with a single message.

"I found her."

Chapter Eight

What's Wrong with this Picture?

The apartment was dark, in shambles, and had the lingering, stale feel of a place that had been abandoned. The main room smelled musty and unused, and decidedly unwelcoming to Allison. It felt like a forbidden place, and while she had been in many similar rooms when she had been an agent for the Purge, something about this felt different to her, and that unsettled her even more. That she, one of the most violent members of the worst terrorist organization ever to walk the planet, felt bad, that alone told her that this was not a good place to be. It was as if the memory of what had happened was still hanging in the air like a silent, angry ghost.

One of the first little details that made Allison uncomfortable was that the apartment was empty. Not just unoccupied, but it had the lingering, cold, vacant feel that a place had when it was no longer loved. Allison had felt it before several times. It reminded her of the one time she had begged Alice to take her back to what was left of her parents' old home. It was a horrible feeling that crept into your stomach and sat there like a cold, slimy stone, and Allison hated how familiar it was.

Upon their arrival, they had been met by a locked door that was further barred by yellow police tape, and as Brandon Vitags cleared a path and held the door open, Allison felt a shiver pass through her as she cautiously stepped over the thin barrier, and entered the darkened tomb. She stood to the side and waited as Brandon made his way in, and then followed, honestly surprised by the state of the main room.

There was blood everywhere. Not just flecks or puddles here and there, but absolutely everywhere. There were large, chaotic streaks along the wall, the television, and the slashed-up couch. There were blood-splattered pictures half out of their frames, lying in piles of shattered glass on the floor.

"Jesus, this is worse than you said it was," Allison managed to get out in a voice that didn't shake. Behind her, Brandon nodded and looked around. He was also uncomfortable here, but this wasn't his first visit. That and, as an investigator for the FBI, the blond superhero was more than accustomed to horrible situations just like this one.

"The police and the bureau have already been over everything twice," he said. "Still, we could use your eyes, if you don't mind. It never hurts to get an outside opinion."

"You know," Allison said as she adjusted her glasses and started to study the scene. "When Victoria said she had something special in mind and that it involved you, I imagined something remotely sexy."

"I'm kind of glad this doesn't fit the bill," Brandon muttered. He glanced towards a door that led to a brightly painted children's room, and closed his eyes. Rob, also known as the super speedster Yeager, had been one of his closer friends. Brandon could not count how many times he had been over and spent time with both Rob and his boy, Matthew. The kid had been small for being 10, and had dreams of being a scientist. Rob had even brought him to Tanner Tower once or twice to introduce him to the R&D teams, and let him see some of the wonders they were working on. Matt had also wanted to be a superhero, and every day he asked his dad when his powers would kick in.

Only a week ago, everything had been different. The floors were messy, the laundry wasn't folded, and there were dishes in the sink. There was a Disney movie left out beside the Xbox, and a stack of comic books leaning in a lopsided pile beside a red futon. There had been messy baths that had led to slight mold damage in the bathroom, and there were slight, black stains in the corners of the ceilings where candle smoke had built up. Looking at all of this, Allison felt her mind drift back to a hazy memory of being 10, and nights of cuddling and reading under mounds of blankets. This place had been messy, chaotic, but most of all, warm. It had been a home.

On a small desk in the corner, Allison saw a series of photos in frames. One of a young man holding up his arms to show off his muscles while sitting on the shoulders of Superior Force. Another was of the same boy and a smiling, familiar-looking man at what looked like Disney World. Several showed what looked to Allison like the Bow Bridge with the young man holding a remote control in his hands.

"They would go to the park, and sail a remote-controlled boat on the weekends. It was Matt's favorite thing. God," Brandon said under his breath. "I hope this was quick."

Allison had shaken off her feeling of discomfort by focusing. She was examining the walls as she replied, "It wasn't."

"Thank you," Brandon said in a tone that suggested he wasn't all that grateful. "These were my friends, you know."

"Sorry," Allison muttered, her eyes still on the pattern. "You had your analysts in here to check the patterns, right?"

Brandon wandered over to her side and nodded. "Uh, yeah. The day it happened. I did the examination myself."

Allison nodded and continued to study the walls. She slowly followed the pattern of splattered blood along the wall to the couch, and then across the stained fabric to the next wall. "Okay. What was your conclusion?"

"Multiple attackers," Brandon said as he slipped into what Allison thought of as Professional-Mode. His voice got slightly louder and deeper, and he was making an effort to stay focused on the job at hand. "The splatter pattern suggests the attackers used bladed weapons. This line pattern is consistent with a quick slash from a blade or other sharp object."

Allison nodded. "Agreed. Plus, there aren't any bullet holes anywhere. Lotta blood, though."

"From what we could tell," Brandon continued, "the attackers came in the middle of the night. They entered through the main door, and either made enough noise that...that Matt came out to investigate, or he was already on the couch. The splatter pattern suggests at least five slashes, possibly from two different weapons based on the thickness of the strand marked K." Brandon pointed to the forensic marker that had been left attached to the wall. Allison glanced at it, as well as the others that dotted the apartment.

"And Yeager?" Allison asked. "Why didn't he just zip out here and deal with this instantly?"

"Inhibitors," Brandon said as he glanced towards Rob's room. "Our guess is they had one to slow him down. They charged his room, and took him out before he was able to get out of bed. The room is in shambles."

Allison glanced towards the door. It was hanging open, and she had a good line of sight to his bed. The mattress was slashed and covered in blood, and the room looked completely destroyed.

"Hey, Brandon," Allison asked, her eyes trailing back to the blood. "Why did the killers use bladed weapons?"

"Probably because this took place at night. The neighbors noticed the open door at around 6:00am the next morning."

"Okay, fair enough," Allison said with a nod. "Until one accounts for things like screaming. Did Yeager have anything special or secret hidden here? Money? Bonds? Collective Good stuff?"

Brandon shook his head. "No, I don't think so. Just a normal apartment. He liked to live simple."

Allison glanced towards the kitchen, and, for a moment, the oven. She closed her eyes and suppressed a shudder. This felt entirely too familiar to her, and she wasn't comfortable with it at all. "This doesn't add up for me," Allison said.

"Well, we're still piecing it together," Brandon chimed in. "The bodies were missing when we arrived. We're not sure what happened to either of them, but based on the damage and the loss of blood, we are working under the assumption that they both died in the apartment."

"The blood type matches?" Allison asked.

"Yeah, we checked that almost first thing. It was theirs."

"So," Allison said as she finished glancing around. "I did a lot of wetwork in my teens. I... don't look at me like that. It was a long time ago."

"It was just a couple of years ago," Brandon pointed out a little too quickly.

Allison glare at her boyfriend. "As I was saying, I've done a lot of jobs. Some were smash and grab, some were stealthy, some were a mix. Couple were botched. You know what they all had in common?"

Brandon shrugged. "Someone got murdered?"

"Beyond that," Allison said as she glanced at the overturned furniture. "Each job had a purpose. Kill a diplomat, steal some superweapon, something. You went in with a purpose, especially if you went in with a team. Tell me," Allison turned to face Brandon. Her arms were crossed, and her face was set in a grim expression. "What was the purpose of this hit?"

"To kill Yeager and his son," Brandon said automatically.

"Okay," Allison nodded. "And they used bladed weapons?"

"From what we can tell," Brandon gestured to the walls.

"Why?"

"I would guess to keep the noise down."

"People scream, Brandon." Allison gestured to the ransacked apartment. "Why go through the trouble of messing this place up this badly? All of this would have negated the whole keeping-it-quiet philosophy. Why not just gas everyone and be done with it? Why not pull the building? This doesn't fit with what you're saying. Why did they destroy the apartment?"

"Maybe it happened during the struggle?" Brandon offered.

"I don't think so," Allison said. "This place was completely ransacked. The living room is trashed, the kitchen cabinets were emptied, everything here is a complete mess. If his son was murdered in the main room by as many blades as you said, it would have had to have been done spectacularly fast. I'm talking Aika-level fast. I've seen her get going, and for what you described, and for this much blood, and for this wide of a pattern, the hits would have been huge, the blade would have had to have arced out, and the swing would have gone completely through."

To stress this point, Allison mimicked slashing with a sword. Brandon watched as she brought the imaginary blade out in a wide arc, almost like a golfer practicing a swing. "That's a bit excessive, isn't it?" Brandon asked.

"You don't deal with sword attacks much, do you?" Allison asked.

"Honestly, it's not the forefront of most of my investigations. I've seen some; there was a machete victim last month in the Bronx. Guy was on PCP, and had the strength of an ox. God, that was a mess. So, would you consider Aika a suspect in this?"

Allison shook her head. "No. Aika is as close to an artist when it comes to things like this as you can get. This," she gestured around her, "was sloppy, chaotic, not her at all. If it had been Aika, the kill would have been more... elegant."

Allison looked to the wall, and then continued to swing her imaginary sword. "It would have been two blades," she said to herself. "Wide, and then back," she made the motions with her hands, studying the blood and then going through the motions she saw in her mind. "I wish I had known. I would have brought Aika to confirm this, but I'm pretty sure. Two blades."

"So, someone with some strength," Brandon said. "That we figured. Professional?"

"Not *that* fucking professional," Allison snorted. "Listen, I realize how this sounds, but you've really got to get some power and have a good stroke behind your swing to make a pattern like this. This is freaking crazy, and for this many slices? I mean, no offense, but the kid was probably dead after the first swing. This was blatant, sadistic overkill. Whoever did this," Allison looked around and whistled. "Whoever did this had a grudge going. I mean, this is some serious hate right here."

"Tell me about it. The bed looks like something out of a horror movie," Brandon said. "The mattress is completely covered in blood, to the point where it was stuck to the frame."

Allison shuddered again. "Jesus. I...wait."

Allison suddenly walked past Brandon and entered the bedroom. She stared at the mattress for a good ten seconds before calling over her shoulder. "Hey, Brandon?"

"Yeah?"

"So, we've established that the killer or killers had a hate hard-on for Yeager and his kid, right?"

"I think so," Brandon answered.

"Okay," Allison muttered. "So, what's wrong with this picture?"

Brandon came up behind Allison, and glanced at the bedroom. He had looked in here dozens of times over the last few days, and each time, it left him feeling cold. "It's horrifying?"

"What's wrong with the bed?"

Brandon stared for a moment at the mattress. There were three slash marks running across its surface in a crisscross pattern, and the blood had caked around the slits. "I'm not getting you."

"Well, I mean, look at it!" Allison said. "That is an excessive amount of blood. I mean, that's like, 80's action movie levels. Yeager didn't have blood sacks lying around, did he?"

Brandon shook his head, slightly annoyed at the joke. "He had a super metabolism. He could regenerate extremely fast. I thought it was excessive, too. Then I remembered, this is the guy who could heal from being shot in the side after five seconds. They probably had to really work him to kill him."

"Brandon," Allison said with a frown. "I know why Victoria had me come in on this. Yeager…Rob was your friend. You're far too close to this to catch what's happened here."

Brandon started to open his mouth to argue, and then thought better of it. Despite his bruised ego, he knew that Allison was right; he was too close to this one. He was normally detached from his work, and extremely methodical, but the entire time he had worked this case, he had found himself getting overrun with emotion. He was good enough at what he did to know that he wasn't in the right frame of mind to deal with things. At least, not on this case. He had insisted on handling it, though. Rob was his friend, and he was determined to see things through.

"Okay," Brandon said in a calm voice. "So, what have I missed?"

"Why didn't Rob come out in time to save his son?"

"I told you," Brandon said with a gesture. "Inhibitors. They strip away all powers and abilities. Everything. He would have been as helpless as your standard groggy, middle-aged man at 2:00am."

"If there were inhibitors," Allison asked, "then why are there 12 gallons of blood on the bed? I mean seriously, this is ridiculous. If he was under the influence of an inhibitor, his metabolism would have reverted to a normal person's, wouldn't it?"

Brandon started to speak, and then froze as what Allison said hit home. "You're right. I… You're right. He would have had to have had his powers when this happened."

"None of this adds up," Allison said to herself. All around the bedroom were smashed picture frames containing pictures of Rob and his son. In a corner above a small desk were framed newspaper cutouts, each showcasing Yeager stopping a criminal, or averting a disaster. Allison looked from frame to frame.

"Dude had a regular rogue's gallery, didn't he?" Allison asked.

"Yeah, he had some regulars. We all do. There was the Iron Mountain, Atomico, Commander Chaos..."

Allison shook her head. "Lightweights. Petty criminals or mad scientists. This isn't their M.O. This was brutal, sadistic, almost insane in execution. Those idiots don't fit the bill. Tell me, who was his absolute worst?"

Brandon thought about it. "There was one. He was... have you ever heard of the Grey?"

Allison froze.

Brandon noticed, and nodded. "I'll take that as a yes."

"He's dead."

Brandon shrugged. "Most of us have died at one point or another. You know that term is pretty loose in our profession."

Allison walked to a frame that showcased Yeager in a torn costume, looking miserable and holding his arm as he stood atop a piece of rubble. There was smoke in the background, and surrounding him, out of focus, were firefighters desperately trying to put out a blaze that was just out of the frame.

"The Grey killed Rob's wife, didn't he?" Allison asked. "Several years back. Bank job gone sour."

"It was more than that," Brandon said, nodding. "The Grey had taken 99 hostages and hidden them all over the city. Yeager had one minute to find them and get a key from each. If he retrieved all 99, he had a chance of unlocking the bio-rhythmic bomb strapped to his wife's chest. He saved 83, and then ran out of time."

Allison remembered the day. It had been shortly after she and Alice had retired, and they had read about the event over coffee at the local café down the street from *Rare Gems*. Even Alice had admitted that it was going a bit too far.

"You don't hunt family," Allison said with a frown. "Most villains try to hold to that, you know. Seriously. You fight people who are walking Gods, you know what they could do if they became unhinged, so there's like this unspoken thing. We don't hurt yours, and you don't go after ours. Aunt Alice made a point of stressing that in the Purge. Keep it focused, and keep it professional. It royally pissed Prometheus off, but he complied most of the time."

"Rob went on a manhunt after that," Brandon said. He put his hand on Allison's shoulder, and gave it a light squeeze. "They ended up fighting on top of the Brooklyn Bridge. No one knows exactly how it ended but Rob. According to him, the Grey 'slipped and fell.' Rob didn't exactly see a need to save him."

"I can see that," Allison said. "So, possibly the Grey, possibly not. This raises too many questions. I..." Allison jumped as her phone started to vibrate in her pocket. "Shit!" She hissed. "Oh, shit."

"Everything okay?"

"Yeah," Allison said, turning the reminder on her phone off. "It's just, I totally spaced on the time. I've gotta go."

"Need a lift?" Brandon asked. "Honestly, I don't want to stick around this place any longer than I have to."

Allison paused, and then smirked. "Well, now that you mention it... mind swinging me by my place to pick something up?"

"Not at all."

"And then dropping me off at 1WTC?"

Brandon grinned as he lifted the tape blocking the door. "What floor?"

Chapter Nine

Broaching the Subject

Alice sat in a small, brown seat at the KornerKafe, a breakfast diner about a block away from her mother's apartment. Across from her, in a wheelchair and wearing a nice floral dress, was Dorothy Gailsone, who was busy cutting into an omelet and grinning. "This is so nice!" The older woman said as she took a small bite. "You never come to visit in the mornings! I was under the impression that you didn't know what the dawn looked like."

Alice coughed, and sipped her coffee. "Yes, well, today was a special day. Holly started school this morning, and I wanted to make sure she got a decent send-off, and I'm up early quite a bit, thank you. I *do* run a store, you know."

"And I am proud of you for doing so, what with you being a ...," Dorothy leaned in and lowered her voice, "... a superhero and all."

"Mom, geez!" Alice leaned back and blushed. "I am not. I just help out from time to time, you know? Like a consultant. A very nicely paid consultant."

"You saved the world," Dorothy pointed out. "That makes you a hero, hon."

"I've also tried to destroy it a few times. I saved *you*. The world can go hang, mother."

"So you say," Dorothy said with a sly smile. "So, to what do I owe the pleasure of your company this morning, dear? Does this mean that our lunch date is off?"

"No," Alice said as she picked at her eggs. "I just realized I haven't been to see you in a bit, and I wanted to make sure you were okay."

"Oh, I'm fine, dear. My new medications are working well, and I've never felt better, honestly."

Alice eyed her. Dorothy had lost some hair since their last meeting, and looked to have dropped at least ten pounds. Her chair was updated to an automatic model, but this one had an oxygen mix tank on the back and a special monitor for vitals. When Dorothy was slicing her omelet, Alice could see a purple mark on her wrist from something having been recently attached. And while she was fussing with her food, she had only taken two bites of her omelet total. Dorothy kept her hands moving, but when she forgot to do so, Alice noticed the tremors, which she was trying to mask by toying with her food.

Alice looked at her mother, and debated with herself. Finally, she smiled and said, "That's good to hear. I was worried."

"Oh, well, you shouldn't be." Dorothy leaned in and took a small sip of tea. "Mr. Tanner has done his best to try to make me comfortable, and, at my age, that's all I could ask for."

"Forget comfortable. Let's get you cured, and back on your feet," Alice said. "With everything out there, all these wonders and technology, there's no reason we can't find a way to fix you up."

Dorothy smiled, but then put her silverware down and slid her hands under the table where Alice couldn't see them. "Then what?"

Alice blinked, her fork halfway to her mouth. "I'm sorry?"

"Then what, dear? I'm old, remember? Very old. I had you late, remember? Your father was so surprised, but he usually was by things. I remember he used to just kiss and kiss your little, purple mop of hair."

Alice quietly fidgeted. There were few topics that could make her uncomfortable, but without fail, one of those topics was her father. Dorothy glanced over, and noticed her daughter's anxiety. Smiling, she brought her hand out, and took Alice's. "It wasn't your fault, love. I know that, and I made peace with it long, long ago. He loved you very much, and he would have been so proud of you."

Alice sighed and looked away. "I'll have to take your word for it."

"As I was saying," Dorothy continued. "I'm old, hon. I've lived a good, long life, seen things people don't normally get to see, travelled places that I never imagined could exist, and had a wonderful time of it. I met your father on my travels, you know."

"I know, Mom," Alice said, familiar with her mother's stories. "Still, old or not, that doesn't mean you just give up on a person."

Dorothy squeezed Alice's hand. "But it does mean that, sooner or later, and probably sooner in my case, the medicines and treatments won't matter. I'll fight because you want me to, and because I want to keep seeing the wonderful woman you are becoming even moreso. I keep hoping for some grandchildren, but I guess that's not in the cards right now, is it?"

Alice shook her head. "Sorry, Mom. That is definitely not happening."

Dorothy was about to make a comment about Alice's love life when she noticed the look on her daughter's face. "Alice," she asked. "Why are you so sure of that?"

Alice was about to take a sip of her coffee, but her mother's question made her pause. She set her coffee cup down, and looked at it for a moment before saying, "Because I know. No matter what you would like, or what I might someday like, that is definitely not happening."

Dorothy held her breath, feeling equal parts embarrassed and mortified for broaching the subject. "Oh, my. Oh, my sweet, little girl. I always thought so, but I never knew how to ask you. Is it because of your powers?"

Alice flinched. It was slight, but Dorothy caught it. Before Dorothy could say anything else, Alice smiled, picked up her coffee, and said in a chipper voice, "You'll have to settle for Allison and Holly."

"I'm so sorry," Dorothy said. "I mean, I suppose I should have guessed, but I just thought... and you never brought it up, and I just..."

"Hey, it's cool. I mean, we've had a lot to catch up on, and not a lot of time." Alice gave her mom a smile. "You're going to have to work harder than that to offend me."

Dorothy frowned, but decided it would be best to let the subject drop. After all, Dorothy didn't see a point in prying. "Wouldn't they be your nieces?" She asked. "Or niece and grandniece?"

Alice cleared her throat. "Depends on how closely you look at the paperwork. Look, I just, I want you to get better, is all. That's been my main motivation in putting up with Alan Tanner's crap, and I know they can do it. I *know* there's a way."

"Hon," Dorothy said softly, "I am so, so grateful that I have you all in my life. You've been such a blessing to me. Please," Dorothy asked in a voice that was beginning to shake, "Please promise me something."

Alice suddenly became concerned, but nodded. "Of course, sure, what?"

"When I'm gone, one... don't look at me like that. When I am gone, one way or another, promise me you won't let all of this go."

"Mom? Where is all this coming from?"

Dorothy sighed and closed her eyes for a moment. Alice couldn't tell if she was thinking, or if she was in pain. "I know you, hon. You like to run. You ran when you had that accident with that skater boy in the back of his car, and from that women's shelter, and then from the Purge when things got bad. It's your default, and you get that from me."

Alice wanted to argue, and then realized she was doing everything she could to not get up and run away from the table. She conceded that her mother might have a point.

"Please," Dorothy asked. "Please don't let this fall apart. What you've done here, with Allison and Holly, with your career and your work, all of it. This is why I've hung on so long, hon. This is what I was *waiting for*."

Alice took her hand back and wiped her face with her napkin, careful not to meet her mother's gaze. "Dammit," she muttered. "I, you, thank you, Mom. I just, I, dammit."

"I love you too, dear. Now" Dorothy said as she picked up her fork. "I think I'm going to pretend to eat this a little while longer while you pretend to not notice that I've been lying about my condition, and I will focus on drinking my tea without throwing up and making wonderful small talk with my beautiful daughter."

Alice sighed and picked up her fork. "So," she said in a falsely chipper voice, "How's the new nurse?"

Dorothy smiled and took a sip of her tea. "Oh, she's a total bitch, dear."

Alice smiled as she took a bite of her eggs. Her mother was deteriorating, and she wasn't sure what she could do to stop it at this point. Still, as long as she was still here, Alice figured that there was still hope.

Chapter Ten

Atomico

Then

***

Robert Parker raced through New York at a breakneck pace, covering a mile a second as he frantically made his way across town to his next challenge. He was running himself into the ground, but he couldn't stop. For a man who was faster than thought, he found himself running out of time. He had already completed over eighty challenges, and while he was setting a personal speed record for himself, he knew that he only had minutes before his hour was up.

One hour. Yeager lived from second to second, stretching each one out into hours, and even with the advantage of speed on his side he was falling behind. The Grey had given him an impossible task, and as much as Rob wanted to quit, he knew he couldn't. He was pushing himself beyond his limits, and his blue and green uniform was torn and tattered from friction burns. His feet were blistered lumps swimming in their shoes, and his legs were on fire. He wanted nothing more than to stop and rest, but if he did, people would die. If he did, she would die.

His last challenge had been trying to free a grandmother from a block of ice. Before that, it had been twins that were strapped to the top and bottom of an express elevator car. Each challenge the Grey had setup seemed more ridiculous.

What bothered Rob the most was how much time this was all taking. To him, with all of the distractions and the elaborate death traps, it felt like things were taking twice as long as they should. That made Rob feel like he was wasting time, and that was the one thing Rob absolutely never did.

Maybe it was a coincidence that Rob had lost track of time. Maybe it was also coincidence that he happened to be where he was when the bomb went off. For the rest of his life, he would tell himself that the Grey had triggered the blast early. It didn't ease the pain of failing, but it helped.

The explosion was so powerful it knocked Rob across the street and through a storefront window. He went tumbling into a fall fashions display, as glass shards peppered his body. Across the street, the apartment complex he had been racing by was obliterated. The smoke and fire pouring out of the hole in the second floor of the building was so thick that even across the street, Rob could barely breathe. As he struggled to his feet, he heard clapping.

Rob looked up. Amidst the running and screaming people in the street stood a lone figure in a trench coat and fedora. He was clapping and shaking his head, calm as could be. Around him the citizens of New York scrambled and fled from the fire, completely oblivious to the faceless, applauding man.

Rob could barely stand. The Grey didn't talk; he never did. He never had to, though, for Rob to get the drift of what he was trying to say. Rob instantly knew what had happened. He knew he had failed, and that the Grey had just detonated his one hundredth prisoner.

Rob felt his whole body start to shake with rage as the Grey made an exaggerated no-no gesture with his index finger. He then pointed down the street, nodded, and vanished before Rob's eyes.

Rob felt his whole body shaking with rage and frustration. He could hear sirens and knew that the emergency services would be there soon to help the people that were trapped under the rubble from the apartment. Any other time, he would have gladly helped. Today though, was different. Today, the Grey was going to die, and nothing was going to stand in Rob's way.

In an instant, Rob tore off down the street towards their first meeting place. The Brooklyn Bridge.

Now

***

The first thing Alan Tanner recognized as he came to was that he was tied up. He could feel the binding on his wrists. Tight, scratchy. It felt like thick twine. He tried to get to the knot, but his wrists had been secured, and he couldn't bend them properly to reach it.

The next thing Alan noticed was that it was dark. Not pitch black, but dark enough that it took his eyes time to adjust. The room was dimly lit from what looked like thin strands of light that were slipping through slits in a window that had been hurriedly painted black.

The third thing he realized was that he was on the floor. He had been left in a heap. No chair or anything else to keep him secure. It was like someone had opened a door, tossed him in, and then left. Not that Alan was complaining, but it seemed sloppy to him.

Last, but certainly not least, Alan noticed the raging pain in his head. He felt dizzy, but lucid. Like his consciousness was forcing itself forward. He felt like he should be groggy, or at the very least drunk, but instead he was just massively hungover. The pain behind his eyes was immense and stabbed his brain with every twitch of his body, but he did his best to block it out. He was alive, he was conscious, and that alone gave him some hope.

Alan waited until his eyes adjusted a little more, and then looked around to see if there was anything else in the room that could be of use. Surprisingly, he noticed that he wasn't alone.

"Hey," he called to the crumpled form on the floor beside him. The figure looked familiar, but it was difficult for Alan to make out much of anything. "Hey, you okay over there?"

There was a muffled response, and the figure shifted slightly. Alan could see that his mystery partner was gagged. Shaking off his headache, Alan looked around the room for anything that could help. The room itself was barren. There was a table, a lamp, a table phone, and a window covered in painted newspapers. While it was hard to see, Alan could see that the walls had dirty, flowered wallpaper that was torn in random places. The smell that lingered in the room was enough to make Alan suppress a gag; it was the thick, sweaty, pungent smell that was almost like overly ripe feet. Over the course of his career, Alan had come to associate this smell with corpses.

Aside from that, the room was empty. Alan scooted towards the flimsy table and gave it a kick. The lamp toppled and shattered into thin, ceramic shards on the dirty, wooden floor. Alan shifted until he could feel the shards with his fingers. Gingerly, he started to slice through the ropes that bound his wrists.

After a few moments, the ropes split, and Alan quickly righted himself. He made short work of the ropes binding his feet, and then turned to the figure on the floor. "Hey," he said as he turned them over. "Hey, are you okay? I... oh, no."

Lying on the floor beside him was the super villain known as Atomico. He looked starved; his once massive bulk now a skinny, pale rag of skin on bone. His costume, a bright yellow bodysuit with the symbol of an atom within a skull on his chest, hung limp on his frame. His hair had mostly fallen out, and his skin was covered in sores. His executioner's hood was gone, revealing a scruffy, long, pale face and sunken cheeks. Alan pushed back the urge to vomit on the spot, and instead carefully removed the man's gag.

"Can you tell me what happened?" Alan asked in a low voice. Atomico coughed and sputtered as a thin line of dark blood trickled down his chin.

"He can't stay still," the tortured villain mumbled. "He can't stay still. He can't...he can't..."

"Easy there," Alan said as he placed a gentle hand on the starved man's shoulder. "Let's get you out of here, and then you can tell me all about it."

Alan stood, and looked around again. Atomico was a bruiser, and typically combined his superhuman strength with a radioactive attack. It made him deadly in a long brawl, and Alan had fought him plenty as Blackthorne. The thing was, despite his powers, Alan never saw Atomico as much of a threat. He was always more of a B-grade villain, more interested in a quick payday than committing acts of savagery. While Alan had no love for the man, he had never wished anything as horrible as this on him.

Alan scanned the ceiling and walls until he saw what he was looking for, a white disk hanging near a corner. To most, it would look like a smoke alarm, but to Alan, it was painfully obvious it was an inhibitor. He grabbed it off the wall and with all his might smashed it against the floor. It broke on the third impact, and Instantly his headache was gone.

"God, that's better. Hey, Atomico? I took down the inhibitor. You can use your powers again. Atomico?"

Alan turned to see Atomico still on the floor, coughing up blood and mumbling, "he can't... he can't stay still."

"Okay, no help there," Alan mumbled. He tried the door to the room, but it was locked. Not knowing if anyone was listening, how many people might be on the other side, or what his situation truly was, Alan didn't want to risk breaking it down. Instead, he turned his attention to the window. He undid the latch and carefully slid the wooden frame upwards. He blinked as a shaft of sunlight hit his eyes, partially blinding him. Looking around, he saw a busy, rundown urban street. He guessed that he was about four stories up, and thankfully, he saw that there was a fire escape nearby. He could make it by himself, but with Atomico, it was going to be difficult.

Alan weighed his options. He considered leaving the villain and coming back for him. It would be the fastest solution, but there was a strong chance that Atomico would not last, and then his death would be on Alan's hands. Alan considered trying to take Atomico with, but even with his frame greatly reduced, the atomic bruiser had to weight over 200 pounds. He was a massive man, towering at close to eight feet tall, and Alan dreaded trying to fireman carry him along a window ledge.

"Dammit," Alan mumbled. "You're damn lucky I'm such a softie. Come here, big boy. We're getting the hell out of here." Alan squatted down and carefully lifted the gigantic man onto his shoulders. "Oh my God, how much did you weigh *before* you almost starved to death?"

Atomico kept mumbling. Alan, not wanting to waste any time, carefully made his way onto the ledge. Almost instantly, he nearly fell as Atomico shuddered. The massive man was proving to be too much, even for Alan to hoist. Normally, Alan would have been able to carry him, but with the ledge being as thin as it was, Alan quickly realized how impossible his task would be. He needed an alternative.

Alan glanced down. They were along what looked like a thin, cluttered side street, and there were some older cars parked along the thin sidewalk. Alan noticed that there was an old, brown van parked almost directly beneath them, and smiled.

"Hey, Atomico?" Alan casually asked. "Remember that time you fought Blackthorne and broke his arm in that car door?"

"He can't...what?"

Alan nearly slipped, and made a quick judgment call. "You've got a healing factor, right?"

Before Atomico could answer, Alan pushed up and forward, and threw the giant man off his shoulders. Alan watched as he sailed through the air before slamming back-first into the rooftop of the brown van below. The windows on the van exploded outward, and several passersby screamed and rushed to the crippled man's aide.

"That'll do," Alan said to himself. While he knew it probably wasn't a good idea to throw a crippled and malnourished man off a building, this particular man was superhuman and extremely tough. He'd wind up in the hospital, but he was free, and that was Alan's primary concern.

Quickly and carefully, Alan made his way to the fire escape, and then to the street below. After calmly dusting off his hands, Alan proceeded to start running as fast as he could into the gathering crowd. People were running to the site of Atomico's crash landing, and Alan quickly realized that he was the only white person in sight. He looked around, and quickly determined from what signs, vehicles, and storefronts he could see that he was not in the United States. He had no money, his wallet was gone, he hadn't eaten in God only knew how long, and he felt dehydrated.

"Okay, no biggie," Alan said to himself. "I can do this."

As if on cue, three large, Asian men with automatic weapons at their sides quickly emerged from the building that Alan had just escaped. Alan glanced back just in time to make eye contact with one of them, and see him start to scream at the others. A second later, all three were training their weapons on him.

Alan dove for a nearby alley as the three men opened fire. He ducked around the corner as the cheap brick of the building next to him erupted in a violent haze of dust and debris. Alan kept his head down and ran as fast as he could past the maze of dumpsters and trash cans that lined the narrow passageway. Behind him, he could hear people yelling, and the sound of heavy footsteps.

Alan rounded a corner, and the alley widened into a backstreet that was currently occupied by several children playing soccer. Alan froze as the kids, six in all, stopped and stared at the dirty American businessman in the torn suit. He looked around, but there wasn't anywhere else to run to in time . Alan glanced at the soccer ball that had rolled to a stop and ran towards it. As the gunmen rounded the corner, Alan spun around and gave the ball a hard kick. The ball went sailing through the air and crashed into the closest man's gun, knocking it back and up, and into the man's face. The man stumbled backwards, cursing as the other two opened fire. Alan cried out as a bullet nicked his arm. He spun and scrambled behind a nearby dumpster as the men fired their guns and laughed.

Alan heard them call out something in a language that sounded to him like either Tai Lü or Shan. "I'm in Myanmar," Alan said to himself as he glanced around. There wasn't much available, but Alan did spot a beer bottle lying nearby. He picked it up, smashed it on the ground, and quickly gathered the glass shards. His hands were shaking, but he forced himself to focus as he heard the sound of one of the men approaching. He grabbed his suit coat jacket and tore off a strip, and hurriedly wrapped three pieces of glass up with his fist, making a makeshift glove with spiked, glass shard knuckles.

As the shooter came around the corner, Alan jumped out at him. He knocked the gun barrel aside, and slammed his fist right into the man's face. The man screamed, and arched backwards as Alan spun towards the other two shooters and flung his remaining glass shards. They sailed through the air, finding their targets easily. The men collapsed to their knees, and then crumpled to the ground, glass shards protruding from their throats.

Alan steadied himself against the dumpster and took a shaky breath. He was losing blood, and it was hard for him to focus. He looked up to see that the children from before had vanished, leaving him alone for a moment. Alan looked around, trying to figure out his next move. The alley looked like it continued on for a while, and it might open up into a busy part of the city. From there, he could get a cab and find a hotel. Alan had safe hotels set up in nearly every major city on the planet, each ready to accommodate a member of the Collective Good if they ever found themselves in a bad situation.

Alan had only taken three steps before he heard the sound of the boys behind him. He turned, and his breath caught in his throat. The boys had led a man in a grey trench coat and fedora to his location. The man had his hands tucked casually in his pockets, and most notably to Alan, did not have a face. Instead, there was just a pale grey surface.

"I remember," Alan said as he turned completely around, and straightened what was left of his jacket. "You came to my apartment, didn't you? You're the one who took me."

The man in gray flickered in and out for a moment, like a bad signal on a television. It almost looked like he was blipping in and out of existence. There was only one person Alan knew of who could do anything like that. Alan felt his chances of escape start to disappear. "You're the Grey, aren't you?"

The Grey took a gloved hand out of his pocket and handed the young boy beside him a wad of bills. The boy's eyes lit up, and he held up the bills and shouted to his friends as they ran down the alley, cheering and laughing. Alan watched them go and sighed.

"Why didn't you just kill me?" Alan asked in as calm of a voice as he could muster. "That's what you do, isn't it? Why keep me alive? Why torture Atomico?"

The Grey stood and silently stared at Alan. Alan repressed a shudder, and looked at his options. He knew the Grey's power set had never been officially determined, but that he was a heavy hitter. His battles with Yeager were the stuff of legend, and Alan didn't know if he could take him on a good day, let alone in his current condition.

Alan clenched his fist, and then realized his shard wrappings were gone. The cloth, the glass, all of it had disappeared from his hand. He hadn't even felt them leave. He looked to see if he had any more shards, but they were gone, too. Alan looked to the Grey, and saw the glass pieces neatly piled at his feet.

"That's cute. That's a cute trick," Alan said. He turned and bolted for the other end of the street, but before he could take a step, he felt a massive force slam into his stomach, dropping him instantly. He let out a wheeze, and a stream of blood flew from his mouth. "God," Alan moaned as he doubled over. "Why are you doing this?"

Alan looked up to see the Grey standing over him. The Grey didn't answer, and the last thing Alan saw before slipping into a numb blackness was the Grey's hand reaching towards Alan's face.

Chapter Eleven

The Truth About Anna May

In its heyday, the Purge boasted over 300 active facilities worldwide. Every capitol city contained a Purge center, a base of operations that could be used by any member of the organization at any time. The bases offered shelter, an armory, laboratories, global communications, and everything else needed for military and scientific endeavors. These facilities cost a fortune, but they were always viewed as a long-term investment by Prometheus, the enigmatic leader of the Purge. He saw their organization less as a terrorist organization and more as a global industry. They were capitalists in the business of terror for profit, and they were the best.

At least, they were until the *Argent* incident. After that, the Purge was devastated, both in finances and in manpower. It had taken two short months to round up the majority of Purge soldiers, scientists and employees after the disaster over the skies of Pittsburg. Once Prometheus was declared dead and Dyspell went missing, the organization crumbled. All of their money had been riding on the *Argent* project, and without funds to pay the troops or keep the facilities going, without investors lining up to help the struggling, leaderless terrorist organization, its members fled in droves. Only a few isolated cells remained, but they were nothing compared to the organization's former glory.

As a result, many of the facilities were boarded up, abandoned, or simply forgotten. Only recently, with the grand push to capture Superior Force, had many of them been activated. Even then, that activation had been to destroy them as well as anything surrounding them. While this push had worked, it left the Purge drastically low on manpower and facilities.

This left the remaining forces in the Purge uneasy. There were whispers of their leader not being the tactical genius she was billing herself as. Stories of her mental instability were spreading, as were tales of what happened to anyone who dared to cross her and her horrifying Totallus. Because of this fear, Anna retained her power. Still, terror could only stretch so far before money was needed, and money was becoming a serious concern for Anna.

Her hovercraft was a light armor detail, designed primarily for troop transport and not for close combat. It had limited stealth and anti-radar capabilities, but even so, was a risk to fly in heavily-populated areas. As a result, her crew put down several miles outside of New York, near an old Purge subway station that was designed to look like an abandoned Taco Bell.

Once the craft had cleared the retractable roof of the faux restaurant, Anna disembarked and boarded the dusty, slightly rusted passenger car that was waiting for her. She was followed by several straining shock troops, who were doing their best to stay behind the brooding Totallus that marched with them. Anna took a seat near the front and waited in silence as the doors noisily slid shut and the car, groaning and creaking, made its way into the heart of the city.

They arrived 20 minutes later at a subterranean command center underneath the GE building in midtown. As soon as the transport rolled to a stop, the soldiers in the sub base instantly set to welcoming Anna and her Totallus, standing at attention with their guns at their shoulders. Anna watched them for a moment, and then headed for the comm center.

The room smelled of processed air, and the lights were only partially working, but the giant LCD screen lit up just fine. A moment later, a black skull with a camera on its side returned her gaze.

"Are. You. Finished?" The electronic voice box on Kogoura's throat said in a broken, monotone voice. Anna tried to ignore the wet, exaggerated movement of her tactical adviser's throat muscles as he spoke.

"Just about. Our new Senator is sadly even more incompetent than the old one. You were right though, he was the one who activated our old Totallus."

"It. Does. Not. Matter," came the synthesized reply. Anna nodded, only somewhat paying attention.

"I suppose you're right. Still, he claims that he can clear out the remaining Collective Good. That should help with things once we launch. Do you have all of Superior Force drained yet? We need that power."

"We. Only. Need. A. Portion."

"Fortunately, that's what we happen to have. Have Diamond blip on by - I have a side job for her."

"We. Are. Wasting. Time."

Anna sighed. "You know, you're probably right. Still, the Purge keeps its word. We'll just move the timetable a bit. How's your end of the plan coming along?"

"I. Set. The. Wheels. In. Motion. Three. Days. Ago." He said in his cold monotone. "We. Will. Finally. Be. Charged. And. Ready. For. Launch. In. Roughly. 12. Hours."

"About fucking time," Anna mumbled. "I still can't believe it's taken this long to get the engines up to full efficiency. I mean, doesn't our little battery have unlimited power? Why couldn't we just drain him in a day?"

"He. Is. Nearly. Dead." Kogoura said. "To. Draw. At. A. Greater. Rate. Would. Kill. Him."

"Fine, whatever. I've waited this long, I can wait a little longer," Anna smiled. "This whole plan of yours has come together rather nicely, Kogoura. You know, I have to admit, the Purge dropped the ball by not hiring you sooner."

There was no emotion fro the skull on the screen. Admittedly, without facial features or a voice that could inflect, Anna wondered at how she could tell at all if Kogoura was happy, sad, or suicidal. She figured that as long as he did his job, he could feel however he wanted to.

"Do. Not. Be. So. Casual. This. Is. A. Dangerous. Game. You. Have. Decided. To. Play."

Anna rolled her eyes. "Yes, mother. Now, if you'll excuse me, I need to prep for my big reunion tonight. Tootles!" She killed the video feed before the general could respond. She considered her jumpsuit, and thought about leaving it on for fun, but then decided against it.

"This has to be perfect," she mumbled to herself. "I need to get ready. This has to be just perfect."

***

Kogoura watched as the monitor before him switched off. He was on the bridge of the *Metatron*, sitting still in his wheel chair as the oxygen pump attached to its back wheezed and hissed with each breath. Beside him, Danica Lewis, also known as the Diamond, small-time teleporting thief and newest recruit to the Purge, stood with her hands on her hips. She had traded her normal outfit, a simple gray catsuit, for a black Purge operative's getup. Her giant aviator goggles stayed, though. She would be dead before giving those up. "She's awfully flippant about all of this, isn't she?"

Kogoura sat perfectly still in response. Danica thought the crippled general had passed out, but then nearly jumped when his voice modulator squawked to life. "She. Is. Crumbling. This. Will. Undo. All. That. Has. Happened."

"You really think so? I mean, aren't people like her *supposed* to be a little crazy?"

Kogoura turned his chair to face the jewel thief. "No. She. Is. Broken. And. We. Will. Not. Win."

Danica 'harrumphed' and glanced at the gigantic cathedral of glass that was the front window to the *Metatron*. Outside, she could see the black and blue hues of ice that relentlessly pressed against the titanic ship's frame.

"Well, we've got the strongest hero on the planet as our personal battery. We've got a senator in our pocket that is going to use the government to hunt superhumans like they're deer in a preserve. We've destroyed the public's faith in their heroes. Hell, we have a colossal warship, ready and waiting to take the entire country. How, *exactly*, will we lose?"

"She. Ignored. Me. About. Victoria. Green. And. Has. Remained. Focused. Completely. On. Alice. Gailsone."

"Well, that's good, right? I mean, one more player off the table?"

She looked to Kogoura, who was still focused on the black monitor before him. "The. Gailsones. Will. Be. Her. Undoing."

Danica let out a laugh, and strolled around. She glanced over at the steel cocoon that was Superior Force. It was glowing with energy that was flowing through thick, steel cables to the Phoenix statue that sat on a makeshift, mechanical pedestal in the center of the Bridge. "In a matter of hours, we're going to launch this bad boy, and take over the world. What can those women do, exactly, that can even *begin* to touch us?"

"That. They. Exist. Is. Enough. To. Cripple. Anna. Alice. Is. Not. To. Be. Underestimated. She. Defeated. My. Previous. Employer. And. She. Will. Kill. Us. All. Before. This. Is. Finished."

"Why would she bother? Seriously, what's so special about this Dyspell woman that the boss hates her so bad? I mean, you say her name, and she just goes off."

"Anna. Insists. On. Making. This. Personal. She. Is. Going. To. Strike. In. A. Way. That. Cannot. Be. Ignored."

"Well, again, isn't that the point?"

"No. Not. Like. This." Kogoura turned his chair to face Danica. "She. Is. About. To. Cross. A. Line. That. Will. Lead. To. Open. War. With. The. Gailsones. Her. Revenge. Will. Hail. Her. Destruction."

"...What is she going to do? What don't I know?"

"The. Truth. About. Anna. May." Kogoura said. Danica waited for more, but the faceless soldier turned his chair and slowly rolled off the Bridge, leaving the young thief feeling troubled.

Chapter Twelve

An Object Lesson

At 10:50 AM, Alice Gailsone walked into the lobby of Tanner Tower with her chin up and her gaze steady. Her high heels clacked loudly on the smooth, obsidian floor as she made her way to the elevator banks. Around her, people stopped and stared as they recognized the woman known as Dyspell sporting a Tanner Industries ID badge proudly on her lapel. She was smiling, and her sunglasses were tucked in her breast pocket, revealing her purple eyes for the world to see. With a flash of her badge, she took the second bank of elevators to their topmost floor, and when she could ride no longer, she got off and took the stairs to the roof.

It was a gorgeous, albeit cold day, and the wind (while a bit strong for Alice) was actually pretty mild for their height. She slipped her oversized white sunglasses out and put them on as Victoria, smartly bundled in a brown jacket, saw her from across the helipad and waved. She was standing with a group of nervous-looking individuals and what looked like a cross between a trashcan and a mini-fridge from the 1980's, but with legs.

"Hey, I was starting to think you weren't coming." She called out with a smile. She grinned back and walked briskly towards the group.

"Had to make some stops, some calls, you know. Business stuff."

Victoria nodded. "I'm just glad you showed up."

Alice looked around. "Have you spoken to Alan yet? I thought he was attending this."

Victoria glanced to the side for a moment and paused before speaking. It was slight, but enough for Alice to notice. "Alan is taking a personal day or two."

Alice studied Victoria for a moment. "Hung over?"

Victoria declined to answer. Alice shrugged it off and figured that whatever was wrong was Alan's fault. "Well, regardless, it doesn't matter. He put me on this. He knows I don't need a babysitter...most of the time. So, do we have everyone?"

Alice looked at the group in front of her. There was a tall, bald, African American man in a green windbreaker and sunglasses standing in the center of the group. Beside him was a short blonde sporting long, messy hair and huddled in a pink coat. There was a small, slim Hispanic woman with long hair who was in a giant sweater that looked like a Canadian flag. This was offset by what looked like blindingly bright red yoga pants (or tights. It was hard to tell.) Her face looked chiseled, with high cheekbones and a thin mouth. Her stare was locked on Alice. Next to her, dapper as ever, was Phillip Gelery. The man known as the Bleed was looking calm and collected, dressed to the nines in his blood-red three-piece suit. Alice was impressed that his fedora was managing to stay on despite the breeze. Off to the side stood Golomous, the Machine that Walked. He was beeping a musical tune that sounded like a washing machine chiming at the end of a cycle. Alice took it to mean hello.

Alice took out her PhoneBuddy, sent a quick text, and said, "Hi everyone, thanks for coming. I need everybody to gather in the middle of the helipad, and then we can begin the presentation. Trust me, this is going to be of benefit, so just give me a sec and you'll see what we've cooked up."

"Shit!" The blonde yelled. Alice and Alan both froze as the petite woman's hands crackled and glowed with electricity. She then lobbed a lightning bolt at Alice, who only barely had time to dodge. The purple-haired witch tucked, rolled and quickly got to her feet in a fighting stance. Sophia lifted off the ground, her hands balled into fists. The bald man in the back instantly started chanting as a green glow surrounded his body.

"Woah! Woah now!" Alice said, her hands out in front of her. "Wha-ha-hat the hell?! This is a bit extreme." Alice was leery, but ready to slip into a fighting stance if she had to. Well, as ready as she could be in heels. To the side, Victoria already had her hand at her belt, ready to go.

Phil was the only one who remained calm. "Everyone," he said in a loud, but level, tone. "Please stand down. She doesn't know. I would remind you that last time, it was not her."

Alice glanced from Phil to the group, swallowed, and said, "I have no idea what this is about, but I assure you, I am not here to fuck with you. Okay? Calm down now? Please? You do not want to start something. Here. And especially with me." Alice glared at the group with that last comment. While she didn't particularly like the idea of getting into it, her knockout record was impressive. If these assholes wanted to start off by causing trouble, the former General of the Purge knew *exactly* how to handle it. "Jesus, if I had known you'd get this twitchy, I would have met with you sooner."

"How did she know?" the bald man was shouting. "How did she know, huh? Is this some kind of sick joke?"

Alice looked to the man, and gestured for calm. "Paul Dasher, right?"

He looked at Alice and after a moment, nodded.

"Look Paul, I'm a little confused as to what set you guys off so hard, so fast. I promise you, I'm just here to help with the orientation process. That's it."

"Why did you say what you said? Just then?" Paul half-shouted.

Alice shrugged. "I don't know, because it's true? I was trying to be, um, nice? Please calm down."

The group looked from Alice to Phil, who was glaring at the tense villains. "Everyone," Phil said. He had a thick, eastern-European accent that caused his l's to be accentuated. "This is Alice Gailsone, formerly known as Dyspell. The *real* Dyspell. I can assure you, we are quite safe. Now, please stop embarrassing me."

One by one, the group powered down. Phil nodded and then turned to a confused Alice and Victoria. "Please forgive them. The warehouse incident I informed you of? Those exact words you just said were uttered before many of our comrades were murdered in front of us. You'll forgive my new associates if this is somewhat suspect."

Alice blinked, and then smoothed out her skirt. "I can see that. I'm impressed at how accurately they portrayed me, but I can see that. Look, you're safe here. You're at Tanner Tower. There is nowhere safer on the planet for people like us."

"Like us? Villains?" Angela asked. Her hands were still crackling with electricity, but not as violently as before.

"Former, and I want to stress that word, *former* villains. You're safe here. Promise."

"We've *been* safe here," Angela snapped. "We've been stuck here for weeks being 'safe here'. I'm starting to wonder if all we did was sign up for a cushier prison than what the State could offer us."

Alice nodded. "I can see why you'd think that, but trust me, that's not the case. Outside of my family, you're the first super team that's been officially recruited under the Open Hand Act. That, and you've been in a makeshift Witness Protection Program. Today, we stop focusing on the latter, and put some serious work into the former. I want to see you out and in public, and using what you've got for more than just running through tests in the Tower."

Sophia, still scowling, looked around. "So, why the roof? Why not a conference room?"

Alice smiled, and gestured to the skyline. "For starters, if you all had pulled that lightning bolt crap in a conference room, we would have considerably more problems to deal with right now. Second, out here, you can stretch your legs, and really show us what you can do. Third, I don't quite trust you yet."

"What does being on the roof have to do with not trusting us?" Sophia asked.

Alice grinned. "Do you see the One World Trade Center tower about half a mile yonder?"

"Yeah, what about it?" Sophia asked.

Alice allowed herself a little chuckle. "Twenty minutes ago, my very pissy niece somewhat-illegally made her way to the roof, popped a juice box, and is currently trained on you with a 408 Chey Tac that she affectionately calls Armand."

The group froze. Angela scoffed. "You're bluffing."

Alice nodded, and looked to Victoria. "Hey, boss-lady. You got something I can use for an object lesson?"

Victoria nodded, and slipped a flask out of her jacket. It was silver, with the initials "AT" engraved in an ornate cursive across the side. Alice nodded a thank you, and took it from her. "Figured you would confiscate one of these." She then walked to Golomous, and set it on his head.

"Don't move, old friend," She said with a grin. The living computer beeped in response.

Alice stepped back, raised her arm and gave a thumbs up towards the OWTC.

Five seconds later, the group (save for Alice) jumped at the sound of a loud clang. The flask jumped high into the air, and then bounced several times across the helipad. Alice nodded towards the distant tower, and then calmly walked over to pick up the flask. She held it up so that the group could see the large hole in its side. Still smiling, she tossed it to Victoria, who looked at it, frowned, and then tossed it over her shoulder.

"I believe in second chances," Alice said in an upbeat voice. "I believe that people can change. It sucks, and it takes time, but it can happen. I believe that people can choose to act against nature, and that they can grow. However, I'm also the former head general for the Purge, so I'm not fucking stupid. You're a group of scared and desperate cons who have signed the Open Hand Act because you have no other options available to you. Now, I have been asked to help with this, as I have experience, but do not for one second think that I am so naive as to just accept your story without question. You get one pass, but that's all you get. You try betraying us? You want to make a mess of things? You'll get shut down. Hard. So, I get that we have had a little mix-up, but you try to start shit with me again, and I will *fucking end you*. Understood?"

The group nodded.

"Wonderful. Now, we need to figure out how to best utilize you. Victoria and I talked, and we're of a mindset that you shouldn't be shelved. You've got good abilities, and we can and should put those to good use."

"What if we don't want to use our powers anymore?" Angela asked. "What if we just want to walk away?"

Alice shrugged. "Then you walk away. That's fine, but God help you if you use those powers in public again. The Open Hand Act has a clause that says if you go back on it, it's the Lunar Gulag for you. So you might wanna think about your actions. I just figured that you'd like to use your existing talents to draw a massive, government-funded paycheck."

Angela crossed her arms in front of her and hugged herself. Alice watched, and nodded. She approached Angela, and said in a softer voice, "I read what happened. I get it. I really do. If you want to leave, then hon, you can walk, and no one here will stop you."

Angela started to take a step. "But," Alice continued. "What sounds better? Running from what happened, or getting some much-deserved closure? I can't promise you revenge, or that if you get it you'll feel better. I do know if you don't try to do right by your sister, you'll go your whole life wondering if you should have made a different choice."

Angela paused, Alice's words running through her mind. Alice gently patted Angela on the shoulder. "Think about it for a second, okay?"

Angela sniffed and nodded. Paul put his arm around her, and she leaned into him.

Alice turned to Sophia. "Hi, you must be Halifax. I think I tried to recruit you a long time ago, didn't I?"

Alice extended her hand. Sophia paused, and then took it. "Yeah, like, just before that Pittsburg thing."

"You made a good call. I'd like to see what you can do, if you don't mind?"

Sophia levitated a few feet off the ground. "Well, I'm a flyer. Nothing really beyond that, but flying is still pretty awesome."

Alice nodded. "Hey, I can't do it, so no arguments here. How fast can you go?"

Sophia grinned. "Pretty damn fast."

Alice raised an eyebrow. "I'd like to put that to the test, if you don't mind?"

Sophia shrugged. "Hey, sure. You want to clock me or something?"

Alice laughed, and shook her head. "Actually, I was going to use Eedee."

Alice raised her voice. "You ready, hon?" A moment later, there was a whoosh of air, and in front of the group floated a tan blonde in a blue, skintight bodysuit. Her hair was done up in a braid, and she was grinning like a kid at Christmas.

"I can't believe I get to do this! This is so cool!" Eedee was vibrating in midair. Alice gestured for her to calm down.

"Reel it in, hon. This is a speed test, plain and simple. I want to see how fast Halifax can go, and I need you to accurately log it. Can you do that?"

"Heck yeah! Watch me, mommmmboss! Boss!" Eedee corrected herself in a panic once she saw the murderous glare Alice was shooting her. Alice grumbled under her breath as Sophia floated up to meet Eedee, who was positively beaming with joy. "So, you're a flyer too, huh?"

Eedeee nodded. "Sure am! And I can do other stuff, too! What about you?"

Sophia shrugged. "I just fly, s'all."

Eedee nodded. "Right. So, does your suit constrict blood flow to your legs? How do you survive at higher speeds? What anti-G tech are you wearing? I don't want to kill you on a test run."

Sophia and Alice blinked.

Eedee sighed. "You have a flight suit and helmet, right?"

Sophia nodded and descended to the roof. She slipped off her sweater to reveal her red and white shiny flight suit. "This was designed for me by Tolarius. The price was high, but I can get some good speed out of it."

Eedee nodded. "Cool. Helmet?"

Sophia walked behind the group to a small duffel bag and slipped out a sleek, red helmet with a solid, reflective front. She put her hair up in a bun and then securely fastened the helmet to her head. A moment later, she was floating beside Eedee, who was nodding in satisfaction.

"Wonderful! I'll try to keep it below 5 G's. Don't need you passing out and/or dying."

"What makes you think I can't go faster?" Sophia's voice was metallic and hollow through her helmet, making it hard to tell if she was male or female.

Eedee giggled. "Well, unless that suit is magic, pressurized, or made of something totally awesome, your brain will most likely shut down at around 630 miles per hour. Now, assuming that we do a steady climb and limit the amount of pressure against your body, we still would be lucky to get you to 8 or 9 G's tops. At that point, without a full-on flight suit and cockpit to keep you safe, and considering you probably fly head-first, your brain will protest by draining of blood, and you will pass out, have an embolism, and die before you hit the ground."

Eedee kept her chipper smile throughout the conversation, but Alice knew the android was doing exactly what she had been made for. She had been on the design team, after all, and knew how capable Eedee's brain was. Despite her ditzy nature, Eedee was first and foremost designed to know a human's weak points, and how to exploit them. Still, Alice couldn't help but underestimate the bubbly android. As smart as she was, Eedee had proven on multiple occasions that she was still socially naive.

Sophia shrugged and gestured to the open sky. "Look, you just try to keep up, missy. How far you wanna go?"

Eedee looked to the west. "Let's shoot for 30 miles offshore. I'll go for close; how does 40.66 by -72.34 sound? That'll still put us near shipping."

Sophia paused. "What? Who the Hell knows lat/long coordinates like that? I... You know what? Okay, whatever you say. Point the way. You ready?"

Eedee nodded and gestured towards the east. "Rock and roll, sugar bowl!"

Alice sighed. Again, she was very smart, but at times Eedee was practically a child.

Sophia wasted no time. In a heartbeat, she took off like a rocket towards the west. The group watched her soar over midtown proper and out over Suffolk. A moment later, Eedee was gone, following behind and then beside the red and white blur.

Victoria had moved beside Alice and was watching the two go. "Wow. She can really move, can't she?"

Alice nodded. "They both can."

"I'm guessing the reason Eedee is doing this, and not Susan, is because you want a more accurate read?"

Alice nodded. "Susie is cool, but yeah, Eedee can give me a pretty damn accurate measure on speed. Besides, Miss Major shouldn't have to step away from her day job for a field test. Now," Alice turned back to the group. "Who's next?"

***

Sophia (who was now going about as fast as she normally dared) was pushing against a wall of wind and was starting to feel some exhaustion. She was over the ocean at this point, and the strain of keeping up her top speed combined with the wind resistance was getting to her.

Beside her, Eedee was cruising along, her hair whipping in the morning air. "Great job, Halifax!" Eedee yelled over the roar of the wind. Halifax could hear her clearly over her comm in her helmet, which bothered her. She wanted to ask how Eedee was able to talk to her, let alone do anything without a helmet, but she was a bit preoccupied to give it much thought. The bubbly android continued, "I have you traveling at 334.25096 miles per hour. That's as fast as a jet plane! Well, a slow jet plane, but still! Nice!"

Sophia barely heard her. Eedee was right, that *was* a great speed, and Sophia felt proud that she had managed to get going so fast, but then she glanced at Eedee. The blonde was soaring along without goggles, or protective gear, or much of anything. The blonde seemed relaxed, while Sophia was starting to breathe heavy from exertion.

'She's not even trying!' Sophia thought to herself. *'I'm killing myself here, and she's not even trying! Who is this woman?!'*

"Just hold on!" Sophia shouted. "I'm gonna go...a little...faster!"

Eedee heard her and frowned. "Please don't! I have your heart rate at 168bpm, and your muscle tension is high! If you continue to push yourself, you will pass out and cease your forward momentum. If this occurs, you will experience close to 32 G's at once. That could sever an aortic vein!"

Sophia blocked out the woman to her side and focused. She sped up, going faster and faster. She could feel the wind against her like a thick, constricting blanket. There was a steady, pounding roar in her ears that she could feel vibrating throughout her entire body. She was going faster than she had ever gone before. Faster than she had ever dared. She...

Sophia glanced to the side and saw Eedee, still keeping pace with her, still staring at her without the least bit of effort on her face.

Surprised by this, Sophia turned a little too far and paid for it. She felt the force of the wind against her head catch her and whip her around. Just as Eedee had predicted, all of this caused her to put on the breaks, and she tumbled through the air at ultra-high speed. The combined G forces, along with the loss of control and exhaustion, forced her to black out. Still moving at a high speed, Sophia started falling helplessly towards the crashing surf below.

***

Alice stared at Angela. "How about you. You're one of the Dynamo Twins, right?"

Angela nodded. "I was. My sister, she..."

Alice held up a hand. "I know. I'm sorry. I honestly don't know who killed her, but we are working on finding out."

Angela sniffed. "Thank you. I just, I really don't know what I'm doing here. We, I can't do anything without her. My powers..."

"Worked just fine a second ago," Alice said. "I think you used each other to help prime and focus your abilities." Alice looked around and settled on the giant antenna array on top of Tanner Tower. "Here. Go ahead and blast that."

Angela looked at Alice and then the antenna array. "I don't know that I can."

"Um, please don't. That's a cellular antenna," Victoria pointed out. "We get rent for that."

Alice promptly ignored her. "Shoulda put in some targets, Vic. Let 'er rip!"

"Hey," Paul said as he gave Angela's shoulder a squeeze, "you can do it."

"No, I can't!" Angela bit back. "I can't do it! My powers don't work without her! Look!"

She pointed her hands at the antenna array. Everyone watched as nothing happened.

"Oh, thank God," Victoria muttered.

"See? Nothing!" Angela said, flustered. "That back there? It was a fluke. That's all. I can't, I want to go home."

Paul kissed the top of her head and hugged her, while Alice nodded in understanding. "Yeah, you're probably right." She chuckled and smirked at the depressed blonde. "Obviously, Cindy was the *real* power behind you two, anyway. Pity you let her get offed."

Phil closed his eyes and made a low, grumbling noise. Paul glared, but before he could say anything, Angela sputtered out, "What? What did you just say to me?"

From off to the side, Victoria closed her eyes and held her forehead with her hand. "Dammit, Alice..."

Alice turned around, and crossed her arms. "I should have known you were fucking useless. You couldn't even keep your own sister alive, and I'm supposed to recruit you for a team? What are you going to do when there's trouble? Cut and run, and leave us for dead? God knows, you know *how*."

"Say that again," Angela yelled. "Say it to my face!"

Victoria sidestepped out of the way. "Alice..." she warned.

164

Alice turned her back to Angela, her arms still crossed. She glanced back over her shoulder and smirked. "Okay. You're a fucking waste who got her sister killed. She was obviously the head of your two-bit operation, and you decided the hell with her the second things got hard. Poor little Angela." Alice fake-pouted to drive the point home.

Angela was shaking with rage. "You, you fucking *bitch*! Fuck you! FUCK YOU!"

Before anyone knew what was happening, Angela extended her arms in front of her and screamed. A blast of electricity exploded out from her and slammed into Alice, full-force. The lightning bolt threw Alice across the helipad and slammed her into the side of the stairwell access entrance. She slid down the stone wall and slumped on the ground, her front now a black, smoking mess.

"Alice!" Victoria shouted as he ran for her. She was by her in an instant. "She's not breathing. I can't detect a heartbeat!" Victoria had her PhoneBuddy out and was shouting for the tower paramedics to get to the roof immediately. Angela, still in shock over what she had done, had dropped to her knees and was shaking uncontrollably. Paul made sure she was okay, and then ran to the prone form of Alice.

"Step back, please." Paul said as he reached for Alice. Victoria moved to stop him, but then realized what he was doing. With a nod, Victoria moved back as Paul placed his hands over the smoldering wound on Alice's chest. Instantly, his hands and eyes began to glow with a harsh, white light. There was a thin, brilliant film of silver that seemed to glow around Alice for a second, the brightest spot being on her chest. Then, with a gasp, Alice sputtered and coughed back to life.

Paul stepped back as Victoria moved to her side. Alice gratefully took his hand as she coughed and shook from the experience, and then (with no small effort) made her way to her feet.

"Your powers are yours, not a result of contact with your sister," Alice said in a trembling, hoarse voice. "You allowed them to be channeled when she was near because of the emotional connection you felt with her. That's become a handicap. Your powers can be triggered just fine."

"I'm sorry," Angela said. "I don't, I'm not a killer. I just rob banks! I swear, I've never, I didn't know that I…"

Alice coughed again and held up a hand. "Angela, *I'm* sorry. I pushed you hard, and said some very bad things. I didn't mean them, I just wanted you to see you could do it. I knew you could when you took a shot at me."

"You knew she'd electrocute you?" Victoria asked. "Are you wearing your suit under that?"

Alice glared at Victoria. "Despite your fashion choices, a black bodysuit does not mix well with a skirt and blouse. No, the only thing I am wearing under this is a rather expensive Victoria's Secret underwire, one of only two I own that comfortably fit, which I believe might now be fused to my breasts, so I've got that going for me." Alice gingerly checked herself and then hissed from the pain. She looked at her front, which was now healed, and very exposed. "I feel like a microwave dinner. Paul, as my jacket has disintegrated, please give me yours. No boobs for you."

Paul (who had, admittedly, been looking) blushed slightly as he took off his jacket and handed it to Alice, who eagerly accepted it. "You could have been killed!" Victoria snapped. Alice felt her hand on her shoulder, and she smiled.

"I know. I wanted to see what the legendary Chalice was capable of."

Angela, Paul, and Victoria stared at Alice. "You knew I would kill you?" Angela asked in a small voice.

Alice nodded. "You throw lightning bolts. Yes, I strongly suspected that would kill me. I also knew that if something bad were to happen, this was as good a place as any. Nice job, Chalice."

"That is horribly irresponsible," Victoria muttered as she held her head, a headache already starting.

"You *knew*?!" Angela sputtered again.

"Of course I did." Alice said, still touching the seared metal and flesh, and hissing to herself. Her hand glowed purple for a moment, and the remaining metal disappeared. "Paul, little help? Got some blood." Paul rushed over to quickly do a patch heal while Alice continued. "Why do you think my niece didn't open your head up? I prepped her ahead of time."

Angela looked to Victoria, who was rubbing her temples. "You let her do this to me?"

Victoria held up a hand. "This is her show today. I gave her full authority as an active member of the Collective Good. Also, aside from myself, she is honestly the most qualified person on the planet to train super-powered individuals. I'm here to supervise. Honestly, if I had known how insane this was going to be, I think I would have reconsidered. Thank you again, Chalice."

"It's Paul." Chalice blushed and scratched the back of his head. "It's okay. I, uh, I got a lot of practice from healing bad guys."

Alice nodded. "I remember. We hired you out a few years back to do cleanup after my niece botched a job in Gary. Good work then, good work now. I'd say the four of you have shown what you can do."

Victoria looked at the group, and then at Alice. "Alice? You didn't have Golomous or the Bleed do anything."

Alice smiled at Victoria. "Hey Golomous," Alice called out. "Can you open the helipad?"

"Of. Course." The walking robot blared. A moment later, the party jumped in surprise as the giant helipad everyone was standing on suddenly split down the middle and slid outward to reveal a black, sleek-looking jet underneath.

"It can talk?" Victoria said.

"He can do a lot of things," Alice said for him. "Golomous and Phil are old friends of mine. I helped Golomous out when he first lost his body. The Purge wrote the algorithms that kept him from going insane from sensory loss. When I put Alan's flask on his head, I slipped a mini-flash drive into a side port on his, um, brain-thingy. It had a text file on it with a laundry list of instructions, one of which was to completely hack the Tower. He passed."

Victoria glanced back at Golomous. "Why didn't you give him a Totallus body? God knows you had enough of them lying around."

"The Totallus body isn't a catch-all shell. It was specifically designed for a syntho-cellular brain. It was revolutionary, and has yet to be perfected outside of Purge laboratories. I think your Ifrit program proved that. The nerve connections are totally different from a human being. That box," Alice gestured, "was custom-built to provide a worthwhile, livable environment for our good friend there. Also, people tend to overlook something that looks like it was a prop from a sci-fi movie."

Victoria looked around. "What about the Bleed? Are we just going off the fact that you've got a history?"

Phil chuffed. "Please, Ms. Green. I believe in formalities, and I think you will find that I have also passed Alice's test for the morning."

Victoria furrowed her brow. "Really? What exactly did you do?"

Victoria felt a light swish of air, a presence, and then something thin and cold pressed against her neck.

"We meet again, Ms. Green."

Victoria froze as Aika pressed a blade to her throat, but she did not betray any outward nervousness beyond an unnatural stillness. Beside her, Alice said, "It's okay, Aika. I'm fine. Really. Calm down and put that away. Please?"

Victoria felt Aika lean in, to the point that the assassin's breath was against her ear. She then heard an almost inaudible whisper.

"Tag."

There was a moment, and then Victoria felt the blade disappear from her windpipe. She turned around to see Aika standing a good three feet away. She was in a loose, white blouse with her arms relaxed at her sides. Her face was unreadable, and there was no blade visible on her person.

Victoria suppressed a shudder.

Alice relaxed. "I told Phil to drop Aika on the roof during our presentation via text message. I wanted to see if he could be discreet with his portals, and apparently, he can. Nice job, Phil."

Phil tipped his hat with a smile.

"Um, excuse me?" said a friendly voice above them, "but is there a good medical team here? I think Halifax could use a doctor."

They all looked up to see Eedee holding an unconscious Halifax in her arms.

"Huh," said Alice. "You broke her."

Chapter Thirteen

"That could have gone better."

Senator Carter twitched and frowned as he watched the news scroll across his flat screen. Reports were coming in about a foiled assassination attempt on the CEO of Aegaeon Holdings by an unknown assailant. Details were sketchy, but it was looking like the attacker was foiled by an as-yet unnamed superhero. Further reports showed that the CEO, Chris Ellswood, was already recovering.

George angrily turned the television off, and then swiveled his chair around to view the Manhattan skyline from his office window. The air was unusually clear, and George could see for miles in every direction he glanced.

"Are you familiar with the term 'decimate'?" George asked. Off to the side, a tall, stoic figure turned its head.

"It's okay," George said with a smile. "I know you can't really respond. I was talking to myself, mostly. Decimate. It's such a wonderfully soul-crushing term. Most people think it means to completely destroy something, but that's not it at all.

"It was a way of making an example in ancient Rome. Prisoners would be lined up, and a soldier would walk down the line, chopping off the head of every tenth one he came to. One tenth of the total prisoner population would be wiped out. It didn't matter if it was for a minor or major offense. Didn't matter if the prisoners were compliant or not. The point was that it made an impression. It taught respect. It taught fear."

George folded his fingers in front of him and idly tapped them together. With a forced smile, he began to rock back and forth. "Despite what the media might say, I don't want all superhumans gone. I just want to set a big enough example to keep the rest of them in line. They need to know their place. Murdering Poseidon would have helped with this. Instead, he is alive, and I am down a Totallus."

George stood, and started to stroll around his desk, his fingers lazily trailing across the mahogany surface. "He will be too well-guarded from this point forward, and I do not want to risk any further resources for such a mediocre target. I already wasted too much time accidentally nabbing that worthless Aquatica, and the ratings for her were horrible. I don't want to risk further issues on these pathetic fish people. No, we need something more extreme. Something more...prominent."

George slid his smartphone out of his pocket, and scrolled his favorites. A moment later, a voice with what sounded like a hybrid British-Asian accent answered, "This had better be important, Carter."

"Good afternoon, Yoshi. I want to change the fight card for our next broadcast," George said with a smile. "Is it too late to advertise a title bout?"

"This is highly irregular," Yoshi said with a growl in his voice. "We have already advertised the next match to our global subscribers. To change now would cost us money."

"What if I gave you someone better than Blackthorne for the ring?" Carter asked.

There was a pause. "Go on," Yoshi said.

"What if I gave you Dyspell?"

There was a very long pause.

"Dyspell recently did us a rather large service. I am hesitant to use her."

"Is that a no?" George asked.

"I am hesitant," Yoshi replied. "However, I cannot deny that televising her death would yield a massive return. The Dead Talon would entertain broadcasting the execution of Dyspell, provided you can deliver her within the next 24 hours. I will not risk such a show being given to the Black Cloak's broadcast time."

"That shouldn't be a problem," George said calmly. "She'll be on your doorstep in a matter of hours."

"A bold claim for someone so new to this."

"I was raised Purge," Carter said, his smile growing firm on his lips. "Do not forget that my father made his career promising impossible things, and then delivering on them. If I say you'll get Dyspell, you'll get Dyspell."

"And your patron in the Purge, what about her? I understand that she has an obsession with Dyspell."

"That's an understatement if I've ever heard one. Don't worry about her. I have a feeling this will be big enough that she'll be satisfied, even if she's not the one twisting the knife."

"Fair enough," Yoshi said. George could practically hear the shrug in the Asian man's voice. "Now, what is the cost of having such a valued contestant for the broadcast?"

George grinned. "Well, now that you mention it, running an emergency election campaign is expensive. $50 million upon her delivery."

"$20 Million, and an additional million for every minute she survives once combat begins."

Carter thought for a moment. "Make it thirty, and we have a deal."

"Agreed."

Carter nodded to himself as he hung up, and started dialing again. A moment later, the line picked up, and George could hear ragged breathing on the other line. "I have a new job for you. One target. Female. I will have my office text you the details."

The voice on the other line spoke in a hoarse whisper, and for a moment, George could swear it sounded like two voices speaking over each other. "Who is it?"

"Dyspell. Will this be an issue?"

"No," the voice responded in that cold, throaty echo.

"Good," George said as he quickly hung up. "Christ," he muttered to himself. "I hate dealing with him. Most of these mercenary types are all business, but this guy? When I found him…God. I would have sent you," George turned to face the motionless black silhouette by his desk, "But I have another task in mind."

George flipped through the images in his phone until he found one sent to him just that morning of a young girl. "As it turns out, I need your help to pick a naughty little girl up from school."

***

"Well, that could have gone better," Phil said as he stood next to Sophia's bed. She was currently being tended to by the RN on duty for the Collective Good crisis ward. Alan had set the facility up several years back. No matter what, Tanner Tower always had a medical team on duty 24 hours a day. This wasn't just for unlucky heroes - anyone in the tower that had an issue could take advantage. Also, insurance-wise, it didn't hurt to have an on-site medical team. Sophia was just coming to as the nurse inserted some painkillers into her IV.

"Where am I?" she asked in a haze. The nurse glanced over, and gave her a bored look.

"Welcome back, darling. You're in our clinic. Please try not to move. You've suffered several force impact injuries, and your neck is sprained. Just rest, you're not going anywhere for a while."

Sophia tried to nod, but found that moving her neck hurt. Instead, she mumbled "okay" as the nurse left the small, but cozy, recovery room. Beside Sophia, Phil was scooting his chair so that he could talk to her without her having to turn her head.

"Well, now," Phil said in an annoyingly parental tone, "What did that android do to you?"

Sophia blinked in confusion. "Wait, she wasn't human?"

"Goodness, no. I thought you knew that, dear. She's an artificial life form, designed to meet or exceed the limitations of most flesh-bound superbeings. Were you trying to outdo her?"

Sophia glanced away. "This morning was such a blur. I thought she was just another superhero, you know? I don't keep up with the circuit. I don't know who's in and who's out. All I know is that purple hussy showed up, gave us some assignments, and then I was off. So, um, did we pass?"

Phil sighed. "Somewhat. This was a test of our abilities. The general consensus is that we all can serve a valuable function to the Collective Good, and as such, may seek employment there. While money at this point is a nicety for me, I have to say, the amount being offered is tremendous. Something about endorsements. Anyway, as far as official field work, the answer is, 'we require further analysis.'"

Sophia bit her lip, and sighed. "It's my fault, isn't it? I fucked up, and we all got punished."

Phil shook his head. "I think it had more to do with the fact that we're all former villains. They need to see they can trust us before they put us out in the field. And I don't blame them. Right now, we're here only because a former villain requested we be given a chance. That's not much, in terms of credentials."

"That purple woman? She was Dyspell, wasn't she?"

Phil nodded. "She very much *is* Dyspell, and reformed or no, she is still extremely dangerous. She's been working with the Collective Good for a while now, and she's built up some trust and a name for herself. She's also a friend, which is why I trust her when she says we will be considered members of the Collective Good. For protection, if nothing else."

Sophia grunted. She wanted to turn her head to focus on Phil a little easier, but she was so sore that she was doing well just to keep her focus on Phil. "Why are you doing all this?"

Phil sat back and let out a small sigh. He glanced off for a moment, and Sophia could see his thoughts were a million miles away. "I've lived a very long life, my dear. I don't really have a firm belief in good or evil, just in the choices we make as people. I believe that I have made some extremely selfish choices, and those have benefited me greatly.

"Now, someone has actively tried to murder me, and it is within my selfish interests to stay alive. This path, this 'going straight' nonsense, is the best way available to accomplish that. That's all. I see this all as a way to ensure my survival, and my continuing quest to find some meaning in life."

"So, why me?" Sophia asked, a bit of trepidation in her voice. "Why spend so much time focused on me? I mean, you're fun and all, and I'd like to think I'm pretty decent, but we don't know each other that well. You didn't have to be here. You didn't have to stick around any of us. So why? Am I just for your own selfish interests, too?"

Phil smiled and gently patted her leg. "Well, I would be lying if I said I wasn't being selfish about you. I find you attractive, and I am enjoying your company, and... truth be known, you remind me of someone from a very long time ago. I see the same fire in you that I saw in them, and that attracts me. I like you, and I like where this is for now, and if we decide to be selfish later, we can deal with that as it happens."

Sophia thought on this, and then did her best to shrug. "Hey, that's a better answer than what I've gotten from my last two boyfriends. I'll take it."

"I'm flattered," Phil said, dryly.

They considered each other for a few moments before Sophia looked around the room. Her gaze settled on nothing in particular as she said, "'We require further analysis' usually means we fucked up, doesn't it?"

Phil nodded. "Angela nearly killed someone today. Despite proving she can use her powers, she has shown that she is reckless and still extremely unstable after the death of her sister. Ms. Green still doesn't trust any of us, and the fact that Golomous hacked her security seems to have put her on edge. And then there was you, the woman who pushed herself to the breaking point to outdo a machine. Yes, my dear. We fucked up. We are nowhere near being ready for fieldwork, but we have jobs, we have protection, and we have the prospect for a future. That's more than I can say for anyone who was in that warehouse with us."

Phil leaned back and slipped a phone out of his pocket. "I do love these little toys. Modern sorcery, complete with Faustian contracts. Rest, my dear. I'll keep watch until you're able to leave that bed, and I'll make sure you get the care you need."

"I still don't get why."

"Well, you said it yourself. Apparently, I'm your 'boyfriend', which is a fancy title for courting nowadays. That, and I meant what I said. I enjoy your company, Sophia. Provided you enjoy mine. Now, I know you're in pain, but our day is nowhere near done. Get a little rest, and then we need to get you out of that bed."

"And then what?"

Phil swiped the screen on his phone and opened a puzzle game. "Well, then we go and train as an honest-to-God team. I've been appointed this backwards squadron's leader."

"I mean for us?"

"Oh," Phil chuckled, "well then, depending on your interest, and your health, I hope to get you right back into bed."

"Dirty old man," Sophia muttered under her breath as she relaxed.

"Dirty young lady," Phil countered, his attention on his game.

***

"So," Victoria asked once she and Alice had made their way back to her office, "What did you think?"

Alice ran her fingers through her hair and shook her head. She felt a massive headache forming. Her chest was screaming in pain, but her pride was preventing her from showing it. "I think they have the potential to be something, but for now, they're 50/50 on the whole sucking thing," Alice quipped. She drifted around Victoria's office, and noted the titles of the books on his shelves. "They have great abilities, and they could be complementary to each other, but they've obviously never worked in a structured environment before. Well, aside from Phil."

Victoria took a seat behind her desk and leaned back. "Agreed. And to be honest, I still think this is a horrible idea. You okay?"

Alice gave a quick nod, and bit her lip as she felt a stinging pain run through her chest. "You didn't say that when you hired me," Alice pointed out, smiling.

"I didn't hire you. Alan did."

"And he never consulted with you?"

Victoria coughed, and went silent.

"Ah," Alice said as she continued to study Victoria's bookshelf. "So, shelve the newbies for now?"

Victoria nodded. "Gonna have to. They're too raw, and we can't afford to have any more screw-ups in the public eye. They need training, and I'm too short-handed at the moment. I am being audited by the IRS, and I have been informed that Tanner Tower may, in the very near future, be the focus of an FBI-led investigation. You and your little side team may want to avoid coming here in the next couple of weeks."

Alice nodded, and, without looking at Victoria, said, "You can keep Allison for now, if you need her."

"Why would you say that?"

Alice crossed her arms. "Because she's a good field agent. She and Brandon work well together, and she's very analytical. Hell, she's nearly OCD when it comes to methodology. She can help on your Yeager murder investigation beyond what she's already done."

Victoria grew very still as she studied Alice. "What do you know?"

Alice held up her PhoneBuddy. "It's called texting. I know you're fucked. I know that I'm standing in your office and not Alan's after trying to audition B-grade villains for the Collective Good. I know that instead of having one of the other heroes on that roof, I got the honor of working with the vice president of Tanner Industries. I know that you are drowning in work, and that you, not Alan, are being audited. Now, why would you be audited, Ms. Green?"

"I was referring to the company. I..."

Alice shook her head and held up her hand. "No. You're too anal about things like that. You would have said Alan was getting audited, but instead you said I. Singular. Why would you be audited, Ms. Green?"

Victoria stood, and adjusted her jacket. "I think we're done here, Alice. I'll make sure you're reimbursed for your wardrobe, and feel free to grab a new outfit from our fitting department. You know the way out."

Alice crossed her arms and stared Victoria down. The flippant attitude Alice had been showing melted away, only to be replaced by a glare of hardened steel. "I don't think so. This doesn't add up. The other night didn't add up. There are no heroes here. None. The building is virtually abandoned of supers, and I haven't heard from or seen Alan, and now you're being audited. Why would you be audited?"

"Go home, Alice."

Alice smirked, and dug in. She knew this was aggravating Victoria, but Alice wasn't sure she cared. After already dying before noon, the former villain found she really didn't care about a minor verbal conflict. That, and she felt she was owed at this point. "Alan doesn't have a board of directors. At least, not a real one. He's the sole owner and CEO. If Tanner Industries is audited, the feds would be focused on Alan, not you. No, there's only one reason you would be audited, *Ms. Green.*"

"Dammit, Alice!" Victoria shouted. She got within inches of Alice, and then crumbled. In a second, her angry expression melted into a sob. She wiped her eyes, and with gritted teeth, gave the bookshelf next to them a hard punch.

"When?" Alice asked in a soft voice.

Victoria took in a long breath, and when she spoke, her voice was quieter than Alice had ever heard her get. "He went missing five days ago. I took over as acting CEO immediately afterwards. I've had Brandon looking into it, but...God. I was hoping to keep it quiet. I've told no one, and I made him promise not to tell Allison. I trust you, but with everything going on, I just... I was trying to keep a lid on this."

Alice blinked. "Oh."

Victoria glanced at Alice. "Oh?"

Alice blushed, and rubbed the back of her neck. With a nervous grin, she said, "Yeah. Um, I was talking about the fact that you two were married."

Victoria went white as a sheet. "How the *hell* did you know that?"

"You took over control of his company!" Alice said, exasperated. "I mean, come on! You can't just magically do that unless you were already a co-owner, and the most logical and quickest legal way to do that without ruffling any feathers would be if you were married. I'm guessing it was around the time of the cruise, wasn't it?"

Victoria nodded. "Yeah. It was right before. I thought we were going together, but then he ended up going with you and Aika, and we had a fight..."

Alice nodded to herself. "That's what he was distracted by. Huh." She suddenly felt her cheeks flush from embarrassment. "Oh, God. I kissed your husband. On what was supposed to be your kind-of honeymoon. I'm so sorry. I didn't know!"

Victoria put up a hand. "Alice, it's cool."

"No, it's not! I totally made out with your guy! I mean, I knew you guys were dating, but things seemed on the rocks, and you had been a bit of a bitch to me, and..."

"Alice..." Victoria said, her voice growing impatient.

"And he was so into it! I feel so dirty now! And not 'good' dirty! I mean, shit! Crisis aside, I was ready to screw him right there on the bomb!"

"*ALICE!*" Victoria shouted. "That's enough. Thank you."

Alice blushed and nodded. "So, who do you think is your traitor?"

Victoria blinked, and then shook her head. "How the fuck..? Have you been using Holly to probe me?"

Alice shook her head no. "No, but good idea. You're keeping something this massive under wraps for a reason. Someone is taking the heroes out, and you suspect there's a mole. You didn't think it was me, but you were covering your bases."

Victoria walked to the window of her office, and held herself as she crossed her arms. "Aquatica, Darkane, Yeager, and now Alan. Also, I got a call from Susan before you arrived. Someone tried to kill Chris this morning with a Totallus. All that's left is myself, Susan, Brandon, and you and your family," Victoria said, turning to face Alice. "And now, someone is trying to publicly discredit all of you."

Alice nodded and bit her lip as she thought. "I probably would have picked up on this earlier if, you know, I hadn't been barbecued on the roof. Still hurts, and I want a new shirt. A nice one. I know what you said, but I want something designer as comp for a work-related injury."

"I would remind you that what happened up there was your fault."

"So," Alice said, blowing the comment off. "Like I said, you need Allison. I figured the heroes were being taken out. She can help. She has experience your people don't. She's got a keen eye, and she knows how to case a scene."

"I agree but she's also unstable. I brought her in for a once-over this morning, but long-term... Alice, I have Brandon on it. He's a special agent. He can do this."

"She's a lot better now," Alice said, all traces of humor now gone from her face. "My girl is better. You're protesting on reflex, but Allison isn't just a world-class assassin. She's also a very thorough planner and analyst, possibly the best the Purge ever had. That's why you brought her in; she may spot something Brandon missed. So, who do you think it is?"

"We're not sure yet, but I spoke to Allison and Brandon on the phone. Her best guess is that we're dealing with the Grey."

"Hooooo *shit*." Alice whistled. "The Grey? He's the one taking out the Collective Good?"

Victoria nodded. "What can you tell me about him?"

"Not much, honestly. I never worked directly with him. We tried, of course. He wasn't one to play well with others. Wouldn't take any money, didn't want to work with a team, and the bastard wouldn't stop twitching. We tried to scan him the one time he met with us, and we couldn't read him."

"What now?"

Alice nodded. "Seriously. It was like he didn't exist. I had our analysts pour over the data, and as best as they could figure, he was flickering in and out of reality. It was like he was there, and then he wasn't."

"Interesting," Victoria said, thinking. "That's... hmmm. Thank you, Alice."

Alice wanted to ask more, but she saw the look of stress on Victoria's face, and heard the strain in the woman's voice, and knew a breaking point was swiftly approaching. Without another word, Alice nodded, and then excused herself.

Finally alone, Victoria stood in the quiet of her office, took a long breath, and sighed heavily as she let her gaze drift to the bustling street beneath her office window.

Chapter Fourteen

The Broadcast

Then

***

Brandon had been searching for his friend and teammate for hours when he got a tip over the comms that Yeager had been sighted atop the Brooklyn Bridge. In a heartbeat, Brandon blasted off from midtown to make his way there. He had been trying desperately to help Yeager with his time challenge, but he knew he was mostly hoping to get lucky. He had never seen his friend move so fast, and Brandon had been sure it would be enough. He had never seen Yeager fail, especially when every second counted.

Until today.

That morning, Brandon had arrived as the swarm of police and paramedics were combing through the remains of a midtown hotel. The blast damage had been extensive, but they had still been able to identify the charred body of the woman that now lay in the morgue. The bomb used to kill Rob's wife had been in the back of a delivery truck, while she had been tied up in the front seat. Rob had failed, and the Grey had done what no other villain had dared to.

Brandon knew in the back of his mind that this was a very real danger for people like him, Rob, and the rest of the Collective Good. There was always that chance that some whackjob would go too far, take that extra step, and then there would be no line left. It had happened before, but usually in accidental or extreme cases. It turned out that most of the villains had families and lives, too. Over time, there had been an unspoken code about it; you don't mess with mine, and I won't mess with yours.

The Grey was different, though. Brandon had to admit, he had never been up against anyone like him. They had traded blows twice now, and both times, the Grey had won. He may not have looked it, but Brandon had to admit the man was formidable. Each time they had fought, the Grey had hit him so hard that Brandon's entire body vibrated from the impact. Other heroes had said the same thing. Superior Force had once said that being hit by the Grey was like being hit by a thousand people at once.

Brandon spotted his friend from about a mile away, but he didn't see Rob fighting anyone. Instead, he was just sitting with his legs dangling over the side of the bridge. Scared that something terrible had happened to his friend, he put on a burst of speed and arrived in moments to find Yeager sitting peacefully with his hands in his lap, staring at the sunset.

"Rob!" Brandon touched down beside him, and frantically looked around for any trace of the Grey. "Where is he? Did he escape? What happened?"

Brandon looked to Rob, and then froze when he noticed his friend's completely relaxed state. Scared, he leaned in to touch Rob on the shoulder. "Hey," Brandon said. "Rob, you okay?"

Rob slowly blinked, and then turned his head to look Brandon in the eye. Brandon's heart broke at the sight of his friend's face. Rob's eyes were bloodshot from crying.

"Rob," Brandon asked in a quiet voice. "What happened?"

Rob glanced back over the water. "I killed him," he said in a quiet, soft voice.

Brandon stiffened. He had known Rob since high school. For a superhero, Rob was something of a pacifist. He was one of the shining examples of standing up for what was right in the Collective Good. In fact, the man's zeal for justice and solving problems without the use of violence was such that it tended to piss most of his more violent coworkers off. Brandon had always written it off as the byproduct of a good upbringing.

"You did what?" Brandon asked, more surprised than anything.

"You heard me," Rob said. His voice never wavered or changed in pitch. It was like he was reading something aloud in a library. "I caught up to him right here." He patted the stone he was sitting on. "Right here. I faced him, and I killed him."

Brandon nodded, taking all of this in. "Okay. Okay, I get that. Um, are you okay?"

Rob looked back over the skyline, and gently shook his head. "No," he said.

Brandon looked around, this time with a bit more scrutiny. There was no blood, no sign of a struggle, and Rob didn't appear to have any wounds whatsoever. When Brandon had fought the Grey, he had to have two healers work to save his left arm after the bone was virtually turned to powder.

"Where is he?" Brandon asked. Rob didn't respond at first. Brandon put his hand on Rob's shoulder and asked again. "Rob? Where's the Grey?"

"I killed him," Rob said again. Brandon stepped back as Rob got up, and gently dusted himself off. "He's gone."

Brandon eyed his friend, and then looked over the edge of the bridge. "You mean you tossed him over? Is he down there?"

Rob looked at Brandon again, and even though he didn't change his pitch or tone, Brandon got the feeling that Rob was being as direct as he could at this point. "I killed him. He's gone."

Brandon looked over the edge again, and then back to his friend. "Okay, pal. He's dead. I get it. What about you? Do you need a doctor? Did he hurt you?"

Rob looked at Brandon, and started to laugh. Brandon stepped back in shock as Rob was busting up in front of him. "Did he hurt me? Did he... I have to go home now. I have to tell my boy that this morning, I wasn't fast enough to save his Mom. I have to plan a funeral. Did he hurt me? Did he..." Rob was overcome with hysterics at this point, fresh tears now streaming down his cheeks. Brandon didn't know what to do. He had never seen his friend like this, not even when his father had died when they were teens.

"Rob, I'm sorry," Brandon began. "I just meant..."

There was a whoosh of air, and in the blink of an eye, Brandon found himself standing alone atop the Brooklyn Bridge. He sighed, shook his head, and looked again over the edge and into the waters below.

"I guess I'll help file the report," he murmured to himself as he took off towards Tanner Tower, his worry for his friend still fresh in his mind.

Now

***

"Bullshit."

Brandon frowned at Allison as she proceeded to dig into a cranberry salad. They were seated at a small, curbside café, grabbing a quick lunch. Allison, seemingly unfazed by her boyfriend's judgment, continued attacking her food.

"What?" she asked, slightly offended. "You brought me in for my professional opinion, and I gave it. Dude we're after is the Grey."

"Allison, the Grey is dead."

Allison took a sip of orange soda, and shook her head. "Nope. I downloaded the official report on him while I was camping out. If you read it, Yeager's report is awfully vague about what actually happened."

Brandon coughed as Allison continued. "There was a scuffle, the Grey was cast into the water, and that's about it."

Brandon raised an eyebrow. "He didn't actually use the word 'cast'."

Allison nodded. "Yep. Dude has a flair for the dramatic. Kinda like you. Anyway, a guy who can seemingly bend reality isn't going to be killed in a simple bridge scuffle."

Brandon frowned. "You're basing your conclusion off some pretty shoddy evidence."

Allison took a quick bite, swallowed, and shook her head. "No, I'm not. Did you look at that apartment? I...sorry." Allison flinched as Brandon closed his eyes at her words.

"I forgot. I'm sorry. Seriously though, I *did* look. Not at the mess, but at the walls. There was a framed news clipping that was smashed. It was the only one that seemed to have any real damage."

"Let me guess. The Grey?"

"The article about his defeat." Allison nodded and allowed herself a grin. She loved one-upping her detective boyfriend. "Look, there is a very short list of people who could be doing what's happening, and you know it."

"There are others," Brandon said, his voice now carrying a slight note of doubt.

Allison nodded. "Yeah, but not a lot. There's the Bleed, but he's on our side, and this is honestly not his scene. His son might have done something like this, but he's super dead. There was that one guy with the shadow knives. Schatten Messer? Not sure whatever happened to him, though."

"What about a professional assassin?" Brandon asked.

Allison shook her head. "Best ones are girls. This was a dude."

"What makes you think it couldn't have been a guy?" Brandon asked.

Allison gave him an are-you-kidding look. "The best ones are girls."

"Say you're right," Brandon said, leaning back in his chair. "Say the Grey is out killing superheroes. Say he's decided to wipe the board. Where would we even begin to look to find him? He had no known haunts, no friends, nothing. Besides that, there's a good chance it would be a wild goose chase."

Allison set her fork down, and looked over the rims of her glasses at Brandon. "Sweetie, why did Victoria ask me to help you?"

Brandon gave an exasperated sigh. "Because you're good at analyzing things?"

"I'm a problem solver," Allison said as she crossed her hands under her chin. "When it comes down to it, that's what I do. I solve problems that other people can't. I do it with data, I do it with weapons, and for over half my life, I've done it with people. I look at an impossible situation, and I see how it can work. I was trained by a world-class organization throughout my teens on how to look at something from every angle. I admit, I'm not FBI," she said with a wink, "but I'd like to think that my experience is worth a little something."

"Okay," Brandon said, mulling this over. "I know this. You know I know how smart you are. Still, unless you've got some rock-solid evidence, I just can't..."

Allison reached into her pocket, pulled out her PhoneBuddy, swiped to her photos, and slid the phone across the table to Brandon. Brandon glanced at the image and immediately turned pale. "Holy shit," he muttered. On the tiny screen was an image capture from the security cameras of a local convenience store. "That's Darkane."

"Yep. And look who he's talking to."

While the image was a bit fuzzy, Brandon could still make out what looked like a man in a trench coat and hat standing just inside the frame. He shook his head and looked back at Allison. "This is too blurry. I'm sorry- that could be anyone. That could be the Bleed, for all I know."

"That," Allison said as she tapped the image, "bears a pretty damn good resemblance to the Grey. Not solid, but it fills in some gaps. The important thing to take away from this is that girlfriend is right. This line of thinking is important."

"Allison, how did you get this image?"

Allison shrugged and tucked her phone back into her pocket. "It wasn't a big deal. I hacked the local surveillance footage from the stores around where we found Darkane."

Brandon frowned. "So did the FBI, but there wasn't any footage. Seriously, how did you get this?"

"Ah," Allison said with a nod. "You didn't find anything because it had mostly been wiped. Purge-edition media worm. Very thorough, but not *completely* thorough. It purposely leaves a back door. We used to sell the code to hostile governments. If you know where to look, you can find all sorts of things."

"Wait, this was a Purge job?"

"Maybe?" Allison said as she picked up her fork. Her salad looked neglected, and she was hoping to change that. "Kinda hard to say. We sold that code to a lot of parties, and the Purge has been all over the place lately. Still, I figured when nothing showed up there had to be a reason, so I looked and bam. Purge worm."

"Huh," Brandon said, impressed. "You really are all brains."

"Was that a compliment?" Allison asked between bites. "That was a horrible compliment. Just tell me I'm awesome."

"You're awesome."

"Thank you."

They sat in silence for a moment, broken only when Brandon rubbed his face and sighed. "Well, this is good to know, but it doesn't help us. If it is the Grey, we still don't know why he's doing this."

"Dude's getting paid. If he were acting on his own, he probably wouldn't have been able to do such a clean sweep of the data. He's a merc."

Brandon nodded. "Okay, fair point. Now, who is he working for? Why is he working for them? Also, what do they want? Why would you target high-profile superheroes? I mean, besides the obvious. Why so many, so fast? If this were a takedown, I figure it would have been done last month when that weird blood bender and his team tried to take over the tower. Wouldn't it have made more sense to just pile it on, then?"

Allison thought for a moment as she tapped her fork against her plate. Suddenly, her eyes went wide. "Salt."

"Sure." Brandon reached for the table salt as Allison started shooing his hand away.

"No, no, no. Salt. When we searched the convention center, we found salt. And cameras, and… I need Aika."

"You've totally lost me." Brandon said as Allison quickly dug her PhoneBuddy out of her pocket and set it to speaker as she dialed. A few moments later, a monotone voice picked up.

"Yes?"

"Aika," Allison asked as her mind raced. "Do you remember the Broadcast?"

There was a pause before Aika started cursing in Japanese. Allison grinned, happy to be on the right track. "Great. Thought you might."

"How did we miss this?" Aika asked, her voice seething with anger.

Allison quickly adopted a soothing tone. "Hey, we all did. It's been a while."

"I thought there was something familiar about the other night," Aika said, mostly to herself.

"What's the Broadcast?" Brandon asked, slightly confused.

"One sec, hon." Allison said to him as she held up her hand. "So, who would have the next one after the Purge? That would be the Dead Talon, wouldn't it?"

"Yes," Aika said, her voice back to being level.

"Okay. Let Alice know, and have her poke around. See if she can confirm that they had Aquatica on. That would at least answer one mystery. Also, see if you can find out who was in charge of the Broadcast here."

"I will do what I can," Aika said before hanging up.

"So what the hell is 'the Broadcast'?" Brandon asked, slightly irritated.

Allison fished out a couple bucks for a tip, stood, and quickly headed out with Brandon in tow. She was rushing, mostly from the excitement she was feeling from putting things together. "A long time ago, the three major criminal organizations on the planet decided to try their hand at global marketing. We called it the Broadcast. Once a month, give or take, one of the organizations would host a global spectacle that high rollers all over the world could tune into. The show would consist of henchmen being slaughtered in creative, arena-style ways. Sometimes there would be a requested political assassination, maybe some ex-soldiers dueling to the death, stuff like that. On rare occasion though, we would get a superhuman and put them through some horrible, and usually ironic, battle to the death."

Brandon paled as Allison continued on, her voice almost chipper. "Jesus, *you* did this?"

Allison shook her head no. "It was a bit before my time as an active soldier. I watched a few, though. It was actually aunt Alice who put a stop to it. The Black Cloak had used their turn to murder a shipment of tween sex slaves and took bets on who would last the longest in a death maze. It was too much for Alice, so she pulled the plug when it was time for the Purge's show."

"So you think the room you found the other night was a Broadcast room?"

Allison nodded. "It would make sense. The Purge is desperate for money, and nothing brought it in faster than a global death spectacle. Sacrificing superhumans always brought in the most customers, and if they used my files on Aquatica, they would have... they..."

Allison stopped as she felt Brandon's hand on her arm. He whirled her around, and Allison's excited flow of words dried up when she saw the look on his face. "What files?"

Allison suddenly realized that she wasn't sharing a portion of her life that others would readily understand. When she was younger, she had poured countless hours into the study of superhumans. Who they were, what made them tick, and most of all, how to kill them. Her work was considered revolutionary in the field, and was cited by every major terrorist group that was willing to pay the Purge for her insight. She had loved the attention and the praise, and more than once it had caught the eye of Prometheus himself. She realized that all of this, that all of her wonderful accolades had been for figuring out how to brutally kill the best friends of the man in front of her. The man who she cared for. And here she was, going on about her former organization's creative ways of murdering people right after what they had seen.

For someone who didn't miss much, Allison felt like she had been incredibly obtuse about what was going on.

"I'm sorry," Allison said in a quiet voice. "Brandon, I'm sorry. I just... It was a long time ago, and it was when I was extremely young. I... Aquatica has one major weakness, and that is being dry. In the event that we ever had her for the Broadcast, I recommended... I don't think I want to say."

Brandon stared at her with a look that could have melted lead. "Please do."

"I recommended that she be bound in rags caked in Epsom salt to dry her out, and that the humidity in the room be turned down to near zero. The contest would be to see how long she could fight before dehydrating to death."

Allison stood silently in front of Brandon and unconsciously rubbed her arm. She waited for Brandon to say something, but he just continued to stand there, staring at her. Finally, she felt her guilt being replaced by anger, and she decided to chime in. "It was a long time ago, okay? I never thought I would be, that all of this would..."

Brandon said in a quiet, shaking voice. "I know you're different now. I know it wasn't actually you. I know that, but... she's dead now, and it was done in a way you created. This... God, I don't even know what this is. She was my f..."

"This is me feeling like shit for something I was asked to do as a young girl," Allison said with a little more steel. "I get it that it was fucked up. Most of my life after 12 was pretty fucked up, in case you didn't notice. Look, it was one of those things that you don't really think about long term, alright? I'm sorry. I'm sorry you feel like I killed your friend."

She was beginning to tear up a bit as Brandon closed his eyes and shook his head. "You didn't kill her. I get that," Brandon said. Allison noticed that he was looking off to the side, away from her. "I know that, it's just that she was... you said it. She was a friend, that's all."

Allison stared at Brandon for a moment before her eyes widened in realization. "That's why you've been so revved up about finding out who did this. It wasn't just because of Yeager. You wanted to find out if your ex was still alive!"

Brandon's head jerked up in shock. "What? How did you know that?"

Allison gestured towards him. "Oh please, it's written all over you. You and she were together. That's why you're taking this so hard. Look, it's cool." Allison took a small breath, and tried to give Brandon a reassuring smile. "You had a life before me, just like I had one before you. I mean, you didn't think I would do something nuts like put a bullet in her head, did you?" Allison paused and looked off to the side. "Except for me being an assassin and all. Also devising the method she was killed via. Come to think of it, yeah, okay, fair."

Brandon opened his mouth to answer, but Allison held up a hand. "Don't respond to that. The point is, I understand. I really do. And Brandon, I am so, so very sorry. I didn't know. I swear to God I didn't know. This is just awful for everyone involved, but I can at the very least try to help, okay? Please, would you at least let me do that?"

"You seem to be fairly okay with all of this," Brandon said, eyeing her.

Allison dug into her salad.

Brandon thought about it, and then nodded. "You had Holly read my mind, and tell you about my past relationships, didn't you?"

"Fuck yes, I did." Allison said while chewing.

"When did she...?"

"Second date. Remember when you were all sweet, and offered to take us both to the movies? I bribed her $50 to suggest something she had already seen, so she wouldn't be distracted and had her go through you like a Rolodex. And before you get all offended, please remember who raised me, and her understanding of boundaries. Besides, my little girl has my back."

Allison saw Brandon's face, and withered a little. "Um...Sorry?"

Allison felt herself relax a little as he leaned in, and gave her a hug. Honestly, hugging wasn't something she did often. Holly was changing that, but hugging another adult was still kind of odd for her. Even one she was romantically involved with.

"You're not mad?" Allison asked.

"Oh, I'm mad," Brandon said. His mouth was against her hair as he spoke. "But I was a royal asshole a few minutes ago, so you kinda gave me an out. Besides, most crazy girlfriends go through sock drawers. I figure this is the superpowered equivalent."

"You're not mad," Allison murmured as she smiled.

"Don't ever do that again," he said.

"Ha," she murmured. "That's funny. You're funny."

"So," Brandon asked. "What's the plan?"

Allison reluctantly pulled away. "The plan is to have Aika place a call, and find out if the Broadcast is actually happening," Allison said as she took his hand and started leading him down the street. "If it is, we find out who is hosting it here. We find that out, we know who is employing the Grey."

"And what makes you think these events are connected?"

Allison let out a small, frustrated sigh. "As I said, there is a very short list of people who could take down multiple superheroes like this. When you factor in the fact that one of the few known things about the Grey was that he was a contract killer, it would make sense that whoever had the resources to run the Broadcast would also have enough resources to bring the Grey out of retirement."

Brandon nodded. "Sounds solid enough to me. Where are we going?"

"To meet Holly at the bus stop," Allison said smiling. "This was her first day of school, and I want to be there when she gets home."

"Okay, but take it easy. You're going to rip my arm off."

Allison was smiling as she continued to walk fast. "You can lift a city bus. You'll be fine."

"Allison, the bus doesn't arrive for another two and a half hours."

"And we're going to be there on time!" Allison snapped. "I am going to be there, and I am going to give her a hug, and take her to dinner, and I am going to ask a thousand questions and embarrass her and do everything moms do. And when we're done, we're going to start hunting us a supervillain."

Brandon raised an eyebrow. He debated pointing out the use of the 'm' word, but let it drop. Allison was doing her best to focus on something, and he suspected it was to try to distract them both from the awkwardness of the fact that she had been involved with the Broadcast.

Allison was also trying to distract herself. Partially because of the guilt she felt over Aquatica's death, and how it had hurt Brandon, and partly to turn off the tiny voice in her head that said she was missing something important.

Chapter Fifteen

Open War

"Dammit, I knew there was something familiar about all that!"

Alice was fuming as Aika was speaking in what could only be described as terse Japanese into her phone. As soon as Aika had gotten off the phone with Allison, she had caught Alice up on what was going on. Her employer's response was one of the most expletive-filled rants the former assassin had ever heard. Considering they were standing in the middle of Tanner Tower lobby, Aika felt vaguely self-conscious.

Alice was busy grumbling to herself as Aika hung up, and slid her phone into her pocket. "As I am no longer a member of the Dead Talon, they see no need to extend the courtesy of an invite to the Broadcast. Additionally, they..."

"Oh, I'll give them a reason to extend a fucking invite! Those fucking, motherfucking sons of fucks!"

"There are other curses in the English language," Aika muttered under her breath.

Alice continued on with her rant, oblivious to her friend's embarrassment. "I cannot fucking believe they fucking did this! I..."

Aika cleared her throat. "Additionally, they stressed that..."

"FUCK!" Alice screamed. Across the lobby, a four-year-old started crying as her mother hurried her away.

"...Additionally, they stressed that they unfortunately could not extend you an invitation, as you are no longer affiliated with the Purge."

Aika waited for another stream of curse words, but it never came. Instead, Alice shook for a moment and then let out a long, loud sigh. "Of course, they didn't. That would make this nice and neat, wouldn't it?"

Aika raised an eyebrow. "Impressive. I thought you would resume cursing."

Alice shrugged. "Seems kind of rude to do it in public."

Aika shot Alice a disbelieving look. Alice adjusted her jacket and continued on. "So this … quit giving me that look. Little kids cry all the time. So, this explains the attacks on superheroes lately. Wipe out the major players, reserve the weaker ones for the Broadcast, everyone wins."

"Was this not part of your Red Rook strategy?"

Alice nodded. "Unfortunately, yes it was. I came up with it with Allison's help, so chances are this is doing wonders for her self-esteem. I just cannot believe they *did* this. I threatened open war with them if they ever tried to do this shit again."

Aika followed Alice out of the tower, and onto the sidewalk. She watched as Alice attempted to hail a cab, and failed. "Why?"

Alice looked over her shoulder. "What?"

"Why did you threaten war?"

Alice continued to wave as a checkered cab flashed its lights, making its way towards them through the busy traffic. "They were murdering kids. Kids that had already been through too much. I told them no. They said there was 15% more profit if the audience got to see little girls instead of big, bad superheroes. I told them that they could shove 15% up their asses. No kids, Aika."

Alice turned to look at Aika, and Aika nearly flinched at the unforgiving, slightly-unhinged look in her eyes. "My one and only rule. You can burn the rest of the fucking world down, but no kids. Ever. I told them to screw off, and that the Broadcast was *done*. I also told them if they skipped the Purge's turn I would shove a nuke up their asses."

For a moment, Aika regarded Alice with respect.

"I survived a nuke, you know." Alice said. "Did I ever tell you that? Have I mentioned that before?"

The moment passed.

"Your threats seem to have gone unheeded," Aika pointed out.

Alice shot her a glare, but then continued on. "We need to find out who's behind this. My guess is the blonde, whoever she is. Also, more immediately, this business with the Grey. If Allison is right, we might need some help. Mr. Man is not small potatoes."

"Who would you suggest?" Aika asked, mildly curious.

"There's only one man I know who would know something about the Grey, and maybe how to take him down," Alice said. She glanced at Aika. "Is there a gas station near here?"

***

Alice did not like to dwell on her past. As second in command of the Purge, she was involved in situations that gave most professional villains nightmares, and she was known for handling said situations with aplomb. She was revered for her tactics, her tenacity, and, above all, for her good business sense. Prometheus may have been in charge, but every bad guy and girl in the game knew that if you wanted to get something done, you talked to Alice.

As a result, Alice had a little black book that was larger than most. She was a professional above all else, and when she decided to go rogue, and eventually 'good', she never turned over the information she had collected during her years in the Purge. Her contact list was a closely guarded secret, and one she did not like to use if she could help it. Unfortunately, they were running out of options. It looked like it was finally time to dust it off, and ring up an old acquaintance.

A slight rain was beginning to fall, and Alice and Aika made their way back towards the businesses lining the busy street. Alice stood under an easement, and did her best to read through a jumble of chicken scratch entries in her worn address book as Aika stood behind her, frowning. Alice might have commented on this, but frowning seemed to be Aika's go-to expression.

"You should not be doing this," Aika said in a voice that dripped with disdain, and possibly fear. It was hard for Alice to tell at times.

"What?" Alice asked without looking up. "Books can't be hacked."

"No," Aika said. "I meant calling people from your past."

"Chill, I got this." Alice shrugged off Aika's warning, and tapped an entry in her book. "Here we go. Thought so - he retired to Arizona. Least, that's what he told me once. I need the not-mine phone. Aika?"

Aika held up the bag that contained the cheap flip phone they had picked up from a nearby gas station. Alice nodded her thanks, and rotted the packaging away with a tap. "Best fucking use of my powers, if there ever was one. Now, lessee…"

Alice tried to quickly activate the phone as Aika shook her head. "I realize you believe you know what you are doing, but he is not someone to contact. Dealings with him do not end well for anyone. Even you."

"Except for me, you mean," Alice corrected. "Look, the grimy old bastard may have been the worst human being to ever draw breath, but he owes me. We had a good, professional working relationship. Besides, I've heard that people mellow with age."

"You left him for dead, and it was only three years ago. He will not be forgiving."

Alice made a 'tut' sound as she dialed. "Look, dude owes me. Too much shit is going down all at once, and I could use some outside advice. That's all."

"So you say," Aika said with a scowl.

Alice waited patiently as the line rang. Then, a tired, gravelly voice piped up. "This is Edward."

"Hey, Ed," Alice said in her usual, upbeat voice. "How's tricks?"

There was a long pause before the voice slowly answered, "Alice?"

"Hey!" Alice greeted again. "Good to hear your voice, you crazy old bastard. How have you been?"

There was a cough. "You left me for dead, Alice."

Alice bit her lip, and shrugged before she realized he couldn't see her. "Eh. There was a lot going on that day. Honestly didn't mean to."

"I was thrown out an airlock at two miles up."

Alice shrugged. "But you lived!"

Ed coughed, and cleared his throat. "I'm 84 years old. Do you know how many bones you break being thrown out of an airlock at my age?"

Alice cringed. "Um, all of them?"

"All of them," Edward said as Alice was finishing her sentence. "I was in traction for 11 months, and I have a nanite-infested bloodstream to help repair damage."

"Ed," Alice said with a groan, "are you really gonna try to guilt me? It was a bad day for everyone."

Alice heard a long, tired sigh through the phone. "What do you want, Alice?"

Alice started walking as she talked. It was something Aika noticed the purple-haired woman did when she was nervous. "Well, I need a favor."

"Isn't this just the week for them?" Edward asked quietly.

"Eh?"

"Oh, nothing. It's just that you're not the first young lady that's come to me asking for things this week. So," Edward cleared his throat. "What can I do for my former superior officer?"

"Not the first?" Alice asked.

"Now, now," Edward said. "I don't discuss clients with one another. You know that."

"Ed, what do you know about the Grey?"

There was an even longer pause. "Alice, why do you care about the Grey?"

"Business-related. I'm trying to find something out for a friend, and I have shockingly little on this guy, other than that he's supposed to be dead. What do you know about him?"

"Not too terribly much, I'm afraid. I can tell you that despite what most believe, his powers are not magical in nature."

"Really?" Alice asked, her eyebrow unconsciously going up. "I always figured that with everything I read about him, he was some kind of super-wizard."

"Nothing of the sort," Edward laughed. "He's superhuman, but his powers are not magic by any means. Tell me, you're not dealing with him directly, are you?"

Alice shook her head, and then remembered she was on the phone. "No, not directly. Not yet, anyway. So, what do you know?"

"Only that you should leave well enough alone when dealing with him. I know you're after something of value, but I'm afraid I cannot help you. I always had trouble getting anything off of him. Too much vibrational interference." Edward said. "Now, if you'll excuse me, I must leave you be. It is getting time for my medications, and I don't like to be off-schedule."

"Of course," Alice said with a deflated tone. "Thank you, Dr. Tolarius."

"Always a pleasure, my dear," he said before hanging up.

Alice looked over to Aika. "He wouldn't tell me."

"He knows who he is, does he not?" Aika asked.

Alice nodded. "Pretty sure. Probably keeping quiet out of professional courtesy. Damn. I was really hoping we could wrap this up quickly. I... say, where's Allison?"

Aika looked at her Phonebuddy for the time. "She is on her way to pick Holly up from school. She wanted to take her out as a reward afterwards."

Alice nodded. "Cool."

***

Allison was waiting with her arms crossed outside of Margaret Mead Middle School. The bell had rung roughly two minutes ago, and Allison was already tapping her foot, and fidgeting impatiently. She mentally took note of each student as they exited the school. Some were heading for their buses, while others were hopping into cars or walking off in packs to God-knows-where. Allison scanned each of them between short glances at her phone.

"Weren't we supposed to go back to your place, and wait at the bus stop?" Brandon asked.

"And what if something happened to the bus?" Allison asked in a clipped tone. "What then? No, this is safer. This makes sense."

Brandon was about to reply, but Allison pointed at him and said, "If you say I'm acting crazy…"

"Nooo," Brandon said, his hands up in defense. "See? There's other parents waiting for their kids. In cars."

"See?" Allison said, her attention on the kids that were coming out of the school. "This is normal."

"Holly's fine, trust me," Brandon said. He slid his hands into his pockets as he watched along with her. "You texted her, and she always has her phone on her. She saw it."

"She didn't reply," Allison mumbled as she continued to scan the crowd.

"She saw it," Brandon said with a nod.

"Hmmph," Allison grunted at him as she continued to scan the crowd. She finally spotted Holly as she was exiting the school with what looked like a pale goth girl. They were talking, and both on their phones. In retrospect, this was probably why they didn't notice what was going on before Allison did.

Brandon!" Allison cried out. He looked up to see a tall, jet-black figure in what appeared to be full body armor floating above the buses. The figure appeared to be focused on where Holly and her friend were making their way through the crowd.

"HOLLY!" Allison screamed as she reached for her sidearm. Brandon was gone in a heartbeat. He had instantly powered up in a blur of crimson, and blasted towards the figure who was now holding a hand towards Holly. Energy was beginning to crackle in front of the armored being, and the air was thick with ozone. It wasn't until the Ifrit let out an energy blast that the crowd as a whole noticed, and at that point, the children looked up to see Brandon fly between them and certain death.

Brandon took the blast full force. He pushed back against it, and eventually matched the blast with enough of his own energy to forcefully swat it into the sky. The blast sailed off a good 300 feet before exploding in the air.

Below, the children screamed and panicked as they fled in droves. It was a scene of mass chaos, and for a moment, Allison lost sight of Holly. It wasn't until Allison heard a frantic *"I'M HERE"* screaming through her brain that she looked to her left, and saw Holly running towards her, the goth girl following close behind.

"Holly, get behind me, and get to safety, now!" Allison screamed as she took Holly into a quick hug.

"Jean, come on!" Holly shouted to her friend. She then turned her attention back to Allison. "It's one of those things!" Holly said in a fearful voice. "It's like the one from the park, it's..."

Allison leveled the sights of her Beretta at the floating figure in black. "It's an Ifrit," Allison said through her teeth. "Someone sent an Ifrit to your school."

Holly covered her head, and pushed Jean down as Allison let off eight quick shots in succession. Around her, the children were screaming and crying as they ran for cover. Jean looked at Allison, and then Holly. "Who is she?" Jean asked.

Holly glanced back, her hands over her ears. "That's my Mom," she said with a small smile.

Brandon wasted no time. As Allison unloaded her clip into the Ifrit, Brandon blasted towards it, slamming into it with both fists. The two went flying into the brick side of a nearby building. They exploded through, sending debris flying in all directions. Allison switched out magazines for a quick reload, and looked back to Holly.

"Holly, Brandon is going to need help. Where's Fudo?"

Holly looked around for a moment, and then pointed to a nearby alley between two apartment buildings. "He's there! He's asking if I'm okay!"

Allison nodded as she quickly turned, and herded Holly and Jean off the street towards the alley. Sure enough, there stood the giant, ten-foot-tall stone golem. Allison was never so happy to see it in her life.

"Fudo, please go help Brandon kill the Ifrit," Allison asked. The golem stood still for a moment, but then Holly put her hand on it, looking up at its emotionless, stone face.

"Please, help us," Holly asked.

Instantly, the titanic stone monster lumbered forward. It gently brushed the soft humans in front of it aside as it emerged from its hiding place, and headed towards the building that Brandon and the Ifrit had just sailed into. Before it was even halfway there, Brandon came hurtling through a window and bounced on the cracked pavement of the street below. Fudo stopped a few feet from where Brandon came to rest while the Ifrit slowly floated out of the broken window.

Brandon coughed and looked up at Fudo. "Hey, pal," he said in a shaky voice. "Don't suppose you could lend a hand?"

Brandon got himself to his feet, and turned to stand beside Fudo. The Ifrit, seemingly unfazed, floated just above the ground roughly twelve feet away. All three were still for a few moments, but then, as if on some unspoken cue, all three moved at once. Allison, Holly, and Jean were all watching from the alleyway in amazement. Jean was just shocked at what was going on, but Allison and Holly were more impressed with the sheer speed that Fudo was moving at. They had never really seen him cut loose before, aside from one or two moments of extreme danger.

"What is that thing?" Jean asked, slightly terrified at just about everything happening.

"That's Fudo," Holly said, mesmerized by the action. "He's a friend."

"Seriously?" Jean asked. "And the Red Guard? That's the Red Guard, right?"

"Yep," Allison said with a smirk.

Jean looked from Allison to Holly with eyes the size of saucers. "Is he your dad?"

"Nope," Allison said.

"Not yet," Holly said with a sideways glance at Allison.

The older woman turned beet red. "And on that note, we need to get moving. Come on."

Allison took Holly by the hand, who in turn grabbed Jean. Together, the three of them made their way down the alley.

"Wait, shouldn't we help?" Jean asked, still in shock from what was going on. "I mean, call the police? That man..."

"That man," Allison said as they emerged one block away, "is connected to a star. He can survive in space. There is nothing that stupid little toy robot can throw at him that he can't handle."

Holly glanced at Allison, and frowned as she heard her thoughts. "Are you sure?"

Allison kept her gaze forward as they quickly made their way through the neighborhood towards a nearby convenience store. "Dammit," Allison muttered. "Half a mile to the nearest public transport. I knew I should have chosen a school closer to a subway. Stupid, stupid rookie mistake..."

"Hey," Jean said with a tug on Holly's arm. "My home is a block from here. We can hide there."

Allison glanced at Jean as if seeing her for the first time. "Does it have a basement? Lower storage area? Anything?" Allison asked.

Jean nodded. "Yeah, but it's gross."

"Don't care," Allison said. "Sooner we get you to shelter, the better. Lead the way, um..."

"Jean," she said.

"Cool. Move your feet, Jean," Allison said, as the homes around them shook from the sound of explosions.

Holly tried to speak up at this point, but Allison was already dragging them along towards Jean's home.

Meanwhile, the fight in the street was turning into a scene of pure chaos. Brandon had heard stories from Allison about the Ifrit that had attacked her and Holly in Central Park, but that one had been a damaged prototype. Brandon, as well as the rest of the senior members of the Collective Good, knew there had been one more android. A full-scale production model had been commissioned, but then dismantled, or so they had been told.

Brandon braced as the Ifrit raised its hand. A blast of blue and white fire engulfed the robot's arm and then shot out towards Brandon, who blocked with crossed arms as he floated back. The Ifrit was insanely powerful, but temperature was something that didn't bother Brandon. He charged through the wave of fire, and punched the Ifrit as hard as he could in the faceplate. The android went reeling head over heels into the concrete below. The street shook as the impact left a small crater in the middle of the road.

"Fudo," Brandon called over his shoulder. "We need to keep it down! If it's allowed to build up enough energy, it's going to…"

Brandon was cut off as Fudo lumbered past him. Before Brandon knew what was happening, Fudo leapt into the air, and landed with a deafening crash atop the Ifrit. The android had just been gathering itself, and starting to get up, when the massive golem slammed down on top of it. Without skipping a beat, Fudo started pummeling the Ifrit. Each hit shook the nearby windows of the middle school, but the Ifrit wasn't stopping. It continued to try to get up, even with Fudo slamming into it with all his might.

Brandon sailed into the air above Fudo, and drew a bead on the Ifrit. He then closed his eyes, and whispered to himself. "I need you," he said. In his mind's eye, he was trillions of miles away. He was suddenly in the void of space. Before him was a star, a red giant. Brandon could hear the radio waves emanating from its poles as they washed over him. Their song was one of fire, of love and devotion. He heard his own heart beat in time with the solar flares that rhythmically jumped underneath him as he whispered.

"I need your help, love. Help me take his fire. Will you? Will you let me?"

The star pulsed. The solar winds ebbed and flowed, and Brandon felt them envelop him completely. In their cosmic whisper, he heard their answer.

Brandon opened his eyes and focused on the chaos of the fight below. Fudo was trying, but the Ifrit was still getting to its feet. Brandon could see energy building up around it, crackling and bubbling as it began to charge. Under the crushing weight of Fudo's attack, the Ifrit raised its hand towards the stone golem's face.

"HEY!" Brandon screamed. The Ifrit turned its attention towards Brandon as Fudo stopped for a moment. Then, a titanic wave of energy erupted from the robot's hands. Brandon put out his hands, closed his eyes, and focused. As the energy hit him, he felt it pull into his being, fill him, and then seemingly disappear. Smiling, he wrapped his hands around the stream of fiery energy and focused on pulling it in further.

The android seemed to realize what was happening and tried to stop, but then paused as it realized it couldn't shut off its beam. The Ifrit then tried to physically pull away, but again, Brandon held on to the energy beam and continued to pull the energy into his soul.

At this point, the Ifrit was trying to tear away as hard as it could, but nothing was working. Its arms were starting to glow white hot and buckle as the energy was pulled from it. Its entire body was a blur of erratic shudders as it dug in its feet, and did its best to twist away. It couldn't break the flow of energy as it continued to pour out, overloading the robot's circuits.

"That's it," Brandon said as he felt his body starting to reach its limits. He was turning white from the vast influx of energy. The air around him crackled with electricity and ozone. Light around his frame was starting to bend as the massive increase in energy was enough to alter the gravity that was surrounding him. In that moment, he was just as much the star that powered his heart and essence as he was a flesh and blood man, and the power was at once overwhelming and intoxicating.

The black armor of the Ifrit was now melting off. As Brandon looked down, he could see the half-finished robotic face of the Ifrit finally exposed from behind it's shiny, solid faceplate. The camera eyes were wide and cracked, and there were tiny metal bars holding the structure of the head in place. From where Brandon was, those bars looked like an open mouth.

"You can't talk," Brandon said through clenched teeth, "but let's see if you can scream! FUDO!"

If the Ifrit saw what happened next, no one could tell. Fudo raised his gigantic stone fists, cupped them together, and brought them down like a massive hammer right on the Ifrit's body. This was the tipping point for the murderous android as its shell buckled, and its core finally overloaded. Brandon felt a sharp, cold snap in his chest as the beam of energy was abruptly cut off. Instantly, there was a blinding explosion in the middle of the street. Cars went flipping through the air as every house window for two blocks around shattered.

In the middle of the flaming, smoking crater that had been Coney Island Avenue stood Fudo, his stone skin burning where oil and fuel had splashed his cracked, ancient frame. He stood over the shattered, smoldering remains of the Ifrit with his foot where the robot's chest had been. In one oversized hand, he held what was left of the Ifrit's head. Without looking down, he clenched his fist, crushing the head with no more effort than a child would use on a paper airplane.

Brandon slowly floated down to stand beside the stone warrior. His street clothes had burned away completely, revealing his red and black Red Guard uniform. His skin was still crackling with the leftover energy from the Ifrit. Shaking a bit, he put a hand on Fudo's shoulder.

"Nice job, partner," Brandon said with a forced smile. "Thanks for the assist."

The golem just stood there, unmoving.

"Say," Brandon said as he caught his breath. "I don't suppose you know where our ladies ran off to, do you?"

Amid the smoke, fire, chaos, and swiftly approaching sirens, the golem turned its head, and then took off in an impossibly fast sprint.

Brandon nearly fell over as Fudo tore down the road. In a heartbeat, he was in the air and following. He didn't bother asking what was wrong. Brandon knew about Fudo's connection to Holly. He also knew that there was only one thing that would make the Golem suddenly take off like it had, and that made Brandon's charged and boiling blood instantly turn cold.

Chapter Sixteen

"Where's the girl?"

As the three women entered an older-looking apartment complex, Holly couldn't shake the feeling that something was wrong. It had been nagging at her for the last couple of minutes, but she was having trouble putting her finger on it. It wasn't until they were inside, and heading towards a door by a worn, white staircase, that she stopped cold and wrestled her hand out of Allison's grip.

"This isn't protocol," Holly said.

Allison stopped, and turned to look at Holly. "What are you talking about? I've got to get you to safety. Come on, let's get in the basement."

Holly took a step back, as Jean and Allison stood with looks of annoyance on their faces. "No," Holly said. "This isn't protocol. We're supposed to call for a quick pick up from the Collective Good. Victoria briefed me on this. She said she briefed you, too."

Allison shook her head. "Look, that's all well and good, but first I'm getting you underground in case of an explosion, and then I'm calling Victoria. Your safety comes first. Now get in the basement."

Allison reached for Holly, but the young telepath jumped back. "How did you know where her apartment was?"

Allison blinked. "What?"

Holly felt a cold knot starting to form in her stomach. "How did you know where Jean's apartment was?"

Allison scowled. "I asked her, remember?"

Holly shook her head. "You told her to lead the way, and then you took off. She didn't lead you here, you just came."

Allison frowned. "I didn't, I...I..."

Holly watched as Allison's eyeballs rolled back in her head. She went limp, collapsing on the thinly carpeted floor. Behind her stood Jean, who was smiling.

"Jesus, Princess, it took you long enough."

Holly clenched her fists and glared. "What is this? How did you do that?"

'How do you think?' The voice was loud as it echoed through Holly's head. Holly nearly fell over from shock as Jean let out a little laugh.

"We've been waiting for you, you know," Jean said as she smugly crossed her arms. "When we got the tip that your guardian had registered you at 209, we made sure to slip in ahead of time."

"You're a telepath?" Holly asked, still shocked by what was happening.

Jean nodded. "Maybe you should have spent more time focusing on what was going on around you instead of trying to make new friends. Seriously, who do you think you are?"

The white basement door opened, and from it emerged a well-dressed blond man. He turned his eyes on Holly, and gave her a wide, toothy smile.

Holly felt her heart stop. The man in front of her was instantly familiar, but she couldn't place him. Every time she tried to focus on his face, the image got blurry, and her head started to hurt. Holly then let out a small cry as a wave of pain rolled through her skull.

"It's a side-effect," Senator Carter said, as he adjusted the sleeves on his finely tailored suit coat. "My powers naturally obscure me when people look at me. I have to use an inhibitor just to operate day-to-day, and let me tell you, when your job is being a recognized public official, having a natural masking ability is a total bitch."

Carter slid a small, white inhibitor disk out of his pocket, and tossed it in the air, lazily catching it while keeping his gaze on Holly. "Thing's got to be cranked up so high that most people get a migraine." He stopped, and gave Holly a wide smile. "I have missed you so very much, Holly."

Holly felt her head spinning. "You," she mumbled. Her sense of balance was starting to go on her as light-headedness was overwhelming her. "You're Mr. Russ."

Carter nodded as he slid the inhibitor back into his pocket. "And you're little Holly Bedford, back from the dead, and ready to come home."

Holly went rigid. "No."

Jean wandered next to Carter, and crossed her arms as she smirked at Holly. "You really thought you could have all this? A rich, superhero mommy? You thought you could walk away? Bitch, please."

Carter put his hand on Jean's shoulder. "Jean is another one of my special little girls. Unlike you, though, she actually enjoys her work. Still, as good as she is, she's not you. I want you back, Holly. You know too much, and you're just too damn good to waste on these fuck-ups." To emphasize the point, Carter gave the unconscious Allison a kick.

Holly shook her head as her adrenaline was starting to go into overdrive. "No."

Carter frowned. "It wasn't a question. You're worth the effort, but only to a point. Don't make me regret doing this."

"Oh, you're going to regret it," Holly said as she began to shake. She was reaching out with her mind, doing her best to try to get into Carter's head, but she was having trouble. It was like there was a brick wall protecting him. No matter how hard she tried, she couldn't get through.

Jean slid a syringe out of her pocket. Holly glanced at her and growled. "So, all of it was fake? Brent, too?"

Jean snickered. "Dude, he's one of us. There were, like, six telepaths at that school. If I didn't make friends with you, we had multiple backups."

"What about all that crap you gave me about your friend Roger?"

Jean snorted. "Who do you think outed him? How's it feel to be played, Princess?"

"You tell me."

Holly focused again, but not on Carter. Jean's smirk quickly turned into a look of horror as the hand holding the syringe started to tremble. "Stop that...Stop it..." Her voice was coming in a strained cry as her right hand drifted up and towards her neck. With a scream, Jean forcefully plunged the syringe into her own jugular. She suddenly started convulsing and dropped to the floor. Both Carter and Holly watched as a mass of froth appeared on Jean's trembling mouth.

"Well shit," Carter mumbled. "All you're doing is making things harder on yourself, you know." A light buzzing sound was heard as Carter fished out his cell phone. "Hmm, he's early," he said with a smile. "Guess we didn't need to drug you after all."

In the blink of an eye, a man appeared beside Senator Carter. He was in a long, concealing trench coat, and his face was mostly hidden by his tall collar and fedora. Underneath those, all Holly could see was a blurry, gray form. Whoever it was, they were giving Holly fits as she tried to focus on him. She kept hearing one thought, then another, like they were overlapping. It was like listening to two songs over the radio at the same time, and it made it impossible for her to focus on either one.

"Mr. Grey," Carter said, "perfect timing. I..."

Carter was interrupted by the thunderous sound of something large and fast slamming into the front of the building. The entire structure shook as Fudo crashed through the front door, disintegrating it as he did so. The golem wasted no time as it stormed down the tiny hallway towards Holly.

"The girl!" Carter screamed as he bolted for the back entrance. "Get the girl, and get us out of here! Now!" Carter turned and made a break for it, leaving the Grey to stare down the massive golem that was still smoking from its prior encounter with the Ifrit. Carter made it three steps before he felt something roughly grab him from behind. There a rushing of air, and a blur of motion, and George Carter suddenly found himself standing in the middle of his office.

Trembling from panic, he steadied himself on the side of his mahogany desk and tried to catch his breath. "What the fuck was that thing?" he asked himself. He took several deep breaths to help himself calm down, and then smiled at the sound of something being dropped on the floor behind him.

Carter had been waiting for this moment for months. Holly Bedford had been the absolute finest telepath he had ever found. After having spent years cultivating children with special abilities, he had finally found his crown jewel in the young brunette. She had provided him with endless hours of blackmail material, and done so effortlessly. He had often wondered just how powerful she truly was, but he supposed it didn't matter.

His ability to block telepaths had proven immensely handy when dealing with children like her. Of course, there were other things that helped such as nanites, the procedures his father had put him through, and so on. Everything one would need to be virtually untouchable by those with psychic abilities had led to him being the king of information. Mr. Mysterious, as he had referred to himself in his youth. Nowadays, he kept it to Mr. Russ while working, but the thought was still there.

When he lost Holly, he had been genuinely concerned that Senator Stengles had finished her off. As it happened, she had been adopted, and was living not ten miles from where he had been mourning the loss of her abilities. Now though, all of that was past him. It didn't matter if it cost him an irreplaceable Ifrit. '*After all*,' he told himself, '*I can always just buy a new Totallus with the money she'll make for me.*'

His triumphant smile firmly in place, he turned to address his long-lost prize possession, but the words dried up in his throat. There stood the Grey, and at his feet was not the angry and frightened form of Holly Bedford. Instead, there lay a still unconscious Allison Gailsone.

Carter stared in mute shock for a solid five seconds before asking in an entirely too quiet voice, "Where's the girl?"

The Grey pointed to the prone Allison.

"Not *that* girl!" Carter shouted. His entire body was shaking with rage. Flecks of spit were shooting out from between his teeth, and forming in tiny, pale strands on his chin as he erupted. "WHERE'S THE LITTLE GIRL?!"

The Grey cocked his head as if thinking. George Carter, meanwhile, completely lost his shit. He started screaming and flailing about his office. He knocked the small spinning desk clock he had perched at the edge of his work space into a wall, shattering the memento. Papers scattered in a whirlwind as he thrashed about, throwing everything that wasn't nailed down in what an outsider might refer to as petulant child's tantrum.

"You had one job!" He screamed at the impassive Grey. "ONE! FUCKING! JOB! I told you to grab the girl! Holly! The LITTLE FUCKING GIRL! That was all you had to do! What in the blue Hell am I supposed to do with her?"

"This was not what you hired me for," the Grey said. His voice was a mixed whisper. It sounded like several voices barely in tune with one another. "You asked me to fetch Dyspell."

"Another job you haven't completed!" Carter screamed. Grey turned to leave, but Carter put his hand up to stop him. "No! No! Don't even fucking bother at this point. You botched this, you'll definitely botch that." Carter got out his phone, and started furiously texting. "This is going to cost me so damn much. I'm not risking another fuck up on this." Carter hit send with enough force to crack his phone screen and then pointed at Allison. "This bitch cost me my Ifrit! I've lost two of my prized possessions in one week, and now you can't even get me one little girl? No wonder you were where I found you! Can you even tie your shoes right?"

Carter stormed over to Allison, and yanked her head back by her auburn hair. He reached into his jacket, and slid a chrome-plated 9mm out of a side holster before putting it to Allison's temple.

"You cost me more than you'll ever know. Least I can do," he said as he started to squeeze the trigger. At the last moment, he noticed that she was sporting a holster and side arm.

"Huh," he said to himself. "You a cop? Is that it?" He took her Berretta out of its holster and examined it briefly before tossing it aside. "Last thing I need is a dead cop in my office. Let's see who we have here," he said mostly to himself. He reached into her pocket and fished out a thin, leather ID holder and examined it.

Carter sat back on the floor, letting Allison fall to the ground yet again. He then started to laugh to himself as he set his gun down, and fished out his slightly cracked cell phone. Still chuckling, he went to his recent calls, and hit a number.

"Hey," he said. "Change of plan. How much would people pay to see *two* Gailsones die?"

***

When Brandon arrived, he found Holly clutching Fudo and sobbing. The building they were standing in had a humongous hole in its front. The hallway they were standing in had long cracks and tears in the plaster from where Fudo had charged in, but, despite the damage, no one was moving. Even after what had just happened, it was a sight that stopped Brandon in his tracks.

Holly looked up when he came in, and then ran to him. She collided with him, and wrapped her arms around his mid-section tightly, still sobbing as she cried out, "They took her! They took her!"

Brandon looked around. There was a pale girl with black hair on the floor who appeared to be twitching, but, aside from that, there was no one else. No sign of anyone - including Allison.

Brandon gently untangled Holly from his person, and asked in a gentle voice, "Who took Allison?"

Holly was a snotty mess at this point, and couldn't stop sobbing. Brandon smoothed her hair, and nodded. "Okay, honey. Okay. Focus. Who took her? Do you know?"

"It was Mr. Russ," she choked out. Brandon tensed slightly.

"The man who used to force you to..."

Holly nodded, still weeping. "He, he was trying to take me, but then Fudo came in, and he told this guy to grab me, but he grabbed Allison instead, and then they were gone, and then you were here, and they're gone! She's gone!"

Holly erupted into tears again as Brandon did his best to soothe her. "Which way did they go?" He asked. "If you stay with Fudo, I could..."

223

Holly shook her head. "They just left, he and the other guy, they disappeared. Like, completely disappeared."

"Do you remember what they looked like?" Brandon asked.

Holly shook her head. "Mr. Russ blocks people from being able to see him. He's all blurry when you try to focus on him, but his voice is familiar."

Brandon nodded. "Okay, but what about his friend. What do you remember about him?"

"He was all gray," Holly said. "He was wearing a gray trench coat and hat. I couldn't see his face, it was all blurry. He was the one who took Allison."

Brandon closed his eyes. "Okay," he said to Holly, who was slowly calming down. "You did alright, kiddo. Even if we don't have a lot to go on."

Holly stepped back, and wiped her nose. She got a look on her face that was strikingly familiar to Brandon. It was one he had seen on Allison's face more than once, and always when they were arguing.

"I may not know where they went," she said as she turned to stare at the shuddering, passed-out Jean, "but she does."

Chapter Seventeen

"Time for you to die."

It was late afternoon, and Alice was sitting in a plastic chair outside of a local café. She was sipping an espresso, and playing a game on her PhoneBuddy as she waited for her mother to arrive. Shortly after she and Aika had left Tanner Tower, her phone had chimed with a brief text message. Nothing long, just a quick request from her mother to meet her for dinner and shopping. Alice, surprised and pleased that the morning hadn't knocked her mother out completely, quickly agreed.

Alice had been focused on the issue of the Broadcast and dealing with the Grey, but everything went on pause for her mother. Aika had agreed to look into things further on her own, and meet up with Allison and Holly at the bus stop. Alice knew it was important to spend as much time as she could with her Mom now, just in case.

Maybe, if Alice had thought it through a little bit, she would have realized how odd it was that her mother suddenly wanted to go out twice in one day – something that would have been out of character at any other time.

And if she had thought a little more, Alice might have wondered about the choice of café her mother had asked to meet her at - a bit further down the road than her usual haunts. The sidewalks here weren't that level, and were somewhat crowded - not the best choice for a woman in a wheelchair.

In fact, from an objective point of view, nothing about this particular meeting made any sense whatsoever. The truth was, The Most Dangerous Woman in the World was exhausted and distracted. Viewing her mother as the only truly safe thing in the world, her subconscious had simply stubbornly refused to read the signs she had trained her whole life to see.

It wasn't until someone sat down in the seat across from her that Alice blinked, stopped playing her phone game, and looked up. Instantly, everything that she had stupidly missed slammed into her gut like a cold, lead weight, and her heart rate spiked. She was suddenly aware of where she was, and who was around her. Every muscle in her body tensed, and she knew that her careless stupidity had finally caught up to her.

"Hey there, champ," Anna said in a friendly voice.

Alice stared at the woman across from her. It was like looking in a mirror. In fact, Alice had to close her eyes for a moment to get her head around what she was seeing. The woman in front of her was identical to her in every way, save for her hair. Anna was kicked back in her small plastic chair, sporting a white blouse and nice khakis. She was also sporting a familiar-looking pair of oversized white sunglasses that were hanging loosely from her neckline. "You mind if I join you for a minute?"

Alice put her phone face-up on the table. "By all means," she said, as evenly as she could. She continued to stare at the woman who could have been her twin.

Anna studied Alice for a moment before chuckling to herself. "You know," she said in a haunting copy of Alice's own voice, "I played through this about a thousand times in my head. You know, how this would go down? I...what in God's name are you wearing?"

Alice glanced down at the green sweater she was in. It had a picture of two kittens in a basket across the front. Alice self-consciously adjusted her sweater as she spoke. "My clothing was destroyed at work, and I had to borrow some clothes from my kind-of boss."

"But that?" Anna asked as she pointed. "You couldn't have changed? Stopped off at a store? Something?"

Alice gave a tense shrug. "Haven't had time to go home. I was about to, but then I got a text, and here I am."

"Here we are," Anna said, smiling.

Alice blinked, and thought for a second. "What did you mean, 'how this would go down'?"

Anna leaned back, and crossed her arms. "Oh, I just had my own ideas about our meeting."

"Do tell," Alice said, trying and failing to keep eye contact while glancing around to see who else was around. The café seemed moderately busy. From Alice's point of view, there were no less than half a dozen potential Purge agents, but she wasn't sure.

"Oh, don't worry," Anna said, her voice practically oozing confidence. "We're alone for the moment. I just wanted to talk to you first. At least, I thought I might. Like I said, honestly, I wasn't sure what I'd do when we finally, finally met."

"And why is that?" Alice asked, curious.

"Oh, I wasn't sure if I could stop myself from just shooting you in the face," Anna said with a shrug. "But then I thought, 'how many people get an opportunity as rare as this?' and I just *had* to bite. I mean, seriously. This here?" Anna gestured to both of them. "I thought I'd be boiling with rage at meeting you, but I couldn't be happier."

"I wish I could say the same," Alice said with a frown. "You're the person who stole the Phoenix and impersonated me?"

Anna nodded. "That would be me."

"And managed to waste untold billions in Purge resources to capture Superior Force?"

Anna nodded again. "Guilty."

Alice smirked. "Well, congratulations there. I have to say, as someone who used to be in your shoes, that was no small feat."

Anna laughed as Alice studied the blonde doppelganger.

"In my shoes," Anna said between bouts of laughter. "Shit. In my shoes. You're something else."

Alice gave a casual shrug, and glanced off to the side. "Of course, you royally fucked it up, but still. Nice effort."

Anna stopped laughing, a hint of a twitch along the side of her face. "Excuse me?"

"Oh, it's nothing. Nothing at all. You obviously know who I am, but despite being incredibly beautiful, you really aren't me, tactically speaking." Alice said with a smile. "Now, what *I* don't know, is who *you* are. I mean, aside from being extraordinarily good-looking."

"My name is Anna," Anna said as she idly picked up a menu from the green, plastic table between them.

"Just Anna?" Alice said, raising an eyebrow.

"Of course not," Anna smirked. She studied Alice's face for a moment as realization set in. "You … you really don't know who I am, do you, Dyspell?"

Alice shrugged. "Not a clue. Evil twin? Clone? Wait. There was a dimensional rift, and you fell through? Murderbot? Long-lost sister? Am I warm yet?"

Anna tapped the side of her face in mock thought. "You *might* have been heading in the right direction on one of those. Gotta tell you, I'm getting a kick out of knowing you don't know. Again, I really thought that would make me mad, but I'm feeling great."

Alice huffed and leaned back, allowing herself a long look around. Admittedly, nothing looked out of place for a typical New York afternoon. "Okay, well, go ahead and pat yourself on the back. You got me dead bang. This was about the sloppiest trap in existence, and I walked right into it. Mom's not coming, is she?"

Anna shook her head.

"You sent the text?"

"Yep," Anna said with a grin. "Smartphones are awesome, aren't they?"

"So," Alice asked as she crossed her arms. "Just making sure I'm on the same page as you. You're the one who attacked the deep-water vessel, and killed all those scientists. It was you that orchestrated the death of the majority of the supervillains on the eastern seaboard?"

"Guilty as charged," Anna said with a smile.

"Ah. Good to know," Alice said with a nod. She leaned back in her chair, and crossed her arms. "So, just so you know, in about three seconds, I'm going to put my fist through your chest. Literally. Just giving you the courtesy of a head's up."

"No, you won't." Anna said as she took out her phone, and brought up a text.

Alice raised an eyebrow. "Really? 'Cause I think I'm gonna."

Anna held her phone out for Alice to see. On it was a picture of Allison, drugged and tied to a chair.

"New plan," Anna said. "You're going to sit there, and not do a thing unless I tell you to. If you refuse to cooperate, my agents watching this exchange will place a quick call. One call, and you can be responsible for the death of yet another person that counts on you." Alice stiffened as Anna's smile never left her eyes. "Do I make myself clear, Dyspell?"

"Crystal," Alice said.

"Good," Anna said with a smile. She gestured to a nearby server. "Then let's get your order, shall we?"

A young, Latina woman came over with a tray. Alice thought she looked familiar, but just couldn't place her. She was wearing a uniform that suggested she worked for the cafe, and her shoulder length hair had a curl to it at its base. Her face was stern, with large eyes that stayed trained on Alice, who recognized the subtle tells of combat training in the woman's stance. Whoever she was, she wasn't a waitress. Alice stopped trying to place her after a second, and instead focused on the syringe laying on said tray.

"I want you to pick the syringe up, and inject it into your left arm," Anna said. "Oh, and you won't be able to break its contents down; there's an inhibitor under the table. Then, we are..."

"Wait," Alice said, confused. "How did you know I'd sit at this table?"

Anna frowned. "Don't interrupt. We are..."

Alice shook her head. "No. Pause right there. This is a little nuts. Are you a magician? How did you know? I mean, I could have sat anywhere, and..."

"THEY'RE UNDER ALL THE TABLES. There, happy? Are you satisfied yet?"

Alice whistled. "Damn. I take it back. You put a lot of thought into this."

Anna nodded. "I like to be prepared. It's one of many things we have in common. Now, as I was saying, you are going to stand, you'll..."

"Huston!" Alice interrupted. She looked to the server, who glanced back in surprise. "You're Lieutenant Huston. I knew I knew you. How's your cousin? She get her BA yet?"

Huston smiled a bit in shock. "Two years ago. She's a vet tech, now."

Anna growled under her breath, and continued. "You'll leave a nice tip, and you will get into that black Cadillac that is parked just down the street."

Alice considered her options. She tried activating her powers, but the buzz she felt in her mind told her that an inhibitor was indeed nearby, just like Anna said. She then considered how quickly she could kill the server and take out Anna, but again, if Anna was telling the truth, that meant that her daughter would die.

There was no decent way out of this.

"One thing before I do," Alice said as she gave Anna a level glare. "Your Purge agents don't touch my niece. She stays safe, and I'll do as you say."

Anna lost her smile, and her voice turned cold. "You're not in a position to negotiate, Dyspell. Your Totallus is babysitting, your niece is my prisoner, your bodyguard is holed up in a bookstore, and your golem is too far away to get here in time. You want to escape? Okay. Maybe you could. Hell, maybe you could even pull off some Hail Mary and save your gal, but what about tomorrow? What about when Holly gets on her bus, and it explodes? What about when Allison finds her boyfriend gutted like a fish in their bed, just like his speedster friend? What happens when I start slaughtering your family, one by one? What's your game then? And even if you manage to somehow stop all of that, I'll still be there, ready to get them the second their guard is down, and yes, that includes good ole' Mom."

Alice bit her lip, her mind racing. *'What am I missing here?'*

"Give me your word you'll leave Allison alone, and I'll get in the car," Alice said. "If not, I make a mess of things, and I get the feeling you don't want that. You've put so much thought into this that you want to see it go off perfectly, so perfect you'll get, but Allison walks. Best deal you're going to get."

Anna relaxed as she shrugged. "You're in no position to negotiate, but I'm feeling whimsical today. Sure. You win, Dyspell. My agents won't touch her. God," Anna said with a sigh. "I thought I wanted your death to be more memorable for me. You know, you and me in a fight to the death, each giving it their all. Still, I have to admit that this is a *far* more lucrative option."

Alice took the syringe from the young woman and rolled back her left sleeve. "Hey, if you wanna go a few rounds, I'm game."

"Tempting, but no thank you," Anna said with a wave. "You, my dear, get to die on camera."

Alice sighed, and flinched slightly as she injected the cold needle into her arm. The liquid inside was freezing, and it stung her veins as it entered her bloodstream. "You were running the murders of the heroes at the convention center?"

Anna shook her head as she took out her own phone, and sent a quick text. "Annnnd sent. Man, Carter must have fucked up something fierce to ask me to do this. He hates owing me. Oh, to answer your question, nope. That honor goes to your illustrious new senator. I'm giving him the fight ticket of a lifetime, and in return, I get a nice little chunk of the door."

"I hope I'm still worth something," Alice mumbled as she flexed her hand. The server handed Alice a towel for her arm. Alice nodded her thanks, and did her best to keep from looking anywhere but on Anna as she cleaned up a trickle of blood on her arm.

"Are you fucking kidding me?" Anna laughed. "Your death is the biggest advertised event in years. The dark web practically melted when reservations to watch your execution were made available. Bitcoin nearly lost its shit over the event. I've got dignitaries, drug lords, supervillains, mob bosses, half the president's cabinet, and everyone else you can think of coming in for tonight's show, so try to make it a good one."

"The Garden," Alice mumbled. "You're using the Garden for tonight? That's ballsy."

"That's a mental leap," Anna said.

"Not really," Alice said as she shrugged. "You want a big show, and there are few places that can handle the crowds you're looking to draw. It's what I would have done, if I were you."

"If you were me," Anna murmured. She shook her head, as if trying to focus. She then locked eyes with Alice as she leaned forward. "I want you to take your finger and try to rot it right through my forehead. No funny stuff, though."

Alice raised an eyebrow. "What the hell do you consider 'funny stuff' if rotting your skull doesn't count?"

"Just do it," Anna said with a smile. Shrugging, Alice put her finger to Anna's forehead and focused.

A few seconds later, Alice's eyes went wide as Anna leaned back and chuckled. "Phew!" Anna said with mock relief. "Boy, good thing that worked. I have to admit, I was a little curious if it would, but hey, what's life without risk?"

"What was in that shot?" Alice asked, now unsettled.

"A special nanite solution, whipped up by one Mr. Alan Tanner. Be sure to tell him thank you when you see him next. I...wait. You injected yourself without asking what it was?"

Alice nodded. "I figured it was either the nanites or something to knock me out. You weren't gonna kill me just then. You put too much thought into this."

"Still," Anna said, "Who does that? I mean, who just … you know what? Never mind. God, tonight is going to be awesome. Die well, Dyspell. I'm going to enjoy watching."

"Alice."

Anna blinked. "What now?"

Alice flashed a small smirk. "You haven't been able to call me by my name since you sat down. At first, I thought it was just a thing, but now I'm not so sure."

"Your name," Anna said in a low voice. "Your. Name. That's not your name. Alice was *never* your name. You're just too fucking weak to admit it."

Alice stared at Anna for five long seconds, and then closed her eyes. She stayed like that long enough that the server beside her glanced down nervously before Alice let out a small, "Oh, my God."

Anna made a shooing gesture with her hands. "Go on. Time for you to die. Shoo."

"Oh, my God," Alice said as she stood. "It figures he never told me. I would have had him jettison the whole batch."

Anna raised a curious eyebrow. "Wait, what?"

"You're my clone," Alice said in a matter of fact voice. "You must have been one of Prometheus's backup plans. He had several of them stacked up for God knows what on the *Argent*. That explains why you could work the Totallus. He was genetically keyed to me, so of course he would be keyed to you. It makes sense."

Anna stared open-mouthed at Alice before bursting into hysterical laughter. She was doubled over, and laughing so hard that Alice flinched when she heard a loud snort erupt from the blonde woman. "*I'm* a clone? Oh shit! *Oh* shit! Oh, my God! I think I just peed a little. Wow. Wow. Hold on," she said as she tried to compose herself. "Okay, fun time is over. Get going...Alice."

"You're not coming?" Alice asked.

"Oh, no. I'm not giving you the chance to pull something out of your ass. Nope, I've got some stops to make. Captain Huston will take things from here."

Alice was about to say something more, but she felt something small and hard press into her back. She noticed Captain Huston, was now behind her. She heard a quiet voice say, "Please, Ma'am. I have to ask that you get into the car now."

Confused, upset, and more than a little nervous, Alice complied. She turned, and obediently climbed into the back seat of the black Cadillac waiting patiently down the street. Captain Huston closed the door, and watched as the car took off into traffic.

Anna kept laughing as she watched the Cadillac pull away, and was at a nearly hysterical pitch a good two minutes afterwards.

Chapter Eighteen

Something Truly Awful

It was late afternoon by the time Brandon and Holly arrived at *Rare Gems*. They came in through the front door, Jean slung over Brandon's shoulder and completely unconscious. Eedee's eyes went wide as saucers. Holly glanced at her. "We're closed, Eedee."

Normally, Eedee wouldn't take orders from a 12-year-old; however there was something about Holly's tone and demeanor that sent Eedee scrambling for the front. She quickly locked the door as she shut off the neon OPEN sign. Outside, she saw a scuffed and dirty-looking Fudo lumber back into his regular place in front of the store. "Um, how was school?"

"Good," Holly said as she opened the door leading to the back, and then started marching up the stairs.

Eedee floated behind. "Who is that? Holly? Who is that girl?"

They made their way to the third floor, where Aika was busy going through a kata in black bicycle shorts and a comfortable sports bra. She was just finishing her third set when Holly, Brandon, and Eedee came in. Aika stopped mid-stroke, and stared for a moment at the scene before her. Holly glanced quickly to Brandon. Using what Aika guessed was a psychic command, she sent Brandon to fetch a chair from against the wall. Holly then met Aika's gaze.

'Rope.'

Aika had heard psychics speak in her head before. However, she realized when the cold, angry word whipped through her mind that it was the first time Holly had directly spoken to her like that. It was genuinely unsettling. Aika found herself repressing a shudder as she growled back, "If you attempt to command me again in that manner, I may forget who you belong to."

Holly looked at her blankly for a moment, and then softened her expression. "Sorry. I, um, I think I'm getting carried away. Please get me a rope? We're interrogating someone." Aika glanced at the girl, and shrugged. She sheathed her katana, and moved to grab some nylon cord from what Allison called 'the pegboard of fun'. Mutely, she handed it to Holly, who began furiously tying Jean up. Eedee floated to Aika's side and whispered, "Aren't you concerned about any of this?"

Aika shrugged, and continued to watch. After a few moments, Aika tapped Holly on the shoulder and pointed at the rope. "Do a Palomar. It's easier than what you are trying."

Holly stared at her work for a moment before Aika shooed her out of the way and quickly bound the girl. "See? Like so. We will practice later."

Once Aika was sure Jean was secured to the chair, she stepped out of the way, and gestured for Holly to resume. "Remember," Aika said, "Do not begin with the worst. Start slow. Anticipation creates results."

Holly nodded her thanks. She then pulled back, and gave Jean a hard slap that echoed around the room. "Wake up, you stupid bitch," Holly barked. Brandon and Eedee jumped slightly at this new side of Holly, while Aika allowed herself a small smile. Brandon moved to stop Holly, but Aika shot him a look that froze him in his tracks.

"If there is a reason good enough for what has occurred so far, I suggest you should allow her continue," she suggested, her indifferent tone barely covering the steel beneath.

Holly was starting to breathe heavily, shaking with her rage. There were hot, thick tears running down her cheeks, as she did her level best to compose herself. "Brandon, my...my mother is missing, and this girl knows where she is. The man who used to hurt me did this. He was trying to take me, and aunt Alli... *Mom* was taken instead, and I have to know where she is before he kills her."

Brandon was about to say something in response, but before he could Holly yelled, "I said wake up!" She slapped Jean again. Jean coughed and mumbled something, slowly coming to. Eedee leaned in and gently touched a bit of spittle running down Jean's chin. She rubbed it between her fingers for a moment as her sensors did their magic.

"This girl has been drugged. Nanite solution. Basic compliance formula, Purge edition, but the dosage is wrong. She's got enough in her to control a full-grown male." Eedee said, her concern rising. "We should get her to a hospital."

"Hell, no," Holly said. "Wake up, Jean. Where was Mr. Russ planning on taking me?"

"Who's Mr. Russ?" Eedee asked.

"Wha-?" Jean mumbled. She looked around, confused. "Where am I?"

"She won't be very coherent," Eedee chimed in. "In fact, I'm impressed she isn't in a coma. She really should be at the hospital."

Aika had heard enough to understand what was going on. "Where is Allison?" She asked.

"They took her," Brandon answered.

Aika tensed. "Who took her?"

Holly slapped Jean again. "Where were you planning on taking me?"

"How could she be taken?" Aika asked, her voice rising. "She is the Mistress of Death. Such an opponent does not go down easily."

"What should we do?" Eedee asked, concerned.

"I don't know," Brandon said in a terse voice. "We were busy dealing with an Ifrit when it happened."

"We?" Aika asked.

"SHUT UP!" Holly screamed.

Aika nodded in understanding. "Give me thirty minutes, and you will know everything this child has ever done." She cracked her knuckles, and leveled a dark stare at Jean. "*Everything*."

Holly shook her head. "There isn't time for that. I…" she looked at each of the adults around her one by one. "I need to do something. I don't want to do it. I, I can get what I need, but it's… it's not nice."

"What's not nice?" Eedee asked. "I mean, compared to this?"

Holly looked to Aika. Of all of them, Holly knew that Aika was the only one who would understand. Aika saw the look in Holly's eyes, and felt the gentle, cold caress of a ghost walking over her grave. She knew that look; she had worn it on her own face more than once. Holly was about to do something truly awful. Without a word, without even a psychic push, Aika nodded in approval.

Holly took a deep breath, counted to three, and lunged at Jean. She grabbed the sides of Jean's head hard, and focused with all her might. Instantly, the temperature of the room felt like it dropped ten degrees, as the chair Jean was sitting in started to vibrate. Brandon and Eedee looked on in horror as Jean opened her eyes wide, revealing nothing but white.

Jean let out a horrifying, inhuman scream as she convulsed under Holly's grip. The wail made Eedee shut her eyes and cringe, and Brandon covered his mouth in shock. Aika stood unmoved. The sound was not one that a human throat should have been capable of, but it was coming out of Jean in a loud, disjointed cacophony.

It only took five seconds. Holly let go of Jean, who was now slumped motionless in her chair. Holly stumbled backwards, and collapsed onto the gray training mats beneath her, panting and crying from exhaustion.

"What did you just do?" Brandon asked in a quiet voice. Aika moved to check Jean's pulse. Brandon's eyes went wide as he untied Jean. "She's unconscious. Her pulse is too low, I think..."

"She's gone," Holly said.

Everyone looked at Holly. She wiped a mess of sweat-soaked brown hair out of her eyes, and glanced at Brandon. "Her mind is gone. I had to take what I needed, and it broke her. She's gone."

"For how long?" Brandon asked.

"Forever," Holly said. "That's why I don't like to do it. It breaks people."

"She is lobotomized?" Aika asked.

Holly nodded. "That's the word."

"Holly..." Eedee started.

"We will need to dispose of her," Aika said. Eedee looked on in horror as Aika cut Jean's restraints and hefted her body over her shoulder. "Give me five minutes."

"We need to talk about this," Brandon said, visibly shaken. "Holly, you can't just..."

"I found out where they are." Holly said. She looked back at Jean's body being hauled out and muttered, "He's taking her to his office building."

"Who is?" Brandon asked.

"Mr. Russ," Holly replied. "But I know who he is now. He's a Senator. Mr. Russ is George Carter, and he's got my Mom."

Chapter Nineteen

Four Minutes

Alice wasn't sure how long she had been out. When she came to, she found herself laying on a black leather couch in what looked like a well-supplied green room. She blinked away her grogginess, and did her best to sit up without inducing an instant headache. After failing miserably, and grabbing her forehead in pain, she mumbled through her teeth, "Where am I?"

Her eyes shot open when a female voice with a familiar Japanese accent answered, "You are in your green room, Miss Gailsone."

Alice looked up to see a young woman standing near a door with a large, smoked glass window. She was dressed in a sky blue gi and was resting her right hand on the hilt of a sheathed katana. The young Japanese woman looked like she was in her late 20's and sported a sloppily cut mop of hair. Her skin was a pale brown, and Alice noticed a scar across the woman's right cheekbone. Her large eyes were trained on Alice, impassively studying her from across the room. Alice instantly recognized her and gave a small nod. "You're Meiyo Mizuki of the Fukijima Assassin's Guild, aren't you?"

Mizuki nodded. "And you are Alice Gailsone, the woman known as Dyspell."

There was a moment of tense silence that was only broken when Alice snickered. "You're about as talkative as Aika."

Mizuki glanced toward the door. "You will need to change," she said. "They will be coming for you, soon."

"What happened to me?" Alice asked. "The last thing I remember, I was getting into a car, and then boom, I wind up here."

"You were knocked out," Mizuki said. "a side-effect of the inhibitor nanites."

Alice growled. She tried to focus her powers, but it felt like they were behind a brick wall. She knew they were there, but she had no control over them whatsoever. "Well, this sucks," she muttered.

Mizuki nodded towards a small, neatly folded set of clothes on the side table near Alice. "You are to change for your fight," she said. "Also, I would recommend stretching, as you seem out of shape."

Alice gave Mizuki a glare. "Well, that settles it. You're definitely cut from the same cloth as Aika. What are you, her sister?"

Mizuki glanced at the door again. "You have roughly ten minutes before they arrive. I would suggest that you hurry."

Alice had questions, but she knew enough to know when to save them. She picked up the small, black pile of clothing, and turned to speak. Before she had a chance, Mizuki nodded towards a door on the far wall and said, "The washroom is over there."

Alice mumbled a thanks, and headed in to change. A few minutes later, she emerged wearing the latest copy of her Dyspell uniform, sans her utility belt. "The belt really brings the outfit together. Mind if I have it back?"

"They mean to kill you on camera," Mizuki said, still glancing to the door. "Your death is the most anticipated event in the history of the dark web."

Alice stretched her arms, and did some twists. "Figured. Well, it's good to know I'm still worth something, I suppose."

"This is not a time for jokes," Mizuki snapped. "When they come for you, they will take you to the Arena. You will not be allowed a weapon." Mizuki paused. "They predict you will last for six minutes."

Alice raised an eyebrow. "And what do you think? I value the opinion of a world-class assassin."

Mizuki studied Alice for a moment. "Four minutes."

"Ha!" Alice laughed. She made a show of dusting off her hands before placing them on her hips. After taking a deep breath, she looked to Mizuki. "So, do I at least look the part? After all, they're paying to see the Most Dangerous Woman in the World."

"You seem quite calm about meeting your death," Mizuki noted.

Alice nodded, and then gave a half-hearted shrug. "Matters of great concern should be treated lightly."

Mizuki raised an eyebrow. "Is the quote for my benefit? Are you trying to impress me?"

Alice gave Mizuki a dismissive wave. "I only try to impress people when I have something to gain from it. Right now, I'm trying to focus on the fact that I'm most likely going to die tonight. You know, like you do." Alice glanced around expectantly. "No M&Ms? What kind of operation is copy-me running?"

"You are posturing," Mizuki noted. "You need to take this seriously. They have your niece. If you fight poorly, they will put her in next."

To help make her point, Mizuki slipped a cell phone from out of her robes, and brought up a video. The footage was short and shaky, but Alice could clearly see the prone form of Allison tied to a chair. There was audio, but that was irrelevant – her niece was clearly unconscious.

Alice thought to herself for a moment. "You're a paid assassin. Is there any chance I could hire you?"

Mizuki shook her head. "My contract cannot be negotiated."

"Of course, it can't," Alice muttered. "Damn honor among assassins and all."

They stood there for a moment silently. Finally, Alice sighed. "I suppose that leaves me with only one option. Please, if you would, let Aika know where my niece is. I know you can't directly interfere, and dishonor your House, but she can. Maybe I can buy her enough time to get to Allison? Would that be doable?"

Alice looked to Mizuki, who stood silent for several seconds. Finally, the assassin said, "My role tonight is to guard you until the fight begins. This is what Senator Carter and the Purge have contracted me for. I have no concerns beyond this."

"Maybe you could look up your old clan sister *after* this?" Alice asked hopefully.

"Maybe," Mizuki replied.

Alice studied Mizuki's face for any sign of a lie or a trick, but she was familiar enough with the women of the Fukijima clan to know that, if nothing e,lse, they were honest in matters of death.

"Well then," Alice said as she stood straight, and looked Mizuki in the eye. "They had better do their best tonight, because now I have absolutely no choice but to kill every last fucking one of them."

Mizuki studied Alice's face. Where before there had been flippancy there was now only a grim resolve. It was as if someone had flipped a switch, and, in the space of a heartbeat, the woman before Mizuki had become someone else.

"I apologize," Mizuki said at last. "I believe you will last longer than four minutes."

"Fuckin' A," Alice said with a nod. The door beside Mizuki opened, and two Purge guards entered the room. Alice strode confidently between them, giving the guard at her left a glance. "Pick that rifle up, soldier!" she snapped. The guard was so caught off-guard by Alice's command that he quickly readjusted his weapon before following Alice as she made her way down the hall towards the main staging area.

Mizuki watched them go, and then slipped her cell phone out of her pocket. "Moshi moshi," she said as the other line picked up. "You were correct; she is here. Yes, yes, I understand." She slid the call button left as she tucked her phone back into the folds of her gi, and then swiftly caught up to Alice on the way to the main stage.

***

"Well, hello," Victoria said as she quickly closed her browser window. She had given up focusing on financials about an hour ago, and had shifted towards running a multi-site search worm to find something, anything, relating to Alan Tanner. She practically jumped in surprise when Brandon, Holly, Eedee, and Aika came barging in.

"Allison's been taken," Holly blurted out. Victoria turned her attention squarely on the young girl. Her hair was a tangled mess, she was as pale as a sheet of paper, and her eyes... Victoria had only seen eyes like that on the most desperate of people. There was a hard edge to them that made Victoria shudder. All of it, combined with Holly's voice, told Victoria exactly how grave the situation was. "Allison's been taken by Senator Carter."

Victoria glanced to Brandon, who nodded. "He made a move this afternoon. He used an Ifrit to distract us, and made a play for Holly, but he took Allison instead."

"Seriously?" Victoria asked. "That's... seriously?"

"It was the Grey," Holly said. "Carter is using the Grey to do his dirty work."

Behind them, Aika jerked slightly as her phone started to vibrate. She slid it out, mildly intrigued that someone was calling her. "Moshi moshi," she mumbled as she stepped away from the group.

"Are you sure?" Victoria asked as she looked from Holly to Brandon. "Are you absolutely sure?"

Holly nodded. "I saw him, and I got... confirmation." Holly growled the end of her sentence. "The Grey is going to be guarding them."

Victoria slammed her fist on her desk. "I knew it! I just knew it! I knew he wasn't dead."

"Um," Eedee raised her hand. "Not to throw things off, but the Grey is one of the more serious superbeings out there. Seriously, he's listed as Do Not Engage in my database. There are only about five people with that distinction."

Victoria nodded in agreement. "I know, but we have you, Brandon, and Aika. That should be more than enough to..."

They were interrupted by Aika hanging up, before screaming something loud, vulgar-sounding and very un-Aika-like in Japanese. She glanced at the surprised crowd, quickly regaining her calm façade. "It appears that they have Alice as well."

"What?!" Victoria yelled. "How? How does this fucking happen? Seriously?!"

"Where is she?" Eedee asked, suddenly sounding far more serious than anyone could remember her being. She stopped hovering, and settled to the floor, her normal ticks and shifting completely gone. She stood upright and at attention, and her eyes were faintly glowing red.

Aika considered Eedee for a moment. "The Purge has taken her for the Broadcast. She is to be publicly executed on live television."

"WHERE?" Eedee asked in a hollow, mechanical voice.

Aika shook her head. "If you charge in blindly, you may end up getting her killed. She is alive for now. Let us keep her that way."

Brandon leaned down, and whispered to Holly and Victoria, "I've never seen her do that."

"She's a Totallus," Victoria said quietly. "As vapid and bubbly as she acts, her primary purpose is to protect Alice. When that protocol is engaged, her secondary functions cease to operate."

"But Alice has been in trouble before, hasn't she?" Holly asked.

Victoria shook her head. "Alice has always had Aika, or Allison, or someone else nearby. Now, she's in trouble and alone, and Eedee can't ascertain the level of threat, so she's gone into full-on murderbot mode."

"Eedee," Aika said. "Alice is being held under heavy guard. If we try to free her without attending to Allison first, there is a good chance that Allison may be killed. We will need to approach this with caution. Do you understand?"

Eedee seemed to be processing what Aika was telling her. Without changing her expression, Eedee responded, "Understood."

"This is bad," Victoria piped up. "We don't have enough muscle to do a two-pronged assault."

"What about Susan?" Brandon asked. Victoria looked to him and nodded in agreement.

"Good call. See how fast she can get over here." Brandon slipped out his phone, and started hurriedly texting. "Okay," Victoria said, taking a deep breath. "That's a little more muscle, but it's still not enough."

"How did you know where Alice was?" Holly asked Aika.

"My sister-in-arms." Aika answered. She looked around at the blank stares that met her. "A fellow member of the Fukijima Clan. Alice is being prepped for combat."

"Can your friend help?" Victoria asked.

Aika shook her head no. "My Clan has been hired to guard her. To turn on her employers is something Mizuki would not do, even if I asked."

Brandon phone beeped. "It looks like Susan is on her way. She should..."

There was a tapping sound on the window behind Victoria. The group looked to see Miss Major floating in her blue and white spandex suit, her white cape fluttering in the cold evening air. Her fists were clenched at her sides, and the look on her face spoke volumes about her level of anger. Victoria pressed a small button on the side of her intercom and the window slid open, letting Susan float in and land beside her part-time employer.

"So," Susan began in a clipped voice. "Who wants to explain how the Purge managed to kidnap my friend?"

"No time," Victoria cut her off. "Now that you're here, and by the way that was *very* fast, thank you, we can split up and..."

"It won't be enough," Brandon said. The others turned to face him. "Look, I've fought the Grey before. Even if we split our forces, we..."

"We're fighting the Grey?" Susan cut in. "Are you serious?"

Brandon nodded.

"He's right, then." Susan said as she looked around the room. "This isn't enough."

Eedee blinked in confusion, the red glow in her eyes diminishing. "Wait. The Grey aside, this should be enough. I have ratings on everyone here, and, by my calculations, we would win in a head-on fight. Miss Major, you and I once fought a giant monster in the bay. You're telling me *this*," she gestured around the room. "This isn't enough?"

"I know it's not," Brandon said, cutting her off. "You've got your rating system, but I've actually fought him. Still, we work with what we've got. There is literally no one else left that could help at this point."

Victoria was about to comment, but then bit her lip. Brandon was right; there was no one qualified to help beyond the people standing in front of her.

Victoria pointed at Brandon and Aika. "You two, your target is Allison. Holly, do you have direct confirmation on where she's being held?"

Holly nodded. "It's a mansion in Churchville. White stone, black shutters. I know how to get there, but I don't know the address."

"That's good enough," Victoria said. "Senator Carter has an estate in Churchville. I've been there for a fundraiser. Brandon, I'm texting you the address. You two, go. Get our girl."

They nodded. Brandon went to pick up Aika, and started floating towards the window. "Hey!" Holly shouted. "What about me? I'm coming, too!"

"The hell you are," Victoria spat. "The Grey is about as serious as it gets. You go, and you'll get killed. End of discussion."

"They'll die if I don't go!" Holly shouted. "You don't understand. It's not just the Grey you have to worry about. Mr. Russ...Carter is even more dangerous! Please! I can help!"

Holly begged, but it was no use. The two adults were already gone, leaving Victoria staring down a growling Totallus, an angry Miss Major, and a furious child. Holly looked to Victoria to argue, but then felt the words die in her throat. She could see inside the older woman's thoughts, and she already knew there was nothing she could say that would change her mind.

"Now," Victoria said. "You two up for kicking some ass at the Garden?"

As Eedee, Susan, and Victoria discussed their strategy for getting Alice back, no one noticed as Holly quietly slipped out of Victoria's office, and made her way to the elevators.

***

While the rest of the super community was burning down, the B Team was completely oblivious to what had transpired. Ever since they had signed on several weeks prior, they had been given an entire floor of Tanner Tower for living and training. That had been the plan, but getting them to work together had proven difficult at best for Victoria, until she threatened to evict them. That said, after their earlier disastrous outing, none of them felt too terribly much like training anymore. All of them, with the exception of Golomus, who was plugged into a socket in the corner of their penthouse common room, were lounging on their sofa and watching TV. Angela and Paul were in their sweats, and cuddled on one corner, while Sophia, now changed into a red, fluffy bathrobe, was cuddled up next to Phil. Phil was the only one still somewhat dressed, having taken off his red jacket and unbuttoned his collar.

They were fairly zoned out when the door to their common room slid open, and Holly came rushing in. In fact, the group was so exhausted, and done with their day, that they only noticed the newcomer when Holly cried out, "I need your help!"

"Well, good evening, littlest Ms. Gailsone," Phillip called out. "Here to visit the rabble?"

Holly looked to all of them before saying, in what she felt was her most professional tone, "You've got five minutes to suit up, and be ready to go."

"Ha!" Paul rolled his head back, laughing. "Excuse me?"

"What the hell is this?" Angela asked. "Is this one of Dyspell's stupid trainings again?"

"Forget it," Paul said. "We already did our training for today. Besides, little girl, Sophia and Angela are worn out. We're done."

"This isn't training," Holly said. "In five minutes, you're going on your first actual mission."

Sophia piped up. "Listen, this has been cute, but you need to reel it in and leave. We've had a day, and I for one am not in the mood for this. You need help, go get your aunt. Hell, go get anyone else."

"There is no one else," Holly said. "Right now, you are the only superhumans left in New York City that can do this."

The group looked to one another in confusion before Phillip asked, "What, exactly, are we doing?"

"You're going to help rescue my aunt Allison," Holly said. "Oh, and probably aunt Alice."

Phil sighed. "Figures. She's gone and got herself in another spot. Still, as appealing as going into the fray is, I..."

Phil froze. The entire group froze. Everyone was as still as mannequins as Holly started to shake. Sweat was pouring down her face, and blood was starting to trickle out of her nose as she concentrated.

There was a beat.

The group unfroze, each slightly dazed. They looked to each other in confusion, and then to the waiting figure of Victoria Green that stood in their doorway.

Holly nearly passed out from the strain of keeping the illusion up. If she had been thinking straight, she would have started off with the Victoria play. It was far easier to fool people continually than to rewrite group memories on the fly. In fact, it was one of the harder tricks for her to pull off, but, for Allison, Holly would ignore how difficult it was.

"Well," Phil looked to the group of villains around him that barely constituted a team. "You heard our illustrious benefactor. A simple rescue mission. How hard can it be?"

***

Alice was being led down a fluorescent-lit hallway, flanked by six Purge soldiers. As they passed through the bowels of the Garden, she saw a mix of troops, supervillains, and what appeared to be medics. All of them stopped what they were doing as she walked by, and each of them, no matter how big or intimidating, took the time to stare in silence as she marched by.

Alice had to admit, under any other circumstance, this would have been pretty damn cool.

One of the Purge soldiers, an older guard to her left, handed her a water bottle. Alice eyed him as they walked. "Thanks," she said as she accepted the gift.

The soldier nodded in return. "Things were better under you, Ma'am," he said, his eyes still straight ahead. "You give the word, and we'll extract you."

Alice shook her head. "You do, and my niece dies. What's your name, soldier?"

"Fredrickson, Ma'am. I served in the 103 out of Houston."

Alice smiled. "God, you guys were good. One of the best groups I ever had the privilege of serving with."

They were approaching a dark tunnel. In front of them, Mizuki rounded a corner, and held up her hand. "You are to wait here," she said.

"For what?" Alice asked.

Mizuki paused, as if not sure how to answer. "Your...entrance music."

Alice blinked. "I have entrance music?"

"Quiet," Mizuki snapped. "They are getting ready to announce you."

"They're going to kill you out there," Fredrickson whispered. "Here," Alice felt something firm press into the palm of her hand. It felt like the hilt of a knife. "It's not much, but it will help. Your first opponent is a bruiser. Some clown in a mech suit."

"Thank you, Fredrickson." Alice whispered back. "And I hope your son is doing okay."

Fredrickson's eyes went wide. His seven-year-old son had been diagnosed with leukemia roughly six months before the battle of Pittsburg. At the time, he had tried to hide what was going on in his personal life, but, roughly two weeks later, he found himself discharged from the Purge for what his file listed as 'Personal Reasons.' Upon contacting his ex-wife, he found that his son had been submitted to a treatment center in Minnesota by parties unknown. Frederickson had never asked who his benefactor was, but the mysterious stranger had paid for all treatments and rehabilitation therapy. Afterwards, Fredrickson discovered the money had been tied to a trust in his son's name.

Fredrickson didn't comment. In fact, he wasn't sure if he could speak around his sudden swell of emotion. Instead, he gave a stiff nod, and let out a short, "Ma'am." A swell of music started to fill the arena that lay just beyond the black tunnel.

Alice smirked. The arena was bellowing with a steady, thunderous drumbeat. It took her a few seconds to recognize it as Mars, by Holst. "Nice," she mumbled as she rolled her neck, giving her arms a quick flex before heading into the tunnel, and out into the blinding lights of Madison Square Garden.

Chapter Twenty

The Queen of Pain

In the heyday of the Purge, the Garden had been the ultimate go-to for their big ticket shows. New York was an ideal location for global events, and there were few facilities that offered better seating and presentation value than the Garden. When the Purge invented the Broadcast, it was the ideal location for their death matches. Beyond that, Alice had found herself here more times than she could count. After all, it had been here that Alice had wound up paralyzing a young scientist named Steve during a sensational heist several years prior. Just another in a series of careless actions that had come back to haunt her.

And now here she was, walking down the runway towards the large ring that lay bathed in spotlights in the center of the arena. She was here because of her carelessness, and yet another of her mistakes, albeit one she couldn't even remember making. She knew this Anna, whoever she was, was her fault. Alice didn't remember making a clone, but to be honest, that didn't surprise her. After all, it could have been Prometheus, or even Tolarius. In fact, as Alice walked down the white runway, bathed in hot lights and surrounded by thunderous applause, she made a silent vow to pay a visit to the old man at his Tucson home to thank him personally.

In the center of the arena stood a man with slicked back, black hair and a sharp tuxedo. He was holding a chrome mic attached to a cord that led into the ceiling, and gesturing in Alice's direction as the music overhead continued to blare. Alice recognized him from her days with the Purge. He was known in the underground circuit as the Announcer. Alice knew him as Carl from back in the day, which didn't have quite the same ring to it. Honestly, of all the criminals that had refused signing on to the Open Hand Act to do something mainstream, this one had surprised Alice the most. The man had a voice that could melt glaciers.

"Ladies and gentlemen!" Announcer Carl was using what Alice thought of as a radio voice. "Making her way to the Ring of Death is our special guest contestant for this evening's Broadcast! At 5'1" and weighing a hefty 135 pounds..."

'If I survive, he dies first,' Alice thought to herself.

"...The Queen of Pain, the Most Dangerous Woman in the World, DYSPELL!"

The arena nearly exploded with cheers. Alice could feel the energy in the room. It was coursing through her, and flowing over everything. Even though she understood the inevitable outcome of the evening, she couldn't help but feel a rush of excitement.

The ring was raised and square, but lacked any turnbuckles or ropes. It was a wide-open floor, roughly twice the size of a boxing ring. Alice did a quick heft of herself up into the ring, and stood for a moment, looking around at the sold-out house. She knew that to get this many people in the Garden, roughly half the criminal leaders on the planet had to be in attendance.

Announcer-Carl quickly scurried out of the ring as Alice approached the center. Her attention snapped towards the entrance she had just come through, as the announcer resumed his introductions. "And for our first competitor, making his way to the ring, weighing in at over eight thousand pounds, is one of the most powerful mercenaries in the world! The monster of the prehistoric world! The scourge of the Cretaceous age! Please welcome, DINOGORE!"

Alice let out a small sigh as Dinogore, now sporting a newly-redesigned Purge biohazard suit, emerged to a swelling roar of applause. He gave a flex, and a primal scream for good measure, before sauntering towards the ring, his eyes locked firmly on Dyspell.

"Remember, ladies and gentlemen, that betting ends the moment the bell rings, so please enter your wagers now. For those watching at home, remember to download our app for Bitcoin transfers." A picture of a smartphone rolled across the titan-tron above the ring as the crowd continued to cheer.

Dinogore stepped into the ring without using his hands. He towered over Alice, standing an easy eight feet tall in his armor. He glanced down at Alice and gave a long, leering grin as he said, "Well, well, well. If it ain't the little lady who humiliated me." He cracked his gigantic, orange, robotic knuckles. "I am going to enjoy watching you die, Dyspell. You've had this coming, and tonight, you don't have those stupid little powers of yours to help you."

Alice crossed her arms, and studied Diongore for a moment. "Is that a Mark IX deep dive suit?"

Dinogore flexed, grinning. "Hell, yes. Three times as durable as the last. Made to withstand environmental pressures at seven miles down. You could literally drop an atomic bomb on me, and I wouldn't feel a thing. So, even if you did have your powers, which you don't, I think my odds would be pretty good."

"LLLLLLLLLLLLLET'S GET READY TO RUMMMBBBBLLLLLLLLLLLE!" the Announcer screamed.

Alice rubbed her chin, as Dinogore licked his lips in anticipation. "God, I've waited for this," he said through his teeth.

The bell rang.

In a flash, Alice dove between Dinogore's legs, smacking a spot above his left thigh as she did so. Dinogore blinked as Alice swung around, and tapped another spot just beneath his right butt cheek. A small panel then slid open, containing a giant, red lever. Alice grabbed it, and yanked.

There was a loud clang, followed by a hiss. Dinogore's armor split down the middle, and fell unceremoniously to the floor. A middle-aged, balding man with a gut fell out. He was dressed in a sleeveless undershirt and light blue boxers, looking completely bewildered.

Alice couldn't help herself – she burst out laughing, leaning against the ropes to keep from falling over. Slowly regaining her composure, Alice tapped him on the shoulder to get his attention. Dinogore turned around to see Alice pointing at the armor. "These suits come with an emergency release, you know, in case divers get stuck in faulty equipment. See? It pops right off."

"Huh," Dinogore said, staring in disbelief.

Alice reeled back, and clocked Dingore with a haymaker. The now-unarmored Dinogore went flying out of the ring, taking out three Purge soldiers.

"Safety first!" Alice called after him.

The crowd erupted. Alice pumped her fist in the air, and let out a victory cry. She was 100% adrenaline at this point, and it felt fantastic. It was the most alive she had felt in years, and she was relishing it. Villainy did have its benefits.

"The winner, DYSPELL!" The surprised Announcer-Carl called out. Several Purge guards entered the ring to move the armor out of the way. Alice turned her attention back towards the path she had walked, and, sniffing, wiped her nose.

"Okay, so who's next?" she asked, mostly to herself.

***

After a quick change at the Tower, Aika and Brandon descended on the white colonial mansion owned by Senator Carter. For being the current headquarters of a supervillain and United States Senator, the house seemed strangely unguarded. Aika was clinging to Brandon's neck, but her focus was on the surrounding grounds of the house. She nodded towards the back entrance. "Over there," she said. Brandon complied, and set down in the backyard garden.

Brandon was in his Red Guard uniform, while Aika had traded her workout gear for a more field-ready black nylon stealth suit. Aika drew her katana, and held it with one hand against her back as she crept silently through the garden towards the back doors. Behind her, Brandon cautiously followed. While Brandon was more powerful, they both knew Aika was superior at infiltration. Aika hesitantly tried the door, and found it to be unlocked. The door swung easy, revealing a well-lit lounge.

"This is not good," Aika mumbled to herself. "They know we are coming. They do not seem to care."

Brandon and Aika looked to each other, and gave a nervous, knowing nod.

The lounge was well-furnished, showing a tendency towards cherry wood. Most of the furniture looked like it was at least 100 years old, but all of it was well-kept. The room reeked with an overpowering combination of Pledge and ammonia.

Aika looked around, and gestured towards a hall that looked like it led to a main entranceway. Around the corner from this was a large, white staircase. Cautiously, Aika made her way up, flanked by the somewhat nervous, superpowered fighter.

At the top of the stairs was a long hall running parallel to the stairway. In the center was a set of open double doors. Beyond was what looked like a library that had been converted into an office. It was a huge room, complete with an ornately-carved desk towards the back. Sitting behind it, drinking something clear, bubbly, and extremely expensive from a champagne flute, was Senator Carter. In a chair beside him, tied, gagged, and unconscious, was Allison.

"Well, good evening, everyone," Carter said, as he raised his glass. He gave a wide smile to the warriors. "Welcome to my…"

That was as far as he got before Brandon erupted in red flames and flew across the room towards Carter. Brandon barely got the words, *"LET HER GO!"* out before he slammed into some unseen force which propelled him backwards and into a bookshelf. Brandon crashed to the ground, gasping and clutching at his chest as Carter let out a -ttt- sound and shook his head.

"How rude," Carter said. "As I was saying before you so rudely interrupted, welcome to my home. Granted, you just committed a break-in, but still, I always try to welcome my guests. Would you like a drink?" Carter held up his glass. "I'm drinking ginger ale, but I won't judge. I know, I know, it sounds childish, but I like to remain sober when killing people."

There was a shift in the room. The temperature dropped. Both Aika and Brandon felt the air pressure suddenly change as a blurry, grey figure in a trench coat appeared at the Senator's side.

"You've met the Grey," Carter said with an unconcerned wave. He patted the Grey on the shoulder and smiled. "Nice save there, by the way. I thought he was going to put a fist through me." Both fighters instantly tensed. Aika raised her sword, while Brandon, now on his feet, powered up. He was glowing red with fiery energy crackling across his body.

"Give us the woman, and we will part ways without further bloodshed," Aika said in a level tone. Carter chuckled, and took a sip from his flute.

"No can do, my dear. This little lady is my insurance policy tonight." Carter picked up a remote control from his desk, and pointed it at a flat screen that was resting above a stone fireplace along the side wall. All of them turned to see Alice tearing through what looked like a gang of armored henchmen as an audience roared.

"And you are telling us this, why?" Aika asked.

"Because," Carter nodded to the Grey. "I already know how this is going to go. I know how you die, Miss Fukijima. You've walked into a situation you can't win, and I am going to enjoy watching it. In fact, my security system is going to record this as an online extra for those that pre-ordered the Gailsone execution tonight." He grinned maniacally. "It's *great* for business."

Brandon raised his glowing, red-hot hand towards Carter, and let loose a burst of solar energy. Aika felt a rush of heat, bracing herself as the blast stopped just a few feet from Carter. The Grey was suddenly standing between them, and, after a forceful rush of air, the blast was dissipated.

"Neat trick," Brandon murmured as Aika charged, her sword at the ready. She swung for the Grey's head, but, the moment the blade would have connected, he vanished.

The Grey reappeared directly behind her. Like lightning, Aika pivoted, and tried to follow through with the strike. Again, the Grey vanished before the blade could make contact. It was a first for one of the world's most deadly assassins. Aika didn't let up, continuing to strike with a fury. No matter what she did, not a single blow hit its mark.

Frustrated, Aika sheathed her katana, and drew a set of shorter, wakizashi blades from scabbards strapped to her side. With one in each hand, Aika pressed the attack, swinging violently while Brandon charged Carter. He slammed into the space where Carter had been standing, but the senator was no longer there.

"What?" Brandon asked, confused. He tried to focus on Carter, but it was difficult. To Brandon, it was as if Carter was phasing in and out of sight. It was like trying to see something at the edge of your vision.

"I know, right?" Carter asked with a smile. "Focusing on me is not the easiest thing, trust me. Not the handiest power for a public figure. Still, it's nice for times like this."

Brandon fired another blast, and followed up with a haymaker. Again, Carter was gone. It was like there were three of the senator, and Brandon couldn't focus on any of them. He knew that if he expanded his powers, and fried the office, he would connect with Carter, but then he would end up killing Allison and Aika.

Brandon shook his head. The constant attempt to focus on Carter was giving him a headache. His vision was cloudy, his head hurt, there was a high-pitched whistle...

Aika was continuing her attack at full speed, to no avail. It was as if she were fighting a shadow – a shadow that could kill.

"I think," Carter called out across the room, "that this has gone on long enough, don't you?" Aika didn't have time to wonder who Carter was talking to. In the same instant, she felt a crunch, and recognized the feel of several ribs breaking. It felt as though a freight train had slammed into her, and she found herself on the ground. She tried to draw breath, emitting a strangled gasp of pain as the broken bones threatened to puncture her right lung.

A moment later, Brandon screamed as his legs buckled at an unnatural angle. Aika watched in horror as the Red Guard, one of the strongest fighters on the planet, bent into a broken mess in front of her. She heard no less than a dozen cracks, barely distinguishable, in the space of a second. Just like that, Brandon was down.

Aika glanced up to see the Grey patiently standing over her, his face nothing more than a grey blur. Beside him was the completely indistinct form of Senator Carter.

"You really didn't have a chance tonight," Carter said as he sighed, and reached for the glass on his desk. "Seriously, I'm not some panicking buffoon like Stengles was. I've been two steps ahead of you, and your ilk, this entire time. This," he gestured to Aika and Brandon, "the explosion on the Hudson, all of it. All of this was by design, and you fell for it so easily it *hurt*."

"You are lying," Aika growled out, panting.

Carter shrugged. "True, I was counting on bringing Holly back, but I work well on the fly. Getting the traitorous General Gailsone was just icing on the cake. It all ends the same way. The Collective Good is dismantled, the Purge gets their resurgence, and I emerge on top."

"You are Purge?" Aika asked. Carter nearly choked on his drink as he started laughing.

"Oh, please," he said as he wiped his mouth with the back of his sleeve. "Just because dad was doesn't mean I am, but it does help to open some doors for me, I won't lie. No, the Purge is nothing more than my partner in getting me on the road to the White House."

Carter gestured to his television. "The world has no time for public, superpowered idiots. You're all menaces as far as the general public is concerned, and they're not wrong. You're a plague, eating away at our comfort zones, making the world feel insecure. Do you know what happens when world leaders, generals, despots, and everyone else starts to feel insecure? Regardless of the reason, it all comes down to the same thing. They panic, they do something drastic, and the world gets plunged into madness."

Carter drifted back towards his desk. Beside it was a beautiful, yellowed globe that he lazily spun with a flick of his wrist. "Granted, this is bound to happen now and then, but what if you knew *how* it would happen? What if you could make it happen in a way that would be of benefit to you? There was no avoiding all of this, but I've made sure that when things start, I'll come out as the most powerful man in the world. Dad would be proud. You and your kind will be dead, but..."

"You are one, too." Aika said in a shaky voice. "You speak as though you were separate, but you are telling people to hate and fear the same thing you are."

Carter shook his head. "No, Miss Fukijima. You all flaunt your powers for the world to fear. Those of us who pay attention keep things to ourselves, and that is why I will win. That is why I am winning tonight, and it is one of the many reasons that you are about to die."

Aika was trying to get to her feet, but her body wasn't cooperating. As soon as she got to her knees, something not unlike a sledgehammer hit her in the stomach, and she was down again.

"Thank you for visiting," Carter said with a wave. "Please know that if nothing else, your deaths will help to increase my profits by at least 20% for my next fight."

Aika felt helpless frustration swelling inside of her. Not 20 feet away, Allison lay tied and unconscious. She had failed. She had let down her retainer and her best friend, and as these thoughts raced through her head, she looked up to see the Grey reaching for her face.

Chapter Twenty-One

You Deserve the Truth

Alice was panting and bruised, but overall, she was doing far better than she had thought she would. After Dinogore, a group of three green, armored fighters came out. Their armor had a bug motif to it, and each fought with small, bladed weapons. Fortunately, they didn't seem to be as skilled as their appearance suggested. It also helped that Alice had taken her knife out and slammed it through the face plate of their leader in the first five seconds of the fight. After that, the other two went down pretty quick. Still, one of them had landed a good hit to her left arm, which she was now favoring.

"So," Alice called out to the Announcer, "How many fighters do you have lined up tonight, Burt?"

Announcer Carl laughed, and spoke into his microphone. "Get ready, ladies and gentlemen. Tonight, we have a special treat for all of you. We know you tuned in to see the death of Dyspell, and we don't plan on disappointing you. We scoured the world looking for someone who was equal to the task of standing with the Most Dangerous Woman in the World, and we finally found him!" The Announcer gestured to the stage entrance Alice had come through. She half-expected to see a Totallus, or possibly some iron-covered monster.

As Alice turned to see who her next opponent would be, the world around her seemed to fade away.

Standing at the ring entrance was Blackthorne. He was in full armor, and he was walking slowly towards the ring, ignoring everything around him. Even under the lights of the arena, he cut a menacing form in his black and yellow attire. His cape, a ratty, unkempt mass of cloth designed to conceal him in the shadows of the alleyways of New York, flowed and billowed as he approached the stunned Alice.

He climbed into the ring, and turned to face Alice. The lenses of his face mask were two white, angry slits, but Alice felt like they weren't really seeing her. In fact, everything about his body language seemed off.

"Alan?" Alice asked quietly. She was answered by Blackthorne charging her, his hands each sporting a spiked pair of brass knuckles. Alice quickly deflected his attacks, and went on the defensive, using her size and speed as best she could.

Blackthorne was using a form of Krav Maga, but Alice noted that he was slipping into a mix of kempo and jujitsu. He was going mainly for her upper torso and head, and, even though Alice had to work to avoid getting in his way, she quickly picked up on the fact that he wasn't moving as fast as he should have been. In fact, after several movements, she realized he was moving in a pattern.

It was almost like fighting a robot, or at the very least, a video game with limited AI. She was good enough to see how sloppy she was, but it didn't seem to be making a difference. Blackthorne wasn't going for the obvious wound on her arm, and he wasn't taking advantage of her openings. If he had, Alice realized she would have been crippled by now.

As Alice fought, she suddenly realized that she had seen something like this before. It had been years ago in a training session, and, while it hadn't stood out to her then, it was definitely coming back to her now. His movements didn't just feel routine - they felt programmed.

"Oh, no," Alice said to herself. She dodged a jab, and swept Alan's leg, sending him crashing to the floor. As he got to his feet, Alice rolled over his back and yanked his mask back, revealing a small, silver circle embedded at the base of his skull. The skin around it was a dark green, and Alice could see his veins through his skin, looking like sluggish purple snakes spreading out in an asymmetrical pattern from the disc.

Blackthorne yanked away and swung around, catching Alice in the stomach. Alice cried out and tried her best to roll with the blow, but Alan managed to bury the spikes of his knuckles into the side of her suit. While it didn't break the material, it was enough to leave Alice smarting.

Alice resumed blocking the pattern of hits, and considered her options. She had seen this before, and back then, it had never ended well. The controller on Alan's neck was enough to input a series of remote commands, but not enough to completely black out all sensory signals. Alice knew that even though Alan wasn't the one attacking her, he knew exactly what was going on.

"Alan," Alice said as he did a sweeping kick just above her head. She dropped, and opted to push him away instead of land a good hit to his solar plexus. Alice remembered how durable Alan's armor was, and didn't like her odds at getting a broken wrist. "Alan, I know you can hear me."

Alan let loose with a flurry of punches towards Alice's head. Alice blocked, swept her foot back for more room, blocked again, ducked, and side-stepped as Alan kept moving forward for a moment before turning to follow her.

"I know you can't stop this," Alice said, panting. While she was wearing down quickly, Alan showed no signs of stopping. Alice knew the controller was probably going to push him past the point of exhaustion. She had seen similar devices force men with torn tendons and broken bones to stand and fight as though there was nothing wrong. Looking at him, Alice could tell that Alan's clothing seemed to be a little too loose, as though he had lost a considerable amount of weight. She wondered how long he had been under control, and when he had last eaten. "Alan, I can't save you," she said, voice cracking. "There's no good way to stop what's going on with you. *This is going to kill you.*"

The look in his eyes changed into a haunting mix of horror, sorrow and pain. While the slits in his mask looked white, if you got close enough you could make out the pupils. Alice was close enough that she could see everything. While Alan might not have had control over his body, in that one moment she knew that he was aware of everything.

"Oh God," she whispered. "You know. Alan, I..."

She ducked another punch and did a swift leg sweep, dropping him to the mat. She scrambled over him, pinning him in a submission hold. Controlled or not, his strength was still greater than hers. She knew it was a matter of minutes before he overpowered her.

"This wasn't how it was supposed to be," Alice said, just loudly enough for him to hear. "You were supposed to settle down with Vic, and you two were gonna be shitty parents, and I was going to be a godmother and spoil the crap out of your kid. Holly was supposed to babysit so you two could go to couple's therapy or get hammered or whatever you two do. Dammit, Alan..."

Alice felt him starting to break the hold she had on him, so she quickly readjusted her legs and yanked hard on his arm, causing him to falter.

"Dammit, this isn't how you're supposed to go! I don't want to kill you." She was crying now. "You owed me a drink, remember? Maybe some sexy flirting? 'You ask and I'll tell you whatever you want to know'. You said that, Alan. Dammit, you promised me one more drink. Please."

Alan bit down on Alice's leg, causing her to release him. They both got to their feet, stepping back. She met Alan's dark eyes.

"Please," Alice whispered. "Please, Alan. I don't want to kill you. I..."

Alice could see it in his eyes. Alan had heard everything, and there was absolutely nothing he could do. Alice thought she saw tears running from under his mask and down his face, but it could have just as easily been sweat. She couldn't tell.

Alice dodged a swipe at her head. "I'm sorry," she said as she let him charge her. She used his momentum to roll him over her shoulder and then swung around, catching him in a sloppy arm bar. As Alan tried to free himself, Alice took the knife she had been given and jammed it between the controller and Alan's neck.

Alan screamed as the controller let out a loud pop and sparked briefly. The smell of ozone wafted in the ring as Alan went limp and collapsed.

"AND BLACKTHORNE IS DOWN! LADIES AND GENTLEMEN, BLACKTORNE IS DOWN!" Burt was going nuts on the microphone as Alice dropped to Alan's side and cradled his head. Carefully, she rolled back his mask from his nose so he could breathe. She was careful to keep the top of his face covered, but he reached up and ripped the mask off completely.

Alice gasped. Alan looked more like a skeleton with skin draped over it. He was beyond gaunt, deathly pale, and his skin was covered in dark purple veins. He looked at Alice and took her hand with more strength than a man in his condition had any right to possess.

"Alice," Alan said in a hoarse whisper. "I'm sorry."

"Shut up," Alice said. Her words were catching in her throat. "You're too weak to talk. Save your strength and I'll get you out of here. Promise."

Alan shook his head. "I'm sorry I never trusted you," Alan croaked. "I'm sorry I didn't believe in you."

Alice let out what felt like a sob mixed with a laugh. "You were one of the only people who did. It's why I..."

Alan flashed a thin smile, and Alice felt him give her hand a weak squeeze. "If things had been different..."

Alice gently stroked his forehead as Purge soldiers started to enter the ring. Alice was oblivious to them until one touched her shoulder, causing her to snap her head towards him with a death glare. Standing there was Fredrickson, and around him, a small group of younger Purge shock troops.

"We need to move him, Ma'am," Fredrickson said in a low voice.

"Two minutes," Alice said. The tone of her voice said this wasn't open to debate.

Fredrickson saw the look on her face and nodded. He looked to the others and waved them back. "Sir?" One of the younger Purge soldiers kept looking from Fredrickson to Alice and back again. "We're still on camera. We should..."

Fredrickson looked the soldier in the eye and shook his head. "Give her two minutes," he said. While confused, the younger soldier gulped and buckled to his superior officer.

"Alice," Alan said. His voice sounded desperate. Instantly, her attention was back on him. "You deserve the truth."

Alice bit her lip, and held his hand tightly. She was worried he was about to further admit his feelings for her or something else sappy, but instead, he whispered, "Look for Project Grail. The password is your mother's maiden name."

Alice blinked, confused. "What are you talking about? Alan? Why her?"

"Tell Victoria I love her so much," Alan said as his eyes became unfocused. "*So* much. Tell her she's wrong. She'll be a good mom. She'll be great. I know she will. I'm so sorry. Alice?"

"Yes?"

Alan struggled to get closer to her and whispered, "I'm glad it was you. I… I thought I would die alone."

Alice stroked a strand of hair away from his eyes. She wanted to tell him he was wrong, that he was going to be fine. Instead, she kissed his forehead and whispered. "It's okay."

"Please take care of them for me," he wheezed.

"I promise."

There was a shudder, and for a moment, Alice felt him grip her hand tightly. Then, just as casually as a breeze stops blowing, she felt him go completely limp in her arms. His eyes stayed focused on something she couldn't see, and his grip on her hand loosened.

Alice felt tears streaming down her cheeks. She did her best not to start sobbing as she covered Alan's face with her hand, closing his eyes.

"Ma'am?" Fredrickson asked. "Please. I promise we'll tend him, but we need to take him now."

Alice nodded, letting her former soldier take her former employer from her arms. Carefully, Fredrickson carried the lifeless body of Alan Tanner, the legendary Blackthorne, out of the arena.

Alice heard Burt calling out the next competitor, but she wasn't focused on him. She stayed on her knees, holding the small, silver controller in her fingers and wondered how things had become so messed up.

Chapter Twenty-Two

"I have been expecting you."

Susan and Eedee were tearing through the night sky towards Madison Square Garden. It was a short trip for the two of them, but, as they approached, they realized that getting inside might prove more treacherous than originally planned. There, floating above the Garden and illuminated by the spotlights that were slicing through the night sky, was Totallus.

He was floating, with his arms crossed and a small smile on his face. His skin reflected a mix of brown and silver in the lights that shone from below as he calmly waited for their approach.

Eedee came to a sudden stop, her fists clenched at her sides as Susan came up beside her. Susan noticed Eedee tense, and quickly recognized the Totallus for what he was. "I wasn't expecting this," Susan said as she glanced from Eedee to Totallus.

"Sister," Totallus said in an echoing, hollow voice. The sound felt like it was coming from a loud speaker, and Susan swore that she could feel it rolling over her skin. "I have been expecting you."

"You," Eedee growled. "How *dare* you show your face after what you did!"

Totallus seemed completely nonplussed by the rage coming from Eedee. Instead, he turned his attention to Susan. "You are Miss Major. You are considered one of the strongest humans on the planet. That said," Totallus's smile grew. "You will not survive this fight. You are not capable of defeating me. I would advise that you leave."

Susan cocked an eyebrow. "That's new. I've never had a Totallus stop to give me the odds before."

"He's not a normal Totallus," Eedee growled. Susan's eyes widened as Eedee yelled, "He's the asshole model!"

Susan wasn't sure what surprised her more, the fact that Eedee had just sworn for the first time in front of her, or that Eedee had just taken off at near supersonic speeds to collide with Totallus head-on. The shockwave from the two of them colliding was deafening, and the force of it sent Susan reeling. She quickly recovered to see the two androids exchanging a series of kicks and punches that were nearly too fast for her eyes to see.

Quickly, Susan rocketed forward to help. She slammed into Totallus as hard as she could, going for his head. In her own experience, most older Totallus units kept their ranged attacks limited to their eyes, so her goal was to take those out first.

Eedee and Susan were pushing the killer android back when his arms began to crackle and glow with bright red energy. Eedee screamed, "Get out of the way!" Susan barely had time to respond as Eedee grabbed her and shoved her through the air. A heartbeat later, Totallus let loose with an energy blast that cut across the Manhattan skyline. Susan cringed as the blast hit a nearby office building, causing the entire structure to shudder.

Eedee rushed forward and locked hands with Totallus, forcing him to focus on her. Susan moved to help, but Eedee screamed out, "GET ALICE!"

"But you can't..." Susan said before Eedee headbutted Totallus. She then followed it up with a gut punch that swept into a midair roundhouse kick. The force of it sent the android flying through the night sky.

"I can hold him! Now go save my mom!" Eedee called out. Susan paused for a moment, but then nodded in agreement as she flew off toward the Garden. She had been in situations like this before, but in her experience, they usually didn't end well. Behind her, Susan could hear the sounds of combat. She was about to slam through the roof when all three flyers stopped as a haunting purple glow erupted from the arena below.

"Oh, my God," Susan whispered as she watched the entirety of Madison Square Garden become engulfed in a blinding, purple orb of light. There was a crumbling sound, and all three of them could hear what sounded like thousands of screaming voices that were abruptly cut off.

Totallus drifted away from Eedee as he watched the purple glow begin to fade. With a quick glance towards Eedee, he shot off towards the west. Eedee suddenly snapped out of it as the sonic boom from Totallus's leaving hit her. She looked to where her opponent had been, and frowned. While she wanted to chase him down, what was happening below was her primary concern.

Eedee floated down to Susan, her eyes glued to the smoldering wreckage beneath them. "What happened?" Eedee asked in a worried tone. She hugged herself nervously. "Is mom okay?" She started to float down towards the glowing orb of purple light that was now where the stadium had been, but Susan grabbed her arm, stopping her mid-flight.

"Don't," Susan said. Eedee looked at her with confusion, but Susan held her firmly and shook her head. "I've seen this before."

"This?" Eedee asked, pointing towards the glowing orb.

"Something like it," Susan said. She felt a cold shudder run through her body as the orb started to recede.

'Oh Alice,' she thought to herself. *'What in God's name did you do now?'*

***

Aika lay prone, expecting her death to finally come at the hands of the Grey. Everything she had ever heard about this mysterious superhuman had proven true. Now here she was, possibly the most dangerous assassin on the planet, about to be slaughtered as an afterthought. She had hoped her death would hold more honor. The Grey reached for her, then paused. In fact, everyone that was still conscious paused at the sound of a high-pitched whistle. It had started while they were fighting, but she hadn't paid it much attention at the time. Now, it was growing louder, and as it did, Carter's eyes grew wide with realization.

"Grey! We..."

Then the ceiling exploded.

Debris went flying everywhere as a deafening crash sent everyone flying. The object that had slammed through the roof continued through the floor, slamming into the ground floor and then through that into the basement. It landed with a crash that shook the foundation of the house, and for a moment, Aika was sure the entire structure would collapse.

A moment later, she heard thunderous booms as something rhythmically stormed through the shuddering home. She heard it make its way up the stairs, which creaked, groaned, and shattered under an immense weight. Then the doors to Carter's office were smashed inward by the massive stone fist of Fudo. He was cracked and covered in dust, plaster, and chunks of house. He looked more like some unbound juggernaut than the calm, passive golem that Aika had walked past daily at *Rare Gems*. This was more of a monster than she had ever seen, and for a moment, she was filled with equal parts terror and gratitude.

A red line appeared in the air next to Fudo. It stretched downward and then bent, and out came The Bleed, followed by Chalice, Angela (now sporting her black and yellow Dynamo outfit), Halifax, and finally Holly. Halifax was hovering with her fists clenched, and Angela was crackling with electricity.

"What …" was all Carter could get out before he was hit by a bolt of electricity. He went flying back into a bookshelf, bouncing off of it before crashing to the ground. A small pile of books, jarred loose by his impact, fell on top of him.

Chalice patted Angela on the shoulder and smiled. "Nice job, babe."

Halifax, who had been hovering just behind Angela, looked at Fudo and then back to Phillip. "How far up did you open the portal for the golem?"

Phillip shrugged. "Oh, about a mile or so."

Halifax patted Phil on the back. "Nice job, babe," she said jokingly.

The Grey looked at the new group, but before anyone could do anything, Holly stepped forward. He looked at her with his head cocked, trying to determine if the preteen was even a threat. Suddenly, he grabbed his head in both hands and reared back.

They all heard the scream, but none of them could tell when it started. It sounded like a chorus of voices all speaking just out of sync with each other. Then, just as suddenly as it had started, it stopped. The group looked around, but The Grey was gone.

"Mom!" Holly cried out as she ran across the room. She knelt next to Allison who had finally been awoken by the sounds of chaos around her. Chalice set to healing Brandon, while Angela and Phillip helped Aika to her feet. Everyone winced at the sound of bones being snapped and reset as Chalice did his work.

Holly finished untying Allison, who instantly enveloped her in a hug. "What are you doing?" Allison asked frantically. She pulled back and checked Holly for any injuries. "What in God's name are you even doing?" She then pulled her back into a tight hug.

The others in the room blinked and looked around. "What is she doing here?" Chalice asked. "And where's Ms. Green?" All of them stared at Holly, who blushed from embarrassment and shrugged. Before anyone could say anything, the pile of books shifted and up sat Senator Carter.

"You!" he hissed at Holly. "You did this!" He struggled to his feet, his shirt scorched and ripped, his once-neat hair now a tangled, sooty mess. After the rooftop incident with Alice, Angela had been fairly drained. Otherwise it was doubtful that Carter would have even been alive. He snarled at Holly and focused with all of his might. "You think you can just waltz in here and take me down? You stupid little brat. I'm in charge, not you!"

Everyone in the room suddenly felt violently ill. All of them dropped to their knees, clutching their stomachs and crying out in pain. Only Holly stood, her fists clenched and her attention squarely on Carter.

"No, you're not." Holly growled out the words. Her entire frame was shaking, and as the two of them stared each other down, the others in the room could feel the electricity between them. It felt like someone was expanding a bubble in the atmosphere of the room around them, pushing everything else away.

Behind Carter, the bookshelf cracked and splintered as it bowed backwards into the wall. Behind Holly, what was left of the beautiful cherry desk was shoved back into the shattered remains of Carter's bay window.

Holly was sporting a massive nosebleed as she started to scream. Not out of pain; she was far past that. She was screaming in rage as she pushed everything she had towards Carter. "I'm not yours anymore!" She screamed. "You can't hurt me anymore! YOU'LL NEVER HURT ANYONE EVER AGAIN!"

Cater dropped to one knee. He put a hand out in front of him as if trying to push back some invisible force, but he was shaking too violently to do anything effective.

"How are you doing this?" he choked out. "You're not this strong!"

Holly responded by pushing even harder with her mind. Carter dug in and tried to push back, but he could feel the immense pressure against his skull building. His vision was going watery, but he could still move. He did his best to regroup and push back, but then abruptly stopped.

He looked down to see the end of a katana sticking out of his chest. A pool of red was forming in the dirty remains of his shirt. He sputtered, a line of spit going down his lips as he tried to turn his head. Standing behind him was Allison.

"No one touches my daughter," she said.

Before anyone could respond, Allison slid the sword out and, with rage-fulled strength, chopped Senator George Harding Carter's head off with one stroke. The head spun through the air, landing with a thud in a pile of rubble. The sword was swung with so much force that it wound up embedded in a plaster pillar that had stood between the shelves.

Aika limped over to Allison, patted her on the shoulder, and then yanked her sword out of the plaster and shook it off. Internally, she was both impressed at the force of the swing and angry about what she would have to do to get it sharp again. Allison looked to Holly and smiled. "Now we're even, kiddo."

Allison was nearly knocked off her feet by Holly, who had collided with her and then gripped her in a fierce bear hug. Allison let out a surprised laugh, and hugged her back.

"Hey, I'm fine, hon." Allison said as she reassuringly stroked Holly's hair.

Holly was sobbing into Allison's shirt. She was trying to talk through her tears, but it was proving incredibly hard. "I thought he was going to kill you!"

Allison hugged her charge tighter and shook her head. "He probably should have, but nope. I'm good." Allison gently pushed Holly back and dropped to one knee, looking her in the eye. "You did good, Holly."

Allison's attention then turned to Brandon, who had collapsed from dizziness. While Chalice had healed him physically, the pain of re-binding bone and tissue had taken its toll. Allison went to his side and helped him to his feet, but he had to lean into her to stand. "What the hell happened to you?" she asked as she shifted her weight to support him.

"I came to rescue you,' he croaked.

'Yeah, I'll keep him,' Allison thought with a smile.

As the group heard the far-off sounds of police and emergency sirens filling the air, they were interrupted by Aika. "Where is The Grey?" They each looked to one another, but no one had seen where he had gone.

Allison was the first to speak up. "I know where he's gone."

Brandon coughed and tried to power up. "Where?"

Allison shook her head no. "Don't even think about it. You're going back with Phil and the others and you're taking Holly with you. Understand?"

Brandon was about to argue, but Holly beat him to it. She violently shook her head no. "I just got you back!" she cried. "I'm not losing you! He'll kill you!"

Allison took Holly by the shoulders and said, "You're staying with Brandon and the others, understand?" Holly tried to argue, but Allison hugged her close. "Holly, trust me. I can do this, okay?"

"I can't lose you," Holly whispered.

Allison held her tight and nodded. "And you're not going to," she said. She kissed Holly on the forehead and then gently steered her to Brandon, who took the girl by the hand. Allison then looked to Aika, but before she could say anything, she was tossed her Berretta.

"Thanks," Allison said as Aika nodded. She then looked to Halifax. "Hey. I saw what happened earlier. Are you good for a flight?"

Sophia stiffened a bit. Phil moved beside her and cleared his throat. "Miss Gailsone, if you need transport…"

Allison shook her head. "No thanks. I need him to see me coming. I need him not surprised. That means you." She pointed to Sophia. "Are you strong enough to play taxi for me?"

"I'll do it," Brandon said. Allison put her hand on his chest and gently pushed him away.

"You can't be there," she said. "Please."

"No," Brandon said in what he hoped sounded like a strong voice. "Let's be honest; I'm the only person here who would reasonably stand a chance against the Grey. I should be the one to go."

Allison shook her head. "It is so damn sweet that you're being like this after what just happened to you, but hon? Shut up. Seriously. I need you, all of you," she looked around the room, pausing to level a glare at Aika, "to trust me. Please."

Aika nodded and moved to stand beside Brandon. "I trust you," she said. "Do not worry. We will be waiting for you at home."

Allison smiled and put her hand on Aika's shoulder. "I think that's the first time you've called it home."

Aika brushed the hand away and shot Allison a look that could melt lead. Allison snickered and then turned to Sophia. "Halifax, right? You ready?"

Sophia lifted off with her arms around Allison's torso. "Where to?" Sophia asked, straining.

"Brooklyn," Allison said. "He's in Brooklyn."

Chapter Twenty-three

It's Not Fair

Alice was sore, battered, beaten, but still standing in the center of the ring. Around her, the crowd was going absolutely nuts. There were deafening chants of "DYS-PELL! DYS-PELL!" echoing throughout the Garden. In a different time, against different opponents, Alice might have enjoyed the victory. Instead, she felt hollow and drained, the death of Alan still weighing heavily on her mind.

While many believed she wouldn't make it past the first match without her powers, Alice had proven many of the bookies dead wrong. After what had happened with Alan, she had won five matches at this point and, while completely exhausted, she wasn't about to give up. She had gone up against what looked like a giant blue businessman known as the Alien Investor. Then there had been the Cobra, someone called Dynamo Dan who had some weird vibro-beam attack, and after that had been the Hurricane. He had tried to electrocute Alice with a bolt of lightning, but she had grounded herself with her knife. Then he had tried to cut her to ribbons with gale force winds, but all he managed to do was give her an extra boost as she charged him, blade-first. She had slammed into him so hard that her knife had smashed right through his chest plate armor and tore through his heart in one hit.

"Just gotta hold on a bit more," she said to herself as her latest opponent, a biker-themed mercenary wrapped in barbed wire, was hauled out of the ring by paramedics. "Just gotta keep this up until Aika can get her ass here," Alice continued. She refused to give up hope that she would survive.

And then Mizuki made her way to the ring.

The moment Alice saw the assassin come out of the main entrance and start down the path to the ring, Alice knew that her luck had run out. While Alice was more than competent as a fighter, both in hand-to-hand and with weapons, she knew her limitations. Even at her best, Alice was no match for the head assassin of the White Lotus. When Aika had left, Mizuki had gone the distance and beyond to fill her shoes. It had long been rumored that if there was anyone alive that could give the legendary Lotus a run for her money, it was the Mizuki, the Night Fox herself.

And now, here she was in front of Alice with a katana in one hand and a tanto in the other. Mizuki radiated an indifference towards Alice that was more chilling than the hatred or rage of previous bouts. Alice twirled the knife she had been given, and gestured for Mizuki to come at her.

"I wondered how long they'd let me do this. I guess someone in the back got tired of waiting." Alice smirked. "You know, you're shorter than the Lotus."

"This will be your last fight tonight," Mizuki said. There was no hint of irony or gloating in her voice. It very much reminded Alice of dealing with Aika.

Alice chuckled. "So, did I last as long as you thought I would?"

Mizuki considered Alice for a moment. "You hide behind your humor. Please, accept what is about to happen with dignity."

Alice gripped her knife and assumed a fighting stance. "Sorry," she said as she crouched. "That's never really been my style."

Mizuki did not respond. Instead, there was a blur of movement. Alice blinked, not sure what just happened. She looked around, only to find that Mizuki was now standing behind her.

"What just..?" Alice started to ask, but then she felt something wet on her side. She looked down to see her uniform sliced neatly open, and a large amount of blood flowing freely out.

"Oh damn," Alice said as she staggered. "Oh damn. That's…" Alice looked up in time to see Mizuki coming straight for her. She tried to parry the blades in Mizuki's hands, but it didn't go well. In one quick motion, Alice found herself disarmed, and with another long gash in her other side.

Alice dropped to one knee. She was bleeding out, and started to feel light-headed. She coughed, and a steam of blood trickled down her chin. She shook her head as she looked at Mizuki, "You know," she said in an unsteady voice. "This is not how I thought I would go out, but I'm glad it was like this." She glanced around the arena. "There are worse deaths."

Mizuki flicked the blood from her blades, and did a quick wipe on her knee before sheathing her blades. "My work is finished here," she said with a short bow. "I take my leave of you, Dyspell."

Alice blinked in confusion as Mizuki turned and headed for the edge of the ring. Around them, the crowd started to boo and hiss. Alice was grateful for still being alive - but also massively confused. "Wait!" she cried out.

Mizuki turned and raised an eyebrow as if to say, *'really?'*

"I'm not complaining, but why?" Alice asked.

Mizuki shrugged. "They only paid me to guard you. This was a favor."

Alice wanted to ask what she meant, but the assassin leapt out of the ring and quickly made herself disappear into the crowd. Alice watched her go until the lights of the arena blinded her to Mizuki's path, and the warrior was lost in a black sea of screaming people.

Alice remained on her knees, clutching her sides and shaking as shock was beginning to set in. *'This is it,'* she thought. *'I'm going to bleed out right here on the mat with a hundred thousand people watching, and there's nothing I can do about it.'*

Alice felt hot tears starting to gather in the corners of her eyes. Not for herself; she actually felt a growing sense of peace at the thought of finally being done with everything. Her only concern at this point was her mother. She felt a growing sense of shame that she couldn't be better for her. That for all her talk, she was never going to be able to cure her. She had harbored fantasies of her mother getting better, and of the two of them having a few more years before nature couldn't be avoided anymore. Now there was a very real chance that her mother would die, either due to the cancer or at the hands or Anna. Despite what she had been told, Alice did not truly believe her mother was safe.

As several Purge soldiers approached the ring to collect her body after the fact, Alice's thoughts turned to Victoria and her baby, and how her child would grow up never knowing its father. This made Alice think back to her own childhood, and, in that moment, she suddenly felt a wave of anger wash over her.

"It's not fair," she whispered. "It's just not fair. None of this is fair. None of this!" Alice felt her hands clutch at the floor of the mat, and then, to her surprise, they went clean through.

Startled, Alice staggered back. The Purge soldiers around the ring suddenly froze, the lead soldier had his hand up to signal the others that something was wrong. Around the arena, the audience quickly looked on in concern and confusion.

Alice froze in shock as she stared at the faint purple glow that surrounded her hands. "How?" she asked herself before reaching down to her sides. She looked at the blood on her hands and slowly began to understand what had happened. With a deep breath, Alice closed her eyes and concentrated.

Her powers weren't completely back, but Mizuki's attack had helped to bleed out enough of the nanites that Alice was able to access *some* of her power. Not all, but enough that she could start to burn out the rest. She felt her power starting to surge within her, and throughout her body she felt a hot tingling, not unlike when a limb had been sat on wrong and is only just starting to regain feeling. It was swelling inside of her, like the chorus of a barely audible song. With each haggard breath, the chorus of power within her rose, blotting out the pain of her wounds. It was loud, frantic, and to Alice's surprise, it sounded so very *angry*.

Alice slowly got to her feet. It was hard to do, as she was still bleeding out, but with each second she could feel more and more of her strength returning. She looked at the Purge soldiers who stood just outside the ring, and then to the crowd that surrounded her. She could now feel her power coming back to her in waves that were crashing against her like the ocean against a rocky shoreline, and as they did, her entire body began to glow with a bright purple light.

The Purge soldiers in the ring were still backing away as Alice, now crackling with energy, actually started to hover. The audience watched, transfixed, as the wounds on Alice's sides briefly glowed white and then disappeared. The Purge soldiers started gasping and dropping to their knees, not realizing that Alice's powers were radiating out in all directions to the point that they were breaking down the air molecules and solid matter around her.

There was a pulse of energy from the center of the ring. The lights in the stadium sparked and popped like a series of poorly timed fireworks, and the titan-tron exploded with a shower of sparks. The only light left in the arena was coming from Alice. It washed the entire arena in a purple hue, and soon, it became blinding.

If one could see past the shining glow, one would see that it wasn't solid. In fact, it looked like hundreds of thousands of tiny purple lights that were flowing throughout Alice's body. It looked like she was a highway of light, endlessly coursing across her skin. It was mesmerizing.

The audience has been sitting in silence, quietly transfixed by the sight in front of them. Then the ring beneath Alice rotted away. This was followed by a chorus of screams from Announcer Carl as he watched his left arm disintegrate, followed unceremoniously by the rest of him. And then the Purge soldiers who were scrambling to get away got caught in the growing orb of purple light that was steadily growing around Alice. It pulsed, and they disappeared in the blink of an eye.

Then the first row disappeared. And then the second.

And then people started to run.

The audience was scrambling for the exits as the Garden erupted into a mass panic. Everyone suddenly realized that they were no longer watching the execution of a has-been traitor; they were trapped in an arena with Dyspell, the Queen of Pain herself. Every person now trapped within the arena now realized with growing horror why Alice was considered the most dangerous woman in the world.

Alice felt her power exploding within her, and for once, she didn't fight it. She just let it flow from her with reckless abandon. Each time she had used her abilities, she had forced herself to focus, to contain the damage so as not to do more than she meant to. Each time, it felt like it was fighting her to desperately break free. For the first time in nearly two decades, she completely surrendered to it, letting it exact her vengeance for her. She screamed, not in pain, but in pure, unbridled rage as she felt her power spread out and consume the world around her. Within her, she felt her magic join her cries with its own. It was free. At long last, for this one horrible moment, it was *free*.

***

Susan waited until the ball of energy started to shrink. As it did, both she and Eedee saw that the Garden had completely vanished. There was absolutely nothing left. No steel, no plastic, nothing. It was as if someone had taken a gigantic ice cream scoop and just scooped the entire stadium out of existence.

In the center of the dimming ball, Susan and Eedee could see a floating figure. As soon as the light faded and the orb vanished, the pale figure in the middle gently floated to the ground and came to rest at the bottom of the smooth crater. Along the crater's edge were a series of parking structure entrances, water pipes that were gushing, and electrical cables that were randomly sparking from being abruptly cut off. In the center, standing stock still with her head down, was Alice.

Susan and Eedee drifted slowly down to her, but instead of rushing her in concern, they set down a little ways away. They were leery both of the naked woman who seemed to be standing with a relaxed demeanor, and of the threat of electrocution from the exposed wiring around them. All three were silent, the sounds of the city around them muted by the shape of the crater they were in.

Susan finally cleared her throat, and cautiously called out, "Alice? You okay?"

Alice took a second to respond. She looked up, only noticing Susan and Eedee just then. Her expression was completely blank.

That part was what scared Susan the most. She had seen Alice happy, manic, angry, and when she was at her lowest, but she had never seen anything like this. This indifference was something that Susan was chalking up to extreme shock. As a medical professional, she understood, but it still unsettled her.

"Suzie?" Alice asked. Slowly, Alice looked around at the crater. Susan slowly approached Alice, taking her cape off as she did so. She put it around Alice's shoulders as Alice moved a purple strand of hair out of her eyes.

"When I was little," Alice said in a quiet, flat voice, "I remember I wanted to see what I could do. What I could *really* do. I remember running to the edge of our property where there was this forest. It had a little creek, and this neat little alcove. It was where I would sit and write in my journal. Did I ever tell you I had a journal, Suzie?"

Susan shook her head. "No, you never did." Behind Susan, Eedee approached nervously.

"I went there," Alice continued, "and I decided I would see what happened if I just let go. I mean completely, totally let go. I had never done that before, you know? I had always been too scared to. My mother had forbidden it. She told me it was the worst thing I could possibly do, but I had to know, you know?"

Alice paused to look around. "When I did it," she said. "When I really, truly let go, there was this blinding light. It was the most incredible thing I had ever seen. I felt myself start to fly. Did you know I could fly?"

Susan shook her head. "Well, I can," Alice said. "Only when I really let go, though. And it's more like hovering, I guess. It was incredible. It was the best I had ever felt in my whole life and the music, Suzie. Oh God, the song that I heard when I did it. It was so beautiful. It was something that couldn't be recreated. It was like hearing the essence of joy. That's the closest I can come to. I did that, and when it was done and the light went away, I had made a crater a quarter mile wide. It turned into a lake by Autumn."

"Mom?" Eedee asked. Alice ignored her as she gently clutched at Susan's cape and started to slowly walk around. She then turned to look at Susan.

"The Garden was full, Suzie." Alice said. Alice looked at Suzie with eyes that made Susan feel cold inside. Alice's voice grew louder, but still sounded flat and hollow. "I let go. I had to. They took my powers, and then when they came back, I couldn't stop. I didn't *want* to. I just let go. Completely and totally, without any direction. I just let go," Alice paused to look around again. "I just killed them."

Eedee was now beside Susan and tugging on her arm. "Miss Major? We've got to go. The police are arriving."

Susan nodded and walked to Alice, gently gathering her up as she did so. With Alice cradled in her arms, Susan and Eedee quickly took off as a swarm of police cars were pulling up to the crater's edge.

Chapter Twenty-four

"Sometimes it's like this."

The night air was clear enough that they saw him from a mile out. He was sitting on the ledge of the Manhattan-side tower, staring out at the city lights. In the distance was a massive, swelling wail of police and fire. Overall, however, they could see that the city was carrying on as it always did, indifferent to what may have been going on just a block over.

Allison nodded towards a spot near to where the man was sitting, and an exhausted Sophia gently set her down. She made sure to land rough, hoping that the noise would help to alert the man to her presence. Sophia, familiar with stories about the Grey and what he was capable of, immediately floated back and out of the way.

"How did you find me?" the man asked. He didn't turn, but Allison knew he was talking to her.

Allison hugged herself. It was shockingly cold this high up, and the wind was unforgiving. "I figured you would want to come here to end it. This is where you tried to end it before, isn't it?"

The man stiffened, but he didn't interrupt. Allison took that as a cue, and slowly approached him. "In our line of work, whenever there isn't a body, that means the other guy is most likely still out there. Sometimes heroes are okay with that. Sometimes they use that to sleep at night. That whole, 'you can't prove I killed them, so my conscience is clean' shtick. I get it. It's nice to be able to sleep at night."

Allison was only a few feet from him now. He was surprisingly small this close up. Not nearly the terrifying figure she had seen earlier. Instead, he looked shrunken as he sat with his hands gripping the edge of the dirty, stone tower.

"In your case, it was different," Allison continued. "It occurred to me that if someone killed the person I loved and destroyed my life, I would make damn good and sure they were dead. Now, from up here that would be pretty hard for a person like me, but for someone who could move so fast they could walk on water, or run up and down walls?" She sat down and looked beside her at the small, prone, and shaking form of Robert Parker, also known as the superhero Yeager.

"There was no fight that night, was there? You never battled the Grey up here at all."

Rob crew in a shaky breath, and started to sob. Allison looked at him and frowned. "Or am I wrong? Maybe you've been fighting him this entire time."

There was a long, uncomfortable silence. Allison waited patiently as Rob struggled to find the right words. When he spoke, his voice sounded like it was on the verge of cracking.

"I don't even know when it started," he whispered. "I just knew that he was trying to hurt me, but I didn't know why. He knew everything about me. Where I lived, who I was, who my family was, everything. I just couldn't figure it out. And then, when my wife… when I found her… I knew I had to end it. But then I found her ring in my pocket, and I just knew. It was like someone had turned on a light, you know? I just knew."

Rob looked out over the lights of the city, and let his tears run silently down his cheeks. Allison noted how gaunt and pale Yeager looked, like the life had been drained right out of him. "I came up here to kill myself, but then Brandon found me, and I couldn't tell him. I wanted to, but I couldn't. I got scared, so I pushed it down. I made up a story, and they bought it. They weren't going to question me. Why would they? I'm a hero." He let out a small laugh. "I'm a hero."

"You never spoke to a doctor about this, did you?" Allison asked.

Rob tensed, and for a moment Allison thought she was in serious trouble. "They would have kicked me off the team. I have a son to consid ... I *had* a son to consider. I couldn't let him down. They would have taken him from me. They would have..."

Rob trailed off as Allison breathed a small sigh of relief. She still wasn't sure which way this was going to go.

Rob took a small, golden band out of his pocket and twirled it in his shaking fingers. "I really was going to do it. I think I was going to do it. I think I was."

Allison stayed perfectly still. She knew that she was still in danger of setting him off, so she just sat and waited to see what would happen. To her relief, Rob continued.

"When I found my boy, I was still covered in his blood. I tried to end it right there. I swear I did. I swear I did." Rob was sobbing so hard he could barely get the words out at this point. Allison closed her eyes and nodded in understanding.

"You tried to kill yourself, but you couldn't, could you? Your metabolism kept healing you, so you just kept stabbing yourself."

Rob didn't answer. He just clutched at his face and continued to cry.

Allison had heard enough. She stood, dusted herself off, and moved behind the broken hero. "You've been gone for a while, Mr. Parker. You've done a lot of damage while you were under."

"It was that man," Rob said. He wiped his face and sniffled. "Carter. He kept it going. Normally it would only last for a few minutes, maybe an hour. He just... he just kept it going. I don't even know how long. God, I don't even know."

"Do you remember anything from it?" Allison asked.

Rob turned and stared at her. The look on his face was one that would haunt Allison until the day she died. "I remember everything."

"And now?" Allison asked.

Rob shook his head. "It's gone. Whatever that girl did, it's all gone. He's gone."

Allison nodded and took out her gun. "Will this do it?" She asked. "Are you just going to heal again, or…"

"I can slow things down," Rob said. "I can make it so that… I can slow down. It'll work."

"If it helps, I won't tell Brandon."

Rob paled. "What will you tell him?"

"I'll tell him the same thing I'll put in the report," Allison said as she cocked her gun. "I'll tell him you fought bravely and that, together, we took down the Grey. I'll tell him you died a hero."

Rob looked at her, and then nodded as he turned to look back out over the city.

"Thank you," he said quietly.

The sound of the gun firing wasn't even heard by the people driving below. It was just one more quick sound on the wind. The same could be said of the splash at the base of the bridge.

Allison shuddered, and holstered her gun. She turned back to Sophia, who had been watching the entire exchange. The young flyer had been so tense that she didn't realize she had been holding her breath until she let it out.

"He was done," Sophia said, her disbelief bleeding into her voice. "He said it himself. He would have come back with us."

"Why?" Allison asked. "He just woke up from a waking nightmare where he murdered his son, his teammates, and betrayed everything he held dear. If I had taken him back, it would have hurt him, Brandon, Victoria, everyone associated with the Collective Good. That includes my family, and also you and your team. This way," Allison nodded towards the spot they had sat at, "he dies a hero, his family can rest without the press tearing them apart, and the Grey is defeated once and for all."

"Why did you bring me here?" Sophia asked. "Seriously, that whole 'he needs to see me coming' line was bullshit. You knew he would be like this."

Allison shook her head. "That wasn't why at all. I brought you here because you needed to see that sometimes it's like this."

Sophia cocked an eyebrow. "Like what?"

"That sometimes it's not all right versus wrong," Allison said. "Sometimes our job is just a big ball of bad, and there is no happy ending. That's why for every hero, they need people like us."

"I don't understand." Sophia said.

"Halifax," Allison said in her most professional voice. "The Collective Good will be lucky to recover from this. You and your team are next in line. You've got potential, but you push yourself beyond what you can handle. In the field, that can translate into some bad situations. I needed you to see that sometimes, you'll get nights like tonight. Sometimes there is no good way out, and that means sometimes you have to make a call."

"Like shooting a man who had given up?"

Allison turned to look out at the city. "Yeah. Like shooting a man who had given up." Allison sighed as she shook a stray lock out of her face. Her ponytail had come out, and the wind was making her hair dance in the night air.

Chapter Twenty-five

"You didn't. Trust. Me."

With a thin slice of red through the night air, they arrived at *Rare Gems*. The golem resumed his post, some debris from the Senator's house still on his shoulders. Phil left them be, considering his own team still needed to be transported back to the Tower. He was slightly confused as to what had happened, and the more he tried to focus on what had occurred, the more his head began to hurt.

Next was Alice, Susan, and Eedee. They landed on the roof, and came to the main room. Alice drifted to her spare room. Even though she found herself sleeping there more than her apartment, she adamantly refused to call it her bedroom. She fished out a green pair of sweats and an oversized purple sweater, yanked them over herself, and then shuffled back into the main room. She drifted to the couch, sat down, and closed her eyes as a long breath escaped her. She wanted a shower. More specifically, she wanted to curl up in a ball on the shower floor.

Susan sat down beside her and checked her over as she did so. Aside from some signs of shock, there didn't seem to be a cut or scrape on Alice anywhere. Susan rubbed Alice's back and said, "Hey, are you okay? I mean, physically?"

Aika stood across the room, arms crossed and with a blank expression. She was also studying Alice, and frowning. "I saw you on television. You were wounded."

Alice glanced at Aika, and gave a slight shrug. "Magic. I healed myself."

Aika raised an eyebrow. "I thought that was difficult for you."

Alice studied her hand, slowly turning it back and forth. "Huh. Well, this time it wasn't."

"Mom?" Eedee asked. "Are you okay?"

"Don't call me Mom," Alice murmured. "I'm fine. I'm just processing everything. I've never gone that big before."

"What about what you told me?" Susan asked. "When you were a kid?"

Alice gently shook her head. "That was different. This felt more powerful. More... just *more*."

"What about the cruise ship?" Aika asked,

Alice shook her head. "That was different. I was focused on a task. That was surgery. This was letting everything go. Everything." Her body shuddered with a light laugh. "It was so beautiful."

Brandon came into the room, rubbing the back of his neck. "Is she okay?" He pointed to Alice.

Susan glanced at him and gasped. Instantly, she was on her feet and had a penlight in her hand. She examined his pupils and asked, "What happened to you? Was this quick-healed? They missed some damage. Did they check for internal bleeding?"

Brandon shooed her away. "I'm fine. How's she?"

Aika walked over to the kitchen, while Susan continued to check on him, despite his complaints. "She had a rough night," Susan said. "Her powers overloaded." Aika came back with a bottled water, and tossed it to Brandon, who nodded a thank you.

"Where is Holly?" Aika asked.

Brandon took a long drink and wiped his mouth. "She's in the bath. She wanted some alone time after everything that happened."

Aika nodded and glanced down the hall. "She has had a rough evening, too." She started to head down the hall, but then her pocket buzzed. She slipped her PhoneBuddy out and checked it. "We were popular tonight," she said as she scanned her messages. She started furiously texting someone as Allison came down the stairs.

"Allison!" Brandon said as he went to her. Allison let out a small yelp as Brandon nearly tackled her. He hugged her tightly and said, "I can't believe you're okay. God, I am so sorry. Are you okay? You look okay. I was so worried. How did you..?"

A very red-faced Allison gently pushed him away and, after an embarrassed look around the room, muttered, "I'm okay."

"What happened?" Brandon asked. "Did you find the Grey?"

Behind them, Sophia drifted down the stairs and into the room. She wanted to go back to the Tower, but she was exhausted and needed a moment to rest. She didn't expect to walk into a family moment, and she instantly felt out of place.

Allison gently pushed away from Brandon and nodded. "Yeah. Yeah, we found him."

"What happened?" Brandon asked again.

Before Allison could answer, Sophia said, "She distracted him by shooting at him long enough for me to get to him. Let's see him survive being dropped from two miles up."

Allison's head snapped towards Sophia, who shrugged in response. Allison bit her tongue for a second, and then said, "Yeah. Halifax was a huge help. She really came through. They all did. I'm recommending to Victoria that their team be greenlit for active duty."

Aika watched the exchange and raised an eyebrow, but said nothing. Allison then turned her attention to Alice. She sat down beside her and put her hand on her shoulder. "Hey, what happened? Why are you all spacy?"

It was Brandon who answered. He had gotten a text when Allison had pulled away, and had just now checked it. "Oh, my God," he said. "Did… did you blow up Madison Square Garden?"

Allison's eyes widened in shock. Alice just shrugged in response.

"They know it was you," Brandon said. He held his phone out, showing a picture of Alice next to a picture of the crater that had been the Garden. "There were diplomats there, billionaires, heads of state, good God." Brandon shook his head as he put his phone away. "You've become the most wanted woman on the planet."

"Again," Alice said. "You forgot to add an 'again' there."

Aika took off down the hall. In less than a minute, she was back with two duffel bags over her shoulder, along with several long objects wrapped in cloth. She looked at everyone before setting her stare towards Alice. "We have very little time. If what he says is true, then the authorities will be here in a matter of minutes. Even your status as an agent of the Collective Good will not protect you."

Alice blinked as if coming out of a long nap. She looked to Aika, sighed, and nodded. "You're right," she said. "You're right. I should get going, I guess."

"Where are you going?" Brandon asked.

"It is not your concern," Aika snapped. She turned to Alice. "I am extracting you in one minute, regardless of how ready you are."

Alice nodded, and looked to Brandon. "I'm not spending my days in a lunar gulag. This isn't the first time I've had to disappear. Besides, they'll only be after me. The rest of you should be in the clear."

Allison, who was still trying to take all of this in, shook her head and leapt to her feet. "What? No! Fuck no! You were fighting for your life! You can't, they can't just..."

Alice turned, and put her hand on Allison's shoulders. "I just killed forty thousand people."

Allison opened and closed her mouth, but couldn't find an appropriate response. Alice brought her into a hug. "Yeah, that's about right. I'm gonna take a little vacation, okay? Can you hold the fort down for me?"

Allison opened her mouth to comment several times. Finally, she grabbed Alice and started dragging her into Holly's bedroom. Before anyone could say anything, Allison slammed the door and spun around to face Alice.

Alice took a deep breath. "Look, I..."

Allison cut her off with a hard slap to the face.

"How dare you," Allison seethed. "You just couldn't help yourself, could you? COULD YOU?"

Alice rubbed the side of her face as she glared at Allison. "Ex-fucking-scuse me?"

"You did it again!" Allison threw her hands up in exasperation. "I don't know how or why, but you went off half-cocked and did it again! You had to go out and make a fucking spectacle of yourself, didn't you?"

"I did it to SAVE YOUR LIFE!" Alice yelled. "You were captured, and that Anna bitch was holding all the cards. If I didn't compete, they were going to kill you!"

Allison shook her head. "No. No, no, no, that's not true and you know it."

"You don't know this one, Allison," Alice said. "This new player, Anna? She's insane. I could see it. She would have done it just to prove that she could."

"In case you haven't noticed, things are different now. Alice, we're not alone anymore. We have a family now. We have friends! Alice, I was saved by an army of supers. I was fine. We were fine!"

"You don't know that!" Alice rubbed her forehead in frustration. "This new Purge is organized. They weren't about to let tonight go off without me. They..."

"So, you what, had to perform for them? You had to go out there and show them that you're still this almighty badass queen? Alice, listen to me. You went out there because A, you didn't stop to think for five seconds about the fact that we're no longer alone, B, you had to go relive your fucking glory days at the cost of everything around you, or C, you Didn't. Trust. Me."

"I DID IT BECAUSE I LOVE YOU!" Alice shouted. "Goddammit, Allison! Everything! Every single thing I have done over the last three years has been because of you! Running away, settling down, all of it. It's all been for you!"

"Why?" Allison asked, tears starting to form in her eyes. "I didn't ask you to quit. I didn't ask you to do any of this."

"You're my...you're my charge. I'm responsible for you. I raised you, I..."

"I DIDN'T FUCKING ASK YOU TO!"

Alice froze. Allison was shaking, her breathing coming in gasps. Tears were now flowing down her cheeks and dripping from her chin. "I NEVER asked you to. You... You ruined my life, Alice! You ruined all of it. Everything that happened to me, everything was your fault. My parents, my sister, that was on you."

"That's not fair," Alice said as she took a step back. "That was not me, and I did what I could to fix that."

"Fix it?" Allison let out a choked laugh. "Fix it? Fixing it would have been putting me in foster care. Fixing it would have been leaving me with my uncle, or letting someone who wasn't a goddamn sociopath terrorist adopt me. I should have been with people who would have let me grieve. I should have had counseling, learned how to cope, gone to school, lived a normal life, anything but this! I should be able to go to sleep each night without wondering if I'm too broken to be a mom, or a girlfriend, or a decent human being. I should be able to close my eyes and not see my sister pounding and screaming from the other side of an oven window. I should have been normal, not... I should have been normal!"

Alice hugged herself and shivered as she felt her own tears starting to run down her face. "I gave you the best life I could. You know that. I didn't know what I was doing, but I tried..."

"*Tried*? Oh, that's what you call handing me off. You didn't raise me, you did the bare ass minimum you needed to so that your conscience would let you sleep. You had everyone else around you train me and when you felt like it, you'd step in, pat me on the back, say 'good girl.' That, in your mind, made things better?"

"I get it, alright? I was a shit parent!" Alice yelled. "Look, I just, this isn't fair! Allison, I know that, I, we need to talk about this, but this isn't the time. I'm sorry. I am so, so sorry. I..."

"You have to run away again," Allison huffed. "You went overboard, fucked up royally, and now you're running away." She then got within inches of Alice's face and stared her in the eyes. "Where have I heard this one before?"

"This wasn't my fault," Alice whispered.

Allison turned around, and shook her head. "Save it. It's never your fault."

"Allison..."

"Would you just get the fuck out of here?" Allison snapped. "Just run away. It's what you do."

Alice wanted to say more. She wanted to scream at Allison, hug her, beg for forgiveness, and slap her silly, but she could practically feel the anger radiating off her niece.

No, more than that. Her daughter.

At that moment, Alice was able to fully admit that to herself. Allison *was* her daughter, and she did love her. She loved her more than Allison would ever know, and the fact that it was only now that she could realize it fully made Alice hate herself all the more.

Without a word, Alice walked out of Holly's room. Allison waited until she was gone and then collapsed sobbing on Holly's bed.

***

Alice emerged to a sea of wide eyes. She realized that with all the shouting and the paper-thin walls of the apartment, everyone present had most likely heard every single word. With a quick wipe of her face, Alice tried to regain some shred of dignity.

"I'll contact you all when I get to where I'm going," Alice said.

"Where are you going?" Eedee asked. She was growing increasingly concerned and confused, and was worried about what Alice would say next.

"I'm going somewhere safe, Eedee." Alice sniffed and wiped her nose. "Tell Allison that I'm going to the last safe place. She'll know what I'm talking about."

Outside, the sound of sirens was steadily growing. Alice stepped away and looked back at Holly's door. "You know, I was told that I could never have kids, but I wound up having one hell of a daughter. I just wish…" She looked over at Brandon. "Be worthy of her."

Brandon tensed, but nodded. Alice grinned at him and winked. "Take care of my girls," she said as Aika put her hand on Brandon's shoulder.

"I will contact you when we are safe," Aika said. Brandon tensed, not used to any type of physical display of concern from Aika. He then nodded, and took Aika's PhoneBuddy. She then turned to Alice and said, "You, too. Nothing that can be tracked."

Alice tossed her PhoneBuddy to Eedee, who sniffed and said, "That includes me too, doesn't it? They can find you if I come."

Alice shook her head and smiled. "Eedee, I am officially ordering you to guard Allison and Holly. You are to protect them no matter what, do you understand?"

Eedee straightened, and nodded. "Yes Mom. I promise I will."

"Don't call… never mind." Alice said. She looked to the room, nodded, and said, "I'll see you all soon. I promise."

Aika grabbed Alice's arm as the sound of sirens grew louder. "We must leave now."

Alice nodded. She looked at each of them, wanting to say more. Instead, she gave a slight smile. "Tell Holly I said bye. Tell her to be good, okay?"

Eedee nodded. Alice was about to say something else, but then stopped. Without another word, she turned and left down the stairs with Aika.

Not two minutes later, the sound of the front door to *Rare Gems* being kicked open was heard, and the roar of stomping feet. There were over a dozen SWAT team officers sweeping through the store and the apartment – but the most dangerous woman in the world had officially left the building.

***

Across the world, deep under the ice of the arctic, Anna May watched the new broadcasts that were playing on loop. She was back in her white and pink one-piece jumpsuit, drinking a glass of wine and lounging in her quarters. She wasn't sure which glass she was on, as she had lost count a while ago, but she didn't care. She watched a large flat screen as the newscasters talked about the devastating attack and the woman responsible, the Purge terrorist, Dyspell.

There was a soft chime as the doors to her quarters slid open, and Totallus entered. He showed some damage from his fight with Eedee, but nothing that went too far beyond being superficial. Anna glanced to him and waved. "Hey Totallus, how was your evening?"

Totallus approached, but came to a rigid stop a good ten feet from Anna. "I failed in my duties, Mistress."

Anna let out a laugh, and gestured to the television. "Are you kidding me? Have you not seen the news?"

"I was instructed to guard the Broadcast and ensure that Dyspell would not escape. I was intercepted by the other Totallus. The female."

Anna raised an eyebrow at that. "She's still kicking around, eh? Ah well, it doesn't matter. Look, tonight couldn't have turned out better if I had planned this myself. I knew she would crack eventually, but this?" She gestured with her wine glass to the screen. "This was perfect! I almost feel bad that I wasted all that effort and energy setting up those Purge workers at that convention center, or whatever it was. I mean, that footage combined with this is just the icing on the cake! God, this is like Christmas!"

Anna downed her drink, set her glass down on a side table, and gracefully slid off her sofa chair to face Totallus. "Please inform the bridge crew that we will be launching ahead of schedule. I want us airborne by morning."

Totallus paused. "The Master has ordered that we wait another two weeks to charge the engines."

Anna glanced at Totallus. "He ordered?" She giggled and covered her mouth. "Really? He thinks we need two more weeks?"

Totallus nodded. "He said the engines are not yet ready for a full-scale assault. We are currently operating at 78% efficiency. He feels it is wise to wait until we have reached 90% or higher."

Anna smiled. She patted Totallus on the chest. "Come with me." She strutted out of her quarters with Totallus closely following behind. She easily navigated the labyrinthian maze of metal corridors that led deep into the heart of the *Metatron*. Before long, they found themselves standing before a sealed double door. Anna quickly punched some numbers into the operator panel to the side of the door. With a hiss, the doors slid open to reveal a dimly lit room. It was long, filled with marble statues and decorative pillars, a beautiful gold trim lining the wall, and a thick, white shag rug underfoot.

In the center of the room was a medichair. It was a large plastic and metal pod that could easily shift into a bed. One side was covered in touchscreens that gave a series of vital statistics. Inside the pod, connected to a series of tubes, was an ancient-looking, bald, wrinkled man. The sounds of his gasping made Anna wince as she approached him.

Anna gave a mock bow and said, "My lord Prometheus, I bring good news! I've just spoken with our engineers, and they say the *Metatron* is ready for launch. We merely await your word."

Prometheus opened his eyes, and looked to Anna. "They told me I would be young again," he gasped. "I felt it. I felt it flow through me. Just for a moment."

"My lord," Anna gently took his hand in hers and leaned in. "We're ready to launch. The world will scream your name once more, and the Purge will assume its rightful place as the rulers of the world. I just need you to say the word."

"They burned green when I came here. The cities. They all burned green. It was beautiful," Prometheus whispered. He turned his gaze outward to something Anna couldn't see.

"My lord?" Anna asked, growing slightly inpatient.

"I want to see it happen," he said. "Take me to the bridge. I need the Phoenix again. I need it. I need to feel it flow through me."

Anna nodded. "As soon as you give the word, Alexi. Please," she bent closer. "Give the order. Let us launch."

Alexi glanced with yellow eyes to Anna, and then gave a weak nod.

Anna kissed him on his liver-spotted forehead and grinned. She turned to Totallus and pointed to the door. "There. Now he's ordered it. Tell the bridge to prepare for launch."

Totallus looked to Prometheus, and then back to Anna. "Mistress," he said with a nod.

"Oh, and Totallus?" Anna called out as the android was about to leave. "Send me Diamond. There's something I've been waiting to take care of, and I'm thinking that if I'm ever going to get the chance, tonight's the night. Send her to my quarters. I'll be there shortly to meet her."

"Mistress," Totallus said again with a nod.

Chapter Twenty-six

The Head of the Dragon

Behind a cluttered desk, bathed in the light of a dozen monitors blaring a dozen different news reels, sat Victoria Green. She looked over the frenzied text messages that had been sent her way from Allison and Brandon, from Susan and the rest. She had already conducted frantic calls with the Attorney General, the DA, and the Commissioner. There were scores of meetings that were waiting for her the next morning, dozens of press conferences, and throughout all of them, the one, gigantic question that was hanging over not only her head, but the entire Collective Good.

Why was Alice Gailsone never locked up?

Victoria knew what was coming. There would be inquiries, demands from Congress, and eventually all of it would culminate. If Victoria was lucky, it would only result in the destruction of the Open Hand Act. At the very worst, the entire Collective Good would be dissolved.

Victoria knew all of this was coming. She knew what it would mean for the people in her care, for Allison and Holly, for everyone that had come forward in the past. She knew that this would be seen in the history books as the tipping point.

She just figured that she would have a little time, first.

Victoria picked up her PhoneBuddy for what felt like the thousandth time that evening as it buzzed to life. She was ready to ignore the call until she saw it was from her old boss and mentor, Federal Director Randy Collins.

Victoria closed her eyes and mentally composed herself so that she would sound somewhat professional as she answered the phone. "Victoria here," she said in a voice that betrayed how exhausted she was.

"Victoria, it's Randy. Is this a good time?"

Victoria would have laughed if a ball of nerves wasn't forming in her gut. "Hell no, but go ahead. What do you have for me tonight on top of everything else?"

She was expecting him to go on about the destruction of the Garden or to hear another rant about Alice Gailsone, but instead he said, "Senator Carter was found dead tonight. He was found decapitated in what was left of his home."

Victoria sat bolt upright in her seat. "Do you have any idea who was responsible?"

"It's hard to tell. The home was demolished by what looks like an aerial assault. We've got a team onsite, but it's hard to tell what's what, considering the damage."

Victoria tensed as something occurred to her. "While I appreciate the update, why are you telling me this?"

Collins paused before continuing. "It is the opinion of the team onsite that this was the work of superhumans, possibly in response to his anti-superhuman legislation."

"Little early to be making a call like that, isn't it?" Victoria asked.

"Christ, Vic. Look at what's happened tonight," Collins snapped. "The Garden is destroyed. Thousands dead, from what we can tell by a superhuman, *your* pet superhuman I might add, and now a senator that adamantly spoke up about this very thing is found with his head missing on the same night?"

"It wasn't my people," Victoria said. "And we're still trying to determine what role if any Alice Gailsone had in the destruction of the Garden."

"You know damn well there's video of her doing it," Collins said. "The internet exploded with it. Vic, they're going to shut you down."

Victoria felt that cold tension in her gut race up her spine. "What do you mean?"

"I got a call from a friend on the Hill," Collins said. "First thing tomorrow, the President is signing an emergency Executive Order. The Open Hand Act is being revoked, and any superhuman that operates openly from this point forward will be considered a criminal. This includes any and all members of the Collective Good."

"They can't do that!" Victoria shouted into her phone. "There are people who have come forward and made a legitimate effort! They've reformed, and now they're going to be viewed as criminals again? Just like that?"

"People like Alice Gailsone?" Collins asked, his voice laced with sarcasm. "And no, not 'just like that.' Vic, we just had the world's most recognized terrorist commit the biggest televised terrorist attack in recorded history. I have reports that she's gone underground, but it's only a matter of time before someone finds her. She was one of yours, Vic."

Victoria slumped in her seat. "I know what you're going to ask me, and no, I don't know where she is. She's apparently gone into hiding."

"Are there others like her?" Collins asked. "Other former Purge members? Vic, we need to know."

Victoria shook her head before she realized he couldn't see her. "No. No other former Purge. No one who would know."

Vic," Collins asked. "I need you to be sure on this. When she came forward, did anyone else?"

"I'm sure," Victoria said. "Sir, you can check the records yourself. To date, there has only been one official registered Purge officer that has come forward, and it was her."

It wasn't *entirely* a lie, Victoria told herself. After all, Allison was technically registered, but her record with the Purge had been scrubbed from the Collective Good's database. Victoria had seen to that herself when arranging Holly's adoption paperwork.

"Thank you," Collins said. "That's what I needed to hear. Also, it would do you well to have that boy toy of yours in front of the press tomorrow. The public will need the Collective Good to separate themselves from this as much as possible. It won't change what's happening, but it might buy your actual heroes some amnesty."

Victoria heard Collins tone soften. "When I put you on this assignment, I never thought that it would turn into all of this. I..."

Victoria cut him off. "Sir? I've got to go. I don't think I'm getting any sleep tonight, and my phone is already buzzing at me. Thank you for the head's up about tomorrow."

She heard Collins sigh through the phone. "Of course. Good luck, Vic. When this blows over, come and see me. If you want, I'll be happy to provide you with a reinstatement to the Bureau and an assignment of your choosing. You've earned it."

"Thank you for the offer, but I'm needed here, Sir."

"Vic..."

Victoria gently slid the End Call button on her phone and stared at it. "I earned it," she murmured.

While Victoria was looking at her phone, it started ringing. The screen said unknown caller, which was a bit surprising considering the level of tracing tech the Tower had on hand. She slid the call open on her screen. "Hello?"

"Hey, Blackbird."

Victoria froze. "Alice?"

"It's a throwaway phone, so don't bother tracing, "Alice said. "Look, I needed to let you know..."

"Did you do it?" Victoria asked. "Did you really destroy the Garden?"

There was a pause.

"Yeah," Alice answered. "Yeah, I did. It was me."

"Alice," Victoria said. "I know about the Broadcast. I can... if you turn yourself in, we can spin this. I can let everyone know what really happened."

Alice laughed. "Vic, are you serious? Do you even know who was there? No, you get away from me and save yourself. You put that blame 100% on my head. You tell them that I was Purge all along."

"Alice, I'm not about to throw you under the bus like that."

"You'd better," Alice said. In the background, Victoria could hear a car honking. "It's the only way to save yourself from this."

"I don't need to save myself. The Collective Good has been in bigger trouble than this, and..."

"Victoria, Alan is dead."

Victoria felt every muscle in her body tighten. She wasn't aware she had stopped breathing until she heard herself whisper, "What?"

"They killed him," Alice said. "He was being manipulated by a controlling disc. It had been on him for days."

"How did it happen?" Victoria asked. She could feel her legs starting to turn to rubber as she spoke.

"They put him in the ring with me. I got the controller off, but it was too late. I'm sorry, Vic. He's gone."

Victoria felt the phone start to slip in her hands when Alice said. "I thought it was only right to tell you directly. You deserved to know. Vic, this is why you have to blame me. You're in charge now. Whatever happens next, you're the head of the Collective Good and Tanner Industries. You're the head of the dragon."

"What?"

"It's a Purge term," Alice said. "It means the person who is actually in charge as opposed to who everyone thinks is in charge. I guess you always were, in a way. When I was in the Purge, it was me."

"Alice," Victoria asked. "Where are you?"

"Before I forget," Alice continued, "he said something to me before he died. He said her loved you, and that you're going to be a great mom."

Victoria felt a sob forcing its way up her throat. "Alice…"

"I've got to go. Look, when you do finally find me and take me down, I'll let you win, okay? Just promise me that you'll look after Allison and Holly, and promise me that you'll make sure my mother is taken care of."

"Alice," Victoria felt herself starting to shake. "Where are you?"

"Promise me."

"I don't know that I can. This is huge, Alice. This is worse than that Central Park incident. I can't…"

"Please."

Victoria shook her head as a feeling of defeat washed over her. "Fine. I promise I'll do my best to keep them safe, and that your mother will continue to receive the best care. And Alice? I'll tell her the truth. She should know."

Victoria's Phonebuddy beeped in her hand, signaling the end of the call. She let it drop to the floor as she hugged herself and stared out the windows of her office at the bustling city lights below. Tomorrow she would have to be at her best. There would be press statements, summons from congress, the whole nine yards. Tonight though, she was done. Tonight, she would cry for the loss of a man she told herself over and over she didn't love, and the loss of a friend that she swore she didn't care for.

Her PhoneBuddy started once again to ring from across the room. It could wait, Victoria told herself. Tonight, she would mourn.

Tomorrow, she would lead.

Tomorrow, she would become the head of the dragon.

***

Across the city, Holly was finishing up in the bath. She had heard everything that had happened with Alice, and had even seen it through everyone else's eyes. She knew how everyone was feeling, but more importantly, she knew she had something she had to take care of before it was too late.

Long term memories were almost impossible to get rid of. They were like something large sinking into the ocean, drifting down through the water, and then settling into the deep sands of the mind. Things that had time to settle could almost never be removed, but things that were freshly drifting through the waters of the mind tended to be manipulatable.

Things like how she had deceived the members of the B Team and used them for her own ends. How she had made them help her and tricked them into thinking she had been Victoria Green. When she had done this, she saw that they all were extremely skilled, valuable in a dire situation, and also easily manipulated.

Holly wasn't a bad person, at least, *she* didn't think she was. She knew some of the things she had done might seem bad, but she hadn't had a choice. That's what people like her did, after all. That's what heroes did, or at least, the children of heroes did. They made hard choices.

When she was done bathing, she wiped a fresh stream of blood from her nose, haphazardly put up her hair, dressed in her favorite Hello Kitty pajamas, and then crept down the hall to Alice's "spare" room. As the police were frantically searching around her home for any trace of Alice or a clue as to where she had gone, Holly blocked herself out of their minds and calmly went about her business. She was still careful about her noise level. When she was tired, it was harder to block both sounds and visuals. She had to mentally coax three investigators out of Alice's room before she could approach her dresser. She then felt around the edge of said dresser until she found the release for a secret drawer located at the very top. The drawer slid out, and inside, Holly found a small box containing a syringe along with the nanite inhibitor solution.

By the time she decided to be noticed, she appeared next to Allison downstairs as everyone was being questioned. As far as everyone in the room was concerned, she had always been there, patiently sitting and waiting for the police to finish what they were doing.

Holly *knew* she wasn't a bad person, but she did understand the merit in keeping secrets. She also knew that sometimes, no matter how much the people who love you may want to keep you safe, it didn't hurt to have a little extra insurance.

It was another two hours before the police were finished and left, and not once did anyone notice the small case that rested in Holly's hands.

Chapter Twenty-seven

A Little Extra Touch

Dorothy Gailsone had lived a long and eventful life, and had seen many incredible things. She had travelled abroad a lot in her youth. She had seen many wondrous lands, fantastic sights, and met many interesting people. As she got older, she settled down, got married, and did her best to attempt a family. When she found herself a single mother of a baby with powers, she found her life had set out on a completely different journey, but not one that she regretted at all. She loved her daughter, and she was immensely proud of the woman she had become.

Not necessarily of who she had been, mind you. Still, even Dorothy had to admit that her own past hadn't been completely without incidents. Her philosophy of late had been to try to focus on the present, and to let the past stay where it was.

Despite all of her experience and her newfound view of the world, Dorothy wasn't without vices. One in particular she refused to admit to anyone but her daughter, and she was happily indulging in it as the evening rolled on - she was addicted to sophomoric, late-night television. At the moment, she was busy enjoying the Late Show while knitting a dark red sweater. The sweater was for Holly, whom she had met during a lunch with Allison a week ago. Dorothy had been so impressed by the girl's manners that she wanted to do something special to welcome her to the family. She was especially taken with the curtsy. That was something Dorothy had done when she was younger, too.

Tonight, catching anything that wasn't the news was proving difficult. She kept seeing something about an attack downtown, but each time it would appear, she would quickly change the channel. Dorothy had a strict rule about watching the news after a certain time of night. She found that if she did watch it, she tended to sit up at night with worry. Besides, anything that was important in the evening would still be important in the morning, and it wasn't like there was anything she could do about it anyway, so why worry?

Her nurse had gone on break about twenty minutes ago and left to grab a snack, which meant Dorothy was alone when she nearly jumped out of her skin at the sound of a knock on the door. She summoned her strength, and pushed herself up out of her chair. With her walker, she made her way to the door. "Yes?" she called out. She was a little too short to see out through the peep hole, a fact that she had complained about to her landlord, and climbing on a stool was out of the question.

"It's me," a familiar voice called out. Dorothy smiled, and quickly unlocked the door. There, on the other side, stood Alice. She was in a black sweater, sporting her purple hair, and looked extremely nervous. In fact, the expression on her face was so severe, Dorothy nearly gasped. "Oh, hon. Are you okay? Come in! What brings you by here so late? Are you okay? Would you like a drink?"

Alice smiled and shook her head as she entered the apartment. Dorothy let Alice close the door. "No, but thank you. You asked if I was okay twice, you know."

Dorothy shrugged, and gestured for Alice to come closer. She gave her daughter a huge hug, and smiled. "I'm just glad you're here, dear. What did I do to deserve two visits in one day? Now, why so late? Did something happen?"

"Kind of," Alice said, looking around. "Um, have you had any other visitors tonight? Possibly some gentlemen in blue?"

Dorothy eyed her daughter. "No, not yet. Why? Have you been up to something? Did you get into trouble, dear?"

Alice shrugged and grinned. "Oh, a little bit. Nothing big. It's just that something is about to happen, and I just wanted to visit you first, you know? I mean, if that's okay and all."

"Of course!" Dorothy smiled and gestured to the flower print couch in the living room. Alice, still moving cautiously, sat down. Dorothy watched as she looked around the small apartment, seemingly taking it all in.

"It's so small," Alice said under her breath. Dorothy, who was hobbling towards the kitchen, stopped and turned her head.

"What was that, dear?"

"Oh! Nothing. What are you doing?" Alice asked in a voice that sounded a little too forced. Dorothy gestured to the kitchen.

"Well, I thought I'd make you some evening tea, for me if not for you. I'm just so excited that you swung by!"

Alice watched Dorothy as she hobbled along with her walker. The older woman was already in her blue, flower-print nightgown, and her thinning hair was in curlers, despite the fact that she almost never went out. Alice suddenly said, "Sit down. I'll make it."

Dorothy smiled warmly, and nodded her thanks. "Thank you, dear. I appreciate it."

Alice stepped into the kitchen and paused. "Um, where do you keep it again?"

"The tea is in the cupboard over the microwave."

Alice moved through the kitchen like a woman in a trance. She found the tea kettle on the stove, and ran her fingers over its dinged, brass side. It was ancient, and looking at it brought a small smile to Alice's face. "Is this the same tea kettle from back home?"

"Yes," Dorothy called out. "Same one."

"I remember you making me hot chocolate on the stove with this," Alice said softly. Her eyes caught her reflection in the warped copper side of the kettle. She shook her head as though she were coming out of a daydream. She ran some water and cranked the stove to high before coming back into the living room. "Tea will be on in a few," she said.

"Please, have a seat, hon," Dorothy asked. She gestured to the couch again. Alice complied, and did her best to sit still. The whole time, she was wringing her hands and fidgeting in her seat. "Now," Dorothy asked after muting the television, "what brings you by so late?"

Alice kept looking around the apartment, as if searching for something. Occasionally, her gaze would fall on a picture frame, or a knickknack on a shelf, and linger. "Something's going to happen tomorrow," she said in a distracted voice. "Something big. I've been working towards it for a very long time, and I've been struggling to get everything in place to make it perfect. Now, I'm almost ready. There's only one more piece left to add. It's a minor one, but it adds a little icing to everything, you know? Just a little extra touch, to make it all personal."

"Does this have anything to do with the fact that the news networks have been going crazy tonight? Or maybe with that handsome Alan Tanner?" Dorothy asked with a wink.

Alice glanced at Dorothy, and chuckled. "Why, yes. Yes, indeed. Alan Tanner is very much a part of what is about to happen. Or, he was, anyway. Not the biggest piece, but still; very good guess, there."

"I thought so!" Dorothy said, beaming. "After that cruise, I wondered to myself if there wasn't something more between the two of you, and here you are! But what about his lady-friend? You had told me once that you thought she and you might be friends someday. What was her name? Victoria?"

"Oh," Alice said with a smile, "I wouldn't worry about Victoria Green. I think she's got more than enough on her plate to worry about."

"Well, that's good," Dorothy said, settling into her puffy, brown chair. "You shouldn't start something with an involved man, I always say. Too many potential problems. Still, he is quite a catch. I'm so happy for you, sweetie."

"Yeah," Alice said with a nervous chuckle. "Me too. So, um, I came by for a reason tonight, and the more I sit here, the more that reason is slipping from me. I, um, wanted to talk to you about something. And I wanted to ask a question. Can I ask a question?"

Dorothy gave her daughter a warm smile. "Of course, dear. What's on your mind that you would come here so late?"

Alice sat and stared at her hands for a long, long time. Dorothy was concerned, but waited patiently for her daughter to continue. The only sound in the apartment was the ticking of the small, wooden cuckoo clock on the wall. The pine cone weights that hung underneath it on tiny chains were close to the ground, and reminded Alice of when she used to play with them as a child.

After struggling with the question for what felt like forever, Alice asked in a small voice, "Why didn't you ever look for me?"

Alice finally looked up, her eyes starting to brim with tears, as she waited for an answer. She could see the look on Dorothy's face, the shock and surprise at being blindsided. Before she could answer, Alice continued. "I was a General for the Purge. I had access to every type of search engine known to man. I had police records, moles, data feeds. I wanted to know if you had ever looked for me, and when I searched, all I found was a police report. One report, and that was it. You filed it two days after Danny's parents reported him missing."

Dorothy tried to speak, but found the words dying in her throat. Alice shook her head and continued. "And then, after *St. Agnes*, after everything that happened there, when I went to the Purge, I thought, 'Maybe she's dead? Maybe that's why?' but no. You were alive, and right here in Brooklyn. I thought maybe you were buried out at the farm, you know? But no, you just... you gave up on me. Why?"

"Hon," Dorothy said in a quiet voice. "Oh hon, I *did* look. The police were so unhelpful. They just wrote you off. They thought you had run away with Danny, but..."

"He died," Alice said abruptly. Dorothy let out a small gasp and covered her mouth with her hand.

"Oh dear, I am so sorry."

Alice shrugged. "I killed him. It was an accident. We were...together, and my powers flared up, and I killed him."

"Is that why you left?"

Alice nodded. "That's why I left."

"Hon," Dorothy said. "I hired a private detective who eventually had a lead on a rumor about a superpowered, purple-haired young lady at a shelter for young women. I came to New York and spoke with the people at St. Agnes, but they had no official record of you, and the girls there were so scared when I bought your name up. I just, I was afraid that you would just run from me. I was worried you would think I thought everything was your fault. Hon, no. I did not give up on you. I never, *ever* gave up on you. That's why I moved here. I wanted to be close, so I could keep looking. I *never* stopped. Never."

Alice started to cry, but forced herself to speak. "You don't know what they did to me. They, they wanted to make sure I could use my powers. That I could control them, but I couldn't! I couldn't, and people were dying. I killed so many people! This girl, oh God, this one girl," Alice started heaving with sobs. "I put my hands right through her face, mother. Do you have any idea what that does to a person?"

Dorothy paled, her hand over her mouth in shock. "Oh dear. Oh, my poor dear." She wanted to get up and hug Alice, but she was frozen in place as Alice continued.

"They, they, God, when they realized, when Prometheus realized I couldn't, I just, I wanted to leave so bad. I wanted to run, but they wouldn't let me, and then they, they said they could fix it. I believed them, and they, they took me to the room with the table, and the cameras, and they, God. Alexi said they 'wanted to film it for posterity.'" Alice made quote signs in the air as she continued to sob. "They said it wouldn't hurt, but I felt it. I felt it! I felt every second of it!" Alice was visibly shaking, her voice going up and down as she spoke. "They ripped, they ripped my *soul* out, Mother! They ripped my soul right out of my body! And they took pictures and they didn't even care *and I felt everything!* Oh God, why didn't you come for me?"

Dorothy reached out to the daughter that was breaking down in front of her. Alice was sobbing uncontrollably, her entire body shaking with sobs. "Sweetheart! Oh, my dear. Oh Alice, I..."

"NO!" Alice stood up suddenly, which surprised Dorothy so much that she fell out of her chair. Alice's face had instantly twisted into a picture of rage, and as she stood, Dorothy notice something odd about Alice's purple hair.

It was sliding off.

"Don't you *dare* call me that!" The menacing woman hissed. Dorothy watched in shock as the purple wig finished falling off to reveal a head of matted, blonde hair. "That is not my name! That was *never* my name! That was a nickname that you wouldn't let go of!"

Dorothy recoiled in horror. "Oh, my God. Who are you? What do you want?"

The angry young woman stared down at Dorothy, who lay cowering on the floor. "Are you serious? Are you fucking serious?! You know who I am! How could you *not* know who I am?! My name is Annalicia May Gailsone! *Anna! Licia! May!*" Anna roared. "You could *never* bring yourself to call me that after dad died, could you? No, I was named after his mother, and *God forbid* I have her name after rotting her son to death! God forbid you love *me*, but that thing? That purple-haired *throwaway*? You're just ready to give her the fucking *world*, aren't you?"

"You're not Alice," Dorothy said in a panic. "What are you? *What are you?*"

Anna leapt for Dorothy, who screamed as she tried to scramble for her chair. She was crawling across the floor towards her phone, but Anna was on top of her in an instant, and had Dorothy turned around to face her. Dorothy tried to swat her away, but Anna had her hands on Dorothy's neck.

"Why couldn't you just love me?!" Anna screamed as she started choking Dorothy. "What was so special about her? She was a clone! Just a fucking clone they threw together and jammed my fucking soul into! I was your daughter! Not that fucking puppet! Didn't you even realize? Even *once*? Didn't it ever cross your scared little judgmental mind? DIDN'T YOU EVER NOTICE SHE WASN'T ME?"

Dorothy tried to speak, but Anna was squeezing her throat so tightly that only a hoarse moan came out. Dorothy was weakly clawing at Anna, who was growing quieter and quieter in her ears.

"WHY DIDN'T YOU NOTICE? WHY WASN'T I GOOD ENOUGH FOR YOU? *WHY DIDN'T YOU LOVE ME?*" Anna screamed in hysterics. She was throttling Dorothy, slamming her against the floor with every choked sob of a scream. Even after Dorothy had stopped fighting and her hands had fallen limp, even after her body sagged like an old, broken doll in Anna's hands, the angry blonde did not let go. She just kept pounding Dorothy into the floor, a scream of "WHY?" accompanying each sickening thud.

"WHY?"

Dorothy felt the tightness in her chest let go. The room was getting darker, and everything had a blur to it.

"WHY?"

There was a noise. Was it Alice? She was sleepy, and so warm. Was Alice sad? She thought so, but it was hard to tell. Something felt loose inside her. Her whole body felt loose. She felt weightless. There was a clicking sound in the distance.

"WHY?!"

There was a soft, green light. Gentle, and familiar. It felt *so* familiar. Something she hadn't felt for so long. A feeling of peace. Friends. Comfort. People and places she hadn't seen since her youth. Her husband, smiling with his hand out. He was so handsome. And beside him, so many wonderful people, so many wonderful faces. It was something she hadn't felt for years. It was a feeling of being home.

"..."

Finally, Anna ran out of steam. She slowly unclenched her hands and let Dorothy's lifeless body fall to the floor with a thud. She stayed hunched over her for several minutes, breathing heavily and sobbing. Finally, she sniffed, wiped her face, and made sure to put her hands all over Dorothy's dress before standing up and straightening her own suit. She calmly and neatly shut the door behind her as she left, never once looking back.

Outside in the hallway stood Danica Lewis, the Diamond, who had been listening. She watched Anna with wide eyes as the head of the Purge turned to her, smiled, and said, "There now, all done. Take me to the *Metatron*. The engines should be about charged. It's time we made ourselves known."

Danica paused for a moment, still in shock over what had just happened. Then she saw the look on Anna's face. It was a smiling, twitching mask that Danica knew could easily split apart into a violent, murderous rage at the slightest provocation. "Sure thing, boss," Danica said, hoping her voice didn't betray her fear.

Danica put her hand on Anna's shoulder and focused. With a quiet blip and a small flash of light, they were gone.

TO BE CONCLUDED

96855985R00209

Made in the USA
Columbia, SC
03 June 2018